MAN OF HONOR?

Lyla tugged at the top of her corset. "Are you a man of honor, sir?" she asked.

"I'm the most honorable man I know, Miss O'Riley."

Lyla allowed him a moment to consider her predicament, then smiled. "If you're gentleman enough to fasten me up without getting handsy, I'll reward you with . . . a little kiss."

Thompson felt a grin spreading slowly over his face as he approached her. "I'd be pleased to assist you, miss," he said. He tugged on the laces until the two halves of the stiff undergarment came together over her spine.

"Tighter," Lyla gasped.

His green eyes glimmered above hers, and then he was pulling her back against himself, kissing her with splendid, lush lips that refused to let her go.

"I—I'm sorry!" she whispered when she could get her breath. "I should never have asked you to—"

"Never apologize for kissing me that way," he breathed. "Now turn around and let me finish buttoning your dress before I . . ."

"Thank you," she murmured, as he looped the last button. After adjusting her lace-trimmed bodice, she faced him with the most demure gaze she could manage. "What did you say your name was?"

CAPTURE THE GLOW
OF ZEBRA'S HEARTFIRES

AUTUMN ECSTASY   (3133, $4.25)
by Pamela K. Forrest

Philadelphia beauty Linsey McAdams had eluded her kidnappers but was now at the mercy of the ruggedly handsome frontiersman who owned the remote cabin where she had taken refuge. The two were snowbound until spring, and handsome Luc LeClerc soon fancied the green-eyed temptress would keep him warm through the long winter months. He said he would take her home at winter's end, but she knew that with one embrace, she might never want to leave!

BELOVED SAVAGE   (3134, $4.25)
by Sandra Bishop

Susannah Jacobs would do anything to survive—even submit to the bronze-skinned warrior who held her captive. But the beautiful maiden vowed not to let the handsome Tonnewa capture her heart as well. Soon, though, she found herself longing for the scorching kisses and tender caresses of her raven-haired BELOVED SAVAGE.

CANADIAN KISS   (3135, $4.25)
by Christine Carson

Golden-haired Sara Oliver was sent from London to Vancouver to marry a stranger three times her age—only to have her husband-to-be murdered on their wedding day. Sara vowed to track the murderer down, but he ambushed her and left her for dead. When she awoke, wounded and frightened, she was staring into the eyes of the handsome loner Tom Russel. As the rugged stranger nursed her to health, the flames of passion erupted, and their CANADIAN KISS threatened never to end!

Available wherever paperbacks are sold, or order direct from the Publisher. Send cover price plus 50¢ per copy for mailing and handling to Zebra Books, Dept. 3730, 475 Park Avenue South, New York, N.Y. 10016. Residents of New York and Tennessee must include sales tax. DO NOT SEND CASH. For a free Zebra/ Pinnacle catalog please write to the above address.

CHARLOTTE HUBBARD
COLORADO MOONFIRE

ZEBRA BOOKS
KENSINGTON PUBLISHING CORP.

For Johnny Lynn, a friend like no other.

*With many thanks to Bronna Flanagan—
boss, friend, and Waldenbooks manager
extraordinaire—who goes above and beyond
the call to promote my books.*

ZEBRA BOOKS

are published by

Kensington Publishing Corp.
475 Park Avenue South
New York, NY 10016

First printing: April, 1992

Printed in the United States of America

Chapter 1

"You get first pick of the women, McClanahan!" a voice called out over the crowd.

"What the hell?" another man exclaimed. "It's your last night as a free man, so we'll let you have 'em *all!*"

The Golden Rose's parlor rang with the laughter of its gentlemen revelers and with the twitter of the ladies in question as Matt McClanahan rose a few steps higher on the grand staircase to address his well-wishers. He looked supremely confident, dressed in a dove-gray frock coat and a white shirt that set off his swarthy face and easy smile.

"Miss Victoria," he said with a bow toward the Rose's madam, "I'm delighted to be honored at this bachelor party in Cripple Creek's finest establishment—not to mention flattered by my friends' confidence in my ability to entertain your lovely ladies," he added suavely. "But I'll toast my bride-to-be rather than deprive these men of their evening's sport. Emily's a helluva woman—"

"Hear, hear!" the men cheered.

"—and if it weren't for Marshal Thompson here, neither of us would be alive. And I wouldn't be the happiest man on the face of the earth." McClanahan's voice vibrated with his gratitude. He raised his glass in a solemn salute as he gazed at the lawman.

"So here's to you, Barry, the finest friend a man ever had—"

"To Thompson!" Silas Hughes led the crowd in lifting their drinks.

"—and I bequeath to you my skills and reputation as Cripple's legendary lady-killer," he finished with a devilish grin. "Not that you need them."

Laughter filled the opulent parlor house, making the prisms of the crystal chandelier clitter with the crowd's gaiety, and then all eyes focused expectantly on Barry Thompson. Ordinarily he would've shot Matt a comeback—his friends were awaiting one of his flippant remarks—yet the words didn't come. Despite the whiskey punch and the camaraderie of the wealthy men in the room, and his sincere happiness for McClanahan and Emily, an inexplicable emptiness clutched at his heart. "You're marrying a fine little lady," he replied, "and if I hear you're not treating her right, by God, you'll answer to me."

He might as well have announced he was closing down the whorehouse. Miss Victoria and Matt appeared stunned, and his ominous tone had hushed even Princess Cherry Blossom and the giddier girls in the crowd. Barry felt lower than a midget's heel for sounding so brusque, but before he could amend his statement, Frazier Foxe stepped up beside McClanahan on the staircase. Foxe was intensely British; his monocle glistened above his waxed mustache as he addressed the gathering in his clipped accent.

"I believe our honorable marshal speaks to our highest intentions," the stockbroker stated as he adjusted his eyepiece with a gloved hand. "And we join him in wishing Mr. McClanahan all the best."

Matt's polite smile reflected the tightening Barry felt beneath his belt. Foxe was known for promoting his latest business schemes every chance he got, a trait that caused secretive snickers among Cripple's mine owners and bankers. Nobody could argue with the Englishman's talent for turning a buck, though. And

6

his contributions to charitable causes spoke for themselves, so the locals usually indulged his windiness.

"And while successful beginnings are uppermost in our minds," Foxe went on, "it behooves me to repeat my invitation for investments in a gold refinery. We're well aware of the expense of shipping our ore to the Springs. Building a mill here in the mining district would save us all thousands of dollars while requiring comparatively little in capital from each of us. It's an investment in Cripple Creek, gentlemen. A down payment on our future."

Thompson snorted. Foxe's plans for a gold mill sounded as sensible as pouring a hundred decanters of brandy down the drain . . . and sampling a bottle sounded like a damn fine idea, all of a sudden. Barry started toward the bar at the far end of the room, until Frazier's crisp voice rose above the guests' murmurings.

"Your marriage to Miss Burnham seems a most auspicious time to contribute to such a worthwhile cause, McClanahan," the Englishman hinted. "May I count on your generous support? Several of your colleagues have already pledged substantial amounts."

Thompson turned in time to catch the roll of his best friend's blue eyes. "I wish you well in your efforts, Frazier," McClanahan replied smoothly, "but the Angel Claire belonged to Emily, not to me. And now that she's deeded the mine to Silas Hughes, we're out of the gold business entirely."

Undaunted, Foxe quickly scanned the gathering. "I say, Thompson—what's *your* reply? Surely your profits from the Flaxen Lassie justify an investment in a mill."

Barry stiffened. It was no secret to the elite company around him that a lucky strike a few years back had made him wealthy enough to retire from his position as city marshal, but he didn't want the source of his bankroll bandied about in common conversation. It wouldn't set well with the brawling miners he jailed if they realized he was one of the anti-union mine owners they got so riled up about.

"Surely you know, Mr. Foxe," he answered acidly, "that the gold in our mines is petering out even as we speak. Building a mill sounds like a damn stupid idea, frankly. So if you'll excuse me, I'll get back to toasting McClanahan's happiness."

Barry felt the Englishman's piercing glare follow him out of the parlor, along with the puzzled frowns of his friends, but he kept walking. A man had a right to speak his mind. And if Frazier Foxe was going to spoil Matt's bachelor party by soliciting funds for a mill that would be bankrupt before it opened, he, as the marshal, had a duty to stop such talk.

He leaned heavily on the walnut bar, gesturing at the slender man behind it. "Brandy, Bob. Your best—and keep it coming."

"Yes sir, Mr. Thompson."

As the first sip of sweet, mellow fire slid down his throat, Barry stared forlornly at his crystal snifter. He wasn't normally this testy, and everyone here knew it. So what was eating him? Why, when he was celebrating the marriage of two perfectly-paired people, in a bordello that Cripple's comeliest doves had bedecked for Christmas, did he feel so damn . . . lonely?

Before he could think of an answer, a feminine hand slithered around his elbow. "You look like a little boy who got caught pissing in the punchbowl, Thompson. Want to tell me what's wrong?"

Princess Cherry Blossom, the Golden Rose's most flamboyant whore, was studying him with a solemn expression—or at least as serious a look as her Indian get-up allowed. The stripes of war paint on her cheek were a seasonal red and green, and her raven hair was plaited with white beads. A nosegay of red carnations and mistletoe graced her buckskin

8

gown's single shoulder strap, and as she rubbed against him, Barry could see every inch of her cleavage.

"I thought it was in damn poor taste for Foxe to start in on his fund-raising, that's all," he muttered.

"So it's Frazier you're worked up about. Funny, I could've sworn you were jealous of McClanahan for catching the most eligible heiress in these parts."

Barry glared at her. "And what's *that* supposed to mean? Neither of us needs her money." He held her gaze, forcing her to look away first, because the Indian princess had hit closer to the truth than he cared to admit.

Cherry Blossom's lips eased into a coy grin and her hand slid down the front of his frock coat. One button . . . two. With a practiced hand she fondled him, chuckling low in her throat. "Money's the least of your assets, far as I'm concerned, marshal," she crooned. "I'm not in the mood to toast McClanahan's marital bliss, either, so I thought we might run a tub full of bubbles and play cowboys and Indians. What do you say, loverman?"

It was an invitation he'd accepted many a time, with no regrets. But as Barry looked at the woman beside him, it suddenly struck him that everything about the princess came from a bottle: her coal-black hair, her mahogany skin . . . the hard gleam in those knowing brown eyes. For the first time in his thirty years he realized how little he had to show for the attention and money he'd lavished on sporting women, and the thought depressed him even more. "Maybe after I buy you a drink. Or two."

His response sounded less than complimentary, but his companion was wise enough to nod and accept her usual tumbler of whiskey. It was a damn sorry day when Cherry Blossom couldn't arouse him, but maybe if he downed enough of this brandy it wouldn't matter to either of them.

I must be getting old—or crazy—if I want to get

9

drunk more than I want to get laid, Thompson agonized. And then the hurried rustling of skirts made him look up and blink. He saw only the back of her, a tiny fairy in lavender and lace bearing a half-empty tray of tarts down the hallway. But there was merriment in her step and sunshine in the light brown hair that shimmered past her shoulders, and in her wake she left the alluring scent of . . .

Peppermints. He was sure of it.

"Who *was* that?" he whispered.

The Indian princess raised a dark eyebrow as she polished off her whiskey. "The new housekeeper. Just started this week."

"Name, woman. I need her name!"

"Lyla O'Riley. Irish. But she's not one of the—"

Thompson didn't care who the girl wasn't. He stepped away from Cherry Blossom's intimate grasp and followed the sweet candy smell of her until he came to the closed pantry door. He heard the stealthy rustling of satin and an uneven gasping that made him wonder what the hell was going on in there. Had Lyla met a lover on the sly? Being Barry Thompson, he wasn't about to leave until he found out.

Lyla whimpered with frustration, cursing the fashion designer—a man, obviously—who'd put so many buttons on the back of her dress. As she fumbled with the last of them and then struggled out of her sleeves, she also muttered choice words at the other man—no doubt a sadist—who'd created the corset no well-dressed woman could be without. She desperately needed to fill her lungs with air, and how she was going to truss herself up again and return to her serving duties was beyond her. Lightheaded to the point of fainting, she clawed at the laces that held her in their cruel grip, and then collapsed against the wall with a moan of profound relief.

When she opened her eyes, Lyla gasped. A tall,

10

sturdy man in a pinstriped suit was staring at her as though he'd been struck dumb. Lyla stilled the impulse to yank her bodice up and took advantage of his dazed state to inventory him. He posed no threat, this huge intruder; sandy waves of hair framed a likable, boyish face. He was a humorous man of deep, tender passions, she sensed, with eyes as gentle and green as the hills of home. But he'd gawked enough.

"Your mama never taught you that it's impolite to stare?" she demanded.

Yere mam nivver tawt ye that it's imp'lite t' steer? Her brogue danced in Barry's ears, and when he could pull his gaze away from two of the plumpest, roundest reasons he'd ever seen for falling in love, he was captured in the spell of her eyes. They were the periwinkle blue of columbines dotting the mountains in springtime, a hue made more intense by the lavender of her gown—which she made no effort to pull up. She just kept watching him, unblinking, as though she knew exactly what he would do next.

"Lyla O'Riley;" he whispered. It was a prayer of thanks to God for delivering him into her presence, a solemn promise to win this woman no matter what it took, foreign as that sounded to a man of his sporting experience. And it was an impish invitation to grin, every time he said it. "Lyla O'Riley," he repeated with a chuckle. "Lyla O'Riley."

"I know my name, sir," she insisted, refusing to flinch beneath his roving gaze. "Now what is it you're wanting in here?"

Thompson swallowed a groan, along with the obvious answer to her question. Her peppermint scent made him feel like a kid in a candy store, or like a young swain flushed with his first bellyful of booze. She expected a rational answer, but the only safe reply he could think of was, "Uh, your dress! I came to tell you how—*flattering*— it is, and to ask where you got it."

11

When he took a tentative step toward her, Lyla knew it was time to escape—no easy feat, given her state of undress. "Thank you, sir," she answered, and then she looked him over saucily. "Mrs. Delacroix made the gown. But as for who gave it to me, well—a girl's entitled to a few secrets, isn't she?"

Once again her lilting voice teased at his insides. But Barry refused to fall for her coy reply, just as he resolved to steal her away from her man, if indeed she had one. "Miss Victoria gets all her ladies' gowns made at that shop," he challenged. "Her maids generally wear uniforms, though. So who bought this for you?"

For the first time since this burly man barged in, Lyla felt naked beneath his gaze. The sudden pounding of her heart warned her that he posed a threat of the most dangerous, intimate kind, and that revealing her benefactor's identity would be a major mistake—although not so drastic an error as accepting the dress had been. With a sly smile, she tugged the top of the corset over her breasts. "Are you a man of honor, sir? A man to whom I can entrust the truth?"

Only a lovesick fool would fall for such a question, but Thompson played along. He was too fascinated not to. "I'm the most honorable man I know, Miss O'Riley. You can ask anybody in the parlor to vouch for my impeccable reputation."

"Good. But I can't go out there looking like *this*, now, can I?" Lyla allowed him a moment to consider her predicament, and then smiled. "If you're gentleman enough to fasten me up without getting handsy, perhaps I'll tell you who bought this gown."

Knowing a line when he heard one, Thompson felt a grin spreading slowly over his face as he approached her. She was looking up at him with that beguiling smile, but Lyla O'Riley was about to find out that he had a few tricks of his own. "I'd be pleased to assist you, Miss Lyla," he replied in a husky voice.

"A man has to wonder why you'd rush in here and start peeling off your corset, though."

"You've obviously never worn one." Lyla turned to face the wall, sweeping her hair up off her shoulders and holding it atop her head with both hands.

It was an extremely sensuous gesture, and Thompson held his breath, hesitating, as he gazed at her arched neck and smooth shoulders the color of richest cream. Her corset gaped at him, held only by its slack satin laces, and it would be so easy to just rip the damn thing off . . . "If—if it's so uncomfortable, why wear it?" he stammered.

"The gown wouldn't fit without it. I've been endowed with too much of a good thing, and no matter what I wear to control it, everything just . . . sticks out."

He reached out to cup her rounded breasts—God, how he wanted to squeeze her alluring little behind while she wrapped her thighs around his! Barry groaned and stuffed his hands in his pockets. Only a cad would take advantage of a young lady who'd confessed such sincere agony about being full-figured. "Honey, I think you're a fine-looking woman," he rasped, "and as far as I can see, you stick out in all the right places."

His words divulged a desire Lyla felt quickening inside her own trembling body. Why had she made such an absurd request of this man instead of insisting he leave? "You'd better lace me up immediately," she said in a stiff whisper. "Before we forget how *honorable* you are."

Nipping his lip, the marshal tugged on the laces until the two halves of the stiff undergarment came together over her spine. It was a *sin* to truss her up this way, and he was ready to rip—

"Tighter," Lyla gasped. "If you don't start at the top and adjust it as you go, you'll never get my gown buttoned."

How had he gotten himself into this mess? His resolve was turning to syrup as the heat of Lyla's curvaceous young body sent her peppermint essence wafting around him. "Begging your pardon," he breathed, "but why didn't you just have the dress made a size larger?"

Figuring nothing she said could possibly embarrass her further, Lyla twisted slightly to look up at him. "The man who ordered this gown prefers his women to fit a modest mold. He says that anything more than a handful is just a waste."

Her flushed cheeks and lilac eyes told Thompson she was utterly serious, ashamed of her generous curves. "Then he's a goddamned fool," he muttered, "or else he's got hands too small to do you justice. I don't have that problem."

His green eyes glimmered above hers and then he was pulling her back against himself, kissing her with splendid, lush lips that refused to let her go. The man's hands *were* large, and as they roamed lovingly over her breasts and stomach, Lyla tried to slap him, but from this position it was a feeble effort at best. Despite a heady warmth that seeped through her body like butter into hot bread, she struggled into a position where she could take better aim.

Barry let her turn in his arms and then he cupped her bottom to lift her to a more comfortable height. Pressing her to the wall, he continued to move his mouth over hers in a breathless kiss. She was soft and silken beneath him, and once she stopped swatting at him she answered his every nuance with subtle responses he'd only fantasized about until now. Her legs had parted when he lifted her, and she was locking an ankle behind his knee, driving him toward a frenzy that galloped through him like a wild stallion.

He pulled away abruptly. "Jesus, woman! You're driving me crazy!"

"I—I'm sorry! I never should've asked you to—" A

14

gentle finger shut off the rest of her protest, and Lyla could only stare at her captor in bewilderment. She'd tried to fend him off—tried to buckle him at the knee—yet at the same time her body had been ready to surrender to this man, and she didn't even know his name!

Barry let out an agonized sigh and slid her down the wall until her feet touched the floor. "Never apologize for kissing me that way, Lyla. It'd be an insult to both of us," he murmured. "Now turn around. Let me button your dress before I forget how trustworthy I am."

Nodding, Lyla lifted her hair again and presented her back to this most perplexing man. He'd entered without knocking, led her to the gates of paradise with his kiss—and she'd *let* him! And her wanton behavior had put her in more than one compromising position, because now that he was fastening her dress, she was supposed to reveal who'd paid for it. A foolish, dangerous confession, given the possessive way he'd nearly made love to her against the wall.

"Thank you," she mumbled when he looped the last button. After demurely adjusting her lace-trimmed bodice, Lyla faced him with the most direct gaze she could manage. "What'd you say your name was?"

Whod ye say yere name woz? Her lilting, childlike voice tickled him until he laughed out loud, forgiving the tension she'd caused him only moments ago. "Barry Thompson. Pleased to be of service, ma'am."

Her mouth fell open and a pang of regret pierced her heart. She had to leave this man immediately, without a *hint* about who paid for her dress. Why hadn't she recognized him from Princess Cherry Blossom's detailed description? Everybody in Cripple looked up to this giant of a man as the marshal, but she'd mistakenly hoped he was the suitor who could set her free.

15

"Maybe I'd better loosen those stays. You look ready to fall over."

"I—I'm fine," she said with a forced smile. "It's just that—well, I've heard so much about the lawman who brought the Angel Claire's blaster to justice, yet I didn't realize—"

"Actually, it was Silas Hughes who nabbed him," Thompson admitted with a shrug. "And he was so crazy for a hit of opium he hanged himself. I just kept him locked up."

Lyla studied Thompson for a long moment, haunted by memories of the destruction Nigel Grath had caused when he had dynamited the mine—a horrible ordeal the marshal's kind smile couldn't erase. "No matter what you did," she replied quietly, "I owe you my thanks. My brother Mick was killed in that explosion. He's the only family I had here in America."

The dew in her eyes tugged at him. "I'm truly sorry, Lyla. Is there anything I can do? Anything you need?"

She toyed absently with the silver shamrock pendant she wore in Mick's memory. "I have a room and a good job here, and this necklace my brother made me. And Miss Victoria and her ladies make me feel very welcome." Lyla smiled suddenly, unable to suppress a sly chuckle. "They discuss you at great length, Marshal Thompson. Tales of your upstanding character and legendary . . . proportion."

The ornery light in her eyes left no doubt as to her meaning, and her ability to rise above her grief made Thompson admire her even more. "Every inch of it's true, Lyla," he said with a teasing wink. "I'm a ladies' man through and through—"

"Is that why you followed me in here with your fly gaping open?"

Barry's jaw dropped, and in the moment it took him to look down, Lyla O'Riley scampered around him, grabbed her tray, and opened the pantry door.

"I have work to do, marshal," she called over her shoulder. "It was lovely meeting you."

She disappeared with a swish of her lavender skirts, leaving him to stare after her. His fly was *not* open, and she'd escaped without revealing who bought her that gown! When Barry could stop chuckling, he realized that this Irish sprite had also chased away his blues and given him a new challenge: he had to see more of Miss O'Riley, and to any man who stood in his way—beware!

Thompson ambled down the hallway and paused to survey the ongoing party in the parlor. The Christmas greenery looked fresher, the piano sounded livelier, and the honey-haired girl passing among the guests with her tray of treats tossed him a teasing glance. An air of satisfaction settled over him, and as he approached Sam Langston, a plan came to him, full-blown and perfect.

"Langston," he said, grinning at the portly banker, "how about you and I stepping over to your office to discuss some urgent business? I'm going to buy myself the best Christmas present a man ever had."

Chapter 2

"You want to *what?*" Victoria Chatterly's jeweled tiara trembled in her white hair as she gaped at Barry Thompson. "That's not only the most unseemly idea I've ever heard from you, marshal, but it smacks of white slavery as well!"

Barry smiled indulgently at the woman who stood with her fists on her hips before the fireplace. He'd expected this outburst from Cripple's most genteel madam, so he'd requested a chat in her elegant boudoir, immediately after the bachelor party. "You're missing my point," he said in his most eloquent tone. "A girl like Lyla has no business living at the Rose with—"

"I pride myself on our level of decency," she interrupted with fire in her eyes, "and you of all people know that, Mr. Thompson. Why you think I'll let you *buy* Lyla is beyond me. Utterly unthinkable!"

"I'm compensating you for her new wardrobe and for the time it'll take to hire her replacement, that's all. Perhaps I phrased my original plan poorly—"

"And how will you phrase your replies when people question this outrageous proposition? What will you *do* with her? Where will she sleep?" Miss Chatterly walked quickly to her bedside table and splashed some sherry into a goblet, her pudgy, ringed fingers quaking with her indignation. Then she turned resolutely toward the marshal. "I can't go along with this, Mr. Thompson. Lyla has an honest job here, and I consider it my personal responsibility to see that she remains wholesome and unsullied until she finds a permanent home. Plenty of men in Cripple would marry Miss O'Riley—decent men, who'll give her the love and respect she deserves."

Thompson considered this as he lowered himself into one of the madam's overstuffed pink chairs. It was late, but he planned to stay until he got what he came for. "What about me?" he demanded. "I can certainly give her a home, and I'm already crazy about her. Don't you consider me decent enough?"

The madam fixed her pale aqua eyes on him. "You're one of the finest men I know, Barry," she replied quietly. "But you live in rooms above a dressmaker's shop. And you've made no mention whatsoever of marriage. I can't be party to the scandal such an arrangement would cause. Now if you'll excuse me, I have some matters to tend to before I retire for the evening."

Thompson settled deeper in the chair, preparing to play his trump. Miss Chatterly was as shrewd as she was alluring; beneath her voluminous silk gowns and voluptuous curves beat the heart of Cripple's most exacting business manager. Though her porcelain features gave no sign of it, he suspected she wasn't laying all her cards on the table.

"Who suggested you take Lyla in?" he asked in a low voice. "Somebody else bought that lavender gown she wore tonight. Is he also paying her room and board, so *he* can lay claim to her?"

Victoria gripped her goblet and glared at him. "I won't dignify that insinuation with a reply," she said in a steely voice. "It's a ridiculous notion and you know it."

"Then who bought her dress?"

"Why is that your business?"

19

The madam's elusive replies confirmed his suspicions, making him all the more determined to pry some information out of her. "I want to know who my competition is. Surely that's not too much to reveal to a good friend, Victoria."

It was a dirty way to fight, since he could close the Rose down any time he wanted to, and he got no pleasure from watching her powdered cheeks color with the knowledge that she was cornered. But damn it, he wanted some answers!

The madam perched on the chair across from him and gazed into the crackling fire, her hands folded in her ample lap. After a long silence, she sighed wearily. "I suppose you've heard how Lyla was bereaved when the Angel Claire exploded."

"Yes. Which is my main reason for concern," Barry said softly. "Cripple's no town for a woman alone."

Miss Victoria nodded. "Silas Hughes told her as much when he made his condolence call to present Mick's pension check, but she remained in their cabin out in Phantom Canyon. Said she could fend for herself. Lyla's headstrong that way."

Recalling how she'd struggled against his embrace, Thompson could well imagine her battering the diplomatic Hughes with her brogue. "What made her change her mind?"

"Loneliness, perhaps. Or the harsh winter we're having." Victoria focused on the fire again, fidgeting with a fold in her turquoise gown. "Being snowbound in a miner's shack is no life for a young lady, and—"

"I'm not buying it." Thompson wasn't surprised that this principled woman would weave a story to protect Lyla O'Riley, but why was it so elaborate? He considered what he knew about the shacks scattered among the hillsides around Phantom Canyon, and then gazed steadily at the madam. "Who was her landlord? Did he force her out, thinking she couldn't

20

pay the rent because her brother was dead?"

Miss Chatterly's aqua eyes locked into his. "You're very perceptive, marshal."

"That's my job. Whatever you may think of my request, my motives *are* aboveboard," he assured her. "I want all these details so I can anticipate any trouble when it comes time for Miss O'Riley to leave the Golden Rose. I may think with my crotch on occasion, but I'd never in a million years do anything to hurt her."

Victoria gave him a resigned smile. "I know that, Barry."

"So tell me who brought her here. The more you stall, the more I'll suspect something underhanded— a situation I may have to investigate, being the marshal and all."

"Frazier Foxe."

Thompson scowled. "Frazier Foxe what?"

With an exasperated sigh, Miss Chatterly rose from her chair. "Frazier *brought* her here! Told her it was unseemly for a young lady to live in the canyon by herself, and encouraged me to hire her as a housekeeper."

The marshal saw the madam's cushiony bosom quiver with her agitation and he burst out laughing. "You British and your *unseemliness*," he said between chuckles. "So you're saying Foxe brought her to a whorehouse to protect her innocence? Hell, he could've taken her to *his* place! Everybody knows he's about as manly as milktoast."

"He's a very proper, generous man," Victoria insisted. "Concerned about Lyla's—"

"And you'd let Foxe have her before I could? That hurts, Victoria."

The madam's chin lifted defiantly and she dented her lush hips with her fists. "Mr. Foxe knew of her situation and remedied it. He found her a place to stay and a job—and yes, he bought her some clothes so I wouldn't be out the expense of her wardrobe.

What have *you* done for Lyla—besides pawing at her in my pantry?"

Thompson cleared his throat. There was no arguing with Victoria Chatterly when she stood on such solid ground, so he led her down another avenue of conversation. "What's in it for Foxe?" he asked bluntly. "You can call him humanitarian names from now until doomsday, but he never takes on a project that won't turn him a profit."

Her porcelain face cracked with a scowl. "It *is* Christmas, and people tend to show more goodwill toward the less fortunate. You could stand to perform a few charitable deeds yourself, Mr. Thompson."

"Which is exactly what I'm trying to do." Barry rose to stand before the plump madam, stooping so his eyes were more even with hers. "Damn it, Victoria," he said in a tightly-controlled voice, "my best friend's getting married tomorrow, and I'm thirty years old, and alone, and I'm tired of it. All the women in this town are either married or whores, or so dried-up they'd crack if you kissed them. I want Lyla and I intend to have her."

"I never said you couldn't," she countered. "I merely objected to the way you proposed to go about it. Keeping Lyla would cause a scandal—the newspapers would make mincemeat of your reputation, and the faith Cripple's citizens have in you would be totally destroyed."

"You're saying I may *court* her, like a proper gentleman?" he asked with a sarcastic chuckle.

"That would be nice," Victoria replied with equal snideness.

"Highly unlikely, what with Foxe paying her way." The marshal reached into his trousers for the bankroll he'd withdrawn a few hours ago. "How much did her dresses cost? And I'll reimburse you for having to hire another girl."

"I don't want your money, Mr. Thompson."

"Then use it to pay Frazier off. Mark my word,

there's more to his generosity than you're seeing." He stepped over to her nightstand and counted four hundred-dollar bills onto its marble top. "That should take care of her clothes, and here's another one to cover wages. I'll come for her tomorrow morning."

He crossed the lavishly-decorated boudoir and bowed at the madam as he opened the door. "Good night, Miss Chatterly. As always, it's a pleasure doing business in your fine establishment."

She arched an eyebrow. "Have you mentioned your plans to Miss O'Riley?"

"We'll discuss them over lunch."

"You'll be sorry, Marshal Thompson."

Barry grinned at the prospect of having Lyla all to himself in just a few short hours. "Judging from the way she pawed at me in your pantry, I sincerely doubt that."

Thompson reached for the restaurant door, feeling like a boy about to open a bright, shiny Christmas present. As they'd walked along the snow-powdered sidewalk, Lyla had chattered eagerly about preparations for the McClanahans' wedding reception, to be held that evening at the Golden Rose. Each time she smiled up at him with those mesmerizing eyes, the waves of euphoria he was riding crested gloriously. The ring he'd bought this morning smoldered in his pants pocket: its large aquamarine mimicked his woman's most stunning feature and was surrounded by diamonds that sparkled like his hopes and dreams. The thought that Lyla would be showing this ring off tonight at Matt's wedding filled him with pride.

"Ever eaten here at Delmonico's?" he asked as he helped her out of her cloak.

Lyla looked across the elegant dining room, with its crisp white linens and fashionably-attired patrons. Aromas of roasted meat and fresh rolls caught her up in their warmth, yet her appetite was edged with apprehension. "No," she mumbled. "This was a bit beyond Mick's means. I—I hope I'm properly dressed."

"Nonsense. I was about to tell you how that red plaid flatters you," Barry said. The gown sported huge ruffled sleeves with a bodice that puffed out in the latest style, much as Lyla did. Its bold colors seemed far too flashy for Foxe's taste, but he suspected Mrs. Delacroix had made this dress, too. Straightening the chain her silver shamrock hung on, he smiled down at her. "You look like a doll dressed up for Christmas. And your brother made your necklace?"

"Aye. Wanted to be a jeweler when he got up the money," she answered quietly. "I wear it so I'll never forget the dreams we had when we came to America."

He wanted to wrap his arms around her and assure her that *his* dreams were every bit as wonderful, but their hostess appeared, walking stiffly between the kitchen doors. Prudence Spickle was a cheerless soul who wore her spinsterhood like a thorny crown of honor. "You have a guest today, marshal?"

Barry smiled as the hostess stared sourly at Lyla. "Miss O'Riley and I would like a table near the back, where the clatter from the kitchen won't disturb our conversation."

With a sniff, Miss Spickle led them between the tables, her head held high by a neck as spindly as a chicken's. Lyla would've chuckled—the woman's behind was so flat she appeared to walk without moving her legs—except for the fact that her stomach was knitting itself in knots. Such elegance, when Marshal Thompson had merely invited her for a bite of lunch! She suspected, from his buoyant air and freshly-pressed suit, that his plans included much more than casual chitchat, and the prospect terrified her.

To make matters worse, she saw Frazier Foxe

24

across the room. Just as Barry was seating her, the Englishman caught sight of them—adjusted his monocle as though scrutinizing their innermost thoughts—and her appetite vanished. Why was everyone staring at her? Surely her new dress wasn't so bright as to be offensive. Surely the marshal brought women here often enough that they weren't gawking at *him!*

"What sounds good?" her companion's voice interrupted her worries. "It's a special treat to be seen with such a lovely young woman, and I want this to be a memorable day for you, too."

His eyes glowed with an emotion so intense that Lyla held her breath. Barry Thompson was much handsomer than she remembered from their first encounter, clearly interested in more than a few stolen kisses behind the pantry door. His smooth-shaven face glowed with a boyish happiness, and compared to the old poop she was to have married in Ireland, he was a dream come true. If only she hadn't—

"You're awfully quiet, little lady. Shall I order for us?"

"Aye—please! I wouldn't have the foggiest notion what to choose." She stared at the stripes woven into the white tablecloth, her cheeks flushing with anguish. The marshal was bound to suspect something: waifs like her never clammed up at the prospect of a free meal! Lyla glanced into green eyes that glimmered like emeralds. She was mortified that his large, warm hand was enfolding hers just as the waitress approached their table.

"What'll you have?" Miss Spickle demanded. Her gaze bored into their clasped hands, but Thompson wasn't about to let go.

"We'd like your roast pheasant dinner, and a bottle of your finest white wine."

"It's a little early, isn't it?"

Barry fixed his gaze calmly on the waitress,

determined not to spoil the ambiance of this occasion. "It's never too early to celebrate life and love, Miss Spickle. And it's never too late. There's no hurry on dinner. We'll be here a while."

The spinster headed toward the kitchen in a huff, calling their order to the chef in a voice shrill with disdain. Thompson grinned. The tiny hand within his own was damp, its pulse fluttering like a bird's. Lyla's eyes were huge as she gazed around the dining room before suddenly focusing on him again. A quick glance revealed Frazier Foxe's presence: the willowy stockbroker's pointed stare made Barry chuckle to himself, and he wrapped his other hand around his companion's, too. She was clearly as excited and nervous as he was, and trying just as hard not to show it.

"I hope you don't think I'm too forward, asking you to dinner this way," he began hesitantly. "The Rose didn't seem an appropriate place to get better acquainted."

"Seems we got *quite* acquainted last night," she quipped. "I'm not that free with every man I meet, you know."

"Of course you're not. And I had no business barging in on you, either. I apologize." The memory of her smooth, supple body yielding beneath his made him shift in his chair; the way she'd hooked her ankle around his knee told him she was as playfully passionate as he was. And this line of thinking would have him making love to her under the table, if he wasn't careful.

Barry tugged at his starched shirt collar. "I—I guess I'm curious as to why you came to this country with your brother," he said with a strained smile. "I hope it's not because he was the only family you had left."

"No, no. My parents are still alive—in the sheep business, they are." Lyla considered Thompson's taut expression and decided not to reveal the real

26

reason she'd fled Ireland. Putting on a flirtatious grin, she added, "Woollybacks don't provide much adventure, actually. So Mick and I stowed away on a ship to come prospecting for gold."

Barry's eyes widened. This little sprite was even spunkier than he thought! "And what'd your folks say to that?"

She shrugged. "They didn't know where we were till I wrote that Mick had a job in the Angel Claire. We thought it was a lucky place for him to sign on, what with our mama being named Claire."

When her eyes clouded over, Thompson gripped her hand. "I suppose they'll expect you to return home now?"

"It took me a while to write them about the mine explosion, and it'll be weeks before their reply comes back," she said softly. "By that time I can tell them I have a good job—that it's safer to stay here among friends than to travel home alone. Unless somebody brings their letter in person."

Lyla grimaced as though she'd swallowed a bitter tonic, and her distaste for returning home made him wonder why she'd really left. Not that it mattered. He didn't intend to let her go back, either alone or with a family friend. It seemed the perfect time to reveal his own plans.

"Honey, is . . . is there anyone else? Another man in your life?"

Her eyes flew to his face. How could he know she'd been thinking that the mealy-mouthed fiancé her father had chosen for her would be the most likely person to come fetch her? "I—no! No one I care about."

An encouraging answer, considering the favors Frazier Foxe had done for her. Barry glanced toward the stockbroker, who was receiving his coffee and dessert, and decided to plunge in before he lost his nerve. "Lyla, I want to move you out of the Golden Rose to more suitable quarters," he began. He leaned

27

forward to expound upon his motives, but just then Prudence Spickle shoved their plates in front of them.

"Pheasant for two and wine," she said as she plunked the tall bottle onto the table. She arched an eyebrow at Lyla. "You work at the Rose, do you?"

"Yes, ma'am. I'm a housekeeper," she added pointedly.

"That's what they all say." Miss Spickle turned on her heel and strode to the cash register at the front of the dining room.

Lyla was dumbstruck. No one had ever insinuated that she was a whore just because she worked among them, and a slow burn worked its way up to her face. She sensed that their waitress was sneaking glances at them, and also felt Frazier Foxe looking their way after overhearing Miss Spickle's rude remark. But the real reason her heart was pounding concerned the marshal sitting across from her—a man who'd obviously made plans for her future. A man like Father, so *concerned* about her welfare. And also like her fiancé, Hadley McDuff, who was all too happy to acquire her so he'd have an heir to whom he could will his fortune.

A wave of longing overtook her as she looked at their delectable meal. Rich, buttery pheasant with gingered carrots and new potatoes . . . how could she resist such a spread, after two years of cooking the plain food Mick's salary allowed? A forkful of the tender fowl convinced her Barry Thompson and his schemes could be stalled for a few minutes while she enjoyed her dinner.

The marshal stared at Miss O'Riley, who was forking down her food as though she hadn't been fed in months. Meals at the Rose were sumptuous—he'd eaten enough of them to know—so as he gently grasped her hand, he grinned. "Whoa there, little lady. Much as I'd love to unlace your stays, you don't want me to have to do it here, do you?"

Lyla gaped at the large hand holding her fork a few inches from her mouth and then glanced sheepishly into his sparkling eyes. "Sorry. When I get upset, I speed up."

"Upset?"

She loosened her hand from his grip. "The work I do at the Rose is honest labor. I don't appreciate people assuming that I'm a whore by association."

Thompson realized he'd get no proposals made until the air was cleared, so he stood up. "I'm used to being jabbed by Prudence Spickle's tongue, but you're right—there's no call for her to be rude to you. Excuse me for a moment."

He walked to the cash register at a sedate pace, calling up his most diplomatic air. The last scene he needed was one female lashing out at him while another worked herself into such a frenzy she'd never want to see him again. The hostess was counting another man's change, and then she challenged him with a silent, beady-eyed glare.

Barry cleared his throat. "Miss Spickle, have I ever told you what exemplary service you always give, and how much I appreciate it?"

She blinked as though she hadn't heard him correctly. "Well, I—"

"Your manager surely owes you a raise—"

"Actually, it's my brother—"

"—and I owe you an apology for all the times I've smarted off at you. You're a fine woman, Prudence. A star in the crown of your profession." Thompson paused to let his compliments soak in; it was a rare woman who squawked after she'd been stroked properly. "And being the gracious lady you are, I know you'll tell me—nicely, of course—what it is about Miss O'Riley that offends you."

Miss Spickle's mouth clapped shut, her thin lips working back and forth in her agitation. Then she leaned forward to speak in a conspiratorial tone. "Marshal, I'm worried that being seen with such women will ruin your reputation. You're known by the company you keep."

"I appreciate your concern, ma'am." Barry glanced back at Lyla, whose placid expression and empty plate told him he should move this show along. "Prudence, do you believe in the power of good over evil?"

The waitress stood taller, her beaky nose rising with self-righteousness. "Why, of course, Mr. Thompson. It's the power of our Lord himself."

"A woman after my own heart." He grasped the old maid's bony hands, ignoring the sensation of holding brittle sticks wrapped in tissue paper. "So you'll understand that by taking Miss O'Riley away from the Rose—letting her associate with *me*—I hope to keep her from sinking into that sordid environment. She'll make me a fine wife, but that'll be our little secret, all right?"

When he winked at her, the old busybody's cheeks actually flushed. It couldn't hurt to let her spread his good news, since Lyla would be wearing his magnificent engagement ring within the hour. With a final squeeze of her fingers, Barry turned to finish wooing the woman he loved, only to see the back of her red plaid skirts disappearing through the kitchen doors.

Feisty little imp's going in to ask for seconds, he thought as he strode between the linen-draped tables. He smiled and nodded at a few friends, thinking of a joke about corsets to make Lyla laugh when he caught her coaxing more food from the cook. A glance at their table made him pause, though. She'd picked both their plates clean and had drained the wine bottle!

Barry pushed through the batwing doors and searched anxiously around the steamy, fragrant kitchen, which bustled with men in white aprons and hats. "Did you see a lady in red go through here?" he asked the nearest chef.

The man gestured toward the alley door. "Good luck. She was in a big hurry."

Probably looking for a place to unlace, the marshal reasoned. And he was just the man to help her! But why hadn't she signaled him, or come up front for her cloak?

She didn't want to be humiliated in front of Prudence. Or maybe she's sick. He stepped quickly into the back alley, expecting to find Lyla doubled over, losing all that lunch. Instead, he saw only the clutter of rubbish, the swirl of snowflakes . . . and the flapping of a red plaid skirt turning the far corner.

He broke into a run, sweating despite the chill wind that blasted him. There must be something dreadfully wrong, something much worse than Miss Spickle's rude remark, to make Lyla dash off this way. His snow-muffled footsteps echoed against the shabby buildings as he approached the street. Barry saw her then, leaning against a pillar of the bank, her chest heaving as she tried to catch her breath. If she could run this fast, she sure as hell wasn't sick, so she must be—

As Lyla caught sight of him, her panic-stricken expression stopped his heart. She turned tail like a frightened deer and bounded down the sidewalk, ducking into the druggist's shop. Barry shivered, as much from the icy clutch of Miss O'Riley's rejection as from the wind that sent snowflakes whirling around him.

Damned if he'd chase after a woman who ate his dinner and then stood him up! His friends in Delmonico's were probably already snickering, watching this little drama from the restaurant window. But it hurt like hell to let her run off, because she was taking a lifetime of saved-up love along with her. It amazed him, how much of his future he'd invested in this woman after one brief, enticing encounter, and by God, she wasn't leaving him before she did some tall explaining!

Barry stuffed his hands into his trouser pockets and walked resolutely toward the restaurant's front door. His fingertips found the smooth, cool aquamarine in his pocket. By now everyone who'd paid for a meal had heard he intended to marry that little minx— hell, even Frazier Foxe probably knew! Probably popped his monocle when he heard about it.

The thought made Thompson laugh, and it gave him the gumption to step inside for Lyla's cloak and then continue down the street toward the Golden Rose, to wait her out.

Chapter 3

Clutching herself against the cold, Lyla darted out the druggist's back door. Her dress offered little protection from the wintry wind, and this hide-and-seek was insane! She was a fool to think Marshal Thompson wouldn't corner her at the Golden Rose: he had every right to be furious, and there was nowhere else for her to go. She only hoped Miss Victoria or Princess Cherry Blossom could detain him in the parlor while she found an obscure cranny to hide in.

Desperation made her stick to the side streets, where the snow was up to her ankles. To gain any speed, she had to lift her skirts, which allowed the freezing breeze to flutter up under her petticoats. Her breath was coming out in billowing white clouds after only a few blocks—damn corset! Lyla saw the whorehouse's butter-yellow gables only two lanes away and walked more slowly. She could slip through the back door without being noticed, because the ladies would be preparing the parlor and ballroom for tonight's festivities.

"Cold day to be out without a cloak, little miss. I could warm you up in here, though."

Lyla glanced into the dim livery stable, where a man stood in the shadows only a few feet away from her. She walked more quickly.

"What's your hurry, sweetheart?"

The sharp edge in his voice made her wish she'd listened to Miss Chatterly's warnings about the derelicts who haunted Cripple Creek's alleys. Her heart was hammering as she broke into a trot. She gasped, the icy air slicing her lungs, when the man sprang in front of her and grabbed her by the arms.

"I asked you a question." Her assailant's dark eyes glittered beneath his black hat. He was compactly built, dressed in jeans and a chambray shirt, but he smelled too clean to be a stablehand.

"Let me go! I'm late for work!"

He grinned and pulled her closer. "And where might 'work' be? You're dressed too fancy to be a shopgirl."

Lyla tried to wrench herself free, but his steely grasp tightened around her arms.

"The Golden Rose. Now turn me loose, before Miss Victoria comes looking for me!"

A stealthy laugh rumbled in the man's chest. "One of Lady Chatterly's girls, are you?" he quizzed, cocking an eyebrow. "Why is it you high-class whores think you're too good for us working stiffs? I've got the same equipment as those fat-ass bankers, and I'm just the man to show you how much better I can use it."

Something in the planes of his face looked familiar. Lyla narrowed her eyes and spoke in the most threatening voice she could muster. "You touch me, cowboy, and I'll kick your equipment right up to your ears."

"An Irish lassie who'll give me a fight—God, how I'd love that!"

Lyla forced herself to keep staring him down, despite the man's brute strength and base intentions . . . which might assist her escape. She stopped struggling and took a deep breath, distracting him with the movement of her bosom. "And who might you be, sir?"

"Why do you want to know?"

She forced a sultry chuckle and replied, "I keep a file of randy braggarts like you. So I can call out your name when you . . . shoot me."

His answering laugh was ripe with desire. "The name's Connor Foxe," he breathed. "What's yours?"

"Frazier's brother?"

Foxe's eyes took on a hooded, predatory look. "And how does Frazier know a cute little cupcake like you?"

Lyla chided herself for blurting out her benefactor's name, because this man obviously planned to put such information to use. She glanced nervously toward the Golden Rose, wondering if Marshal Thompson would hear her if she screamed. Or would that be a stupid move? Better to lure Connor to the whorehouse, where Miss Chatterly and the ladies would protect her, than to deal with him in this deserted alley. Fighting the chatter of her teeth, she gazed into Foxe's dark eyes. "We'll catch our death if we stay out in this wind," she said in a husky voice. "Come with me. We'll slip in the back way, and I'll show you precisely what makes me worth more than an ordinary whore."

Connor's low laugh registered his approval and he stepped to one side of her, still holding her elbow in a possessive grip. "Now you're talking, sweetheart. This being Christmas Eve and all, I might feel extra generous and—what the—?"

They were passing a stock trough, so Lyla deftly slipped a foot between his legs and shoved as hard as she could. A tinkle of splintering ice gave way to Connor Foxe's vehement swearing as he tumbled into the frosty water, and Lyla took off sprinting down the lane.

Thank God the back door was unlocked! She scampered inside and up the narrow stairway that led to the third-floor help's quarters, her heart hammering so hard in her throat she nearly choked. When she reached the long dormer room she fell onto her own bunk, wheezing like a winded horse.

Her stomach pitched violently. Her eyes started playing tricks with the pattern of the wallpaper as her head began to dip and spin like a lazy top. The wine she'd guzzled was now racing through her system, and she felt the sudden urge to vomit.

She stumbled into the small water closet and hunched over the commode, but nothing came up. In her frenzied, swaying state she couldn't decide whether to keep hugging this cool fixture or struggle out of her restrictive clothing or just pass out on the floor. A noise made her hold her breath . . . there it was again—creaking stairs!

Instinct drove her into the double clothes closet, which was crammed with the uniforms, dresses, hatboxes, and trunks of the housekeepers and cooks. God help her if she threw up on anyone's things, but the fear of being caught by Marshal Thompson or a lecturing Miss Chatterly was far worse. The footsteps were already coming down the hall! Lyla shut the door behind her and huddled in the close darkness, listening frantically.

It was the heavy tread of a boot rather than the clatter of the madam's pumps. As quietly as she could, Lyla fumbled along the crates and boxes beneath the hanging clothes until she came to her own trunk. She'd had precious little to pack when she'd left the cabin, so she struggled with the latches and clambered inside.

Were her skirts sticking out the lid? She had no time to check, because Barry Thompson was now strolling down the room's center aisle, between the beds. Right toward her.

There was a pause. Lyla's heart pounded painfully and she struggled to rearrange herself. Why had she thought it such a joke to gobble the marshal's meal with all that wine? She was scrunched into a tight square, arms clutched over her breasts and legs folded against her bottom, feeling pinched in half by her laced-up stays. How long could she remain in this claustrophobic box before she either climbed out of it shrieking or fainted dead away?

The doorknob clicked and the hinge whined. Lyla felt her eyes bulging against her eyelids—why she'd squeezed them shut in the dark, she didn't know—as her predator entered the closet. He stood there while seconds of not breathing turned into hours. "Damn," he muttered, and then stepped out and closed the door.

She gulped air as quietly as she could, listening. The marshal swore again as his heavy, measured tread faded in the opposite direction.

Cautiously, Lyla lifted the lid of the trunk. Her face was beaded with sweat, and she didn't know whether to laugh or cry: she'd eluded the tall lawman this time, but there was no avoiding him at the wedding reception tonight. If she was too ill to attend, he'd be the type to come upstairs and check on her.

She climbed out and then curled up on the cool wooden floor, wondering when the pheasant and wine would stop waging war inside her. The heat of her hiding place had accelerated the effects of the liquor. Her thoughts were jumbled, and all she could do was loll there, weaving from one edge of consciousness to another.

Picturing his ruddy, youthful face, Lyla tried to sort out what it was about Barry Thompson that made her run like a rabbit. He had a gentle voice, a humorous way about him that she couldn't help smiling at. Even in her miserable stupor, the memory of his kiss made her ache for his tender caress. He was thoughtful and generous, a popular customer here at the Rose because he so freely admitted his weakness for women.

And he had chosen *her*, and for more than just a game of cat-and-mouse around the whorehouse.

Lyla shifted uncomfortably. The pieces were starting to fit: the moment Father had announced she would wed Hadley McDuff, she'd felt the need to flee. Such a relationship, where she would become just another of the wealthy old codger's possessions, rankled her because she had no say in the matter. Her marriage would've been as stifling as staying curled up inside her trunk for the rest of her life.

Thompson, it seemed, was making the same mistake. By not asking her to say yes, he was forcing her to say no—truly a tragedy, because except for this one regrettable flaw, he was a man whose company she enjoyed.

Lyla started to sit up, and then stiffened. A rustling on the other side of the closet door made her hold her breath, and then she nearly collapsed with horror. Someone had eased onto the nearest bunk! The springs squeaked so softly she wouldn't have heard them had she not been lying silently on the floor.

Minutes ticked by. Was the marshal back, waiting her out, or had one of the staff come up to rest before tonight's party? She herself needed a nap or some sort of relief before dressing for the wedding. Emily Burnham had invited the entire household to the ceremony, and even if she had to be propped up between two of the whores, Lyla would never miss the biggest wedding in Cripple's recent memory. She felt clammy and nauseated, and a huge gas bubble was pressing against all sides of her stomach at once.

Lyla intended to belch quietly against the back of her hand, but the air rushed out of her in a raucous burp that filled the closet with the rude noise. Drunk as she was, she got to giggling—until a voice just outside the door said, "Come on out, Miss O'Riley. We have things to discuss."

Her blood froze in her veins. She prayed desperately for the floor to open up, or for Miss Chatterly and the marshal to come storming in after her—anything rather than facing Frazier Foxe alone.

Slowly she shuffled to the door, dreading whatever it was Foxe wanted. When he'd informed her he was moving her into town, Lyla had tried every conceivable argument: Mick's pension would pay her rent through the winter, and she *liked* living out in the cozy canyon shack with her potted plants and the animals that came calling when she needed companionship. But the landlord had other plans. And as he had urged her to accept a position at the Rose, plus three beautiful new dresses to sweeten the deal, Lyla had had the sinking sensation he'd extract repayment someday soon. Wealthy men never did their tenants any favors unless they had ulterior motives.

Now, as she opened the door a crack, Lyla squinted at a glint of afternoon sunshine Foxe's monocle beamed at her. His close-cropped curls looked freshly brushed, and he was wearing a natty checked suit. He was perched on the edge of the bed, one slender leg draped over the other, with his gloved hands resting atop his walking stick. Why did he *always* wear fitted kid gloves? Some people dismissed the habit as another of his eccentricities, yet to Lyla they signified something . . . clandestine. Something she didn't really want to know about.

"I don't have all day."

Hoping to keep her fear—and her dinner—under control, Lyla swung the door open and leaned limply against the jamb. The lines of Frazier Foxe's face tightened, outlining the slightest of jowls despite his slenderness. He resembled an English bulldog who'd missed dinner, lean and disgruntled.

"You look absolutely *ghastly,*" he said in his clipped accent. "As well you should, after inhaling all that pheasant and wine."

"Thank you," she rasped. She had the sudden urge to throw up all over this sanctimonious fool.

"We have business, Miss O'Riley. After more than a week, surely you've heard what the customers here are saying about my refinery." Adjusting his monocle, he awaited her reply.

"I didn't know I was supposed to be eavesdropping," Lyla answered sourly. "What—am I to listen at the bedroom doors? You've not spent much time in a parlor house, or you'd know—"

"No need to become insolent, dear heart," Foxe said tautly. "After finding you a job and providing three hundred dollars' worth of new clothes, I thought a token of your appreciation was in order. What *have* you heard?"

"Nothing." What she detested most about Frazier Foxe was that he never raised his voice. He was too damn civil, as though loud talk might rumple his suit. "All the chitchat's about Matt McClanahan's wedding, and Christmas . . . and what sort of risqué little pleasures are in store for the next hour," she added, to ruffle his feathers.

Foxe's hands twitched; apparently he thought lovemaking was an improper topic even in a whorehouse. "Well! The talk at Delmonico's was about you and the marshal," he said with a hint of a grin. Frazier twisted one tip of his waxed mustache as though pondering the most pointed way to finish. "I hear congratulations are in order. Am I invited to your wedding?"

Lyla felt the color drain from her face. "I—I don't know what you're talking—"

"Of *course* you do, dear heart," he interrupted with simpering cheerfulness. "Why, the way Prudence Spickle tells it, Barry Thompson's afloat on a veritable *ocean* of happiness—as well he should be, now that I've attired you so attractively."

Her stomach shuddered. This conversation had taken a turn she didn't like; even though he was merely repeating what the real culprit had told him, Frazier's own undertones were unmistakable. "Miss Spickle strikes me as a woman with a very creative tongue," Lyla said in a coiled voice.

"Most women enjoy spreading news about weddings. And it was news she got from the marshal himself," Foxe added smugly. "The way he followed you out through the kitchen confirms it. Barry Thompson *wants* you, Miss O'Riley."

Standing before this impeccably proper man as he tittered at his own jokes about her was the ultimate embarrassment. Lyla stepped away from the door, determined to leave before he let the other shoe drop, but he sprang lithely from the bunk and planted himself in the aisle, his gold-headed walking stick centered precisely between his stylish leather shoes.

"We're not finished," he whispered.

"Yes, we are. I have to help the ladies prepare—"

"Inebriated as you are, you'll knock the crystal from the tables," Frazier replied lightly. "Your job is to sober up, dear heart, and then to adorn yourself for the wedding and reception, where you'll settle that apparent *tiff* you had with the marshal. The silver-blue taffeta gown should do nicely."

"Why?"

Foxe blinked. "Because it's the most exquisite. I chose the fabric to complement your—"

"Why am I to reconcile with Thompson?" Lyla braced herself for a reply she already knew she would despise.

The man before her chuckled to himself. "Did you hear what he said about my refinery idea at the party last night?"

"No. I must've been fetching tarts from the kitchen."

"He said it was *stupid!* And in this enlightened era, we can't—*shan't!*—tolerate such ignorance. So—" he continued in a proprietary tone, "you shall help me educate him. Drink with him, dance with him— seduce him, if you like. You might as well live up to the gossip."

Lyla shot him a look that should've melted his mustache wax. "And what does that have to do with contributing to your mill, Mr. Foxe?"

"Nothing, and everything. If you tell him my refinery's a worthwhile investment, he'll hang on every word. He *adores* you, Miss Lyla."

"And if he refuses to fall for it?" She crossed her arms, feeling sicker by the minute. It was pillars of society like Frazier Foxe who required the deepest dirt to remain standing.

"He'll be eternally sorry he ridiculed me in front of my friends. And so will you." He laughed almost girlishly and ran a gloved fingertip along her cheek. "Take your nap now, dear heart, and I'll make your excuses to Miss Chatterly. I expect nothing short of radiance to rival the bride's tonight. *Radiance!*"

Chapter 4

The church was filling rapidly when the usher escorted Lyla and the others from the Golden Rose to their pews near the front. The ladies spoke with hushed excitement as they glanced around the magnificent sanctuary, which was adorned with lace-trimmed bouquets of red and pink roses. Candles flickered serenely behind the altar and in the bronze sconces on the walls; the fresh scent of pine garlands blended with the flowers' subtle sweetness, enveloping the congregation in a warm, fragrant sense of expectation.

Lyla settled herself between Princess Cherry Blossom and Darla, a henna-haired dove who seemed pleased to provide commentary about everyone around them.

"My stars, would you look at this crowd!" the vibrant whore whispered. "Miss Burnham and Matt certainly know their share of good-looking men. But then, I've known most of them myself, at one time or another."

Smiling, Lyla nodded during appropriate pauses while the redhead chattered on. A nap and numerous cups of strong tea had released her from the wine's wily grip, and all the ladies had complimented her silver-blue gown, yet she fell far short of the radiance Frazier Foxe was expecting. Her stomach was still

43

complaining about her gluttonous lunch, so the thought of the feast and wedding cake that awaited them at the Rose only made her queasy.

At least they were seated far enough down that she wouldn't spot Mr. Foxe in the crowd. Or was it Barry Thompson she wished to avoid? She'd be serving the wedding cake, so confronting him was inevitable. And after learning about her part of the bargain she'd never meant to strike with Frazier Foxe, it was clear she had to dissuade the marshal from ever seeing her again.

". . . and the young colored man sitting down at the piano is Josh LeFevre," Darla was saying. "He and his wife Zenia came back just to perform for Miss Emily's wedding. He used to play at the Rose, you know, until Zenia was nearly killed by a bartender who became quite taken with her."

"Goodness," Lyla mumbled as the pianist began to play. "I'm surprised they'd return to Cripple. Miss Burnham must garner a great deal of loyalty."

"She's the one who got rid of the bartender. Same outlaw who killed her daddy, you see—but that's another story." Darla sucked in her breath and gazed wide-eyed toward the door at the side of the chancel, where three men were entering the sanctuary.

"God, what a man," Princess Cherry Blossom murmured on Lyla's other side. "Every woman here wishes she were Emily tonight. Matt McClanahan's a fine piece of work. A true gentleman."

It was the first time the Indian princess had spoken since they'd arrived, and Lyla heard a deep sense of loss and frustration in her husky voice. Without her war paint and buckskins, the adventurous whore looked positively meek, far less intimidating than when she regaled the Rose's clients with her ribald jokes.

And Matt *did* look stunning in his black cutaway coat with tails and pinstriped trousers. As the robed minister ascended the two steps behind him, the groom swept the crowd with a confident smile and then looked expectantly toward the rear of the church.

But it was Barry Thompson who had Lyla holding her breath. He stood beside McClanahan, a head taller and several inches broader at the shoulders, his hands clasped before him as he surveyed the congregation. When his eyes found hers, she could only stare back, helpless beneath his gaze.

Josh LeFevre played a rolling arpeggio which silenced the whispers and had people craning in their seats as the Wedding March began. The stately chords filled the church, the melody carrying to the high, beamed ceiling even though the pianist was playing with effortless control. A buxom bridesmaid appeared, regally attired in a cerise gown trimmed with ermine and pearls, and Lyla gaped. "It's Miss Victoria!"

"Isn't she something?" Darla whispered back. "She and Emily have gotten real close since Mr. Burnham was killed. Kind of standing in for the mother who died when she was born, you know."

Lyla nodded, somewhat amazed that madams and marshals and millionaire brides meshed so comfortably. Yet Cripple Creek society thrived on such juxtapositions of social status. She flashed Miss Chatterly a grin, admiring the woman's exquisite gown and the proud way she wore it.

Then a majestic piano crescendo announced the coming of the bride, and people were on their feet. It was a poor time to be short: oohs and ahs rose above her head as the crowd around her leaned forward for a glimpse of the illustrious Emily Burnham. All Lyla could see were dark suits and colorful gowns and Cherry Blossom's bare shoulders, until the bridal trio strode sedately past their pew.

"You know Silas Hughes, of course," Darla spoke next to her ear. "Emily's deeded the Angel Claire to him, and that colored man on her right helped raise

45

her at the ranch. Name's Idaho something."

Lyla nodded, struck again by the way Miss Burnham managed to bring such opposites together. The bride was a heavenly vision, afloat in a shimmering gown of white satin with lace-capped leg-of-mutton sleeves that dwarfed her tiny waist. Her golden hair was swept up beneath a gossamer veil which cascaded the entire length of her train. She was so petite and lovely, kissing each of her escorts before slipping her hand under Matt McClanahan's elbow. Lyla despaired of ever being that elegant, or that obviously adored, or of ever having such a perfect lifetime to look forward to.

Thompson, too, had watched the procession with a mixture of wonder and wistfulness. Emily shone like the Star of Bethlehem, radiating a love so complete and serene he could only ache in McClanahan's shadow. He knew he was partly responsible for this glorious moment: he'd saved Matt after an explosion, and then rescued Emily from pining away when she thought he was dead. But it was a fleeting victory. As he watched the couple exchange vows, he doubted the aquamarine in his pocket would ever find its home on Lyla O'Riley's hand. The way she'd run off and then hid from him made her feelings painfully plain.

LeFevre was playing softly on the piano now, familiar triplets that brought Zenia to her feet beside him. This couple, too, basked in each other's love, their brown faces aglow as they cued each other. The congregation behind him held its breath in expectation, for Zenia's voice had made her something of a legend during the few weeks she'd lived here.

> *O holy night*
> *The stars are brightly shining . . .*

The colored girl's words stirred him. Could Lyla feel their power, too? Barry turned slightly, only intending to glance at her, yet her enthralled expression held him captive. Her gown glowed like blue moonlight in the candlelit sanctuary; her hair, pulled into a knot at her crown, shimmered past her shoulders—a style that was deceptively innocent and extremely flattering. Lyla's breasts rose with the volume of Zenia's song. She was spellbound, as he was, and he pulsed with a longing that was as emotional as it was physical. God, but he wanted her to love him!

Till he appeared
And the soul felt its worth . . .

Lyla felt a tugging on her heartstrings and held her breath when she saw how intently Barry Thompson was studying her. His expression held no malice—in fact, it mirrored her own silent desperation. He was so large and so handsome, yet he appeared every bit as lonely and vulnerable as she was, standing there beside his best friend. And Barry *had* made her soul feel its worth: he wanted her for herself rather than for what she could give him or do for him. What would it hurt to allow herself a little more laughter, a few more exhilarating kisses?

Fall on your knees . . .

It seemed God was directing him to forget Lyla's talent for escape and propose to her tonight. Her eyes glimmered like the ring in his pocket, and he sensed she'd be more receptive to his ideas now that she'd seen how the glory of true love could transform them.

O hear the angel voices . . .

Lyla's heart soared with the words of the song. The angels were indeed telling her to listen to her heart and give this man a chance!

47

Barry saw a tear slither down her cheek and his insides tightened. She'd never blinked, never looked away, and her yearnings were written all over her face . . . tender feelings he intended to share the moment they could slip away and be alone.

The song climaxed, and as Zenia's sweet soprano rang out triumphantly, Lyla released a silent sob at the sheer beauty of it. The marshal's gaze faltered only when Matt nudged him for the ring. The rest of the ceremony went by without Lyla's being aware of it, because every throb of her heart told her she could no longer deny her feelings for Barry Thompson.

But a tiny voice in the back of her mind said she must.

The marshal entered the Golden Rose, pausing to brush the snow from his shoulders as he took in the familiar scene. The ballroom was already alive with the excitement of Josh LeFevre and a small orchestra playing a ragtime waltz. Husbands who frequented the parlor house on the sly were here, some dancing with their wives on this very special occasion, and the bachelors were being entertained by the finest doves to be found in Cripple Creek. The candles on the parlor Christmas tree winked at him; the beribboned sconces in the ballroom scented the whole house with hollyberry, accentuated by the pungent scent of the evergreen garlands over the doors.

The Rose's opulence always lifted his spirits—such a contrast from the barren, drafty jailhouse that smelled of unwashed drunks most nights. Barry scanned the crowd. Matt and Emily were waltzing on the dais, while Silas Hughes danced with Miss Victoria. One whole wall was laid out as a buffet, loaded with the choicest cuts of meat, fresh oysters, elegant pastries, plum puddings, and other delicacies only the wealthy ever got to enjoy.

The morsel *he* wanted stood behind the cake table. Lyla appeared to have suffered no ill effects from her double dinner. Her gown swayed provocatively each time she handed someone a plate of cake, and her bodice was cut so low that the silver shamrock pendant glistened at the crease between her breasts. He'd taken his time walking here, planning what he wanted to say, but the magic of her presence spirited away his eloquent thoughts.

From the corner of her eye Lyla watched him approach. She purposely scraped the gooey coating off the cake platter so as not to encourage him. Much as she liked the tall, husky marshal, she couldn't in good conscience accept his advances—especially since Frazier Foxe was watching them from the far corner.

Well aware that the coy Irish girl was ignoring him, Barry grasped her hand as she scraped the wet clump of golden crumbs from her knife onto the platter's edge. "That's the best part of the cake," he mumbled, wishing he had something more profound to say.

Lyla looked up at him, her periwinkle eyes sparkling. "That's why I volunteered to cut—so *I* could have it!"

She stuck a lump of the sweet goo into her mouth and then teased him by very slowly pulling her finger between her lips. Lyla didn't want him to go away angry. But she did want him to go away—for his own good. "So—am I invited to *your* wedding, Marshal Thompson?"

The lady had the uncanny ability to steal his thunder. But at least she was speaking to him, and he could certainly return her fire. "And just where did you hear that rumor?"

Lyla blinked. If she answered honestly, she'd get into uncomfortable territory. But the way Barry was ogling her low neckline, and the way Foxe's gaze was

49

boring into her backside, perhaps it was best to get this ordeal over with. "Apparently it was all the talk at the restaurant."

"And how would *you* know that?"

She shifted her weight to the other leg. "Mr. Foxe thought I should be aware of—he—"

"Did he pull you out of that trunk after I left?"

Lyla's mouth dropped open. The lawman sounded deadly serious, yet when she looked up, his green eyes were twinkling like baubles on a Christmas tree. She grinned sheepishly. "No, I climbed out for some air and then gave myself away by belching rather rudely. That was a fine lunch you ordered for us, marshal. I enjoyed it immensely."

The laughter started in his chest and erupted into a belly laugh such as Thompson hadn't experienced for months. Understatement was another of this Irish imp's talents, it seemed, and he was determined to discover more. "Dance with me, Lyla. It's the least you can do after leaving me to look like a fool in Delmonico's."

She hesitated; swaying in this handsome man's arms would only make what she had to say more difficult. The wink of Foxe's monocle egged her on, though. At least it would appear she was coaxing Thompson to contribute to the refinery fund while she was actually warning him to run like hell in the opposite direction.

As though on cue, the musicians struck up a dreamlike waltz and Lyla was trapped. She loved to dance. And when the tall, tuxedoed marshal opened his arms, the invitation on his ruddy face tugged at the very core of her.

Barry was a surprisingly graceful partner, large as he was, and for several moments she allowed herself to soar on the wings of the fantasy he'd created. He wanted to marry her—wouldn't have started such a rumor if he weren't serious—and she imagined herself floating down the aisle of the church arrayed

50

in shimmering white, just as Emily Burnham had done.

"Frazier's staring at us," Thompson teased softly. "You sure there's nothing between you two?"

"Mr. Foxe is the coldest, most . . ." Lyla sighed and stared at the knot in her partner's white tie, hoping her next words sounded like an effective warning. "I'm not supposed to tell you this, but Frazier vows he'll get even if you don't contribute to his refinery. He hates being ridiculed."

"Get even?" Barry laughed aloud, realizing the cause for his woman's anxiety now. "Honey, he's got to catch up to me first, and that'll never happen. If what I said yesterday hurt his feelings, we'll just give him something more to pout about."

Suddenly she was eye to eye with the marshal, who'd led her into a graceful dip and then swung her effortlessly against his chest, never missing a beat. Her pulse fluttered frantically. He wasn't *listening*—

"Lyla, please," he whispered, "let me speak my piece. Watching you at the wedding, I knew you wanted the same things Matt and Emily have found—the things I've waited so long for myself."

Speechless, she felt herself being waltzed into the curtained alcove between the ballroom and the hall. It was a dim little nook, angled beneath the grand staircase, and as Barry's arm tightened around her, his shadowy face made her hold her breath. He was going to propose! And if she accepted, she'd make him Foxe's target for sure.

Barry leaned back against the wall and placed one foot on the seat of a nearby chair. God, but he wanted her! She was lodged between his thigh and his chest now, her sweet weight pressing into him, her breasts temptingly displayed where he couldn't help but gaze at them. Lyla's eyes were as wide as a frightened fawn's, but with the right words he'd convince her he wanted to love and protect her for the rest of her life.

He breathed deep and pulled her closer to nuzzle

her ear. "Lord, but I love a woman with some shape to her," he murmured. His hands roamed the warm, smooth expanses of her taffeta gown, finding the curve of her waist and then the fullness of her hips. "How is it you always smell like peppermint, honey? It's my favorite sweet, you know."

At last, an answer that could move the conversation back to a rational level! With her legs parted over Barry's thigh and her breasts crushed against him, Lyla could barely think, much less drive him away. "It—it's schnapps!" she replied raggedly. "The Indian princess keeps a bottle in the bathing suite, for a breath freshener!"

Stroking the silky curls that tumbled down her back, he chuckled. He was quite aware of the gadgets and enticements Cherry Blossom stashed in the room down the hall; he had half a mind to carry Lyla there and show her the pleasures they could bring.

But the girl in his arms was too fresh and exciting to make such games necessary. Just the thought of loving her made him stiffen in the tight confines of his trousers. "I'm trying very hard to behave myself, Miss O'Riley," he said in a husky whisper. "But you feel so damn good—so right."

His lips found hers and Lyla closed her eyes against a wave of rapture. One hand was still on his shoulder from their waltz, and the other found the thick, wavy hair at Barry's nape. Her mouth opened beneath his; his low moan made a subtle accompaniment to the languid dance his tongue did with hers. He kissed her again, more fervently, his embrace tightening until she felt his heart thundering against her own. When one large, gentle palm very nearly caressed her breast, it was all she could do to slap him.

"What was that for?" he rasped.

"I—I can't! I'm betrothed to another man."

Barry blinked away the impassioned fog that was

52

muddling his mind. "But you said at lunch there was no one—"

"I lied!" Lyla forced herself to look into his deep green eyes, which were now clouded with pain and confusion. "When my letter about Mick's death arrives home, it'll be Hadley who comes to fetch me back. What with my oldest brothers Dan and Denny claiming the sheep ranch—they're twins, you see— Hadley was gracious enough to accept my hand without requiring a dowry, so I'd be terribly rude to—"

Her rapid brogue betrayed her panic, yet Barry sensed her situation in Ireland was fact rather than fabrication. He shifted her weight, retaining his hold on her. "You don't love him," he said in a tight voice, "or you wouldn't be so set on staying in America. Wouldn't have come over in the first place."

Lyla swallowed. Her attempts at rejection were going nowhere, and he seemed to see through every ruse. Perhaps a touch of the truth would convince him to leave her alone before they both got hurt. "I came to this country to get away from Hadley McDuff," she admitted in the firmest voice she could find. "I *hate* being trapped—*detest* men like my father and McDuff—and *you*—who decide what they want from me without asking what *I* think!"

Thompson flinched. Perhaps he'd come on a little too boldly, but this girl surely realized his intentions were the best. "Honey, I've never forced you into anything. You didn't let on like you *minded* when I found you in the pantry, or kissed you just now, so how—"

"Don't you get it?" she blurted, hating herself for the way she was about to wound him. "I don't *want* you, Thompson. You're coarse and crude and— always *fondling* every woman you see, like—like some *beast!* Like a damn ram who can't stop rutting!"

He was too stunned to stop her when she

53

clambered awkwardly off his lap. And he'd be damned if he'd chase after her and ruin McClanahan's party by starting an argument. Never in his life had any woman accused him of being coarse or crude, and by God, he'd set her straight when they didn't have an audience.

Barry sighed and slid dejectedly into the chair. The music was livelier now. His friends' laughter was getting louder as the liquor flowed . . . and something stronger than punch sounded like the perfect tonic to bolster his bruised feelings. Cherry Blossom kept a bottle of good brandy in the bathing suite, too, bless her, so he ambled down the hallway.

At the dessert table, Lyla was slicing off pieces of tender white cake as though a hundred guests were waiting in line. Nearly sliced her finger, too, blinded as she was by her tears. She should've escaped through the alcove's other door, because Frazier Foxe would be here any second, wondering why she'd come out alone, obviously agitated.

On a sudden inspiration, she picked up two plates of cake and assumed what she hoped was a lovestruck expression. She could pretend to be slipping back in to Barry to continue their tryst, and pass through the alcove to the back stairway instead. Once upstairs, she could figure out a way to leave the Golden Rose and Frazier Foxe behind her forever. It would mean never seeing Barry again, but after the insults she'd just hurled at him, Lyla doubted she could ever face the marshal, anyway.

A pistol barked and her plates fell, shattering on the parquet floor. The music stopped. Amid the ladies' shrieks she heard gruff orders being called out.

"Up against the wall! Take off your rings and watches, all of you!"

The crowd froze, confused, until another shot rang out and had people scurrying toward one side of the ballroom like frightened livestock. As she was carried along in a tide of gasping women and their muttering escorts, Lyla caught a glimpse of the intruders who'd brought the reception to such a drastic halt. There were three of them, dressed in heavy coats, hats, and bandanas that covered their faces. Moving with menacing grace, they waved the revelers into a line with their pistols while the shortest marauder pulled a flour sack from inside his jacket.

"Quit your yackin'!" came his muffled command, and another bullet through the ceiling made the room ring with silence. "If you wanna live to see Christmas, you'll cooperate when these boys relieve you of your valuables, understand? Anybody caught holdin' back'll be real sorry."

Just as Lyla fell into line with the others she saw the marshal at the ballroom doorway. She tried to signal him with an unobtrusive wave, but one of the robbers saw her and then let out a cackle.

"Well, now. I think this lawman wants to be the first to kick in for the cause—don't you, boys?" the cocky thug called out. "He can set an example as to how the rest of 'em should behave. Grab his gun while you're at it."

While the leader pointed his pistol toward Barry's chest, his accomplices frisked the marshal with obvious glee. They yanked the gold watch from his vest pocket and, seeing no rings on his fingers, commanded him to empty his trousers. Lyla's heart was in her throat. She wasn't surprised that Thompson had come unarmed—few of these elite guests would be sporting weapons tonight—but then the shortest thug plucked something large and shiny from his palm.

"Whooo-ee! Looky here, boys," he said as he waved the object in front of them. "The marshal musta had excitin' plans for tonight. Coulda got a hole in his pocket, totin' this big ring around. Which one of these fine ladies was this for, loverboy?"

Thompson had been observing the three men

carefully to see if he recognized any of them. Their insolence irked him. "What the hell do you think you'll accomplish here?" he challenged. "In the first place, you won't make it out of Cripple with this jewelry, and in the second place, you won't be able to hock it. There's not a jeweler in Colorado stupid enough to resell these custom-made pieces."

"Shut up and stand with your nose to the wall, smartass," the man with the flour sack ordered. "One false move outta you and your friends here'll be springin' leaks on this fine dance floor." He gestured for Thompson's assailant to hold him against the far side of the room with his pistol in his spine, and then trotted to the beginning of the line of reception guests. "Let's get a move on. Wastin' too much time. Toss me that ring."

When she saw the huge, pale stone glimmer in mid-air, Lyla felt her breath catch in her throat. It was a beautiful piece—hundreds of dollars Barry must have spent on it. And it was obviously intended for her. She felt the curious gazes of others who'd heard Thompson's engagement rumors in the restaurant and her cheeks scalded with embarrassment. Staring at the floor, she heard the two thugs harassing their other hostages.

"Help us out, damn it. Don't make me yank them rubies off ya."

"You, sir—I bet there's matchin' gold cuff links for that tietack."

"Gimme that cane. Gotta be two hundred dollars wortha gold on that knob."

Lyla glanced up just as an indignant Frazier Foxe surrendered his walking stick, followed by an ornate gold watch, a money clip, and numerous gold coins from his pockets. The short man with the sack gave the orders and watched each piece disappear into his bag, a malevolent Saint Nicholas in reverse. His accomplice held the pistol to the victims' heads, and then turned them toward the wall when they'd contributed. No one was brave enough to protest or make a sound as the two marauders went about their work with quick efficiency.

Emily McClanahan's gold locket and wedding ring . . . Miss Victoria's tiara and diamond pendant . . . Silas Hughes' engraved watch and fob. The whores, too, lost anything that looked like it could be of value, their faces pinched with bitterness as they dropped the items in the sack. Then the pistol was pointed at her ear, and the two bandits were gazing expectantly at Lyla. "Cough up, sugar. A dress that purty means jewels to go with it."

She stared into two eyes that shone like black agate above the thief's blue bandana. Had she seen this man before?

"Get the shamrock. We gotta move."

Lyla gasped as the delicate chain of Mick's memento snapped at the back of her neck. "But that's my only—you *can't* take that—"

"Shut up or you'll be eatin' bullets. Nose to the wallpaper, you little slut."

Her lungs emptied in a rush when she thudded against the wall, but her discomfort was nothing compared with her anger. *I'll get you, you damned —nobody steals my silver shamrock!* she fumed silently. *I will get it back. Or by the saints, I'll die trying!*

Chapter 5

Before the muffled thunder of the bandits' hoof-beats died away, Barry was hurrying toward the door, tugging at his tie. "You folks rest assured, you'll get your valuables back," he called out over the murmuring crowd. "Soon as I get rid of these glad rags, I'll get my deputy and a posse and I'll be on their trail. Stay here where it's warm and safe. Those desperadoes'll shoot to kill."

Lyla was already scampering toward the grand stairway, lifting her dress as she took two steps at a time.

"Don't get any ideas about riding with us, young lady!" the marshal ordered. "You've got no business—"

"*Watch* me!" she hollered over her shoulder. By the time she rounded the third-floor landing, Lyla was free of her bodice. Her dress slithered into a billowing pool of blue taffeta at the foot of her bunk as she dashed toward the closet. "Damn corset!" she muttered, clawing at her tightly-laced back.

Her trunk held a pair of denim jeans and a heavy flannel shirt, work clothing she'd thrown in when Frazier Foxe had announced she was moving to town. The dry, familiar scent of the garments soothed her as she tugged them on—*nobody* would tell her to stay put when her brother's handmade treasure had been carried off! Especially since one of the thieves had had such a familiar air about him.

Lyla slipped into Mick's fleece-lined jacket and crammed his hat down over her hair, wishing she'd brought his pistol to the Rose, too. But there was no time now to hunt a weapon. Her heavy boots clattered on the back stairs and then she was out the bordello's back exit, leaving the agitated chatter of reception guests behind her.

The wind caught her at the corner and she grabbed her hat. Snow had been falling all evening, covering Cripple's buildings and the surrounding hillsides with a thick carpet of white that glowed beneath the deep azure sky. The serenity of Christmas Eve was broken by men calling to each other as they hurried to the livery stable.

"They're headed toward Victor!"

"Probably going to hole up in Phantom Canyon. You boys watch out," came Thompson's warning. "Awfully easy to get ambushed from those cliffs."

Lyla saw the marshal's tall form silhouetted in the stable doorway. By the light of flickering lanterns she watched him saddle his huge buckskin stallion. When he mounted and loped out the door followed by his handful of men, she slipped into the corner stall where her own painted mare stood munching hay.

"Come on, Calico. Time to work off some of that feed," Lyla whispered. She stroked the horse's velvety nose and then quickly buckled the bridle over her head. "You've got to give me your best tonight, girl. We're making this ride for Mick as much as for me."

Moments later Lyla urged the sturdy mare into a trot, out of the shadowy stable and into a twilit snowscape that would've held her in awe had she not been on such an urgent journey. Already the posse's tracks were blurring with new snow. She nudged Calico into a gallop, praying the footing was firm . . . praying she hadn't made herself a target by lagging after the marshal and his men.

Once the lights of Cripple Creek were behind them, a deep, wintry stillness closed in. There were only the sounds of her mare's muffled hoofbeats and steady breathing. Snowflakes whirled around them, borne by a wind that stung her eyes and cheeks. Lyla pressed on, thankful the horse knew the way after the numerous trips she'd made into town from the cabin in Phantom Canyon.

She would stay there tonight after she retrieved the silver shamrock; thoughts of a cheerful fire and the simple, cozy furnishings made her press on across the rugged white terrain. If she arrived in time, she could prove to Barry Thompson that she was a woman to be reckoned with, a woman who set her own terms. Once they'd captured the bandits, perhaps the burly lawman would send his men back to the jailhouse, prisoners in tow, and then explain the glittering aquamarine that he would pick out from among the other items in that flour sack. It would be a night to remember, a night to set things straight between them, away from wagging tongues and the glitter of Foxe's monocle. Barry would understand why she'd called him such ugly names and forgive—

Calico's nicker interrupted her thoughts, and when the mare's ears pricked forward, Lyla listened, too. The whine of gunfire sliced the night silence, and then came answering shots and urgent voices. Somehow the miles had passed, and she was approaching the narrows that led into Phantom Canyon. She stared intently at the snowy trail ahead and discerned two sets of tracks: the posse had divided, some men taking the road between the rugged rock walls, and some clambering the higher, more treacherous trail that ran atop the side of the canyon.

Which way had Barry gone? Lyla reined in, allowing her horse to catch its breath, but another volley of gunfire convinced her to head for the cover of the trees. "Up the trail, girl. Just like we were going home," she murmured, pressing her knees into the mare's heaving sides. "Easy does it. One slip and we could end up on the canyon floor full of bullets."

She let Calico pick her way among the pines, keeping to the shadows as she tried to figure out where the outlaws and posse were. Unarmed, Lyla knew she'd be a detriment to the marshal's cause if she attracted attention. It was best to let the men do their jobs and then move in afterward to help, if they needed her.

A bullet whistled by and Lyla's heart raced. She could hear the thieves trading threats with Thompson now, their shots punctuating the dialog, ricocheting through the night air with deadly urgency. Just as she eased to the edge of a clearing, two shots ended in muffled thuds and she saw the marshal slump in his saddle.

Terror seized her. The two bandits he'd challenged wheeled on their horses, one of them hollering, "Gotta go now, Thompson! Your men'll be real sorry they came along!" Their wicked laughter echoed in the canyon below as they loped off through the trees.

Lyla trotted toward the marshal's inert form, so scared she didn't realize she was holding her breath. There was enough moonlight for her to see the gruesome, dark trickle running down his left thigh. His reins had dropped to the ground and he was clutching his mount's muscled neck, gasping for breath as though he barely had the strength to stay in the saddle.

"Easy, boy. Stay still now," Lyla crooned as she rode alongside the stallion. The horse stood several hands higher than Calico, a powerful animal who was sidestepping with his ears cocked back. "We've got to get Barry out of this wind, to tend his wounds. Help me out now, horse."

"His name's Buck. That's what he'll do if anybody besides me tries to ride him."

The marshal's pallor shocked her, but at least he was coherent. Very slowly, Lyla reached out until she had Buck's reins in her hand. "My cabin's not far from here," she replied in a voice strangled with fear. "You hold on, love. God bless us both if you fall off, because I couldn't budge you."

Thompson grunted and made a feeble attempt to stay on his horse. Through a red haze of pain he recognized Lyla's brogue . . . he had no choice but to ride behind her, because he could feel his strength ebbing at an alarming rate, blood flowing from the gash in his thigh and the hole in his shoulder. Must've struck some major veins . . . the awareness that his posse was in danger glimmered like a candle in the back of his mind, but the light was growing dimmer . . . dimmer . . .

Sensing that Barry would soon be unable to walk, Lyla urged Calico into the quickest pace she dared. The snow was deep enough to disguise irregular spots in the trail, and more than once the horses stumbled over hidden rocks and dips as they cut back toward the hollow that sheltered the cabin. She could see the tin top of its chimney gleaming dully a short distance ahead, and she prayed that she could somehow help the marshal inside and then revive him, enough that they could ride back to the Cripple hospital after she bound his wounds.

"Whoa, Calico. Let's lead him as close to the cabin as we can. Good girl," Lyla mumbled when the horses stood before her door. She dismounted carefully so she wouldn't spook the stallion. He eyed her warily, but allowed her to stroke his neck before he whickered and shook his tawny head. "Good boy, Buck," she said in a low voice. "We're going to unload this fellow, and then you're to follow my mare to the shed in back, understand? No horsing around or heading back to town. We'll need you in a bit."

A glance at Barry told her he was either unconscious or asleep. What if he fell and banged his head before she could stop him? Lyla opened the door and then returned to his left side, her heart pounding. "Barry? You've got to swing your other leg over," she ordered above the gusting of the wind. "Let's get inside so I can stop this nasty bleeding."

Thompson groaned. God, he was tired, and his entire left side throbbed with an agony so sharp it dulled his perception. Somebody was talking . . . *get inside . . . nasty bleeding* . . . Gritting his teeth, he lifted his right leg over the saddle, which sent a burst of pain through the wounded leg in the stirrup. He was pretty sure the scream he heard was his own. Buck shifted nervously, but somehow both feet reached the ground and he held himself upright by clutching the saddle.

"Lean on me, love. We'll get you to the bunk and patch you up," Lyla said with forced bravery. She guided Barry's arm around her shoulder and then gasped when he teetered, landing heavily against her back. Sheer fright propelled her toward the door, which was banging in the wind. *"Walk,* you big bull moose!" she cried out. "If you fall on me, we'll both freeze to death!"

Thompson rallied weakly, realizing there was shelter ahead and a tiny body supporting him as they approached it. They were inside . . . shadows of furniture, and he was falling, helpless. "Christ!" he muttered when he landed on the mattress. And then, thank God, somebody snuffed out all his candles.

Gasping for breath, Lyla hurried to close the door against the swirling snow. "Go on to the shed, Calico!" she called outside. "I'll tend to you as soon as I can."

She fell against the door to close it, and then laid logs for a fire as quickly as her quaking hands would allow. When the flame was licking at the dry twigs, she rushed about the cabin gathering supplies. The earthy scent of all her plants and dry, hanging herbs soothed her; the familiarity of all she'd left behind wrapped itself around her, but there was no time to savor the joy of being home again. Barry's breathing was shallow and irregular. The flickering firelight revealed a pant leg soaked with blood, and now his jacket sleeve, too, was dark and wet.

From the closet she fetched a pail and bandages and the herbs that would cleanse his wounds: lavender, yarrow, thyme, and others, some she'd grown herself, and some in square boxes and corked bottles from the druggist. She put a kettle on to boil, and as she glanced toward the inert form that hung over the end of the small bed, Lyla steeled herself for the teeth-gritting task of getting Barry's clothes off him. It would be like rolling a felled redwood: dead weight. She brought a bottle of laudanum and the last of Mick's whiskey to the bedside, in case she hurt him enough to wake him up.

Lyla paused, thinking. She couldn't cut his clothing off, because he needed its protection during the ride back. Starting with his good side, she wrestled him out of his coat sleeve and one side of his heavy plaid shirt. It took all her strength to stuff the garments beneath him and then turn him from the other side to pull them through. She blanched when she saw the dark, saturated top of his union suit sticking to his shoulder, but there was no time to waste. Thompson was moaning softly, grimacing as she tugged at his boots and peeled his pants down over the other wound.

She chuckled wryly. Barry would be kicking himself if he knew she was stripping him naked and he couldn't return the favor. Lyla reached for his underwear buttons, her hands trembling with fright and awe. He was firmly muscled, far more powerfully built than the miners she'd treated for an occasional cut or wound. Again she started with his right sleeve, stretching the thick flannel over arms and shoulders that dwarfed her own, praying he wasn't aware of the pain she was causing him.

She rolled him as before, gingerly lifting the sticky, bloodied fabric from the matted hair on his chest. Lyla dared not look at his face or at the gruesome hole that gaped above his left armpit. It was all she could do to tug steadily at his underwear, past his waist, where the down of his chest peaked below his navel; past the smooth flesh of his abdomen and a set of privates that lolled between his legs.

Lyla stopped to stare. She'd caught glimpses of Mick and his buddies skinny-dipping, but never had she beheld a man who was so unabashedly displayed . . . or so undeniably huge. Even in his unconscious state, Barry Thompson brought to mind a proud stallion—regally, majestically male. She let out the breath she'd been holding and eased his union suit over his other seeping wound, then down past his knees.

"Now that you've looked me over, am I worth saving, little lady?"

Lyla jerked to attention, her cheeks flooding with color. Barry's eyes were only half open in a face the color of milk. He was watching her with a smile that was half grimace. "I—sorry if I pulled too hard, I—"

"Yanking the way you were, you could revive the dead. No joke intended," he added weakly. Barry could feel the life oozing out of him and knew this was no time to be witty. "Get your sharpest knife. Cut the bullets out."

The air rushed from her lungs. "But I can't—we're taking you to the hospital, as soon as I—"

"I'll never make it. Can't ride . . . probably be ambushed . . ."

Lyla's heart was in her throat when she saw the ghostly pallor stealing over Thompson's slack face. "Wait! Tell me how to—"

"Whiskey," he mumbled, already dimming behind

65

his eyes. "Lots of whiskey, honey. And work . . . fast. I'm drifting . . . drifting . . ."

A sob escaped her as she grabbed for the bottle beside the bed. After a few deep gulps, Barry seemed unable to swallow and the liquor ran in rivulets down his cheek. He let out a long sigh that sounded like air leaking from a tomb, and then went limp against her.

"Don't you die, Thompson!" Lyla screamed. "Damn you, getting yourself shot, and now—"

Spurred on by her racing heartbeat, Lyla forced herself to look at the gaping wounds. Already the mattress was soaked with blood. Getting Barry to the hospital was impossible, and his life forces flickered even as she watched him slip away into numbness.

Lyla prayed to God and to every saint she could name, and then fetched the sharpest knife she could find.

Chapter 6

While decoctions of lavender and thyme and eucalyptus brewed in large enamel pots, Lyla washed the marshal's wounds. She had unflinching faith in the healing powers of her herbs and in her ability to administer them, but *surgery?* To her great relief, the bullet had passed cleanly through Barry's shoulder, but when she washed his blood-covered thigh, the metal stub taunted her from deep inside his muscles.

Quickly she tied a tourniquet around his arm and disinfected the bullet hole with the hot lavender and eucalyptus. To stop the bleeding, she applied a pack of lady's mantle, binding it tightly to let the pressure and the herbs work while she cut the bullet from his leg. Thompson's breathing was so shallow he appeared lifeless on the bed. Clenching her jaw to keep from crying, Lyla went to the fire to sterilize the knife. What if she cut tendons and he lost the use of his leg? What if gangrene set in? What if—

"Quit stalling or he'll bleed to death, you ninny," she muttered to herself. Lyla returned to the bedside, and after a last prayerful stroking of his light brown hair, began her grisly task.

Instinct overcame her fear and revulsion. In a mercifully short time the bullet clattered to the floor and she was cleansing the wound, applying disinfectant oils and a packing soaked in the thyme

67

decoction to staunch the bleeding. She would have to sew him up, another chore she felt unqualified for . . . another matter she had no choice about.

When Lyla had stitched and applied fresh bandages and covered her pale patient with quilts, she fell exhausted into the nearest chair. It was long past midnight. A day that had begun with eating and drinking for two had progressed through a heart-rending wedding, a reception interrupted by robbers, a bone-chilling ride home, and doctoring that had drained her. She stirred chamomile leaves into a cup of steaming water, longing for the rest it would bring.

The wind woke her from a doze. Thinking it was Barry moaning for laudanum, Lyla jumped up to tend him, only to realize that the snowstorm had blown itself into a blizzard. Soon they would be hostages here—the windows would darken, covered over in opaque white, and the door might be drifted shut. The horses needed food and water, the fireplace and stove would consume more wood than the tinderbox could hold, Barry would require broth and fresh poultices . . . the list stretched on and on in her tired mind. With a weary sigh, Lyla bundled up to begin her night's work.

She was grateful that Mick had set in a large supply of hay, and that she'd put up jars of garden vegetables and tins of dried fruits and jerky. And she was thankful that Frazier Foxe hadn't taken in a new tenant before she could reclaim these efforts. Lyla trudged to the shed, through snow that was drifted past her knees, and set out feed and water for Buck and Calico. Countless armloads of wood got stacked beside the hearth and in the stove's tinderbox. Was it enough to last out the storm?

Lyla's only consolation was that she would be snowed in at home, and that the thugs who shot Thompson would be unable to pester them. They had left Barry for dead, and had no idea that she had

68

given him sanctuary in the secluded little shack. It was a safe place to stay until she could get the marshal back to Cripple for proper medical attention.

She dropped another armload of wood into the tinderbox and checked on him. He'd shifted. His jawline was shaded with stubble that made his cheeks pale by comparison; his face was haunted by pain even as he slept. Lyla placed a hand on his forehead. Cool . . . unnervingly so.

She judged it to be about four in the morning when she started dough for bread and put on a pot of jerky and water to simmer. Barry would need food to keep his strength up. She changed his dressings, pleased that the grievous bleeding had stopped, and then slumped into a chair beside the bed, her hand resting on his good shoulder in case he awoke. Exhaustion overtook her swiftly. Lyla drifted off, lulled by the wind's low song and the yeasty warmth from the hearth.

She came awake with a start and found Barry watching her. He was conscious—alive! She slid forward on her chair, called by aromas of broth and bread that needed looking after, but Thompson grabbed her hand.

"Merry Christmas," he mumbled.

Lyla gaped, speechless with joy. Not only had he survived her amateur doctoring, but he knew what day it was! "Does it hurt? I'll get you some water—"

"Bring a pan. Can't remember the last time I relieved myself."

She blushed to the roots of her hair. Of course he would need to perform such basic functions, and he required her help. Lyla rushed to the kitchen, emptied a jar of carrots into the soup pot, and returned to the bedside. "I hope this'll be—"

"It's fine. Get these covers off me."

Swallowing hard, Lyla did as he asked. It was one thing to tend this virile giant when he was unconscious, and another matter entirely when he was watching her flush and fumble. How was she supposed to aim—

"You hold the jar, and I'll take care of everything else," he said with a quiet chuckle. "Almost makes me wish both arms were wounded."

"Right," Lyla mumbled. She looked away until he was finished, and then carried the jar to the door. It was snowed shut. After placing the container in the far corner of the cabin, she returned to the kitchen and washed her hands. The broth needed stirring, and the bread dough had risen high above the rim of the crockery bowl.

"No need to be embarrassed, Miss O'Riley," a soft voice wafted toward her. "I'd be buried in this blizzard if you'd listened to my orders to stay at the Rose. Instead of strumming a harp, I'm snowed in with a good-looking, good-cooking woman."

The gratitude behind his playful words made her chin quiver. "You'd be playing with a pitchfork and you know it."

"Come here and tell me that to my face."

With a defiant glance toward the green eyes peeking out above his mound of quilts, she continued forming dough into loaves. "If you're strong enough to boss me, you're strong enough to wait, Mr. Thompson."

His answering chuckle sent desire spiraling through her insides. "How long can *you* wait, honey?" he teased. "You'll have to change that bandage, down there where I'll be pointing at you. You'll have to sponge off my entire body. You'll have to—"

"Why do I get the feeling you'd play the invalid till spring, if I let you?" Lyla challenged. She set the bread pans on the hearth and then approached the bunk with her arms crossed, stopping a few feet away.

Barry took in her disheveled hair and rumpled shirt, sorry he'd caused the purple half-moons beneath her tired eyes, yet so far gone in love with her his heart hammered in his chest. "Lyla, please hold me," he mumbled, aware that their short sparring match had sapped his strength. "Touch me like you did at first, as though you truly believe this randy old ram is worth saving."

Was it a trick, a play for her sympathies that would land her in his embrace? Lyla hesitated. They still had important matters to discuss before she could allow herself to fall for his kiss again.

Thompson's eyelids lowered and the outline of her masculine clothes blurred before him. "Thirsty," he breathed.

The timbre of his voice told her this was no ruse. Lyla rushed over for fresh water, chiding herself for becoming distracted by a moment's suggestive chatter when Thompson had days of recovery ahead of him. She sat close, cradling his head in her arm as she held the cup to his lips. "You're getting hot," she noted in a whisper.

"Women do that to me."

"Can't you ever think of anything except—" She was ready to dash his face with the rest of the water, until she realized he was already wet. Sweat beaded on his brow and his body temperature was rising rapidly. "Fever. I hope to God this doesn't mean infection," she prayed aloud.

Thompson looked at her briefly before his eyes crossed and then closed. A moan escaped him and Lyla quickly fetched more herbs to brew into potions. Should she cool him with a wash made from sweet basil and burnet, or induce more sweating with sweet Joe Pye or yarrow tea? "Hang on, Barry. Fight with me," she pleaded as she mopped his brow.

71

The hours passed unheeded as Lyla toiled over him. He would smolder with fever one moment and then shiver with chills. His body was so large she couldn't keep him wiped down or covered enough as his temperature fluctuated. When she asked if he could hear her, his moans grew steadily more delirious. Barry tossed and pitched, sometimes jostling his wounds until they bled again. Frantically she replaced the packing and bound him up, wondering if he would slip away never to return, the moment she took her hands off him.

The dim daylight in the cabin darkened into the most harrowing evening of her life. Lyla was afraid to go to sleep, for fear he'd die; afraid not to sleep, for fear she'd kill him with carelessness. Barry was flushed all over, his fever raging constantly now, and nothing she did affected the fire that threatened to consume him. Her movements became lethargic and her eyes closed more than once in the middle of a task.

One last time she sponged him off. Then she removed her boots and jeans, draped the bear rug from the fireplace over his quilts, and crawled beneath the covers with him. He would either sweat his infection out or die from it. There was nothing more she could do.

Chapter 7

Lyla dreamed Barry was making love to her on the bear rug in front of the crackling fire. His large hands roamed over her body, igniting every sensitive spot they touched, while his mouth plied hers with long, delicious kisses that left her weak with wanting him. His lips moved lower, ever so slowly, until his tongue was teasing her nipples into stiff, aching peaks.

"Lyla . . . let me love you, honey," he murmured as he nuzzled her ear. His gentle fingers slipped beneath the waistband of her lacy drawers, and when they slithered between her legs she squirmed uncontrollably, pressing against him in a silent plea to continue this torment until she could stand it no longer.

She felt like a teakettle at the brink of boiling, each caress sending bubbles of desire higher and higher, the pressure building until she was ready to explode. Lyla awoke with a gasp, stifling a moan so she wouldn't disturb Barry. How could her imagination produce visions of such wondrous, erotic pleasure when she'd never been to bed with a man? She shivered with the memory of his touch and then sucked in her breath.

This was no dream.

Barry's hand rested between her legs while his long, agile fingers massaged and probed, producing a new wave of sensation within her. He was lying on his right side, curled around her like a cocoon as she faced the fireplace. Her drawers were tangled around one ankle. Had she squirmed out of them, or had he tugged them down himself?

That seemed unlikely, since his wounded arm was uppermost, lying along her body in a heavy trail of warmth that led directly to her simmering core. Her knees were bent, and her left leg was hooked over the top of his, following the slow, hypnotic rhythm of his hips and allowing his hand access to this most intimate of caresses.

His right arm pillowed her head and held her back against his broad chest, while his hand followed the curve of her waist until it was cupping her breast with a firm, subtle assurance that made her swell to fill his grasp. How had her shirt come undone? She'd fallen asleep with a man too consumed by fever to feel her presence, yet now he was driving her to a frenzy with purposeful, knowing strokes.

Or were they?

Lyla tried to ignore the dizzying delight he invoked so she could take stock of their situation, quietly, in case he, too, had been caught up in an erotic dream. He showed no signs of delirium: his fever had broken, and his breathing was deep and even, interrupted by impassioned sighs—just as hers was. He was rocking against her, lightly, slowly . . . taking his pleasure at an effortless pace that allowed him to avoid hurting himself. Only Barry Thompson could find a way to make love when he was too weak to leave her bed! Lyla struggled to free herself, but his arms tightened around her.

"Barry! Barry, you've got to stop—"

"Lyla," he murmured against her ear. "Lyla . . . let me love you, honey."

Momentarily stunned by the echo from her dream, she went limp. Where did imagination end and reality begin? His lips were lighting tiny fires along her neck. His breathing tickled her ear until she giggled and squirmed, which only inspired her lover to increase his attentions.

This had to stop! Too much remained unanswered between them. He could reopen his wounds if she allowed him to . . .

Lyla swiveled her head and beheld a face alight with love. Barry's eyes were closed and he was smiling sweetly, well aware of the sly trap he'd set while she was asleep. "Thompson, you—"

His kiss knocked her roughly against his muscled upper arm. He was so large, so powerful, and his mouth opened hers while his plundering tongue struck like a snake. Lyla whimpered, caught in a headlock from which there was no escape.

She struggled against the heavy arm that pinned her to the mattress, yet her panic seemed only to spur him on. He was rock-hard against her backside. When his manhood probed for an opening and found the slickness beneath her hips, Lyla braced herself for the battering she knew was inevitable. His fingers continued to knead her from the front while his shaft sought the slender opening that would bring his release. He was rocking faster, smothering her with a savage kiss that made her cry out with the pitiful sound of a mouse caught in a cat's jaws.

And suddenly he stopped.

He released her lips to draw a deep, shuddery breath. "Lyla . . . Lyla."

She gasped for air, reeling from his assault. "Barry, let me go!"

"Lyla, please love me, honey," he whispered fervently. His eyes flickered open, tranquil and green, and he smiled as though she were the answer to his most urgent prayer. "Lyla, please. Love me . . . make me whole."

For a long moment he gazed at her. Her heartbeat slowed to a steady thrum as she studied his handsome face from this intimate distance. Always one to flee a

75

trap, Lyla searched for signs that his words were a noose disguised by silken sentiments, but she found none. His forehead was free of lines and his eyes shone clear and true; his lips, lush yet distinctly formed, relaxed into a gentle, expectant smile. Barry Thompson had declared his interest in her from the first, and his motives remained sincere and unchanged. He certainly hadn't lied to get her into bed with him.

Lyla was about to remind him of the threats Frazier Foxe had made, but Barry's kiss extinguished all rational thought. His lips brushed softly across hers, hesitant, parted in anticipation, and she relaxed against his arm to receive his affection. Again he kissed her, full and sweet, all signs of force forgotten, like a nightmare she might or might not have had. All she could be sure of as she answered his tongue's invitation was that she was achingly, hopelessly involved with a man whose passions rendered all reason incomprehensible—a man who turned her world upside down with his declarations of love while setting her life right for the very first time.

His languid movements rekindled the flames he'd lit in her dreams. While one hand caressed her breast as though it were an exquisite treasure, his knowing fingers resumed their exploration further below. Lyla gasped, awash in a sea of sensations as his warm, insistent tip slid close to where she was throbbing with an ecstatic pain.

Instinctively she turned, flattening her back to his chest, allowing him to work his subtle magic at will. She was rising, rising . . . striving to stay above the soul-consuming rush she sensed was only moments away. Lyla arched against his broad hand, begging shamelessly, and he responded by rubbing up a slick friction that made her crest with a joyful cry.

Barry angled her away slightly, opening her to the advances of his manhood. She reached between her legs to guide him, no longer afraid of what his awesome length might do to her. He inched inside, pausing until she thought she'd go mad with anticipation. Then she gripped the edge of the bed with both hands and bucked against him.

"Barry!" she shrieked.

He muffled his reply against her hair, moving inside her with increasing speed. Momentary pain made way for another wave of wildfire, sweeter and more prolonged than the first, and Lyla gave her body up to an uncontrollable rapture that reached its peak with Barry's final, forceful thrust.

Her head lolled on the edge of the mattress for several minutes before the room stopped spinning. Thompson's hold relaxed; she suspected their love-making had drained him, and his shallow breathing confirmed it. As her own respiration returned to normal, she noticed the coolness of the cabin. The fire was a pile of gray ash with a few red embers. The air still smelled of fresh bread and broth, which made her aware of how many hours had passed since she'd eaten. And then she listened, holding her breath.

The wind had stopped. The snow was over.

When she eased out from between Barry's arms and legs she got a soft snore in response. Lyla stood beside the bed, shivering from the lack of his body's warmth. The lawman's face was haggard, the sickly color of a cold fish, and she regretted giving in to the drive that had seemed to revive him for those wonderful moments of their lovemaking. Would she also come to regret giving herself to this man, body and soul?

It was no time to ponder such a self-centered question. Thompson had lost a lot of blood, and the sooner he saw a doctor the sooner any infection could be cleared up. She seriously doubted that he could mount Buck, much less make the treacherous ride through the canyon, so it was her responsibility to get him to Cripple somehow.

After rekindling the fire, Lyla dressed and ate two

77

generous slices of bread dipped in the rich, beefy soup. The cabin door was still blocked by a drift, so she tried each dull gray window, making her way from the main room to the kitchen and into the curtained-off closet where she'd slept while Mick was alive. At last! The frame loosened beneath her pounding fist and the snow fell away to reveal a mounded, white world that glistened in the sun.

While shrugging into her coat, she glanced at Barry. He was sleeping, smiling with a contentment that made her chuckle. Lyla hoped he would rest well during the next few days, until she figured out how to transport him to town. She pulled a chair to the closet window, stood on it, and yanked the sash high enough so she could wriggle outside. There were horses to tend, a door to shovel out, wood to be carried—chores that Barry's strong arms could perform twice as quickly as hers, ordinarily.

Lyla sighed. Now that she'd given herself to Thompson, she fervently hoped she was capable of taking care of him.

Thompson jerked and groaned. When his eyes opened he saw a cheerful fire. He smelled bread and beef and a muskiness he couldn't identify. The room was small yet cozy, furnished with functional pieces, embroidered samplers, and plants—everywhere, plants! Red geraniums hung in front of the windows and philodendron stretched in leafy profusion across the mantel. The kitchen window was surrounded by shelves full of pots—green shoots and pale flowers he couldn't name—and bunches of dried herbs hung from the rafters. He sensed he was now free of the demons that had waged war inside him for God knows how long. But where the hell was he?

His effort to raise up on one elbow nearly made him pass out. Then he remembered: he had taken two bullets, Christmas Eve, Phantom Canyon. Gingerly

78

he touched his bandaged left shoulder and then let his hand trail down to the thigh that throbbed painfully in its binding. Someone had saved his life . . . but who?

Barry dozed, shifting beneath the weight of his quilts like a dog settling into warm straw. As badly as he hurt, there was no comfortable way for him to situate himself, and apparently no one around to pour any painkiller down him. He heard a muffled scraping from the direction of the door, and then dozed again. The clatter of boots crossing the floor a little while later sounded too distant to be any threat, so he drifted, dreaming of hot bread and whiskey. Lots of whiskey.

When he awoke, he saw a short figure in a plaid shirt and jeans, with honey hair no self-respecting man would wear so long . . . not to mention a behind that strained suggestively against those back pockets when—*she* leaned over. Barry blinked. Why would a woman have boards, a hammer, and nails arranged on the floor around her?

His companion turned, and the pieces fell into place. "Lyla," he whispered.

"High time you woke up," her brogue teased his groggy ears. "We slept through breakfast and I already ate your lunch."

He held back a laugh that threatened to tear his bad shoulder apart. "Doesn't surprise me. What do I have to pay the cook to work an extra shift?"

"There's not a penny in your pants, marshal. I checked when I took them off you."

Thompson considered this statement with a long sigh. He'd been worse off than he thought if this little flirt had stripped him without his knowledge. "My credit's good and you know it. And while you're rustling that grub, you can tell me what all this *stuff* is."

Pleased at his playful tone, Lyla left her tools on the floor to dip up some soup for him. "I'm fixing a sort of fence, for when I take you into town. An ingenious plan, actually."

Barry frowned. His hostess looked smugly serious as she sat down beside the bed with a bowl of heavenly-smelling broth and a slice of bread that had his mouth watering. Hungry as he was, though, his curiosity came first. "A fence? Like for livestock?"

"Good guess. You win a bite of bread." She placed the slice where he could tear into it, and continued. "A wagon'll never make it through this deep snow, but one of the previous tenants left an old toboggan out in the shed. I'm putting a rack all around it, to keep you on board while Buck pulls you."

The marshal nearly choked. "He's not a draft horse, Lyla. He'll—"

"We've talked it over, Buck and I," she assured him lightly. "We've agreed to cooperate, to get you to the hospital. Even if it means I'll be riding him."

Barry tried to rear up in the bed, but he fell back with the effort. "Lyla, I'm warning you! Honey, he'll throw you so fast—and then who'll take care of *you?*"

The concern in his eyes touched her deeply, yet she chuckled. "You've got to trust us on this, Mr. Thompson. I gave him an extra measure of hay and brushed him down this morning. He's a fine animal, as good-hearted as he is handsome."

"We'll hole up here until I can ride him myself. That's final."

Lyla brought a spoonful of soup to his lips, giving him no choice but to swallow it. "Your pride could kill you, marshal. We'll leave tomorrow or the day after—as soon as I can get us ready."

He grabbed her arm with amazing speed, sloshing soup onto her lap. "I'm telling you, he's trained to throw—"

"Buck's much more polite than *you* are, actually," Lyla protested. "You'll either stop fighting me, or you'll fetch your own damn food. Understand?"

The little spitfire beside him looked quite capable

of letting him starve. Her rosebud mouth was pressed into a determined line, and her periwinkle glare left no doubt that she intended to do things her way—the hard way. He released her wrist with a sigh, realizing he was too damn weak to set her straight right now.

His reluctant surrender made Lyla smile and offer him another bite of bread. "I'll brew you some tea that'll help you heal," she said coyly. "I like animals with a little spirit, and I usually have my way with them in the end. I . . . I'm looking forward to your full recovery, Barry."

What the hell did she mean by *that?* Thompson ate gratefully, finishing a second serving of her delicious bread and soup, but he couldn't help wondering what secret was making Lyla O'Riley's Irish eyes shine with such an impish glow. It was just his luck to be snowed in with the woman he loved, yet unable to prove it to her. His ring was missing, he was too sore and weak to do her justice in this puny bed . . . and the strange-tasting tea she gave him made him so drowsy he couldn't talk about his feelings, either. All he could do was sleep.

Lyla carried her boards to the shed to finish nailing them together, so her hammering wouldn't disturb Barry's nap. It was underhanded to lace his tea with laudanum, but he needed to mend so he'd be strong enough for the grueling ride to Cripple. She attached the rack to the old toboggan, grinning. Beneath his rugged facade, Thompson was a cream puff, the lovable, boyish man she'd hoped he was from the moment he walked in on her at the Rose.

In time he would admit she was right about Frazier Foxe and settle that matter of the ore refinery, so the Englishman would leave them both alone. And she did want to be alone with Barry! Memories of his caress made her so giddy she bent three nails before she finished preparing the sled that would carry him.

81

A low nicker made her look up to where Buck and Calico were watching her. The horses stood close together for warmth, absently chewing wisps of hay as she pulled the toboggan over to the shed wall. "What do you think?" she asked them cheerfully. "I'm betting we'll have to tie that master of yours down, Buck, bullheaded as he is. He swears you'll throw me. But we know better, don't we, boy?"

The stallion stomped a foot, rumbling a reply. Lyla removed a glove and slowly reached over to stroke his head, letting him get accustomed to her scent. He was a majestic animal, his buff-colored coat set off by a black mane and tail. Buck nuzzled her hand, as though expecting a treat.

"I'll bring you both carrots next time I come out," she assured the two horses. "And I might as well adjust your saddle, boy. My short legs'll never reach the stirrups."

Four eyes followed her to the corner where she'd stashed the blankets and tack. The marshal's black saddle sat proudly on its hay bale. Its braided decoration and silverwork attested to its fine quality, and even in the cold it remained supple as she shortened it. The leather creaked cozily in her fingers, emitting an earthy, masculine scent that reminded her of its owner.

"Let's see what the marshal's got in his saddlebags," she commented to her two observers. "This one seems awfully full."

Lyla glanced inside and pulled out a tan leather pouch with drawstrings, large enough to hold a day's provisions. She didn't consider herself nosy, but the bag's metallic clatter got her curiosity up. It obviously held something besides food.

And when she looked inside, her mouth fell open. Pocket watches, cuff links, glittering rings . . . the booty from the raid at the Golden Rose.

Her heart fluttered erratically. She'd watched the three thieves carry these items off, so how had the jewelry ended up *here?* No one had seen her approach the clearing where Barry was shot—she was sure of it. The marauders had left the marshal for dead, probably to pursue the rest of the posse.

"And they circled back to town when they realized a blizzard was blowing up," she murmured slowly. "Saw the shed, and stashed their loot here, figuring Thompson would never ride his horse out, and they could come back when the weather cleared to claim it."

Lyla's mouth went dry as she imagined this scenario, because she'd assumed they were so *safe* here, and—

"But they saw Calico, too," she corrected herself in a strained voice. "And they would've noticed the smoke from the chimney . . . lights in the windows." Had they peered inside the cabin to watch her cut the bullet from Thompson's leg?

She dumped the pouch's contents onto Buck's blanket and pawed feverishly through the pile of valuables. Miss Victoria's tiara, Emily's wedding ring, a gold money clip inscribed FF, which still contained its folded bills, and countless pendants, pocket watches, and cufflinks she couldn't readily identify.

Barry's aquamarine ring was missing. So was her silver shamrock.

"Mary, Mother of God, they *did* see us!" Lyla whimpered. She stuffed the jewelry back into the bag with quaking hands, her thoughts racing. Today's bright sunshine meant the thieves might come calling any time now. By tomorrow—or this evening!—they could arrive to reclaim their take. And Lyla was certain the bandits had plans for her and Marshal Thompson, too.

They would have to leave tonight.

Chapter 8

"Easy, boy. Settle down, now," Lyla crooned to the stallion beside her. Buck was prancing nervously, champing at his bit as she led him from the shed with the toboggan trailing behind him. "We're doing this for Barry, remember. We've got no time for nasty pranks."

Eyeing the way the sled followed him in fits and starts, she wondered if the harness straps would hold all the way to Cripple. The gear had been salvaged from a trash heap and was suitable for Calico to plow her small garden with, but in this deep snow, the ride to town might take several hours, through drifts and over uneven trails. Lyla sighed and patted the horse's shoulder, trying to accustom the skittish stallion to her touch. If they didn't leave now, under cover of the night, the thieves might find them. If Buck threw her, or if the toboggan broke loose, she or Barry might not make it to town alive anyway. Nothing about this trip seemed promising, but it was better than holing up here, imagining various methods of sudden, violent death at the hands of strangers.

Now that the horse was in front of the door, Lyla pondered her next problem: could she get Barry from the bed to the sled and keep him in it? He continued to protest about her riding Buck, and he would hurt himself struggling against her. She hadn't told the marshal about the jewelry. She'd stuffed the pouch in Calico's saddlebag instead, figuring Thompson had enough to stew about—and to boss her about.

Lyla checked the provisions one last time: bread, water, whiskey, laudanum, bandages. A thick padding of quilts lined the sled. Her fingers found the marshal's heavy pistol in her coat pocket, and a handful of bullets. Calico stood a short distance away, waiting patiently. She had to move quickly, before Buck galloped off to rid himself of the sled, and she prayed that her plan to get Thompson outside worked.

Draping Buck's reins around the top of the harness collar, she talked firmly to him. "You're going to stand still," she instructed, "and you and I will prove to the marshal that we can *do* this. Understand?" She took the stallion's head between her hands, gazing purposefully into his large, liquid eyes. "Understand, Buck?" she repeated in a low, steady voice.

The horse rumbled at her, and then nuzzled her hand. His breath rose around them in transparent puffs of vapor, white against the night sky. After a moment Lyla stroked his jaw, smiling. "Good boy. When this is all over and we're safe, he'll forgive us for tricking him."

With a final pat on his shoulder, Lyla strode into the cabin. As she'd hoped, the herbal potion Barry drank earlier had left him snoozing, still sitting up against his pillows. Guilt prickled her conscience for sedating him, but it was for his own comfort. And how else could she insure this giant's cooperation, now that things had to proceed like clockwork?

She picked up his clean clothes from the hearth and then set her deception in motion. She'd soaked two balled-up socks in kerosene, and when they landed in the fireplace the flames leaped ominously. "Fire!" she yelled as she ran toward the bed. "Fire, Barry! Wake up!"

The marshal came to with a jerk. His disoriented

expression reflected the glare from the blaze, and then his survival instinct moved the huge body Lyla couldn't possibly have budged by herself.

"Wrap your coat around you! We'll go outside!" she hollered. Hugging the jacket to his broad shoulders, Lyla continued to talk with loud insistence. "Lean on me—you're doing fine, marshal!"

With a grunt, Thompson swung his bare legs to the side of the bed. His thoughts were jumbled, all senses blurred by a curious lethargy that didn't mask his wrenching pain, which tore through his left arm and leg with a vengeance. He moved anyway, aware only of the leaping flames and the petite figure kneeling before him.

"Step into these pants!" Lyla called out. "Can't have you freezing anything off!" She tugged the denim legs over his feet and up past his knees, then hurriedly put his socks on. Knowing his longjohns, shirt, and boots would be impossible, she'd already stashed them in Calico's bags.

Barry was doing amazingly well. He stood up to lean on her while she gingerly fastened his fly. His breathing was punctuated by frightened groans. "Will your coat fit over your bandaged shoulder?" she asked urgently. "We may be outside a long while."

With a valiant groan, Thompson allowed her to draw the sleeve over his wounded arm, and then he shrugged into the other half of the jacket. They started toward the door at a teetering limp, and Lyla hoped to God she could support him all the way to the sled. Every breath he took was a pained wheeze; his face was contorted in a grimace that tore her conscience in two. She vowed that if they arrived in Cripple alive she'd never, ever cause the marshal another problem as long as she lived.

Luck was with her: just as Lyla wondered how to ease Barry onto the railed toboggan, his knee buckled. Gasping, she broke his fall by succumbing to his weight, shoving him toward the thick blankets as she went into a sudden squat. Pain shot through her thighs, but she chuckled softly. Thompson had landed on his back, padding bunched around him, and he resembled an overgrown baby in a huge cradle. Before he could realize what she was doing, Lyla laced a length of rope across his chest and around the toboggan rails, securing it on both sides.

A quick check of the cabin satisfied her: the fire had died back, she had their supplies and clothing, and her passenger seemed content to lie very still. Remorse made her take the whiskey flask from Calico's saddlebag. "Drink up, love," she said near his ear. "We'll make it—you'll see. This'll keep you warm."

He drank gratefully, taking quick breaths between gulps. "Fire! Hurry!" he gasped.

"It's all right now. Buck'll take us to safety," she replied as she capped the bottle. Tucking the blankets in on all sides of him, and then around his head, Lyla kissed him lightly. "Rest now, Barry. We'll have you feeling better in no time."

Thompson nodded, and with a moan he either dozed off or passed out—Lyla couldn't tell which. She walked slowly to his horse's left side, praying the animal continued to behave like a gentleman. "Good boy, Buck. You're doing fine," she said in a soft singsong. "You've got to be the man now. Just do what I ask. Easy, boy . . . hold still."

She took his reins, and then realized the stirrups and saddlehorn were too high for her to reach. But she *had* to ride him! Lyla glanced frantically around the drifted clearing. She could step on the stump where Mick had split firewood, if this skittish stallion would cooperate. "Come on, boy—over here. Don't tromp on my feet, now," she commanded in a low voice.

Buck laid his ears back, eager to be free of the strange collar and his awkward load. He tossed his head, sending vapor clouds around them as he snorted his reluctance.

"Don't tell me you're scared of a *woman*—especially a half-pint like me," Lyla chided gently. "Get on up here. We're leaving whether you like it or not."

With another toss of his head he complied, but he was too dangerous an animal to ignore the warning signs. She stopped him beside the stump, hoping he wouldn't sense the fear coursing through her as she stepped up to mount him.

Buck pranced, his front feet leaving the ground. Lyla hesitated, clutching the reins . . . if she fell and broke her neck, or got trampled to death, she wouldn't have to worry about Thompson anymore, would she? Inhaling the brisk night air, she stroked the horse's pale neck and sang softly. *"Silent night . . . holy night. . . ."*

Buck's ears lifted. He whickered, listening.

"All is calm . . . all is bright," she continued, and then repeated the tune on the words, *"Buck is calm . . . Buck's all right."*

He was standing steady, so she slipped a foot into the stirrup and swung over him. The stallion reared immediately, nearly knocking her out of the saddle before she was in it, and Lyla clutched his neck. "Whoa, boy! *Silent night, you're all right,"* she crooned desperately.

The marshal's horse danced on two legs again, his shrieks piercing her eardrums. *"All is calm . . . all is bright,"* she rasped. "Damn it, Buck, if you dump Thompson before we even get started—easy, now! Put 'em down, that's the way. *All is calm . . . Buck's all right . . ."*

The stallion tossed his head, prancing in place, but he was nickering now, attentive to the tune she sang so close to his ear. Lyla was still hanging on to him with both arms, and she continued the hymn until he let out a long sigh and stood absolutely still.

Cautiously she eased off his muscled neck, stroking him as she sat upright in the saddle. "Good boy, Buck. We're friends now, right? That was Mick's favorite carol, too, when he lay dying in the hospital."

The remembered agony of her brother's death nearly choked her; she nudged the horse with her heels, reminding herself that tears would freeze on her face if she gave in to them. They circled around the stump in a wide arc, toward the trail that led to the canyon, and she whistled to Calico. The mare fell into step behind the toboggan. They were finally on their way.

The night was in her favor, at least. A high, white moon beamed down on the foothills, which slept beneath coverlets of iridescent pearl gray. Evergreens kept watch in their lacy nightgowns; icicles hung over the far canyon wall like pointed doilies, glimmering softly. Had she not been so intent on finding the trail, Lyla would've reveled in the pale, unspoiled splendor around her.

Buck, too, settled into the silent harmony of the snowscape. He plodded carefully along, apparently sensing his important role in getting their unwieldy yet precious cargo to Cripple Creek. Behind them, the mare's muffled footfalls kept a steady rhythm. Lyla congratulated herself on working so diligently with Calico: she'd been on her way to the rendering man because her wealthy owner's children were bored with riding her around a small corral. The horse had shown her gratitude by learning everything Lyla taught her. *That mare would follow you to the fringes of hell and then pull you out of the pit,* Mick had said, and he was right.

Hearing a moan, she turned to look at Barry. The toboggan balked when it passed between drifts, making the leather harness straps creak and groan with its weight. Buck was pulling steadily despite the double burden of being both harnessed and saddled; the sled lurched, causing its passenger to protest weakly. "Does it hurt too terribly?" she called over her shoulder. "Do you want some more laudanum?"

Thompson groaned. He struggled briefly against his bindings before letting out a ragged sigh. "I'll live. You riding Buck?"

"Damn right I am."

The marshal snorted. "Helluva woman. But you'll pay for lying . . . about that fire."

Lyla smiled smugly. "You don't scare me, Thompson. Rest now. Are you warm enough?"

His only reply was a grunt, and when she glanced back, he was snuggling deeper into the blankets. A rich sense of accomplishment tingled inside her: she'd put them on the path to Cripple, just as she'd said she would. She'd avoided the thieves by traveling at night, and she planned to hand the jewelry over to Thompson's deputy right after she got the marshal to the hospital. Great odds and obstacles had been overcome, and as long as she remained alert, they should have no trouble reaching town before daybreak.

Lyla leaned forward in the saddle, helping Buck ascend a rise in the path. The stallion chose his footing with care; his breath came in soft, steady snorts, a duet with the creaking of the leather saddle and harness straps that stretched behind him. He was straining, pitting himself against a weight that challenged his mighty strength. When they topped the rise, she would dismount and let him rest. Judging from the trees she used for landmarks, they were a little better than halfway to town now. He plodded on, stepping, pulling, struggling to heave himself onto the plateau.

With his final surge, Lyla heard a dull *snap*. One of the harness straps broke, sending the sled into a sideways skid that would've pulled them over backwards had the other strap not snapped with the sudden, uneven weight. Buck lunged to keep from losing his balance, and as she grabbed for his neck, Lyla feared he'd gallop wildly over the trail, glad to be free of his load and wanting to toss her, too. Instead he pranced, tossing his head, and then turned as though he sensed something was terribly wrong behind them.

Lyla's heart stopped. The toboggan, bouncing askew against boulders and drifts, had turned until its curved front end was pointed down the slope they'd come up. She watched in horror as the sled went speeding along the path it had just packed down, a path that glistened with heart-rending slickness in the moonlight. Faster it went, ricocheting off rocks and groaning when it hit curves, until it bounced over the edge of the cliff. Barry was now hurtling into Phantom Canyon head first, toward certain death, and she couldn't do a damn thing about it.

"Mary, Mother of God . . . I've killed him." Lyla shoved a gloved fist against her mouth to stifle a scream. She could see the sled diving toward the drifted canyon floor. For endless minutes the sight riveted her, although she knew it was happening in mere seconds. Like a bullet speeding into a target of white, it struck. Then it bounced, ran raggedly along the snowy wall, and came to rest against a huge mound. Puffs of white shimmered in the wind and then settled in the silent night.

Lyla stared doggedly, but what was there to see? A healthy man probably wouldn't survive that plunge; if he had, he'd be too stunned to loosen the ropes and signal to her.

It was over. The burly, boyish marshal she'd come to love was lying lifeless below her. The torment of laying yet another dear friend to rest . . . she'd watched Mick do battle with his burns and demonic hallucinations, struggled to save Barry from two bullets and thought she'd won . . .

But the pain would have to wait. "Come on, Buck, we've got to get down there somehow," she murmured. "Can't leave him for the scavengers. Can't let those thieves find him this way."

Lyla wiped her eyes against her coat sleeve and then blinked. She heard muffled steps and a long snorting breath, and Calico shuffled up the trail toward them. Lyla had been too terrified to think of her poor horse when the sled had broken loose, and the fact that Calico had somehow saved herself from being swept over the canyon wall sent large drops dribbling down her face.

"Come on, girl. We'll give Buck a rest," she croaked. Swinging one leg over the saddle, she jumped to the ground on quavery legs, her fall cushioned by the snow. Lyla stuffed the long leather harness straps into Buck's saddlebag. Then she hugged her mare and mounted, happy to be in her snug, familiar saddle again.

"We'll have to go to Victor, where the trail heads into the canyon, and then double back," she explained tiredly. "Buck, I'm trusting you to follow us. We'll need you to . . . carry Thompson out. And I don't have the strength to hold your reins while I watch the trail. Here we go, now."

Lyla let Calico set the pace along the lip of the canyon. The night's white finery was lost on her now. The wind rattled branches and made crystalized tree limbs clitter restlessly, chilling her. Her limbs felt numb and her mind drifted from one listless image to the next. It occurred to her that she should get help in Victor: how could she possibly bring Thompson's body out, big as he was? The toboggan was shattered, no doubt, and she certainly couldn't sling him over Buck's back.

Yet she went on alone, guiding Calico down into the canyon, dreading each minute that brought her closer to the wreckage. She had to make her peace, had to say good-bye without interference from strangers who'd deride her for hooking an old harness to a decrepit sled. Only a woman would try such a stunt. Only a lovesick little fool would think she could outsmart robbers and conquer a snow-clogged trail along a cliff.

Sniffling, Lyla contemplated the empty life that stretched ahead of her. She had a job at the Golden Rose, but could she ever work there again? Surely Miss Chatterly and the ladies would blame her for Barry Thompson's death—she could imagine daggers in Princess Cherry Blossom's eyes, and worse. And what of Frazier Foxe? He'd be getting no money from the marshal for his refinery now. Would he take revenge on *her*, as Thompson's killer?

No, she couldn't stay in Cripple Creek . . . not with memories of both Mick and Barry to haunt her. Perhaps Hadley McDuff would still have her, despite her flagrant rejection of him a few years back. At least he had money and a grand home . . . begetting an heir would satisfy him and keep her from embarking on any more treacherous journeys. Her wayward spirit had gotten her into this mess, and it was God's way of telling her to settle down before she killed anyone else. Living with a stodgy old poop was her life sentence. Her eternal punishment would be recalling Thompson's magnificent maleness, his uncompromising delight in women, every time McDuff wagged his skinny . . . finger at her.

Lyla tugged on the reins, gazing ahead into the canyon. The moon had moved across the sky, and the cliffs were casting shadows that tricked her. A wintry wind blasted her, funneled between the high, rocky walls. Whirling white powder stung her tired eyes until she had to close them and turn her face away. When the gust blew past, she saw a large, dark object several yards ahead. Was it a boulder, blown clear of its snow? Or was it the sled?

Her heart beating erratically, she nudged Calico

forward. Buck was following close behind, livelier now, as though some scent in the wind had warned him where they were. When he whinnied and trotted past them, Lyla knew why, and the horse's devotion to his master made the tears stream down her windburnt cheeks. Animals grieved, too, and it was a wretched sight to watch.

Lyla stopped Calico a respectful distance from the toboggan. She could see now that its curved front end was tilted upward, lodged between the drifted rocks that had stopped Barry's runaway ride. His head was outlined in the moonlight, above the ropes that still crisscrossed his blanketed chest. When Buck stopped to paw the ground, and then slowly stretched his neck to nuzzle Thompson, Lyla had to turn away.

The stallion nickered, the rumbling in his throat more insistent the second time. She could picture him nudging Barry's cheek, imagine the shock when the lifeless chill of his master's skin sank in with such hopeless finality. Calico shifted, as though to say they should ease Buck's bereavement by sharing it. Lyla braced herself for what had to be done, praying for the physical strength and emotional fortitude to get the marshal back to town. Then she let her mare amble toward the sled.

The wind kicked up again, hissing around the rocks like the sinister laughter of a snake. Its eerie whining chilled her—Lord, she was hearing *voices* now! She was going crazy, alone with a corpse—

"Buck, you old . . . son-of-a-gun."

Lyla's head snapped as she stared at the scene silhouetted a few yards in front of her. The stallion tossed his head from side to side and then nipped Thompson playfully.

"If you . . . lost Lyla in this snow . . . we're in deep trouble, fella."

Before she could even breathe, Lyla was scrambling through the drifts, toward a Thompson who sounded weak . . . but who was *alive!* She stopped a few feet in front of him, too overjoyed to do anything but gape.

Barry, who felt as though every muscle in his body was bruised beyond repair, couldn't resist teasing the wide-eyed angel who stood before him. From the moment he'd heard the harness strap give and felt the sled swooping down the hill, he'd assumed he was sailing out over Phantom Canyon to his own snowy grave. Lyla's herbal concoction had lost its hold on him shortly after he landed, and for the first time in days he felt lucid, bubbling over with life in spite of his pain. *"Whot're ye steerin' at?"* he rasped in his best imitation of her brogue. *"Ye look loik ye've seen a ghost."*

"I thought you were dead, and then—Jesus! Your sled went over the—how was *I* to know you—" Lyla gasped for breath, seeing the grin twitching at his lips before she realized what he was up to. "You ornery *toad!* Teasing me, when I've been worried *sick* over how I'd get you to town, and how I'd *live* without your—"

"How will you?" he asked quietly.

"How will I *what,* damn it?"

It hurt to laugh, or Thompson would have. Lyla was grinding her fists into her hips, her glare hot enough to thaw limbs frozen from the cold and hours of restricted movement. And he loved her dearly for it. "How will you get me to Cripple? I'd have started in myself, but I've been a little . . . tied up these past few hours."

"By the saints, I swear I'll—I ought to just *leave* you here!" Lyla kicked at a drift, sending a white shower over Barry's face and shoulders. When he shivered, she regretted her peevish reaction and quickly wiped him off. "I'm sorry," she mumbled, "but I saw no way for you to survive that fall. From where Buck and I stood, it looked like you hit flat down and then skittered around the jagged rocks until—"

"I angled off a drift, actually." He saw her eyes sparkling with moisture and knew the time for teasing was over. "It wasn't much different from the daredevil way I went sledding when I was a kid, but I can't recommend taking that ride on one's back."

Brushing the snow from his hair, Lyla nodded. She'd been so bravely steeling herself against his death that it was still hard to believe he was watching her, joking with her. Her hand trailed down across the ropes that cut wickedly into his chest. "This must hurt something awful. Let me cut you out—"

"Don't feel sorry for me, honey," Barry interrupted quietly. "If you hadn't tied me in so tight, I would've been flung out over the rocks for sure. What's this make, twice you've saved my life now?"

His tenderness made her heart swell. His face blurred behind a veil of tears. "Barry, I was so sure I killed you, using that old harness to—it would've been all my fault—"

"Just goes to show you I'm too ornery to cash in my chips. I'll be around for a long time yet," he assured her, "but now we do need to head for Cripple. These bullet holes are howling like a bitch in heat."

Lyla wiped her eyes, alert with purpose now. "Should I hitch Buck to the toboggan again? I'm not sure those straps'll—"

"Get me out of this thing. After I sit on a rock for a bit to get my blood pumping in the right direction, I'll ride him out of here."

Her jaw dropped. "Thompson, you're not strong enough to mount him, much less—"

"I won't have to."

"—hang on until we get to town," she protested. "I won't let you rip those stitches—"

"And you won't listen, either!" he rasped. "God love me if I'd landed upside down, and you kept on *talking!* Now cut me loose!"

Stung slightly, Lyla looked at the straining knots on the top side of the toboggan and went for the knife in Calico's pack. Barry had a right to be churlish, after all he'd survived, but damn it, she was doing her best under the circumstances! Carefully she sawed on the uppermost rope, and when it broke she braced Barry's good shoulder and loosened all the ties. Leaning heavily upon her, he limped to a flat rock nearby.

Barry felt like a pincushion, needles and pins jabbing each of his cold, stiff limbs as he sat down. His woman was watching him with eyes that glistened in the moonlight. He'd made her cry when he should've been thanking her, after all he'd put her through. As his good arm got its feeling back, he extended it, inviting her into his embrace.

Lyla stepped forward, her chin quivering. When his hug enveloped her, she leaned into him and let his blessed warmth and forgiveness flood through her. Barry was alive, and he didn't blame her for the terrible ride he'd taken! His lips found hers, coaxing softly until she responded with a kiss that held the love of a million tomorrows, the hope of a harrowing loss redeemed.

He broke away, chuckling. "I'll take up where we left off when I'm stronger, little lady," he whispered. "Lead Buck over here. Better get on him while I still can."

Hearing the ebb of his strength quite clearly, Lyla didn't argue. One look at the sled, which had a wide crack down its middle, confirmed that the stallion was the marshal's only plausible mode of transportation. The horse obeyed, standing still as Lyla lowered the stirrups to their original length. Then she questioned Barry with a glance.

He tried to smile through his pain. "Buck, let's show Miss O'Riley just what sort of rank bronco she broke tonight," he said lightly. "Kneel, boy. Down on your knees."

With a grace that amazed her, the huge horse lowered first his back end and then his front, docile as a house dog. He waited, unflinching, while Lyla helped Barry stumble over top of him to land in the saddle with a heavy groan.

Sweat beaded his upper lip and his head felt swimmy, but by God, he would arrive in Cripple like a man. No sense in causing undue alarm or giving the wrong people ideas about how incapacitated he was. Lyla didn't need to suspect his new resolutions about the way he intended to woo her, either. Close calls with death had given him a new perspective on life and love. The fact that he was breathing after all this was a sign—a second chance to do right by the woman who deserved his respect for the rest of her days.

"Up, Buck," he said with a fond slap on the stallion's shoulder. And when the horse had risen to its full height, he looked down at the tiny, jacketed angel who was knee-deep in snow, the biggest grin he could fix on his face. "Shall we go? By the time we get to town, Doc Geary ought to be wide awake, ready to tell me what a damn fine nurse I've had."

Chapter 9

Lyla dozed in a hard wooden chair, lulled by low voices coming from Doc's examination room. The warm waiting area, dimly lit by the dawn, was the perfect place to nap after the exhausting ride from Phantom Canyon. Barry had insisted on stopping here rather than at the hospital because Dwight Geary was a trusted friend, a man who'd get him back on his feet without gossiping, and without experimenting in any new-fangled treatments, he said.

She'd chuckled at the lawman's comment and wondered how he felt about her unorthodox nursing methods. But when Geary stepped into the lobby, smiling tiredly from behind his spectacles, she knew why Thompson liked him. Dwight was getting on— he was in his sixties, she guessed—and his years of patching up miners and pandering to millionaires at all hours had left him slightly stooped. They'd gotten him out of bed, yet he'd dressed hurriedly without complaining, greatly relieved that the marshal was back alive.

"Well, young lady, you've been through quite an ordeal," he said as he sat down beside her.

"Aye, sir. Twice I thought we'd lost him."

"So he told me. I checked his wounds and put fresh bandages on them, and insisted he go to the hospital for a few days' rest." With pale blue eyes, Geary took

99

in her boots and faded jeans, and her brother's heavy coat. "What'd you put on those bullet wounds, anyway?"

Lyla's stomach lurched. Had she made Barry worse instead of better? "I . . . well, I disinfected with lavender and yarrow, and applied packings of eucalyptus leaves and lady's mantle to reduce the inflammation. I—"

"Bang-up job. You've got grit, and if you'd ever consider becoming a nurse, I'd certainly—"

The door opened, and Matt McClanahan entered with a gust of wind. He looked anxiously from Lyla to the doctor. "That's Thompson's horse outside. Is he here? Is he all right?"

"He'll be pestering us with his bad jokes again in no time," Geary chortled. "Took two bullets down around Phantom Canyon, but this young lady had the wherewithal to keep him alive."

McClanahan's eyes flashed with gratitude, bluer and more direct than the doctor's. He removed his hat and smiled at her. "Lyla, isn't it? From the Rose?"

She nodded, thinking his new bride must spend hours on end gazing at him.

"Well, now. That's what I've been waiting to hear," he continued with a relieved chuckle. "Emily and I postponed our honeymoon until we knew what had become of him. I trust he left those three desperadoes in worse shape than he was?"

Lyla sighed tiredly. "It was an ambush, Mr. McClanahan. They got away."

"Damn!" Matt slapped his hat against his knee. "We'll get those—can I see Barry? If I knew who to go after—"

"Right now you can be better help by assisting me," Doc Geary said pointedly. He stood up and opened the door to the examination room. "I'm checking him into the hospital, and I could use a strong set of arms to boost him into my wagon. He's flatly refused to be seen on a stretcher or in an ambulance."

McClanahan laughed. "Must be feeling pretty spry, then."

"And Lyla, could you see to his horse?" the physician asked. "He seems to put great store in the way you handle that animal."

"Certainly. I have to go to the stable anyway."

She rose slowly, wanting to see Barry off, and wanting to tell McClanahan he could take Emily's wedding ring with him. But a voice from the other room bellowed, "You going to leave me on this table all day, Doc? If I've got to go to the hospital, I might as well arrive in time for breakfast."

Dr. Geary chuckled, shaking his head. "Duty calls, Matt. Why not drop by later to see him, Miss O'Riley? I'm sure he'd enjoy that."

Lyla nodded and watched them disappear through the doorway. Extreme weariness overtook her, and all she could think of was a hot bath and a cozy bed. "I'll be at the Golden Rose if you need me," she called in to the men, but she heard no response.

Outside, the wintry breeze whistled around the corners of the buildings. As Lyla headed down the street with the horses, she wondered where the McClanahans had planned to honeymoon and how soon they'd be leaving now. Or would they stay in Cripple until the robbers were caught? Lyla knew how disappointed *she* would feel if such a nasty episode postponed a romantic trip. Emily would surely be happier if she could at least have her jewelry back.

She entered the dusky livery stable smiling. This afternoon, after she visited Barry, she would find out where Matt and Emily were staying and deliver the locket and the ring. Then she'd turn the rest of the loot over to Rex Adams, Barry's deputy, and explain why the McClanahans' pieces were missing from the

101

leather pouch.

Looking around, she saw that neither Wally Eberhardt, the manager, nor his stablehands were around yet. It was a good time to pick the two items out of the pouch—her meeting with Connor Foxe had taught her not to trust anyone who might be lurking in these shadows. Dismounting, she led Calico and Buck past stalls strewn with musky straw, where horses of all sizes and colors looked over their shoulders, nickering at her. She was in luck: the back two stalls were empty. After wrapping the buckskin's reins around a slat, she led her mare into the corner. "I'll be with you in a minute, Buck. Got a little business to tend to."

Squatting with her back toward the aisle, Lyla picked through the pouch until she found the exquisite diamond ring and the gold locket ornately engraved with the initials EMR. Would she ever wear such expensive jewelry herself? She'd only caught a glimpse of the aquamarine ring Barry had lost to the bandits. She knew it was intended for her, but the thrill of anticipating such a gift was dampened by the thought that the thieves might come after the marshal—or her—before the ring was seen again.

Lyla slipped Emily's pieces into the front pocket of her jeans and pulled the pouch's drawstrings. "Okay, Calico, let's get your gear off and brush you down. You and Buck deserve double rations for getting the marshal and me back safely."

She reached over to unfasten the saddle girth and heard an ominous *click* behind her. "I believe you'll be coming with us, Miss O'Riley."

Lyla pivoted and found herself facing a pistol, held fast in Wally Eberhardt's thick grip. He was standing beside Connor Foxe, his usual toothy grin a sharp contrast to his actions.

"Wally—I—what's going on here?" she stammered. "I was just bringing the marshal's—"

"What's in the sack?" Foxe demanded.

She'd despised his cockiness the first time they'd met, and now his smart-aleck grin really galled her. "Nothing," she spat. "Now if you'll excuse me, I'll tend these tired horses and—"

"Keep her covered, Eberhardt. Looks to me like our lady from the Golden Rose has turned some tricks the past few days. And she hasn't even been at work."

Her cheeks burned when Eberhardt's dumb chuckle made his belly quiver. And as Connor reached for the leather pouch, she jerked it behind herself and backed toward the wall. "You don't know a thing about me! And you've no right to—"

"The marshal's been missing for three days, and you suddenly turn up from out of nowhere with his horse," Foxe said in a stealthy voice. "Let's see what's in these saddlebags."

"I just dropped Barry off at Doc Geary's. Not that it's any of *your* business," she hissed as she grabbed for his arm. "And if you so much as—"

"Get your hands off me. Or Wally'll have an unfortunate accident with that pistol." Foxe shook himself free of her grip and yanked out her emergency provisions, tossing them onto the straw-strewn floor. "Food, water, whiskey. This lady's ready to travel, or my name's not Connor Foxe."

"I'm telling you, I *have* traveled! I brought Barry Thompson in from my cabin above Phantom Canyon—"

"With all *this* stuff?" Foxe's obsidian eyes mocked her. "Okay, so maybe you got a fit of the guilties and took him to the doc, but with this many supplies you're ready to ride awhile, lady. What do you think, Eberhardt? Does that leather pouch look like a great place to carry stolen jewelry? Like maybe the stuff from the Christmas Eve robbery?"

The stable manager cleared his throat. "I thought—they told *me* it was in a flour sack," he replied.

Wally's voice was deep and nasal, making him sound even denser than Lyla suspected he was, but she turned his answer to her advantage. "That's right—I saw that sack myself! So why do you think—"

Connor grabbed for the pouch and she cried out when he wrenched it from her grasp. He looked inside with a triumphant laugh. "Just as I thought. No self-respecting whore would carry loot in a flour sack—not when everybody in town *knows* that's what the thugs hauled it off in. I'm betting you found Thompson in a bad way and cut yourself in on this real sweet deal, after he caught the guys who—"

"He didn't catch them!" Lyla was ready to strangle her compactly-built tormentor, but Eberhardt was just fool enough to pull the trigger. "I cut the bullet out—"

"Tell it to the judge, sweetheart." Foxe spread the contents of the pouch on a nearby hay bale and was pawing through it. "All the talk was about that sparkly ring in Thompson's pocket, which everybody knows was for you, and about how you swore to retrieve the silver shamrock you lost." He looked up from the glittering array of finery and narrowed his eyes at her. "Neither piece is here. Which tells me you stuck them away and figured on hocking the rest after you got out of town. Or out of the country. Ireland, isn't it?"

"That's insane! Why would I hide—" She looked frantically at Eberhardt, hoping to play on his friendship. "Wally, you know I *always* wore my shamrock because Mick made it. So why, if I got it back, would I not have it *on?*"

The stable manager shifted his weight, looking to Foxe for assistance. "Well, I guess—"

"She's got a snake's tongue in that pretty head," Connor cut in, "but she can talk herself blue. I doubt Deputy Adams'll fall for her story, either. Like everybody else, he's been real concerned about

104

Thompson's whereabouts. Let's get her over there, see what he says."

"You've got this all wrong! If you'll ask Barry—or Doc Geary—"

"Sounds to me like they're busy right now—unless you also lied about taking Thompson to his office."

When he yanked her closer, by the lapel of her jacket, Lyla knew she was outmanned—just as she suddenly realized where else she'd seen the glittering, dark eyes that were boring into hers. These men were setting her up to take the fall for the robbery because . . . the pieces didn't all fit, tired as she was, but she had to fight with every weapon she had. "The horses! They've been out all night, and if they aren't fed and—"

"Wally'll see to them after we escort you to the jailhouse," Foxe replied. "Let's get on over there—no tricks or screams for help, if you know what's good for you. And after you're settled into your cell, Eberhardt can bring the rest of your gear over. It might prove interesting."

Settled into my cell? Lyla gasped as Foxe shoved her toward the door, and with Eberhardt on her other side, the pistol in his coat pocket prodding her back, she knew better than to try to escape. As they marched her down the sidewalk, she could only hope Rex Adams would see the real reasons behind her provisions and arrival.

The moment she stepped through the doorway of Thompson's office, though, she knew she'd been framed. The deputy was skinny and carroty-haired, mostly a paper pusher, since Barry was so adept at handling the crimes and crises around town. And when his pale hazel eyes registered surprise followed by secretive comprehension, Lyla lost all hope of persuading him to see her side.

"Well, well. Miss O'Riley, isn't it?" he asked as he rose from his creaky chair. "You've certainly made a name for yourself these past few days."

105

"Get a load of this, Adams," Connor said as he tossed the pouch of jewelry onto the deputy's desk. "She *says* she brought Thompson in to see Doc Geary, and she *says* she took the shot out of him. But she won't say how she came across this booty. Wally and I caught her just before she rode out, with enough food and water to last her quite a ways. Get the rest of her stuff, Eberhardt. And be quick about it."

The stableman clomped out the door, leaving Lyla caught between the intense gazes of Connor Foxe and Rex Adams. They were obviously in cahoots—and Barry knew nothing about whatever scheme they'd cooked up, or he would've fired Adams when he turned traitor. It was best to let these men do the talking. The less she said from here on out, the less information she could inadvertently pass on to be used against herself and the marshal.

"Cat got your tongue, miss?" Adams asked.

He had a soft voice, yet his knowing tone put a knife's edge on his seemingly innocent curiosity. Lyla stuffed her hands in her coat pockets, considering her reply carefully.

"I don't like the looks of this," Foxe muttered, and suddenly he was rifling both her coat pockets at once. "A pistol!" he crowed, wrenching it from her hand. "Awfully big piece for a midget like you."

"Well, well. Looks like Thompson's," the deputy chimed in. He studied the gun when Foxe handed it over, shaking his head in mock surprise. "Miss O'Riley, we're finding all the wrong things on you, honey. You'd better speak up or I'll have no choice but to lock you away until we can get to the bottom of this."

"It's like I told Foxe," she said tightly. "I found Thompson shot, I patched him up, and when I was bringing him into town, I found that bag of jewelry. I was on my way *here*, to turn the pouch *in*—"

106

"With certain pieces missing," the man beside her said.

"*My* pieces, which were gone when I found the sack!" Lyla blurted. "Why would I steal my own pendant? Or the ring everyone claims Thompson was going to give me? It makes no sense—"

"After the way you ran out of Delmonico's earlier this week, everyone in town thinks you're playing Barry for a fool," the deputy answered with a wry smile. "Why should I believe you care enough to act as his nurse? You could've poisoned him, for all we know, and then—"

Lyla threw her hands in the air. "Ask Barry what I did! Ask Doc Geary!"

"I fully intend to, young lady. It's my job, now that Thompson can't investigate for himself." The lanky deputy took her arm and steered her toward the hallway where the jail cells were. "Meanwhile, you're going to cool your heels and get your story straight. You're an immigrant, you live in a whorehouse, and your actions have shed a dubious light on your relationship with the marshal. He's not keen on having his reputation compromised."

"In other words, cupcake," Foxe called to her from the office, "you're in it up to your little pink ears."

When the door clanged shut behind her, Lyla felt as though Adams had locked her into a dungeon and thrown away the key. She collapsed on the smelly cot, staring blankly around the peeling plaster walls, which had obscenities scrawled on them in various languages. Her cell was the last one, a windowless corner cubicle, and all she could see of the office was the door Adams had shoved her through. A chill went down her spine when the scraggly man in the next cell grasped the bars between them, leering at her with a deranged grin.

Hushed murmurings drifted down the hall, as though Connor and the deputy were conferring

107

about their next moves. Lyla strained to hear . . . someone came in from outside . . . Eberhardt's chuckling gave way to a roaring trio of laughter and then Foxe poked his head into the hallway. "Chrissakes, O'Riley," he taunted. "Stealing Thompson's horse and gun I can understand. But what the hell'd you figure on doing with his boots and longjohns?"

She stood and paced toward the wall, her face aflame. Of all the nerve, to insinuate—

"Oh shut up, or I'll steal *your* underwear, too!" she snapped at the lunatic next to her. He was giggling uncontrollably, a new interest kindled on his mangy face, and when he began gyrating against the cell bars, she was disgusted beyond words.

Her only hope was that Thompson and Doc Geary would straighten things out and spring her from this horrid hole. She'd made an unfortunate impression by deserting Barry at Delmonico's, but her friends— Miss Victoria, and the ladies—and Matt McClanahan!—knew her true feelings toward the marshal. If all these people protested her incarceration, Adams would have to release her. As soon as they all heard . . .

Lyla sank onto the rickety cot with a groan. If the deputy and Foxe and Eberhardt were indeed in alliance, they might not tell anyone she was here. Few people were on the street when she entered the livery stable. Doc Geary might've been called out on a case, and wouldn't realize she hadn't come to visit Barry. Neither would Matt, if he'd gone back to the hotel to be with Emily. And Thompson was in no shape to fetch her . . .

As the shadows deepened into late afternoon, Lyla sank deeper into despair. The only person to come down the hallway was a woman who brought meals from a nearby café; Lyla had never seen her before. The biscuits and beans sent up a tempting aroma when she lifted the cloth napkin. Her stomach rumbled; she had not eaten since yesterday about this time.

But when the wooden tray clunked against the ring in her pocket—bless the saints, she hadn't been searched!—she lost her appetite completely. What if Foxe and Adams *did* tell Barry they'd caught her with his horse and his gun and the stolen jewelry? He'd been weak and exhausted enough during the ride into Cripple that he might easily misconstrue her motives now—especially since she hadn't told him about finding the loot in his saddlebag.

Any lawman would have doubts about her, given the fact that his own ring was missing from the pouch . . . given the fact that she'd run out on him and accused him of being a lecherous beast, and then drugged him and frightened him with a fire. And then she'd watched him sail into Phantom Canyon on a wobbly toboggan, and admitted she hadn't expected him to survive.

Evidence was piling up on the wrong side of the ledger, depending upon how Marshal Thompson chose to read it—and whether he believed a long-standing deputy or the feisty flirt he'd met only a few days ago. Lyla set the tray aside, sighing dejectedly. It could be a long, lonely wait, for a fate that seemed less and less promising as the evening ticked by, marked by the tinny chiming of the office clock.

Chapter 10

"Whoa—slow down! You're supposed to be resting, remember?" Matt McClanahan flashed Barry a grin and reached for the crockery teapot on the bedside table. "I'll pour you some of this nice brew, and then you can lay back on those pillows and tell me—"

"Tea!" Thompson snorted. "Had enough of those strange concoctions while Lyla was taking care of me. Whiskey and a good cigar's what I need. Think you could sneak me some?"

"And have Doc Geary on my butt?" McClanahan asked with a laugh. "Now take it easy and tell me what you remember about the ambush. Was it the same three thugs from the reception? Do you know who they were?"

With a thoughtful sigh, Barry accepted the steaming teacup his best friend handed him. It was the damndest thing: some parts of the past few days were as clear as a Colorado sky and others he couldn't recall at all, like having those bullets cut out of him. Lyla would have to fill him in, but for now he pushed aside the cozy images he experienced whenever he thought of her. "Two of the men went up the trail along the rim of the canyon. Hid behind some trees and came out shooting. I assume the other fellow rode into the gulch to attack the posse. Did everybody else make it back in one piece?"

"Far as I know," Matt answered. "Said they heard shots above them and circled back, but you were gone. So they returned to town, figuring you'd ridden on ahead. Your search party barely made it out of Cripple before they were forced back by the blizzard."

"Bad night all around," he replied with a sorry shake of his head. "Adams went up the side with me and followed a set of tracks into the trees, while the rest of the men—only about three, it being Christmas Eve—took the more likely trail into the canyon. After I stopped those two bullets, it was all a blur."

His handsome friend smiled knowingly. "Good thing Lyla doesn't listen to orders. You could've dropped into a drift and we wouldn't have known it until Buck came back to town. And then we might not've found you until spring."

"You trained him better than that, McClanahan. He would've stood beside me till he froze to death." His voice sounded thick with emotions he wasn't accustomed to expressing. He'd never owed anyone his life, and it was a heavy debt. "And Lyla—now *there's* a woman. Who'd have thought that little squirt had the guts to remove my bullets? Had to be her, though. Nobody else could've gotten there."

McClanahan's grin flickered across his face and he looked away to keep from laughing. "So what other kind of medicine did she practice? Three days, snowbound with her in a cabin? Folks'll get a lot of mileage out of that!"

"And they'll have it all wrong," Barry insisted quickly. He ignored the pain in his leg to lean closer and make his point, knowing McClanahan would tease him forever if he didn't set the record straight. "Lyla might work at the Rose, but that doesn't make her a whore. The whole time we—"

"I never meant to imply she was," Matt interrupted quietly. "But it's no secret you've been seeing

111

her, and I *know* you, pal. You can talk a woman naked faster than any man I've ever met. And I don't mean that as a derogatory remark."

The man seated beside his bed was totally sincere, but Thompson shook his head. "Nope. She got my clothes off me somehow, and I vaguely recall her sponging me off, and feeding me after the fever broke. But otherwise, it was all tea and talk. And the tea wasn't worth beans, I can assure you."

Matt cleared his throat as though he wasn't buying it. "You said she sedated you—"

"You think I wouldn't remember dipping into that little honeypot?" He smiled sheepishly at the nurse who'd poked her head into the room. And when she left, he couldn't keep a grin from his face, wondering which of his plans to reveal to McClanahan first. "And just between you and me, ole buddy, I don't intend to take Lyla to bed until she's my lawfully-wedded wife. She's earned my highest respect, and from here on out Barry Thompson's going to behave like the perfect gentleman Miss O'Riley deserves. Somebody else can be the town playboy."

McClanahan choked on his tea. "Thompson, this is *me* you're telling—"

"I kept your woman alive for you when she was ready to cash in, thinking you were dead after that shack exploded," he said in a solemn voice, "and I expect the benefit of the doubt from you in return. I love that woman, Matt. She accused me of being a randy old ram at your party, and she was right. I aim to prove I'm capable of higher moral conduct."

Matt's ruddy face lost all signs of jest. He sat back against his chair, eyeing Thompson long and hard. "Are you sure she wants to be placed on such a pedestal? Lyla impresses me as a fun-loving, affectionate—"

"She is," Barry assured him with a grin. "But she told me herself she despises men who take what they want without asking. And Victoria warned me not to steer her into any scandalous situations. I'm finally catching on, finally *listening* to women instead of assuming they'll fall for all my lines."

"I've got to hand it to you for trying," came his friend's reply. "But if Lyla's anything like Emily, she'll be hurt if you turn her away when she wants to make love."

Barry shrugged. "Emily's used to getting everything she wants. My woman's been to hell and back, for her brother and now for me, and I can't ignore her challenge to change. Not that I'll have to curb my animal passions for long," he added mischievously. "That's where you come in."

McClanahan's dark eyebrows raised in a question.

"You know that piece of property up north, the one that overlooks the whole town? I want you to put a deposit on it for me. Then find out who built Silas Hughes' place and have him come see me, soon as he can."

Thunderstruck, Matt stared at him. "You're sure about this? You fall for every woman you meet, Thompson, and you met Lyla less than a week ago."

"I know what you're thinking, and I appreciate your concern," he replied with his good hand upraised. "But Love-'em-and-leave-'em Thompson has finally met his match. I sure as hell can't ask her to live upstairs from Mrs. Delacroix's shop, so it's time to build a place befitting my bank account. You'd have done the same for Emily—"

"But I—"

"—and it wasn't too damn long after you met her that you refused to live without her," he continued smugly. "Things hit a snag when she accused you of killing her daddy, but look how happy you are now. I want the same satisfied glow I see on your face, McClanahan. It's time for life to stop passing me by."

With a resigned sigh, Matt stood up and placed his teacup on the table. "All right, I'll put some money down on that land and find your architect. Anything else you want?"

Thompson chuckled, feeling as giddy as a kid after his first kiss. "If you see Miss O'Riley—I imagine she'll be here any time now—don't breathe a word about me or the house. You might ask the posse if they got a good look at our thieves. I—I'm sorry I didn't recover Emily's ring, pal," he added more quietly.

"We'll get it back. Just glad we didn't lose *you*, Barry." McClanahan gazed at him for a long moment and then clapped a hand to his good shoulder. "You rest now, and think things over. We've got ourselves a jewelry heist to investigate."

Jewelry, indeed. Thompson settled into his pillows, thinking about how Lyla's eyes matched the aquamarine he'd bought, and mentally designing the magnificent diamond ring he planned to place on her finger the day she became his wife. The chat with McClanahan had tired him. He let himself doze so he'd be fresh when his woman came by, while in his mind he kissed her sweet, willing lips.

He fell asleep with a wide grin on his face.

Lyla jerked awake, shivering and disoriented. Had someone slammed a door? What time was it? She'd heard the office clock strike eleven and midnight, between fits of dozing; her cell was so drafty she couldn't sleep for shaking with the cold. A violent sneeze brought her halfway off the cot, and even in the dark she could see her breath.

She heard a grumbling, shifting noise and regretted waking the vagrant in the next cot. He sat up with a groan, mumbled a string of curses, and then walked toward the front of his cell with something in his hand. The wild cacophony of a tin cup against metal bars soon had the other prisoners muttering, and then he was calling out, "Open that damn door!

Let some of that heat back here before we freeze our butts off!"

When Rex Adams peered into the hallway, his hair glowed pale orange from the light in the office. "What's this racket? Shut up and—"

"*You* try to sleep in this friggin' cold! Give this little girl another blanket before she catches her death."

Adams sighed impatiently, but a moment later he was stuffing a quilt through the bars of Lyla's cell. "Will there be anything else, Miss O'Riley?" he jeered.

"N-no. Thank you." When she rose to fetch the blanket, the deputy glowered at her and then at the derelict next to her, and then he returned to the office. The light cast eerie shadows upon the walls and gave the gridwork of the cell fronts a menacing gleam, but already Lyla was warmer. Or maybe the clanging of the radiator out front made her *think* she felt its heat. Everything took on a different perspective from behind these bars.

The stringy-haired man ambled back to his cot, mumbling the litany of swear words she'd heard a hundred times today. Lyla wrapped the quilt around herself, wondering how to respond to his unexpected kindness. "Thank you," she whispered when he'd burrowed under his blanket again.

He rose on an elbow to peer through the darkness at her. "You're welcome," he grunted. "Can't let those bastards get you down. They commit their share of crimes, too, but nobody catches 'em."

"You've got that right," Lyla said with a heavy sigh. It was anybody's guess how long she'd be stuck here, because it was in the deputy's best interest to keep her and the stolen jewelry hidden away for a while. The clock was striking two, a pitiful, rattling sound compared to the rich bonging of the grandfather clock back home, and the comparison made her ache for the company of her brother. Mick would

115

know what to do at a time like this, would keep her spirits up with his biting wit. But she didn't even have his shamrock pendant to comfort herself with.

She huddled on her cot, ready to cry herself to sleep, when voices caught her attention. The conversation was low and covert, interrupted by the hissing and hammering of the radiator. But what Lyla could hear made her forget all about being cold and lonely.

". . . anyone know she's here?"

"No. Just us three and now you."

"Good . . . rethink our strategy . . . impetuous little bitch fouled us up . . ."

Lyla held her breath so hard her eyeballs bulged. She had indeed seen Connor Foxe's dark eyes mocking her from between his hat and bandana—he'd been the gang leader at the Golden Rose holdup! He had drawled to disguise his voice! Eberhardt and Adams must've been the other two bundled-up bandits, but who was here now, conferring with them?

". . . oughtta snuff Thompson?"

"Yeah! Easy to . . . wrong kind of medicine."

She nearly choked; she felt as if her heart were in her throat. Now they were plotting to kill Barry, as though he'd been their target all along!

"No, no . . . too obvious. Better to . . . and let nature take its course."

Better to *what?* Lyla was sweating now, despite the dankness of her cell. Adams hardly impressed her as the type who'd murder his boss in the hospital, yet the deputy had certainly twisted *her* circumstances around. Who was the fourth man? The damn radiator drowned out—

". . . say we finish him . . . could make it look like the girl . . . perfect alibi, since we caught her with . . ."

"Absolutely not. Geary could trace . . . want your reward, you'll have to keep playing this my way, gentlemen."

116

Lyla let out her breath very, very slowly. That clipped, authoritative accent could belong to only one man—a man who had enough money to plot Thompson's demise without anyone suspecting him, because he was paying some well-placed accomplices to do his dirty work. This revelation didn't really shock her, just as she wasn't surprised to see a tall, familiar form coming down the hallway toward her cell.

He stopped to peer through the bars. Lyla remained motionless beneath her blankets, listening to his measured breathing. What on earth was he gawking at? After several moments of nerve-wrenching silence, he tapped the floor repeatedly with his walking stick, until she wanted to spring off the cot and scream at him!

"I know you're awake, Miss O'Riley."

So? she thought defiantly.

Foxe tapped the floor again, more insistently. "As your benefactor, it behooves me to remove you from these premises now, to avoid further embarrassment to myself or more damage to Marshal Thompson's reputation," he said in a low voice. His precise diction indicated his irritation. Framed between the dark metal bars, his face expressed his displeasure while his monocle glowed like an evil eye. "Gather up your things. We're leaving now, before word gets out about why you're here."

Lyla choked on a laugh. "Why *am* I here, Mr. Foxe?"

"You know bloody well—" Frazier let out an exasperated sigh and glanced around at the other prisoners, who were hanging on his every word. "Miss O'Riley, this is not the time or the place to discuss such circumstances. After the stunt you pulled, I should just leave you here to—"

"Please do," she muttered, "because I'm going nowhere until Marshal Thompson can straighten this mess out." Lyla balanced on an elbow to glare at

117

him, knowing quite well he had underhanded reasons for whisking her out of here at two in the morning.

"Thompson's condition precludes—"

"Then bring Dr. Geary, or Matt McClanahan," Lyla challenged. "I want my name cleared by someone who knows what *really* happened when I came back to Cripple. The charges Adams is holding me on are ridiculous and you know it."

"I beg your—dear-heart, I only tonight learned about your incarceration—"

"Isn't it rather *unseemly* for a paragon such as yourself to be lying this way?" she mocked. "Leave me alone. I'll stay here until someone I trust unlocks that cell door."

She could practically see Foxe's monocle cloud over and hear him prickling with indignation—and that thought would sustain her for days, if that's how long it took to tell her true story. Lyla sensed he intended to use her against Thompson, since she'd apparently fouled up his first attempt on the marshal's life. It was scary to realize what sort of monster resided beneath Frazier Foxe's impeccably-groomed facade. Would he kill Barry merely for poking fun at him during the bachelor party? Or was there something else behind the discussion she'd overheard?

Lyla breathed much easier when Foxe finally left with a miffed sigh. Better to wait him out than to pay for a hasty departure by becoming his pawn again. If he really was the brains behind this robbery and murder attempt, Doc Geary and McClanahan were the last people he'd tell of her whereabouts. Days might pass before Thompson found out why she hadn't come to see him . . . which would be his clue that something was terribly wrong.

Warmed by these conclusions, she decided to plan her escape after a few solid hours of sleep.

* * *

The noon meal was carried in by none other than Princess Cherry Blossom, whose war-painted presence had the male prisoners smoothing back their hair so they could get a good eyeful when she leaned over to slide their trays under the bars. Her braid fell strategically beneath her loose buckskin bodice. The sway of her hips elicited whistles and whoops with each trip she made into the hallway.

Lyla, too, felt her pulse speed up: here was a friend . . . someone who could get word to Thompson or McClanahan! When the Indian princess shoved her covered tray into the cell, she grinned profusely. "By the saints, I'm glad to see *you!*" she gushed.

"Are you?" The mahogany-skinned whore glanced surreptitiously toward the doorway and then reached so far down her front that the mangy man in the next cell yipped like a coyote.

"What's going on here?" Rex Adams' shrill voice called out above the echoing din in the hallway. "Shut up and eat! And *you*—" he said, pointing an accusing finger at Cherry Blossom. "Where's Milly? If I'd wanted some floozy from a Wild West show to deliver dinner, I'd have . . . I'd have . . ."

The princess was smiling demurely at him, her hands on her hips pulling her dress so tight that her every curve was clearly outlined. "I'll bring your lunch in just a moment, deputy," she said in a coy voice. "And maybe when I'm finished here, you can show me your . . . tomahawk."

Raucous hoots and catcalls brought an unbecoming flush to Rex's freckled features. When he slammed the door behind him, the brazen Miss Blossom quickly shoved the folded newspaper page she'd been concealing through the cell bars. "Thought you'd want to see this. You've certainly set

119

Cripple Creek on its ear, honey."

Lyla unfolded the printed sheet and gasped. **MARSHAL RETURNS! DEPUTY JAILS WOULD-BE ASSASSIN** leaped off the front page of the *Cripple Creek Times* in bold letters that stunned her like a slap in the face. And there was her face, sketched two columns wide— a startling likeness of a sly, conniving young angel fallen from grace. It was bad enough to be held on Adams's trumped-up charges, but to be accused of—

"*Assassin?*" she hissed. "Who'll believe—"

"It's all the talk at the Rose today," the princess replied with a shrug. "Special edition. Even the folks who know you are pretty damned amazed at how well all the pieces fit. The men who've seen you and Thompson together are saying it's good he found this out before he gave you that gorgeous ring."

Lyla plopped down on the cot, too flabbergasted to speak. She knew that when Barry heard her out, it would be her word against that of his long-time deputy. But now everyone in town would think she rode after the marshal to kill him and claim the jewelry for herself, before she could explain how she'd found the leather pouch.

"I—I saved his life, damn it!" she blurted, knowing her words sounded like an alibi invented after the fact. Did Cherry Blossom think she was a killer? The whore's eyes shone with their usual hint of whiskey-inspired mischief, yet her direct gaze held heartfelt sympathy Lyla hadn't guessed the dove capable of.

"I never doubted it," the princess confirmed in a confidential tone. "No woman in her right mind would kill Barry Thompson. And who'd care about that bag of trinkets once she'd had the marshal's jewels? Must've been pure hell, being holed up with him for three days."

Her attempt at humor only made Lyla shake her head dolefully. "Nearly lost him—twice. I cut the damn bullet out of him—stayed up night and day fighting his fever, and for what? Some gratitude this

120

town's showing me for saving its lawman."

The whore leaned against the bars and beckoned her closer. "It's not Barry's doing the story got out like this," she suggested gently, "but perhaps . . . perhaps it's for the best. I—I should've warned you about him, Lyla."

She frowned. "What do you mean?"

"Barry is . . . well, he's like a bumblebee, honey," Cherry Blossom whispered with a bittersweet smile. "Flits from one flower to the next, dipping his stinger in. He can swear on a pile of Bibles he loves you, and next thing you know, he's under another woman's dress."

Lyla recalled the tender words Thompson moaned as he made love to her, and felt a flush creeping up out of her collar.

"So I'm too late. He's already stolen your heart—and your flower. Hasn't he?" The whore shook her head, clucking. "You're young, and you'll get over it. But I can tell you it'll take months to forget him. He . . . he promised he'd take me away from the whorehouse and marry me—buy me a big ring and build me a fancy house. And that was the first time he came to my room."

Cherry Blossom glanced toward the door. "I'd better go before I get you into any more trouble." Reaching between the bars, she gave Lyla's shoulder a solemn squeeze. "I'll see if I can find a way to spring you out of here. And meanwhile, try to forget about the marshal. By now he's probably lured every nurse in that hospital into bed with him."

Lyla gazed forlornly after her. Should she believe Cripple's most flamboyant dove, or relive those moments in the marshal's arms over and over, to convince herself Barry Thompson wanted her for keeps? *Lyla, please love me,* he'd begged against her ear. *Love me . . . make me whole . . .*

She shook off the memory of his caress, shocked at how the spark he'd ignited could be rekindled at the

121

merest thought of him, even when he was clear across town.

And when she read the lengthy piece from the *Times,* Lyla realized with a sinking heart that Cherry Blossom's advice was right on target. . . . *Ruthless young hoyden . . . dumped the marshal at Dr. Geary's after stealing his gun and the jewelry taken at . . . was escaping with Thompson's stallion when apprehended by Wally Eberhardt, who wisely delivered her to Deputy . . .*

The story was worded in such a way that she half believed its inaccuracies herself, so Barry would surely refuse to associate with her now. She might as well forget him, because, as the princess hinted, he could certainly find women enough to amuse himself . . . women who weren't would-be assassins.

"That's ridiculous and you know it!" she muttered under her breath. Then she realized she was talking to herself in the presence of other people, as though the strain of being held hostage was already eating away at her sanity.

Beneath the linen napkin was a plate of pork smothered in gravy, with fried potatoes, and she ate so fast the food backed up in her throat before she could swallow it all. She was ravenous, she was frustrated, she was *angry,* because this "special edition" had undoubtedly been the work of Frazier Foxe: his revenge for her failure to comply with his orders. If he had a deputy and a stable manager on his payroll, he could certainly buy a reporter.

Lyla recalled his hushed conference, how he'd implied that she'd messed up his plans. He obviously had a new scheme, beginning with this defamation of her character that would leave her destitute. Who could she work for now? Certainly not the genteel Victoria Chatterly, whose strict code of conduct had cost a few beauties their rooms at the Rose. Certainly not local merchants or bankers, who couldn't turn their backs lest she steal them blind and then shoot them. She'd cost Dwight Geary his patients if she became his nurse . . .

Thank God and the saints Mick's not here to see this, she thought as she gazed sadly at the newspaper. Marshal Thompson was known throughout Colorado, and the tale of his death-defying Christmas Eve chase would appear in every paper in the state—along with her portrait and the shocking story.

It seemed Ireland was the only place she could go now. She had to escape—she knew she could—and if it meant whoring so she'd be sneaked onto a ship, that's what she'd do. Frazier Foxe would use her to lure Barry to his death: the fact that his walking stick was recovered before the loot was planted in Thompson's saddlebag *proved* he was masterminding this plot! And why would Barry want her, when so many more suitable women were willing to lift their skirts for him?

Lyla wrapped herself in the quilt and sat cross-legged on the cot to think. How could she dupe the deputy—or Foxe himself—into opening that iron gate? How could she flee Cripple Creek without getting caught?

Chapter 11

The coffee Thompson drank with his noon meal was now turning to acid in his stomach. He shifted, trying to find a comfortable position in a bed he was disgusted with, but his wounds throbbed relentlessly no matter how he sat. Once more he looked at the front page, at the sketch of his own Lyla, so hauntingly rendered. "How the hell did this happen?" he mumbled. "Why didn't she tell me—"

"I thought you should see it for yourself, before people came streaming in here to quiz you," McClanahan answered quietly. He glanced over to reread the lead paragraphs of the *Times* story, printed in bolder type than the rest of the piece. "Why did she have your gun? How'd she get—"

"She could've left me for dead—could've killed me with a potion from her herb collection. Could've lifted my cash and keys and whatever else I had on me, as far gone as I was," the marshal protested. "It wouldn't make sense to leave my pistol at her place. She probably figured she'd run up against the robbers again."

Matt was already leaning over, pulling the bullet-riddled pants from the drawer in the bedside table. "How much money'd you have on you that night?"

"How the hell would *I* know?" Barry howled. "I changed in such a hurry my monkey suit's still

124

scattered across my apartment floor."

With a sigh, McClanahan looked at the items he took from Thompson's pants. "A key ring, a couple of bucks. That's all you had?"

"My pockets got picked at your reception, remember?" Barry looked at his companion, his exasperation rising. He understood why Inspector McClanahan of the Rocky Mountain Detective Agency was asking him all these devil's-advocate questions that could point up Lyla's motive or guilt. But why was his best friend Matt so willing to see her in a negative light? "What else can you hang on her? We might as well hash this out between us, before anybody else gets in on it."

McClanahan draped the pants over the back of his chair, pursing his lips in thought. "The part about Buck doesn't make sense. You had me train him so he'd throw anybody but you. It took us *weeks* to drill that into him."

"You heard Geary tell her to take him to the stable, didn't you?"

"Her own mare was tied beside him. I assumed she'd ride it and lead—"

"Don't assume anything about that little lady," Thompson interrupted with a proud smile. "I warned her she'd fall to her death if she so much as put a foot in the stirrup. Next thing I knew, we were headed toward the canyon and my stallion—who'd no more pull a plow than fly—was harnessed to a loaded toboggan, with Lyla riding him. Figure it out."

McClanahan's eyes shone bluer as he digested this information. His admiration paled, however, as he formulated his next question. "All right, so she has a way with animals, and Geary attested to her healing skills. You yourself said she kept you sedated . . . what makes you think she couldn't pull one over on you? Why didn't Lyla tell you she had the stolen jewelry?"

125

Thompson sighed and gazed at her portrait again, aching to hear an answer to that in her laughing, lilting brogue. "That's where the fly sticks to the spiderweb, isn't it?" He shook his head, bewildered, and looked McClanahan in the eye. "Maybe if we figured out how she got ahold of it in the first place, we'd know her reasoning. I'd like to think she was bringing it in so people could have their pieces back."

"So would I. But we can't assume anything about that little lady," he echoed with a tight smile. "Let's list the possibilities. What if . . . what if, as the thugs left the Rose for Phantom Canyon, they dropped the bag along the way and Lyla found it?"

"No good. That gang leader was agile as a cat and wouldn't drop a sack of valuables. And if he did, the chances of Lyla seeing it in the snow when no one else did are slim to none." Barry leaned back and clasped his hands over his stomach, eyes closed so he could picture the situations Matt was suggesting. "Another thing puzzles me about that. Those guys dropped our stuff into a flour sack, yet the *Times* says they took it off Lyla in a leather pouch."

"She could've switched it. Less likely to be identified as the loot when she came into town with you."

"True enough," Thompson replied with a sigh. "All right, Inspector, give me another scenario."

Matt cleared his throat, leaning back in his chair. "What if, after those guys shot you, they planted the booty on you? Which would either implicate you as an accomplice, or make you look like a big hero when Buck got you back to town."

"Can't buy that, either," the marshal said firmly. "No doubt in my mind they thought they killed me. Why would they leave all that high-class jewelry with a corpse?"

McClanahan shrugged. "The paper said some items were missing. Maybe they just took what they wanted, since you warned them about hocking such expensive pieces."

"That doesn't smell right. Those desperadoes took everything they could snatch, expensive or not." He glanced over at Matt and felt his insides tightening, because his closest friend only chewed his lower lip when he was contemplating something he didn't want to say. "Spit it out, pal. Better you than the federal boys, who'll surely get called in if we don't crack this case pretty fast."

The detective looked at his knees. "What if Lyla was in on it from the start?" he mumbled, as though the words tasted bad to him. "Let's say the three thieves rode ahead, having told her to do the shooting—catch you by surprise—and then they circled back—"

"Where do you come up with this crap?" Barry said with a scowl. "In the first place, I remember seeing her painted mare in the livery stable when I rode out with the posse."

"Whose mounts were gone?" Matt shot back.

"How the hell would I know that? Honest people had their horses out, too," Thompson snapped. "Besides, Lyla rode in behind me and the bullets hit me from the front. I *saw* my assailants, Matt. This *assassin* malarky is just another example of—"

"All right, all right, keep your nighty on," McClanahan teased. "We're trying to exhaust all the possibilities—even the remote ones, remember?"

"Which we can't really do until Lyla tells the story herself." Glancing at the skimpy gown the hospital had provided, he rolled his eyes.

Matt chuckled and then resumed his thinking aloud. "So we've established she didn't shoot you. But she still could've been in on it, because the paper said your ring and her pendant were missing from the bag. Lyla reclaimed her own piece and took yours as payment for her efforts."

Marshal Thompson thought back to the reception

raid as objectively as he could. He'd had his front to the wall and a gun in his back, but he'd watched the robbery from over his shoulder. And he distinctly recalled the stricken look on Lyla's face when that cocky bastard snapped the fragile silver chain against her neck.

"I don't think so," he murmured, "and I'm not just sticking up for her. There's something else involved here. If we knew who even one of the men was—"

"It's a good thing you're up and talking, because that pigheaded deputy of yours is obstructing justice!" Victoria Chatterly bustled into the room, her ample cleavage aquiver beneath her flowing pink gown. She stopped on the opposite side of the bed from McClanahan, accenting her tirade by smacking her palm with a rolled-up newspaper. "He won't set *bail*—won't even let me *see* Lyla! Frazier Foxe told me *he* had no luck getting her out, either."

Thompson knew better than to chuckle at this white-haired whirlwind, but he certainly wanted to. "I'm glad to see you, too, Victoria," he said suavely. "How was your Christmas?"

The madam's aqua eyes blazed for a moment, but then she let out the breath she'd been holding and laughed. "I—I'm truly sorry, Barry. How are you, dear? Thank God you're alive, because I'm afraid Lyla's in a fix only you can get her out of."

"Matt and I were just discussing that," he said, taking the gem-studded hand she offered between his own. "Sit down beside me and tell me what you've heard. I could use the company of a good-looking woman to cheer me up."

Victoria nodded to McClanahan and scooted onto the edge of the bed. "So you've read the *Times?*"

"I brought it over as soon as I saw it," Matt said. "Figured he ought to know what sort of scuttlebutt he's in for when he gets out."

"Deplorable. Absolutely deplorable," she clucked. "We all know Lyla didn't shoot you or steal that sack

128

of jewelry. How anyone could print such lies is beyond me."

Thompson kept ahold of her plump hand and smiled fondly at her. To him, Miss Victoria was more like a doting aunt—a delectable one, to be sure—than a world-wise madam, and he found her staunch support of Lyla refreshing. No fuss, no analysis; just feminine intuition. And he hoped to God she was right. "So what did my pigheaded deputy say? I imagine he hasn't been here to see me because he's too busy keeping Lyla locked in her cell. She's good at getaways, you know."

Miss Chatterly's chuckle was edged with indignation. "Rex was a veritable *pill.* Claimed he couldn't return my tiara or other accessories until the case was further along—"

"Which was smart of him," Barry conceded.

"—and swore at me—swore at *me!*" she said in a shrill voice, "when I said I'd gladly pay Lyla's bail, or take her into my custody and leave a large deposit, to ensure her presence when the investigation begins."

The marshal frowned. "I'll have to remind Mr. Adams of his manners," he said in a conciliatory tone. "Otherwise, I'm afraid I can't fault him for the action he's taking. Now that this article's causing so much talk, he'll have his hands full controlling the curiosity seekers—even the well-meaning ones."

Victoria's hand fluttered to her bosom and she let out a placated sigh. "I suppose you're right, Barry. But isn't there some way I can help her? Grace got in to see her by paying off the girl who delivers lunches. She says Lyla's still in men's clothing, and looking pale and shivery and pathetic. The poor girl deserves better. Isn't there something you could say, something you could do? We're all she has now."

Ever a soft touch when a woman's soulful eyes were pleading with him, Thompson struggled to sit up. "Hand me those pants, Matt."

"But you—Doc Geary said—"

"Doc Geary can jaw at me till hell freezes over—after I straighten this out," Thompson insisted. "I won't get any rest worrying about her, so I might as well be doing something constructive."

He grinned when he saw the madam eyeing the bare legs his gown didn't cover. "And Victoria, I thank you with all my heart for coming to see me. You tell everybody I'm back in action, and that I fully expect to have their jewelry returned so they can wear it New Year's Eve."

"I knew you'd find a way!" she purred, and she placed a generous kiss on his cheek. "Take care of yourself, though. Back to bed once this is behind us, promise?"

"Promise." He winked and watched her go, then looked at McClanahan. "Did I say something wrong? You look confused."

"It's December twenty-eighth, Thompson. That gives you two days to make good on that prediction."

"No problem. I can't tell you who shot me or stole those valuables, but I know who *didn't* do it," he said as he gingerly stuck his feet into his pant legs. "How would *you* rather start the new year? As a hero who saved his woman's reputation, or as a poor slob who's lost his own? Get my coat, will you?"

Chapter 12

"Do I look like my usual fierce self?" Barry asked as he turned unsteadily before the mirror.

He preferred the denim and leather he wore to corral criminals over this dandified outfit his city position required, yet he knew he cut an imposing figure in his brass-buttoned blue uniform. It was a matter of image. Although he regretted the evolution of his rugged, range-riding predecessors into policemen, he knew bustling towns like Cripple Creek needed street-wise lawmen with savvier crime-fighting techniques.

Even-tempered and heroically proportioned, Thompson was perfectly suited to his post. Yet as he saw the bulges at his shoulder and thigh and contemplated the controversy surrounding the woman he'd come to love, he wondered how much longer he'd want to wear the marshal's star.

McClanahan briskly swatted some lint off his sleeve. "You look like a warmed-over corpse, pal. And if you fall flat in the street from all the blood you've lost, you'll forfeit everything you're trying to prove with this performance."

"That bad, huh?" Barry sighed and slapped his haggard cheeks. Those purplish half-moons under his eyes confirmed Matt's harsh assessment, and he realized he'd be damn lucky to make it through the afternoon still standing. "You'd do the same thing for Emily though, wouldn't you?"

"Damn right I would," McClanahan replied with a wry chuckle. "You think you'll be needing me? I can stick around, if you want me to."

Hearing a hint of other plans, the marshal raised an eyebrow. "Are you two lovebirds finally going to leave on your honeymoon? Get out of here! I can take care of this, I tell you."

Matt smoothed his dark waves and studied Thompson as though he wanted to dispute that last statement but didn't have the heart. "Emily—well, we both want to get back to the ranch until the robbery's solved. She knows that gang wasn't out after her specifically, but the whole episode's been pretty unsettling. At the Flaming B, she'll have things to oversee, and I think she'll feel safer."

"And the new husband wants to start feathering the nest," Thompson added with a grin. "Go to it, pal. I'll get that gold locket and her ring out to you soon as I can."

The stairway from his rooms to the street took more out of him than he cared to admit, and he silently thanked McClanahan for not hauling him back to the hospital. After sending his love to the bride, he watched Matt stride off toward the Imperial Hotel, envying his robust health and the sweet intimacy he'd share with Emily when they got home.

He'd win such a love himself, but it would take a persuasive tongue to convince the people of Cripple that Lyla O'Riley was a victim of circumstance and of an irresponsible press. After accepting surprised greetings from acquaintances who passed him on the sidewalk, Barry looked across the street toward the jail. The way his left leg was throbbing, the walk stretched before him like an endless obstacle course, dotted with horse-drawn delivery wagons and laughing children dashing through the snow, and friends—or maybe the thieves—who would note his shuffle and pallor. But a journey of a thousand miles began with the first step, and he'd limp that distance and more to clear Lyla's name.

He started off at an ungainly shuffle, determined not to favor his injured leg. But by the time he reached the back entrance to his office he was hobbling, covered with sweat despite the brisk wind that whipped down the alley. He leaned heavily against the doorjamb to catch his breath. If he was going to pull this off, he had to look convincing—or at least alive—to Adams and anyone else who might be inside. Drawing deep, head-clearing breaths, Thompson told himself if he could get through the preliminaries, he'd be alone with Lyla. They'd solve this little jewelry problem and get on to more important topics.

Barry squared his shoulders, unlocked the door, and entered the building with a determined grin on his face. It felt good to be back in his own domain. The large safe and messy desk were welcome sights as he hung his coat on the wall peg. He smoothed his hair and opened the interior door, waiting for Rex to notice him.

The deputy's freckled face paled and his Adam's apple bobbed as though he'd been caught at something. "Mar—Barry! Here, sit down," he stammered as he hopped out of the marshal's chair. "Are you sure you should be here? You look a little . . ."

"White? Must be a reflection from the snow." He'd planned to remain on his feet until he got his assistant out of the office, but his chair seemed a more sensible place to land than the floor. He lowered himself with as much grace as he could muster, gritting his teeth so Adams wouldn't see him wince when he settled his bad leg. "Sounds like I missed some excitement. Have you had many people asking about that piece in the paper?"

"Yes sir, most of them wanting a look at Miss O'Riley or asking after their jewelry," Rex replied with a nervous grin. "But I sent them on their way."

"And the jewelry's in the safe?"

"No sir, I had them put it in the vault at the bank. Thought it'd be more secure, what with those bandits still unaccounted for."

Thompson nodded, wondering how many years it would take for his second-in-command to participate in a normal man-to-man talk without shaking like a whipped pup. Rex was a responsible sort who was much more patient with paperwork than he was, though, and from the looks of things, he'd kept order pretty well. "That's what I wanted to hear," he said with a smile. "Anything I should know about? Any leads on our thieves?"

Rex's uniform cleared his skinny wrists when he shrugged. "I—I doubt they'll come in to confess," he said with a tentative chuckle.

"Miss O'Riley giving you any problems?"

"N-no, she's been real quiet. Says she won't talk to anybody but you, even though I told her *I* could—"

"That's why I'm here." Thompson looked up into his deputy's light green eyes and smiled, eagerly anticipating this reunion. "Bring her out here, will you? Then I want you to treat yourself to coffee and one of Milly's cinnamon rolls at the café, and stop by for the jewelry on your way back. Give me about half an hour, forty-five minutes."

The deputy's Adam's apple jiggled again. "Do you think it's wise to interrogate her without a witness, or—or somebody to—"

"When I can't defend myself against a pint-sized woman like Lyla, order me a pine box, will you?" he teased. "She's no more a killer or a thief than you are, Rex."

Adams hesitated, but bobbed his head. "Yes, sir. I'll be right out."

Barry straightened his uniform and shifted in the hard wooden chair, vainly seeking a comfortable position. He pulled the folded *Times* article from his pocket and pressed out its creases with nervous fingers; it was a prop for the interrogation he had to conduct as a formality. Other more personal questions danced in his head, and as he recalled the swell of Lyla's breasts above her silver-blue gown and the lush softness of the body he'd fondled in the pantry at the Rose, he had to force himself to stop these fantasies. *Business before pleasure, Thompson,* he chided himself. *And you've promised to behave yourself until she shares your name.*

A commotion in the hallway made him look up and scowl. "Chrissakes, Adams, take those cuffs off her!"

"But it's our policy to—"

"Miss O'Riley hasn't been convicted of anything, and I doubt she will be," Barry snapped. Leave it to By-the-book Adams to spoil his first moments with Lyla! He extended his hand impatiently, and when the deputy dropped the cold metal handcuffs into it, he closed them over his belt loop, out of sight. "I'll see you in forty-five minutes, Rex. Don't forget to stop by the bank."

He watched the lanky deputy leave and then focused on Lyla, who stood like a forlorn urchin on the other side of his desk. God, but he wanted to pull her into his lap and kiss away the worry on her face! Her periwinkle eyes drank him in as though she, too, longed to dispense with the tough questions they had to discuss. He had to have answers, though— evidence to convince the city of Cripple Creek that Miss O'Riley was as innocent as he knew her to be. "Have a seat, honey. Let's get this straightened out."

Lyla's heart was fluttering so fast she could feel it. The marshal looked even worse than when he'd landed in the canyon after his toboggan flight—or perhaps his dark blue uniform made him appear wan. He'd nicked his chin shaving, and his thick, sandy hair had been blown awry. His eyes were pools of dull green, surrounded by lavender shadows that

135

revealed how close he was to collapse. Yet he'd come to rescue her!

She cleared her throat, wondering why words seemed lost after all the highs and lows she'd shared with this man. "You ... I've never seen you in uniform, Marshal Thompson," she mumbled.

Oi've nivver seen ye in uniform ... His blood was barely pumping, and all she could say was—

Lyla's eyes, as round as plates, stopped the retort he knew was sheer weariness on his part. He'd intimidated her with his uniform—the last thing he'd intended—and she assumed he was here to ship her off to prison for her crimes. Barry found a smile and put it on for her. "I couldn't very well come in my hospital gown," he explained patiently, "and I— well, it's important that people see me looking fit and able to carry out my duties."

"Ah." Lyla's gaze fell to the article on his cluttered desk and her heart sank. "So you think I did it. After keeping you sedated, and lying about that fire, and losing that toboggan, you figure I—"

"I know damn well you didn't shoot me," he interrupted firmly. "But only you can answer to the crimes this article charges you with. Did you have my pistol on you when we came to town?"

"Aye," she responded with a shrug. "But saints preserve me if I'd had to defend us with it, heavy as it is."

Barry nodded, relaxing. "And you took Buck to the stable, and then intended to go to the Rose, like you told us in Geary's office?"

"You know how exhausted I was," she pleaded. "All I could think of was crawling into my own bed after a hot bath—which I'm in sadder need of now, I'm afraid."

Her hair hung limply around her shoulders, and the plaid flannel shirt and pants she wore looked and smelled slept-in, bless her. But he couldn't let Lyla's pitiful condition sway him until he'd heard all the facts. "What happened in the livery stable?"

Lyla sighed, hoping her answers sounded more plausible to Marshal Thompson than they had to everyone else. "It—it was like they were expecting me. I was hardly off my horse before Wally Eberhardt's pistol clicked behind me. He and Connor Foxe were accusing me of shooting you—and planning to escape with your horse, and—"

"Who's Connor Foxe? Can't say I've made his acquaintance."

His tone was cool and businesslike. Where was the man who'd wanted to take her away from the Rose and take care of her? "He's Frazier's brother, I think. Younger, cockier—no manners—and before I could convince the two of them that I'd saved your life instead of plotting to end it, they marched me here. Accused me of trying to flee the country with the jewelry stolen on Christmas Eve."

Barry had to hand it to her for bringing up the subject of the loot. Her palms were on her upper thighs, squeezing and releasing nervously, and his own hands itched to be in their place. "That's the issue that ties the knot in the noose, because I had no idea you'd so much as seen that jewelry. Where'd you get it, Lyla?"

He was trying to temper his voice, but damn it, he still sounded as though he took the *Times* account as gospel! She'd been ready to admit she was removing Emily's diamond when the two men cornered her, but now she kept her right hand over the bulge it made in her pocket. He'd get no more than he asked for until he stopped treating her like a criminal! "I found it in your saddlebags."

Frowning, he searched for signs she was teasing him. "Where was this?"

"In the shed behind the cabin, where I kept the horses," she explained. "After I cut your bullet out and sewed you up, I went out to tend them, and there were the jewels, in a leather pouch."

Either she was telling a truth that wasn't the least bit likely, or she was a bare-faced liar like nothing he'd ever seen. He glanced at the sketch in the paper, wondering if the cunning temptress portrayed there was the woman he'd publicly set his cap for. Or should he believe the saucer-eyed little waif sitting across from him, silently beseeching him to listen with his heart instead of his head? "How do you think they got there?" he asked quietly.

This was the weakest link in her story . . . especially since Thompson would have no qualms about searching her for the missing items. "I honestly can't say," she answered in a halting voice. "I'm guessing the thieves circled back when they saw the storm was getting worse and put them in your tack, figuring you were dead. I didn't *see* them ride in because I was working on you. Why they didn't barge in, demanding shelter, I don't know. They would've noticed my mare, the smoke from the chimney . . ."

She sounded as sincerely puzzled as he was. This theory seemed as farfetched as the ones he and McClanahan had tossed back and forth, yet Lyla was the only person who could give him an educated guess. Unless she was, as Matt had reluctantly suggested, in on the robbery from the start. Thompson shifted, wishing he didn't have to keep his personal feelings separate from his professional duties. "Was everything in the bag when you found it?"

"No. But it's hard to say what all might've been missing." Lyla stalled, wondering how to phrase her reply so she didn't sound presumptuous. "I didn't know how many pieces got stolen at the Rose, you see. My shamrock pendant was gone, as was the . . . ring they got from your pocket. Frazier's gold-headed walking stick was missing, too—but I didn't think about that until last night, when I saw him with it. He's behind this whole thing, Barry—and Wally, Rex, and Connor are his accomplices."

Thompson felt his pulse quicken. "Whoa, wait a minute. You're implicating Foxe because he had a walking stick with him? He can certainly afford more than one, honey."

"They implicated *me* because *my* jewelry was missing," Lyla blurted. "They originally intended to kill you, but when they learned you were in the hospital, they decided I could be blamed for shooting you. Then they—"

Comparing this to his own theories, Barry let her vent the frustrations she'd kept to herself since her capture. The thieves *had* thought he was dead when they rode off, but saying Frazier Foxe and his own deputy were party to that attempt was like—

"—telling you, they're all in on it. Connor and Wally knew I had the jewels on me," Lyla continued urgently, "or why would they have cornered me at gunpoint before I even had time to unsaddle the horses?"

The marshal wished he could get up and pace, but he was too weak and his head was throbbing. What he'd assumed would be a simple matter had become a tangle of wild assumptions and circumstances he was just too exhausted to sort out. When the young woman across from him stopped for breath, he asked the most logical question he could think of. "Miss Chatterly says Foxe came here to get you out, but Deputy Adams wouldn't release you."

"Maybe that's what Frazier told *her*," she said, "but the truth is that I refused to leave with him. I'd just overheard the four of them saying how I'd fouled up their plan to kill you, and then they were thinking of another attempt—finishing you off in the hospital!"

Was she trying to mislead him by telling lies so incredible no one could disprove them? He leaned on his desk, trying to keep his eyes focused despite his relentless pain. "I'm surprised you didn't jump at the chance to get out of here. Wouldn't have been that hard to get away from Frazier, at his age."

"At two in the morning? When they were talking murder? What sort of fool do you take me for?" Lyla fell back against her chair, frustrated beyond words. Either he was too ill to understand what she was telling him, or he thought she actually was a criminal. Which wasn't exactly the thanks she'd expected for saving his life . . . or for giving herself to him, body and soul. She clenched her jaw, determined not to cry.

Barry couldn't ignore the suspicious hour of Foxe's visit, or the fact that Lyla was sincerely frightened of him. She was trembling in her chair, looking away so he wouldn't see her glistening eyes. But damn it, he couldn't let tears soften him up; couldn't discount her story, but couldn't believe it, either. "I'll tell you the reasons why your accusations don't add up, and you tell me where I'm wrong," he suggested heavily. "I need to have your story before I breathe a word of this to anyone or approach any of these men. All right?"

It wasn't a terribly complimentary offer, but she nodded.

"Now, I'm not saying you didn't overhear these men talking, and I'm not saying they didn't make a try on my life," he began, "but I've lived in Cripple a lot longer than you have and I *know* these fellows. Let's start with Eberhardt, who's too clumsy to be in on a heist, and certainly too dumb to be on Foxe's payroll—if we go along with your assumption that Frazier's behind this."

Which you obviously don't, she thought bitterly. Yet it was his job to ask these probing questions, and it was her word against the testimony of men he'd known for years. "Wally's dense, but that makes him the perfect follower. And who would suspect him?" Lyla replied.

"I would've recognized his voice during the robbery."

"One man—the one who held the sack—didn't talk," she countered.

Barry thought back to that fateful night and had to concede to this point. "That still doesn't prove it was Eberhardt, but we don't know who else it was, either. What about this Connor fellow? You act like you've seen him before."

Lyla rolled her eyes. "He propositioned me, on the way back from our lunch at Delmonico's," she said. "He was the gang leader—the shorter man who gave all the orders. I *know* that, because when he and Wally were quizzing me in the livery stable, I remembered those dark, nasty eyes."

The marshal sighed. As many drifters and shiftless men who passed through this boom town, he couldn't possibly keep track of each one, but he wished he'd known Frazier Foxe had a brother in these parts. "So that leaves Rex Adams holding me to the wall with his gun?"

"Aye," she breathed, already knowing she couldn't win this part of the argument.

"Honey, Adams has six kids and a wife he's crazy about," Barry began matter-of-factly. "Why, he's— he's a deacon in the Presbyterian church! He was home with his family that night when I was getting up a posse—"

"The thieves rode out ahead of you, remember?" Lyla challenged. "Wally and Rex had plenty of time to resume their usual places while you changed your clothes."

Barry shook his head. "Rex rode out with me, and—"

"How many men shot at you?"

"Two."

"Was Eberhardt in the stable when you went after your horses?"

Thompson swallowed, thinking. "No, but—"

"So there! Wally and Connor figured you'd follow their trail, and if they missed you Rex would be right

141

alongside as a backup." She crossed her arms smugly. The marshal couldn't refute such facts unless he allowed his biases to overrule his reason.

And Barry was stunned into almost falling for it, except— "But Adams was in church clothes—had just returned from Christmas Eve services when I got to his house. None of the thieves had on trousers, Lyla!"

"And how long would it take to change them, once he rode back here ahead of you?" she protested.

"Nope, sorry. I know every article of clothing my deputy owns, what with a wife and six kids to outfit on his salary," Thompson declared. "And now that I think of it, the man who held me to the wall wasn't wearing Rex's ratty old coat, or his hat—"

"He could've traded with someone!"

"—and I would've recognized his walk, and his build, and his freckled face."

"The bandana and heavy clothing disguised all that!" Lyla hopped to her feet, ready to shake some sense into the marshal, except he looked haggard and incapable of fighting back. "So none of this makes sense to you?"

Barry sighed and rubbed his temples. "The pieces just don't fit, honey. And even though Frazier Foxe isn't my favorite person, I can't believe he'd murder me. He's more likely to milk me for contributions to his mill, or his fine-arts funding—to get even for when the Flaxen Lassie turned out to be a bonanza and his new mine went bust. He'd rather see me broke than dead."

"Do you think I was in on it, then?"

The pain in her periwinkle eyes anguished him, and he knew how ungrateful he must look to her by now. "No," he said softly, "but I still need some answers—"

"So where does that leave me?" She leaned on his desk, her eyes level with his. "Let's say, since you've got no proof about who stole that jewelry, that I'm released from jail. I couldn't possibly work at the Rose any—"

"Victoria tried to bail you out. She'll take you back," Barry interrupted.

"—because the customers couldn't *trust* me," she finished bitterly. "And until you catch the robbers, no one else will hire a suspected thief, either. I certainly won't accept any more of Foxe's generosity, and with Mick's pension about gone, I can't afford to move somewhere else and start over."

Lyla paused to lick her lips, praying her last plea would force Barry Thompson to prove he did indeed believe her—believe *in* her—enough that he'd offer the honorable lover's solution. "I . . . I don't have passage back to Ireland. Which seems my only remaining choice," she said in a faltering voice. "Can't expect anyone to lend me the money, so I guess I'll have to sell myself—"

"That's enough of that talk." The marshal gazed sadly at her, visions of the magnificent house and wedding he'd planned fading dismally. Where was the laughing, flirtatious Lyla he'd waltzed with at Matt's reception? Had only thirty-some hours in jail soured her faith in him?

She'd obviously spent her time planning for the worst. And without any proof to hang on somebody else, she would indeed be a victim of public contempt. This visit hadn't saved her name at all; it had merely created a chasm between him, as the law, and Lyla, as the suspect he couldn't clear. There was only one thing to do, and it involved a great deal of mutual trust—trust he fervently hoped he wasn't misplacing, and trust he could only try to rekindle in her heart if his plan worked.

Barry rose unsteadily, grimacing when the pain shot through his numbing leg. "I'm going to make you an offer, Lyla. It hurts to think you'd stoop to whoring before you'd ask for my help, but considering our positions on the robbery, I suppose I can

143

understand that."

Frowning, she watched him shuffle awkwardly to the back room. What was he talking about? Mother of God, the man could barely support himself on those shaky legs and his face was a sickly green as he returned with his coat and—what was that bundle in his hand? Her mouth fell open as he slapped a pack of twenty-dollar bills onto the top of his desk.

"It's five hundred dollars," he said in answer to her unspoken question. "And I'll give you five hundred more—plenty to settle yourself elsewhere, or sail home, if you decide that's what you have to do—when I come back to the office."

"Wh—where're you going?" She gazed up at his pale face, at the body that lacked the strength to make it to the door, much less anywhere else.

"To round up Rex and Eberhardt, and that other Foxe, if I can find him," Thompson said in a strained voice. "But first answer me one question, and this stack of cash is yours."

Lyla stared, unable to take her gaze from the marshal's pain-furrowed face. Her heart was pounding so loudly she thought he could hear it.

He cleared his throat, hoping to God she'd give an answer he wanted. "Lyla, honey, why didn't you tell me about that jewelry before we came back to Cripple?"

It was indeed a five-hundred-dollar question, the question she knew would condemn her the moment she decided to keep her discovery a secret. "I . . . Barry, you were so sick, and so determined to stay at the cabin until you could ride Buck into town. You didn't need to be worrying about why the jewelry was in my shed, and wondering whether the thieves would come back and kill us for it after the blizzard cleared."

It was true enough. He hoped her honesty and fortitude didn't desert her while he was arranging the next phase of this investigation. "All right, I'll buy

144

that," he said in a voice that was getting wheezy. "And while I'm gone, you think through everything that's happened since the reception. Much as I hate this, it's come down to your word against whatever Adams and Eberhardt say when they get here."

Lyla nodded, dreading the denials that would surely ring around these walls when the deputy and the stable manager confronted her, with Thompson looking on as judge and jury.

"And I guess you know how bad it'll look for you—and for me—if you're gone when I get back."

She let out a long sigh and nodded again.

"All right, then." Watching her sit down, Barry prepared himself for the ordeal of fetching Adams, Eberhardt, and the bag of jewelry without tipping them off as to what they'd be walking into when they came here. A fit man would have to talk his way through it with utmost finesse, and right now Thompson could only hope that if he got the men here, Lyla would be clever enough to catch them in their deception rather than snaring herself.

He struggled with his coat as he limped to the front door, then turned to give her a feeble wave. Lord love her, those eyes took up her whole face, and her shirt buttons were about to pop from the rapid rise and fall of her chest. *We'll dance again, someday soon, in our wedding finery*, he vowed as he stepped out onto the sidewalk. *We'll show this damn town—give those tongues something to wag about.*

Chapter 13

Lyla shivered in the draft from the door and then reached for the packet of cash. Five hundred dollars. The bundle felt firm and cool; it whispered seductively when she riffled her thumb along its edge. This was more money than she'd ever seen at one time, yet the promise of receiving twice as much left her perplexed rather than exhilarated. To be sure, Thompson was testing her integrity. But was he paying her out of guilt, for letting her down after she saved his life? Or was this transaction as casual as the countless times he'd paid Princess Cherry Blossom? The same sort of whoring she'd alluded to while coaxing him to propose rather than to remain her one-time lover?

A heavy *thunk* against the jail's facade brought her out of her musings. Was that a gasp for help, or the wind whistling through a crack in the wall? Recalling Barry's ashen complexion, Lyla rushed to open the door and her worst fears were confirmed: Thompson lay sprawled across the sidewalk, unconscious.

He was breathing, but her urgent slaps didn't rouse him and she couldn't possibly pull him inside. No one was in sight—gone home for the day, she realized frantically—so she rushed in for her coat, stuffed the money into her pocket, and coiled her hair up under Mick's hat.

Lyla sprinted to Doc Geary's office, but the sign on his door said he was making his hospital rounds. *McClanahan!* she thought. She paused to catch her breath, keeping the brim of her hat lowered so the few passersby wouldn't recognize her . . . *the Imperial!* Bless Darla for filling her in on all the McClanahans' comings and goings at the wedding. As fast as her aching lungs would allow, she ran down Bennett Avenue and then turned toward the luxurious hotel, holding her hat to keep it from flying off when the wind fought her at the door.

"I have to find Matt McClanahan—*now!*" she wheezed at the man behind the glossy registration desk.

He blinked, adjusting his spectacles. "And you are—?"

"It doesn't matter who I am! Marshal Thompson's passed out and I need McClanahan's help!"

The clerk's eyes widened with alarm. "I—I'm sorry, but the McClanahans checked out earlier this afternoon. Took the train back to Colorado Springs."

Lyla grimaced, her throat and lungs still burning. "I have to get back to Thompson!" she gasped on her way through the lobby. "Notify the hospital! Get him an ambulance!"

Down the snowy avenue she ran, ignoring the curious stares of the shopkeepers who were closing up. Her lashes were starting to freeze together before she realized she was crying. What if Barry had a concussion? What if he caught pneumonia and never made it out of the hospital before he could—

Lyla grabbed at one of the bank's wooden pillars to stop herself. A crowd was gathering in front of Thompson's office, and above their murmurings she heard Rex Adams calling out shrill orders.

"Get a doctor over here! I *told* him that O'Riley girl would—you, and you! Go find her!" he cried.

147

"She won't get away with this a second time!"

Sobbing for breath, Lyla ducked down the nearest alley, praying Connor Foxe wasn't lurking around the livery stable. Eberhardt was in the crowd at the jail—probably because Deputy Adams had warned him that the marshal would soon be asking questions they didn't want to answer. If she was to get out of Cripple before a lynch mob found her, she had to move like lightning.

The horses shuffled in the musky shadows of the stable, murmuring as she ran behind them. Calico nickered eagerly, and in a matter of minutes Lyla swung into her saddle and was galloping down a side street. Remorse stung her eyes: this was the ultimate betrayal, leaving Barry helpless—maybe dead by now—and looking as though he'd let a prisoner escape. She was adding fuel to the fiery accusations the *Times* had made, sealing her doom if she got caught.

But it was the only way she knew to survive. And if she didn't survive, the real Christmas Eve criminals would go free.

A sharp sting of camphor pierced his nostrils and Thompson came to with a jolt. He batted at the hand holding the smelling salts, struggling against the weight that held him down. Dwight Geary and Rex swam above him, their earnest faces doing a languid dance as voices murmured indistinctly in the background. He vaguely recalled stepping outside . . . waving to Lyla . . .

He fell back with a groan, more embarrassed than he'd been in his entire life. He'd tried to play the avenging hero and had passed out like a prissy little miss with the vapors!

"Thompson, can you hear me?"

The lips above him were moving, yet the familiar voice seemed to come from somewhere else. "Yeah," he rasped.

"You lie there a minute, get your bearings. Then we'll take you back to the hospital—which you shouldn't have left without my releasing you."

Geary was giving him the lecture he deserved, yet he felt curiously detached. His mind wandered . . . warm as it was, he must be in the bed beside the fireplace . . . yet the mattress was hard, like—like that damn toboggan he was strapped to! "Lyla," he breathed.

"She escaped. Probably knocked you on the head! I told you I should've stayed, but—"

The voice whined on: Rex Adams. And as the deputy's words filtered through his murky thoughts, Thompson finally understood that he was back in his office, surrounded by Geary, Adams, Eberhardt, and a few others. And Lyla had run out on him.

"Damn." He shook the last cobwebs from his head and looked at the men above him until he could bring them into focus. Rex was yammering about sending somebody to chase her down, and Wally was nodding beside him. He hadn't fetched either of them, but they were here, together. Did Lyla's story have some truth to it after all?

"Did she get your gun? Was there anything else she could've hit you with?"

The deputy's face was directly above him, and for the first time Barry realized how much his assistant resembled an oppossum . . . a freckled oppossum that looked scared of being cornered.

"Lyla did *not* strike me—nor did she escape," he added on an impulse. "I blacked out and hit my head on the wall."

Rex scowled. "You're still groggy. Miss O'Riley hightailed it out of here—"

"With my blessing. I had no evidence to hold her on," Thompson said in the firmest voice he could manage. "She probably saw me hit the sidewalk and ran for help."

149

"Charlie from the Imperial said someone short, wearing a man's coat but with a female voice, told him to get an ambulance," Geary confirmed with a nod of his head.

"There you have it." Thompson looked smugly at his deputy. "And if she's disappeared, after the way that article called her a killer and a thief, I can't say as I blame her."

Adams let out an exasperated gasp. "But marshal, she was our only—"

"That's quite enough, Rex," the doctor said with a pointed look. "Here's the ambulance—let the stretcher through. This man belongs in bed, and by God, I want no one disturbing his rest until I release him."

Thompson allowed himself to be lifted into the horse-drawn ambulance without complaint, thankful that Dwight Geary had provided an alibi for Lyla. He was disappointed that she'd gone, but not surprised. He had no illusions about Miss O'Riley's skittish nature and only regretted that he wasn't strong enough to give chase. Maybe, in the back of his mind, he'd intended for her to take that money, because instinct told him she'd rather solve the robbery than return to Ireland.

He was counting on that. And thoughts of joining her when he was well helped him pass the next few days in a narrow, short bed that he would've complained loudly about had he not had his fantasies to distract him.

But Thompson wasn't a man who could lie low for long, and Lyla O'Riley wasn't the only topic he had to ponder. He'd stake his life on the fact that Rex Adams was in church with his family instead of robbing the Golden Rose on Christmas Eve, but after that . . . some of the ideas Lyla had spouted during their brief reunion were taking root. After one of Victoria Chatterly's frequent visits he asked her to have Sam Langston stop by, and when the portly banker appeared at his bedside that afternoon, Barry was sitting up, alert and ready to resume the investigation.

"I thought you'd cashed out for good, the way folks talked when you banged your head on the jailhouse." Langston eased onto a nearby chair, chuckling until his chins quivered.

"You've always told me how hard-headed I was, and I guess I proved it," Thompson quipped. "But I'm not getting that robbery solved by lying here. I need your help."

The banker raised his pale eyebrows.

"First, I want another bundle of twenties like we keep in the back room safe for emergencies. Take the money out of my personal account."

Sam's eyes twinkled. "Don't tell me—you've been playing poker with the night nurses."

"Nope. Let's call it an investment in the future."

"Like buying that piece of land north of town?"

Barry studied his financier and decided to let him draw his own conclusions. He saw no need to connect Lyla's name to such a sum of money, since tongues were already wagging full tilt about her disappearance. "You've got the combination. Tell Rex you're putting it in the safe for me—that I had it in my coat pocket when I passed out."

Langston's brow puckered. "Is there something I should know about?"

"All in good time," the marshal replied with deliberate vagueness. "And then I'll need you to bring me that pouch of stolen jewelry Adams put in your vault. If I can't be out doing legwork, I can at least inventory the evidence."

"I'll give you the list I compiled when he brought it in," Sam said. "Since you were incapacitated, I felt it my responsibility to make a complete record of the bag's contents."

Barry nodded, pleased that his deputy had been as good as his word about depositing the valuables. He

151

hated to even *think* Rex was in on the heist, since his family depended upon his paycheck . . . the idea of Theresa Adams raising those six little children while her man was in prison didn't set well with him. Then he noticed Langston's expression was as troubled as his own. "Was there a problem with the deposit, Sam?"

"I . . . haven't mentioned this to anyone," the bank president said with a sigh, "but one of my own pieces is missing—the Masonic ring that belonged to my father. I carried it in my pocket, you see, because it's too small for my finger."

Thompson scowled. "Is anything else gone, that you know of? A lot of jewelry was taken that night, and I didn't get a good look from where I was standing."

"Well, as the *Times* mentioned, your ring and Miss O'Riley's pendant weren't there," he said, watching the marshal's reaction. "And neither was the diamond wedding set Matt McClanahan gave to Emily."

He felt a sick sensation creeping around in his middle. "What about her gold locket that's engraved with the letters E-M-R?"

Langston thought for a moment. "I don't recall seeing that, either. Who'd take such obvious pieces, when everyone for miles around would recognize them as Emily's?"

"Somebody with more greed than sense," Barry mumbled. "Somebody who had access to that bag between the time it left the Rose and the time it arrived in your bank."

"So the thieves picked through it? Or . . . or Miss O'Riley?" The man's vest buttons nearly popped when he let out his breath. "But she's long gone! And surely you can't think Adams—"

"I need one more favor." The marshal spoke in a voice that was deadly calm, despite his growing concern over how much of the jewelry had disappeared. He needed to put a finger on the thieves now, while they assumed he was laid up and unable to track them, and there seemed only one way to tie all these loose ends into a knot that would hold. "I want you to bring Norbert Sykes to see me tomorrow, early."

"That fellow your mine manager caught with his pockets full of ore?" Sam protested. "But he *smells!*"

"So buy him a bath and a clean set of clothes, on me," Thompson said with a chuckle. He reached for a pencil and a sheet of the paper he kept by the bedside, and then scribbled a note. "Give this to Adams. He'll demand proof before he lets you take Sykes out of that cell. Norbert's a decent sort, really, and now that he's sobered up, he might have some interesting things to say about this whole affair. Those jailhouse walls have ears, you know."

Chapter 14

Half frozen and utterly exhausted, Lyla stepped up to the door of the Flaming B ranchhouse. Knowing Foxe's men would trap her at the cabin, she'd urged Calico along the Gold Camp Road toward Colorado Springs instead, and spent the night holed up in an abandoned shanty along the way. Her first view of the legendary Burnham estate gave her pause: the vast network of corrals and outbuildings and bunkhouses impressed her, yet the dark-timbered, two-story mansion with its wrap-around veranda was truly intimidating. Had she not had Emily's jewelry to deliver, Lyla would've turned around. Infamous immigrants who hadn't bathed for several days had no business even approaching such a grand house.

And when a wizened old colored man opened the door, his scowl mirrored her poor opinion of her appearance. She recognized him as one of the men who escorted Emily to the altar. He was dressed in ordinary pants and a shirt now, yet he clearly felt it was his place to send her packing.

"Please don't shut the door," Lyla implored him. Her voice was husky from riding in the cold wind, and he cocked his head in surprise as he listened. But of course he would! She removed Mick's broad-brimmed hat and let her hair fall around her shoulders. "I—I'm Lyla O'Riley. I've brought the jewelry Emily lost at her reception."

The man's chocolate-brown eyes widened, and he motioned her inside. "Come in—why, for a moment I thought you were one of the renegades who . . ."

Lyla watched his wrinkles stiffen as he shut the door, and her heart sank. He recognized her now—was going to throw her out! Quickly she reached inside her coat for the jewelry, but the Negro pinned her to the wall with a viselike grip that made her gasp.

"Don't you dare draw a gun in this house!" he threatened. "You're the girl who shot Marshal Thompson! One of the thieves who—"

"No! I—"

"—ruined my Emily's wedding day! Your picture was in—"

"It was a pack of lies, that story! I—"

"What's going on here?" a familiar voice rang out above them. Matt McClanahan was thumping barefoot down the grand stairway, his face taut as he buttoned his shirt. Then he blinked. "Lyla? How on earth did you get here, unless—Thompson cracked the case, didn't he? Emily!" he called over his shoulder. "Emily, honey, come on down!"

Lyla smiled gratefully at the colored man when he released her, and then she looked at Matt. "Actually, it was his head he cracked, when he passed out and hit it on the front of the jailhouse. He needs your help, McClanahan, because I . . . I left him in a bit of a predicament."

As he smoothed his dark waves into place, his expression turned wary. "What do you mean, predicament? Miss O'Riley, you didn't break out of jail, did you?"

"No! I—Barry had just turned me loose, and he was going to fetch Rex Adams when—" The sight of Emily descending the stairs, her blond hair tumbling in disarray over the robe she was wrapping around herself, made Lyla blush. "I seem to have arrived at an inopportune time. Should've waited until—"

"Don't change the subject," Matt said in a teasing yet concerned voice. He put his arm around his bride's waist and looked at the colored man who'd opened the door. "Let's have some breakfast, Idaho. This is indeed the young lady we read about in the *Times*, and she's as slick as any con artist, to hear Thompson tell it. But Lyla's no more a thief than you are."

Idaho's wrinkles warmed with a smile, and he bobbed slightly. "Pleased to make your acquaintance, Miss Lyla. I'm truly sorry I read you wrong when you came in."

"You were just being careful." Seeing Emily's expression wavering between curiosity and disgust, she again reached beneath her coat. "I apologize for the way I look, but I was rather . . . in a hurry when I left Cripple last night. I—I thought you'd want these back as soon as possible."

When she saw her gold locket and wedding ring, Emily's tawny eyes lit up with sunshine. "Oh, my— Matt, look! Please, put them on me. I . . ."

"Nothing would make me happier," he murmured, and when their eyes met, Lyla wondered if they were going to continue the lovemaking she'd interrupted, oblivious as they were to everything but each other.

She held her breath, her heart beating with joy for them as McClanahan slipped his diamond ring onto Emily's dainty finger and then fastened the locket's chain beneath her disheveled golden hair. Their love was stunning to behold, and Lyla ached to be a part of such a blissful marriage herself. But now that she'd abandoned Barry Thompson, perhaps such a relationship would never be hers.

"Well, now," Emily said, forcing her gaze away from her husband's. "How can I thank you, Lyla? I was so afraid I'd never see my jewelry again, and I never expected *you* to—" Her forehead crinkled, and she focused intently on Lyla. "If you left Cripple last night . . . how'd you get out of jail? Why isn't Barry with you?"

"It's not what it seems," Lyla explained hastily, "and I'm sorry if I smell like I've slept in these clothes for a week, but—"

"Look me straight in the eye and tell me you weren't involved in the robbery," Matt ordered.

His eyes, ordinarily a beautiful blue, now resembled icy bullets in a double-barreled shotgun. McClanahan would haul her back to jail the moment her story faltered, so Lyla returned his demanding gaze as directly as she could. "The pouch was in Barry's saddlebag—when I went out to tend the horses, after I sewed him up," she said in a plaintive voice. "I—I suppose I should've told him, but he was out of his head with fever. I . . . thought he was going to die."

McClanahan's face softened somewhat, but his tone remained serious. "And how'd the jewelry get into Thompson's tack?"

"At the time, I thought the thieves circled back and put it there, to reclaim it after the blizzard. But now that I've talked to Barry about it, I'm not so sure," she replied quietly. "I *do* know that Connor Foxe and Wally Eberhardt set me up, though. They knew I had the jewelry when I left Doc Geary's to take Buck and my mare to the stable. And they marched me over to Deputy Adams, who jumped right in with their story about me trying to kill Thompson and escape with the jewelry.

"Then I found out Frazier Foxe was behind the whole scheme—the robbery, the murder attempt, that story in the *Times*. When I left town yesterday, Barry was being taken back to the hospital and they were hunting me down for supposedly knocking him in the head." Lyla paused to let out a tired sigh. "You've got to believe me, Matt. Thompson can't catch those men while he's laid up, and I can't show my face in Cripple until the crime's been solved."

His eyes, which had followed her every movement as she poured out her story, now ceased their silent interrogation. "You've given me more questions than answers, Lyla. Let's hash this out over breakfast."

Emily took her coat and hat, and they entered a roomy kitchen steeped in the aromas of sausage and biscuits and coffee. Lyla was immediately impressed by the closeness the newlyweds shared with the old colored cook, who limped slightly as he served up large portions of the breakfast and then sat down at the small table with them. She had expected a haughty grandeur—uniformed servants hovering about the long table in the adjacent dining room—but Emily, Matt, and Idaho were *family*, and she felt honored to be included in their circle during the delicious meal.

When they all took second helpings and their coffee cups were refilled, Matt resumed his questioning. "Tell me why you think Adams and Eberhardt are in on this," he began, "and explain Foxe's involvement. I'll make a bigger mess for Thompson if I start sniffing around in the wrong places. And frankly, armed robbery and attempted murder aren't Frazier's style, from what I know about him."

"Barry said the same thing," Lyla replied, and as she recounted the details of the Phantom Canyon ambush, being cornered in the stable at gunpoint, and the clandestine conference the four men held in the jailhouse, she wasn't at all sure Matt McClanahan believed her. He interrupted with shrewd questions, punctuated by those relentless eyes, ferreting out minor points and possibilities she and Thompson hadn't considered.

Idaho quietly cleared away their dishes, and still the questioning continued. McClanahan's skill as an investigator amazed her. No wonder he'd solved the murder of Emily's father so quickly, and won her love in return! Yet as the morning passed by, her exhaustion and the sumptuous breakfast took their toll. More than once Matt challenged her for contradicting a previous answer, until she wondered what really *had* happened the past few days in Cripple.

Emily, who was following the conversation closely, placed her hand on her husband's arm. "Matt, she's worn out. Why don't you ponder all this for a while, and I'll take Lyla upstairs. A bath and a nap would clear her mind, I'm sure."

With a grateful smile, Lyla followed the petite blonde back through the parlor and up the magnificent staircase. The house was large and homey, furnished in greens and golds and blues, with woodwork polished to a gloss. No expense had been spared, yet the decor was anything but ostentatious. The oil portrait above the fireplace was of a woman who looked like Emily but with redder hair, obviously her mother.

"You have such a lovely home," Lyla whispered with a trace of awe. Emily was leading her down the upstairs hall, into a water closet that adjoined a room with a large porcelain tub.

Her hostess smiled, drizzling bath oil into the tub. "It's even better, now that Matt's here to share it with me," she answered in a wistful voice. Then she looked at Lyla with golden-brown eyes that intuitively sought the depths of her soul. "Don't think harshly of him for his pointed questions. Barry Thompson kept us both from dying not so long ago, and we'll be forever indebted to him."

Lyla nodded, inhaling the fragrant steam that rose from the tub. She'd heard the ladies at the Rose discussing how Thompson had hidden Matt away and badgered Emily into recovering, after a miner's shack had exploded around them. Since Mick had died as a result of the same maniac's sabotage, she felt a kinship with Emily Burnham McClanahan despite the fact that the young heiress still had so much while she herself had lost everything.

"Are you in love with him, Lyla?"

She stopped unbuttoning her shirt to study the inquisitive woman beside her. "I don't suppose that's any mystery, after the way I spoke of him downstairs," she answered shyly. "Barry's a dear fellow, funny and sweet. What woman *wouldn't* fall for his flattery and affection?"

Emily frowned. "You think it's only flattery? Several people at the wedding were saying he planned to marry you, and he certainly *looked* serious."

Thinking back over her days with him at the cabin, and then about the things Cherry Blossom revealed about the marshal, Lyla was no longer sure of her feelings for the tall, boyish Thompson. Even though she still had her clothes on, she felt naked beneath Emily's concerned gaze. It would do no harm to confide in her, yet Lyla hesitated to appear foolishly lovestruck and—

"There's no reason to be bashful in front of *me*," the little blonde said with a confidential grin. "Why, when I thought Matt was dead and Barry came around every day to cheer me up, I was sure he intended to court me when I quit grieving. And I might've fallen for him, Lyla. I think those tales about him being such a ladies' man are greatly exaggerated, and they'd die out altogether if he found the right woman to love him."

Who should she believe? As Lyla peeled off her shirt and pants, she compared this woman's glowing account of Thompson's virtues to the furtive confessions the Indian princess had made. There was no denying Barry's passionate nature, yet beneath his burly chest beat a gallant, loving heart. She was so tired and confused. Large teardrops plopped down onto her camisole before she realized she was crying.

"I'm sorry. I didn't mean to pry." Emily's voice

160

was low and soothing, and she dabbed at Lyla's face with a handkerchief from her robe pocket. "You have every right to feel mixed up, what with all the upsetting things that've happened this week. I'll leave you alone now—"

"Let me explain." Lyla let out a long sigh, hoping she wouldn't regret the secret she was about to reveal. Surely Emily could set her straight, advise her in matters about men, since she'd married such a fine one herself. "It's just that, well . . . the last night we spent in the cabin, Barry . . . I curled up beside him to get some sleep, assuming he was too sick to even *think* about . . ."

Emily's face lit up with comprehension, and then she chuckled. "So he *does* want you! Matt says he chattered constantly about all you did for him while he was there, and—"

"You wouldn't know anything had happened between us." Lyla glanced away, embarrassed but too far into her confession to quit. "He gave me five hundred dollars—you tell Matt that, in case he thinks I stole it! I was hinting that I might have to return home to Ireland, since no one in Cripple will hire me, and instead of begging me to stay he gave me that money to travel on. He acts as though . . . as though he never made love with me."

"Oh dear." Mrs. McClanahan looked truly perplexed, as though she couldn't believe Thompson would act so insensitive about such an intimate matter. Then she turned the spigots off and took two fresh towels from the cabinet. "You soak awhile and wash your hair, and all these things will look clearer when you've gotten some sleep. There's got to be a reason for this, and between us, we'll figure it out."

Lyla nodded, and when her hostess closed the door of the little room, she stripped and slid into the chin-high, rose-scented bubbles. It was pure heaven, that hot, silky water, and as the dirt from the past week drifted away, so did her thoughts . . . to a cabin where she and Barry shared their hopes and dreams in preparation for reuniting their love-flushed bodies beside the fire.

But she fell asleep before she got to the good part.

After a cozy dinner that evening, Lyla followed Emily and Matt into the parlor for coffee while Idaho cleaned up the kitchen. The whole house smelled of the old cook's succulent ham and yams and freshly-baked bread, and her clean clothing and hair gave her a more cheerful outlook than she'd had for days. She settled into an overstuffed chair across from the newlyweds, sensing they'd discussed her situation while she took a nap and were about to offer some advice.

"Now, about that stack of twenties we found in your coat pocket," Matt began. He winked at Emily and she scooted closer to him with a secretive grin. "Was that for uh, services rendered, or what?"

Lyla scowled, until she realized the handsome detective was teasing her—which meant he believed she was a victim of circumstance who'd made a few untimely decisions, rather than a hardened criminal. "As I told Emily, the marshal intended that as fare home to Ireland, since I can no longer support myself in Cripple Creek."

"Uh-huh. Well, I don't believe a word of it," McClanahan replied, leaning forward to emphasize his point. "But that's because Thompson's told me a few things he hasn't shared with you yet. If you leave, you'll break his heart, Lyla."

She nipped her lip, wondering how much Emily had revealed to her husband this afternoon. "It'd break mine, too," she mumbled, "but he gave no clue that he wanted me to stay. After coming on so boldly at first, he . . . well, now he acts as though the days at my cabin meant nothing to him, beyond the fact that

162

he's grateful I patched him up. I—I was hoping for more."

"And you'll get it, if you give him a chance to explain himself." Matt glanced at his wife, clearing his throat. "Emily told me about the, uh, situation you're in. Barry's acting so dense because he doesn't remember everything he did at your place, and—"

"*What?*" Lyla rose from her chair, her cheeks blazing. "You can't tell me—he was talking the whole time, asking me to *love* him, and—"

"He was probably still out of his head with fever or those herbal potions you were giving him," her host replied earnestly. "I *know* Barry—teased him about what he did while you were snowbound, and he was utterly serious about denying it. He'll be embarrassed as hell to find out he made love to you and can't recall it, honey."

She stared at the McClanahans, feeling foolish and very confused. "But after I sewed him up, he knew it was Christmas . . . made jokes about my tea, and—and seemed perfectly coherent when he talked to me."

McClanahan smiled and shook his head. "I can't explain it. Perhaps parts of his brain were more affected by his loss of blood than others. Trust me, Lyla. He cares deeply for you, and Barry would never, never make light of your feelings—or of what you gave him because he said he loved you. Thompson adores women, but he's no cherry plucker."

With the same persuasive intensity he'd used to interrogate her, Matt was now defending Barry Thompson. Lyla looked at the dark-haired, handsome man, realizing he knew the marshal far better than she did, but still . . . it was a bitter pill, hearing that the man she loved couldn't remember escorting her into womanhood.

"Don't take it as a fault on your part," Emily suggested gently. "I'm sure once you tell him—"

"Tell him? And what would I say—'Mr. Thompson, I'm so sorry you don't recall making love to me. It was wonderful'?" Her fists drilled into her hips as she paced in front of her chair. "He'll think I'm trying to trap him! What man would admit to a woman that he didn't remember bedding her? Could *you?"*

Matt let out a sheepish chuckle, shrugging. "He can't apologize for an offense he doesn't know he committed. And it's sure as hell not my place to tell him."

"Oh, fine! I'll just march into his room at the hospital and blurt it out. Doc Geary and the nurses would love that!" Stuffing her hands into her pockets, Lyla tried desperately to make sense of yet another dilemma she was in because of Barry Thompson. How could loving him make everything go so wrong?

When her temper cooled, she looked to the McClanahans for help. "I can't return to town, anyway," she admitted. "That sketch in the papers will be on Wanted posters all over Colorado, if Rex Adams has his way."

"Why not return to your cabin? Send Barry a message to meet you there when he's released," Emily suggested. "Perhaps the words will come easier when you're in your own surroundings."

Lyla shook her head. "I'm betting the deputy and Eberhardt have somebody watching it, waiting for me."

"I'll take care of them," McClanahan said. "After thinking about what you and Thompson have told me, I'm going to have some extra lawmen sent in to man the jailhouse while I quiz Wally and the deputy. The one time I met Connor Foxe, I suspected he had no purpose in Cripple other than to cause trouble. The fact that he and Frazier don't associate with each other—at least in public—bothers me, too."

"And if you and Barry talk at the cabin, maybe it'll

164

jog his memory. Maybe you won't have to *tell* him what his best medicine was." Emily glanced coyly at her husband and took his elbow. "Cabins can be cozy, romantic places . . . just the two of you, in front of the fire."

Lyla sensed the dreamy-eyed couple was reliving a scene from their own love story, just as she suspected they'd planned this all out while she was sleeping. Now that she'd delivered Emily's jewelry and convinced Matt to corner the robbery suspects, she had no reason to intrude upon their honeymoon any longer . . . and it *would* be nice to return to her little home, knowing she'd be safe there. "All right, I'll go—"

"And I'll deliver the note for you, when I visit Barry in the hospital," Emily piped up.

Her enjoyment of these matchmaking efforts put Lyla on guard again. "If you breathe a word about this to Thompson—"

"Oh, don't worry. That's your business," the twinkly-eyed blonde replied. "I'll just play Cupid's helper, and prove your innocence to him—and everybody else I see—by telling how you came all the way to the ranch to return my rings. Your reputation needs a little repair, and I'm happy to help. For you, and for Barry, too."

It was assistance she couldn't afford to pass up, and Lyla saw that the McClanahans regarded this mission as an adventure rather than an imposition upon their newly-wedded bliss. She penned the note in her neatest hand. *Come to the cabin, love. I can't leave without seeing you,* she wrote, hoping to entice Thompson into immediate action. She signed her name, sealed the envelope with one of Emily's ornate wax stamps, and entrusted the message to a grinning Mrs. McClanahan. "I hope this works. Plans've tended to backfire lately," she said quietly.

"You leave things in Cripple to Matt and me. Your job's to get Barry to chase after you until you catch him," Emily said with a girlish grin. "And be *merciless* when he realizes you're already his."

As Lyla mounted her mare early the next morning, she hoped Emily's enthusiasm wasn't misplaced. How on earth could she bring up such a delicate subject with a man who'd more likely laugh at her than believe her? What would she do if Barry flatly refused to admit he could've committed such an intimate crime against her innocence? She patted the bundle of twenties in her coat pocket, praying she'd be handing it back to him rather than paying her fare to Ireland with it.

Calico loped along the trail leading out from the Flaming B's tall, timbered gateway. The wind blew powdery snow in loose, spiraling swirls on the path before them. Above the foothills the sky was dove gray, overcast, with a continuous cloud cover. Her mind wandered to the cabin, to the hours she hoped to spend getting better acquainted with her lover, discovering the myriad admirable things about Barry Thompson that Matt and Emily already knew.

He would be stronger this time, teasing his way out of an embarrassing predicament until they'd fall into each other's arms, laughing, kissing . . . in her mind she saw his powerful body tensing, felt his lips nuzzling the hollows of her throat on their way down to suckling the breasts he fondled so lovingly with his large, gentle hands. His manhood probed between her thighs until she opened to him, longing for the rush of wildfire he'd kindled in her before. He claimed her mouth with a searing kiss, clasping her to his chest as he lunged—

Lyla gasped with the reality of her sensuous daydream—until she realized that the tightness around her shoulders was a lasso loop rather than Barry's embrace. Before she could grab the saddlehorn, she was tumbling backward over Calico's rump, shrieking.

"Send that mare on its way!" a menacing voice

called out.

As she hit the ground with a bone-jarring *whump*, Lyla saw a man spring out of a grove of trees and fire his pistol repeatedly to keep Calico from circling back to her. "Stop it!" she gasped. "If you hurt my horse, I can't—"

"Where we're taking you, you won't need such a homely nag, cupcake." The man's laughter sounded frighteningly familiar as his footsteps approached her from behind. She'd been so lost in thought she hadn't realized she was being watched from the trees, an easy mark for two ambushing outlaws.

The rope around her chest yanked the breath from her, and she was spun around in the loose snow to face her captor. "Connor Foxe! You—"

"How nice of you to remember," he replied smoothly. "Nice of you to clean up at the Flaming B, too. Can't stand a woman who smells stronger than I do."

She was about to make a retort, but Foxe jerked the rope tighter, and it cut her forearms with its vicious grip. "Miss O'Riley, I'd like to present Kelly Jameson, my partner in crime—one of many," Connor jested. "You've met him before, though you weren't aware of it at the time."

The man approaching them was lean and tall, wearing a boot-length tan duster that flapped in the wind. Beneath his hat she saw a square jaw set off by reddish-gold sideburns and a smile she'd have found alluring under different circumstances.

"You sure you oughtta be spoutin' off about that?" he drawled as he looked down at them.

"What can it hurt? She won't have the chance to identify you in Cripple. Not that Adams would lock you up if she did," Foxe replied with a smirk. "And with Thompson out of the way, it'll be our little secret. Won't it, cupcake?"

Lyla grunted when the toe of his boot found her backside.

167

"See how agreeable she can be, once you get her attention? Let's hoist her onto my horse before anybody happens by here," Connor said, tugging his blue bandana over his face. "We don't want Nate thinking something went wrong."

When the other man also covered his face, Lyla's heart stopped. Could this be the desperado who'd held Barry at gunpoint during the robbery at the Golden Rose? And what was this talk about Thompson being "out of the way"?

"You'll never get away with this!" she challenged. "I'll break loose and—"

A resounding *smack* made her cheek sting and the coppery taste of blood seeped onto her tongue. "Quit your yammering or I'll gag you," Foxe threatened. "Can't stand a woman who runs at the mouth."

Reeling from the blow, Lyla put up no fight as the two men lifted her between them and boosted her onto a sorrel stallion that was waiting in the trees. Jameson cantered out to the road beside them, watching her as though she might squirm out of Connor's grip. She knew better than to hope they were heading into Cripple, and sure enough they left the main trail when they came to a wide creek. Turning north, Lyla thought.

These foothills and open stretches of pastureland were totally foreign to her, so she soon gave up trying to memorize all the twists and turns they followed. Where on earth were they taking her? She thought fleetingly of her ruined rendezvous with Thompson in the cabin. Would she ever see him again? Would Calico return to town, alerting him or the McClanahans to her crisis? Or would Eberhardt be waiting to hide her mare away . . . or dispose of her?

The way her luck was running of late, it was best not to think about such things.

Chapter 15

The first day of 1899 found Barry Thompson resolute indeed, resolving to clear up the Christmas Eve jewelry heist now that he had enough facts to catch the culprits. Three days of rest had cleared his head. Norbert Sykes, who'd heard the incriminating conference from his cell beside Lyla's, had backed up her story word for word. Rex Adams, Wally Eberhardt, and the Foxe brothers were all involved, even if the pieces of the puzzle didn't quite fit . . . yet.

He sat on the side of the hospital bed to pull on his blue uniform trousers. Doc Geary had released him with the condition that he'd stay off his horse and out of his office for at least a week. He could live with that, could have Sam Langston do some of his legwork and contact McClanahan about starting the investigation in earnest. The hardest part would be locking his deputy away. Because it was Sunday, Barry refused to accost Rex when he was coming out of church with his family. He had plenty of other things to do first, like getting the jewelry returned to its owners. And maybe finding out where Lyla was.

Barry smiled at the thought of the impish Irish lass. Who else could alert an ambulance and then disappear with five hundred dollars before anyone recognized her? He chatted amiably with the hospital attendant who gave him a ride to his apartment, all the while studying the people on the street, hoping to see the elusive Miss O'Riley in her heavy coat with her hat brim pulled low.

He saw her, all right—in practically every storefront window along Bennett Avenue. The sketch from the *Cripple Creek Times* had been enlarged and reproduced on Wanted posters that made him chuckle despite the bold black headlines charging her with an attempt on his life, among other things. He'd keep one as a memento they could laugh about in years to come. Waving to his driver, he waited for the hospital carriage to turn the corner and then walked slowly toward the Golden Rose. Most of the people he needed to see were probably there, and he hoped they weren't too hung over from New Year's Eve festivities to assist him.

Thompson was greeted with cheers and back slaps when he entered the bordello parlor.

"Marshal! Good to see you up and around!"

"Come toast 1899 with us!"

"Barry, by God, that little Irish whore didn't get the best of you, did she?"

The marshal held up his hand for silence, returning the smiles he saw on these familiar faces. Some had bleary eyes and booze-reddened noses, and the ladies drooped as though they'd entertained long and hard while ushering in the new year, but seeing them made his heart swell. These were his friends, whether fabulously wealthy or heavily indebted to Miss Chatterly for the clothes on their backs. The concern in their eyes told him just how worried they'd been about losing him, strengthening his resolve to settle this robbery business quickly and decisively.

"A couple things need to be said, since several of you were here on Christmas Eve," he began. "First of all, Miss Lyla O'Riley has been greatly wronged by the papers and falsely accused of several ridiculous crimes. Let there be no mistake—she saved my life

170

after I was shot while chasing the bandits, and she was imprisoned because my deputy became over-zealous about protecting me. I released her with no qualms whatsoever before I blacked out."

A gasp circulated among the guests, who glanced at each other and then studied him expectantly.

Barry chuckled. "If you think I'm defending her honor because I'm sweet on her, you're right. But we owe Lyla our thanks for pointing me toward the real culprits, and I'd appreciate it if you'd spread the word about her innocence. Poor girl's afraid to come back to Cripple because the crowd around me at the jailhouse sounded a lot like a lynch mob. Didn't it?"

The men murmured among themselves, until Daniel Klegg, a mine owner, asked, "So if Miss O'Riley didn't shoot you or steal our valuables, who did?"

"I'd rather not divulge that until I have the suspects in custody," Thompson replied. Then he smiled at Sam Langston. "I can, however, let you reclaim the jewelry you lost, since there's no point in holding it any longer. Sam, let's have everybody register a detailed, written description of their stolen items with you, and then they can pick up what's theirs at the bank, starting tomorrow. How's that?"

"Fine by me," the banker replied.

"And to help you out," Barry continued with a slight bow toward the Rose's madam, "Miss Victoria can make a list of all the guests who were here for the McClanahans' reception. Some of the pieces that were stolen weren't in the pouch when it was retrieved, so please don't get alarmed if all your items aren't returned just yet. Once our crooks are behind bars, my first priority is to locate what's missing."

"And how do we know you won't go sniffing around to find Miss O'Riley instead?"

It was a brazen challenge, one Barry knew was intended to make him stammer. But he smiled, hooking his thumbs through his belt loops as he addressed the buckskinned beauty with the sly brown eyes. "Princess Cherry Blossom, I can assure you it's in my best interest to find the pieces that're missing," he replied suavely, "because if my aquamarine ring doesn't show up, Lyla will be terribly disappointed. And you know it's not my nature to disappoint a lady."

Laughter filled the crowded parlor and then the men replenished their drinks and came up to ask about his health. Sam and Victoria situated themselves on a settee with pen and paper, where they could make their lists on the marble-topped coffee table as the guests and whores reported the necessary information.

Darla brought him a plate of sandwiches, pickles, and cookies from the buffet and exchanged pleasantries until Silas Hughes placed a snifter of brandy in his other hand and dismissed her with a polite smile.

"Glad you're back among the living," the new owner of the Angel Claire said, "and it sounds like you've got the robbery situation well in hand. Or was some of that little speech designed to placate the natives until you've had time to find some real answers?"

Barry chuckled, not the least bit offended by Hughes' astute comment. "I'm doing what I can, considering Doc Geary's keeping me off my horse for a while. Going to have Matt round some renegades up, and then send those two on their honeymoon."

"Fine idea. I hope you find Emily's ring and locket, too," the silver-haired magnate replied. "Poor girl, loses her father and then gets robbed on her wedding night. Makes you wonder if any of us are safe in this town. No reflection on you, understand."

Barry nodded and bit into a thick ham sandwich so he wouldn't have to comment. Hughes' concern was genuine, since the man reported to his mine every day not knowing whether his employees might blow the

172

Angel Claire up again, by accident or on purpose. Every mine owner in Cripple lived with that threat: the unruly nature of blasters, muckers, and other laborers made for conditions as volatile as the explosives used to free the gold ore from the bowels of the earth.

But how did Hughes know Emily's diamond and pendant were missing? Had Langston leaked that information, or had the newspapers reported it when they mentioned his and Lyla's pieces? Damn, it was lousy to be out of circulation—and out of his head for part of that time! Barry hated wondering if any more of his friends were tied in with the heist somehow. He glanced at his banker, who was taking down descriptions, and hoped his trust wasn't misplaced. Sam Langston and Silas Hughes had no reason to be parties to the robbery. But then, neither did Frazier Foxe.

And Frazier wasn't here today, he noted. The man with the monocle was a tough one to figure: frequented a whorehouse but never lay with a lady, had a brother he didn't acknowledge in public . . . masterminded a robbery, paying honest men in opportune positions to do his dirty work. In addition to his brokerage house on Bennett and part interest in numerous Cripple Creek businesses, he owned the largest sheep ranch in Colorado, north of the Springs a ways. Barry sensed he'd be paying the ranch a visit if Foxe didn't show up around town soon.

He didn't realize Hughes had gone to talk to Miss Chatterly until a hand slipped under his elbow and a warm, angular body was rubbing against him like a cat. He smiled down at the Indian princess, who was tipping his snifter for a sip of brandy. "Feel better, now that you've shot your arrow?" he teased.

She batted her black-lined eyes with a decadent air he knew well. "I'll feel better when you shoot *yours*, loverman. Deep down inside me," she purred.

Barry chuckled and gave her an apologetic shrug.

173

"Not sure I could even take aim, much less fire, sweetheart. I lost a lot of blood, and this bum leg—"

"Thompson, comes a time *I* can't get a rise out of you, you'll be holding up a headstone." Cherry Blossom gazed at him with a coy grin, her breasts thrust forward in a blatant come-on beneath her beaded bodice. "And even if you can't attack, you can still nibble, or squeeze, or kiss me . . . you know where."

Her seductive whisper didn't fool him for a moment: the war-painted woman running her thumbnail up his fly was testing him. Seeing if he'd succumb, after he'd declared his intentions toward Lyla in front of all his friends. These men wouldn't think of informing his beloved of his infidelity, but they'd file it in the backs of their minds just the same.

"How about a bath, then? For old times' sake," she coaxed. "A steamy soak would do those stiff muscles good. It's the least you could do for a poor working girl whose favorite turquoise combs were stolen by those big, bad robbers."

"They were?" Barry glanced at the beaded rawhide she'd plaited into her hair. "Did you report it to Sam?"

"You're changing the subject," Cherry Blossom said with a roll of her eyes. "Frankly, I'm doing you a favor, Thompson. These men would never mention it, but that perfume you're wearing leaves a lot to be desired."

He wasn't wearing any . . . this hussy was telling him he stank! Barry cleared his throat sheepishly. He couldn't remember the last time he'd had more than a sponge bath administered by a meek nurse's aide.

But he'd be damned if he'd let this crafty dove get the upper hand. She couldn't care less about his money—friend and confidante though she was, Princess Cherry Blossom was jealous of Lyla and intended to trap him, with a trick he knew he'd regret. He gave her one of his most suggestive once-

174

overs, chuckling low in his throat. "All right, foxy lady, you win," he murmured. "Go start my bath water. I'll be in as soon as I tell Sam about your combs."

"Of course, marshal—anything you say." She left the parlor with a victorious sway of her hips, but then turned in the doorway to waggle her middle finger at him, a gesture they often exchanged when they romped in her room or in the bathing suite.

Thompson laughed out loud and approached the table where the banker and the madam were nearly finished taking names. "Sam, jot down that Grace Putnam's minus two turquoise-and-silver combs," he said. "And Victoria, I'd appreciate it if you'd poke your head into the suite down the hall after a bit. That wild squaw of yours says I need a bath, but her brown eyes are flashing green lightning over Lyla, and she just might try to drown me."

The madam smiled knowingly and waved him on his way.

He had his brandy refilled at the bar while he polished off his lunch. It was a stall tactic, because he wasn't sure how to approach the woman who awaited him in the bathing suite. Dozens of times he and Cherry Blossom had cavorted there—she was his favorite, and he'd told her so. Neither of them expected more than a few hours' entertainment from the other, yet Barry knew damn well that beneath her Indian get-up beat the heart of a Grace Putnam who would've had a husband and children, had fate dealt her a better hand.

Those dreams would never disappear, no matter how much mahogany dye she put on her skin or how many jaded little games she invented for her customers. And Princess Cherry Blossom wasn't about to let him go without a protest of some sort. Thompson knew her—*understood* her. Yet as he slowly walked down the hall, he had no idea what to expect from the raven-haired whore who was run-

175

ning his bath water.

She was leaning over to turn off the faucets when he slipped in and shut the door. Her buckskin dress was short enough to reveal shapely brown calves and tight enough to strain across her narrow, flattish bottom. *At least she's still dressed,* he thought, and to avoid any unnecessary temptation he began to remove his uniform himself.

Cherry Blossom turned, smiling at him. "Can't wait to have me caressing you? Or afraid I'm up to some nasty little stunt?"

"The thought crossed my mind, yes," Barry admitted. He walked over to the room's brass bed, his wariness masked by a subtle grin as he draped his clothes over one of its posts. "I wasn't just putting you off, sweetheart. These bandages are the mark of a man who's got to live a careful life for the next several days."

As he gingerly tugged his union suit down over his wounded arm and then past his midsection, the princess's eyes widened with concern. "I . . . I thought about some sort of revenge," she confessed softly, "but it wouldn't be the same if you weren't able to fight back."

"Were you worried when you heard I got shot?"

She bowed her head. "I didn't want to think about you dying, Barry. Saw enough mangled bodies to last my lifetime when the mine blew up." Cherry Blossom came over to him, her dark eyes and voice still subdued as she reached hesitantly toward his shoulder. "Can these bandages get wet, or should we take them off?"

"We'll unwrap them."

Her touch was gently cautious as she unwound his shoulder, and Thompson thought it best to take the binding from his thigh himself. It was the first time he'd ever been nude in front of her that he wasn't rock hard, and the first time the Indian princess hadn't fondled him shamelessly in the places she knew he

176

liked best. When she saw his scabs and stitches, she paled visibly.

"Guess I wasn't cut out to be a nurse," she mumbled.

Barry smiled, surprised at her squeamishness. "Most women wouldn't make good whores, either, scared as they are of sex." Before the words died away he realized the cruel irony of them and grasped her hand. "I'm sorry, Grace. I didn't mean to imply—"

"I'll accept that as the compliment you intended," she said with a wry smile, "and for God's sake let's stop acting like a couple of old fogies at a funeral. Get in that tub! You're making my eyes water like I was peeling an onion."

Was it another of her little acts, or was the notorious savage of the Golden Rose truly affected by his brush with death? Thompson stepped into the bathtub and then eased himself very carefully into the steaming water. Bless her, the princess knew just how deep he liked it and how warm, and she'd scented it with musk rather than the flowery oils most of the ladies preferred.

He watched her fetch a washcloth from the vanity, still leery of her motives. Best to get her grievances aired before he became any more vulnerable. "Now that you've got me where you want me, how're you going to pay me back for falling in love with Lyla?"

Cherry Blossom's eyebrow shot up. "Love at first sight, was it? That's almost too cute for words, Thompson." She walked behind him and began scrubbing his shoulders with firm, thorough strokes. "Seems to be contagious—first McClanahan and now you. But I learned my lesson. Made a last-ditch effort to seduce Matt and he got up in the middle of it. I felt like a fool for days."

The marshal sighed, wishing there were an easier way for her to vent her frustrations. "He never told me that, so your reputation's safe," he said in a gently teasing voice. "It's not like either of us begrudges you

177

a husband, Grace."

"But you neither one made me an offer, either," she snapped. Then she sighed and brought the washcloth to rest on his shoulder, sending little rivulets of water down his chest. "I've got no right to expect matrimony. I *know* that. But damn it, Barry, with you it's—well, we're *friends*. We talk about things and joke with each other, and . . ."

"And we get along better than a lot of husbands and wives we know. Is that what you're trying to say?" He turned in the tub, truly sorry for the lone teardrop racing down her war-painted cheek, but smart enough not to blot it. "I can't explain it, sweetheart. Even before she saved my life, I wanted to marry Lyla. She's had her share of problems, yet she—"

"Is she any good in the sack?"

Thompson cleared his throat. "I honestly don't know. Every chance I've had to—"

"Maybe she's frigid. Better think twice before tying yourself to a woman who'll freeze you out of bed, marshal."

The princess resumed her scrubbing with a vengeance that matched her tone, until he had to swallow his laughter and grab hold of her hand. "If that happens, you'll be the first to know," he said in a low, serious voice.

He wasn't leading her on, exactly. It was just better to let this wily woman see a glimmer of hope than to leave her feeling totally abandoned—nicer for her, and healthier for himself.

Cherry Blossom smiled subtly. "That's a fact, isn't it? I should know that, with as many hungry husbands as I cater to."

Chuckling, she continued her ministrations with utmost tenderness. Although she knew every nuance that could drive him to a frenzy, Grace's touch remained as coolly detached as that of the nurses who'd tended him in the hospital. She was silent now, her dark eyes following the washcloth's progress over his chest and stomach as though she was memorizing each mole and ripple.

Barry let himself relax, satisfied with their truce. The warm water lapped softly around his shoulders. He lifted first one leg and then the other to let her lather them, aware that this ritual wasn't half so much fun when his partner wasn't in the tub. He envisioned Lyla bathing with him, her breasts bobbing in the bubbly water, and decided the first request he'd make of the architect was a room like this with the longest, deepest tub he could find.

"Here—you do the rest while I get some lotion," Cherry Blossom murmured. "Those muscles and scabs'll benefit from a good rubbing."

Thompson blinked. She wasn't going to wash his privates, usually the highlight of their foreplay. He wasn't sure he could resist her once she started a massage, but how the hell could he say no at this point?

"I'm not going to rape you," the whore teased as she set out a bottle of oil. "Here's a towel. If you dry yourself, I won't charge you for this little farewell session. I don't want you to think I'm a sore loser, or you'll never come back."

He nodded, puzzled. When he stood up, Grace's gaze followed the flow of water down his chest and thighs and then lingered on his manhood. Damn her, she was arousing him with just a look, from across the room! Self-consciously he dried his midsection, feeling like an utter fool when the towel tented out despite his efforts to control himself. He couldn't turn his back because she was watching him, smiling smugly. So he dried quickly and wrapped the towel around his waist.

"Don't tell me marriage is going to make you a modest man," the princess said with a giggle. "Why marshal, do I foresee you sleeping in your union suit, or—dare I say it—a nightshirt?"

179

"I don't own a nightshirt," he muttered.

"I'll give you one for a wedding present."

Something told him he should dress and leave before things got out of hand. The Indian princess hadn't once tried to seduce him, which meant she had something truly humiliating or unthinkably cruel on her mind. But how could he walk out now without appearing henpecked and foolish?

Barry dropped his towel and stretched out on the bed, stomach down, so his manhood wouldn't mock him while Grace massaged his backside. Her hands gripped and stroked. As the lotion seeped into his thirsty skin, he felt the muscles between his shoulders relax and a languid warmth spreading through his body. He would miss this woman's touch. As much as Lyla's innocence appealed to him, she would require time and patient instruction before she could give him as satisfying a massage as Princess Cherry Blossom did.

The whore hummed while she worked. She was straddling him; her dress was hiked up past her thighs, allowing her the fluidity of movement to slide her palms around his forearms and down his back. Her thumbs followed the hollow of his spine into the crevice of his hips . . . she kneaded the halves with tender thoroughness, and he felt himself drifting . . . drifting. His mind followed his body into a delicious state that floated between wakefulness and sleep, and he sighed contentedly.

The princess raised up and whispered, "Turn over now, loverman. Nap if you want to. I'll shut the door when I leave, so no one'll disturb you."

Eyes closed, Barry nodded. Despite all the rest he got in the hospital, a short snooze sounded like a fine idea. He was still weaker than he cared to admit, and his masseuse was working out the kinks caused by an uncomfortable hospital bed. A cold pooling of liquid on his chest made him hoot, and then Grace's palms spread the lotion in wide, warming arcs that fanned

180

out from his collarbone to his armpits.

"Hang onto the spindles while I rub your sides," she murmured.

Thompson obeyed, grasping the cool brass headboard as he always did. Hard to believe the Rose's most raucous dove was being such a sport. She was leaning into him . . . squeezing, releasing . . . brushing his face lightly with her breast as she worked her magic up the length of his right arm. She took his hand and slowly rotated it until his wrist was limp in her grip. He breathed deeply . . .

The *click* didn't register until he felt a cold bracelet of steel close around him. By the time his eyes flew open, the whore had handcuffed his left arm to a brass rail as well.

"What the hell're you—" Barry jerked, rattling the short chains that bound his hands to the headboard. "If this is some sort of joke, I'll—"

"It's a new game I devised, just for you," the princess purred. "I call it 'Shackled by Love,' because that's what you'll be when you marry Lyla." She crossed her arms and with one swift movement pulled her dress over her head. "But for now, you're *my* slave. Long after I set you free, you'll remember this little rendezvous, Barry honey."

Grace vaulted nimbly over him and went to the chair where his underwear was draped.

"How'd you get ahold of these—"

"Handcuffs?" she asked coyly. "When I took Lyla's lunch to her cell, the other prisoners got a little rowdy. Rex went in to settle them down, and I couldn't resist—these two sets were just lying there on your desk. I fastened them to the bed while you were talking to Sam about my combs."

"You little bitch." Barry watched her pluck his cloth bandages from the chair and whirl in a circle, wrapping her mahogany body like a maypole as she cavorted. He managed a chuckle. If he kept everything light, kept her laughing, perhaps she'd turn

181

him loose unscathed when she'd played out her little game.

Cherry Blossom stopped beside him, and with a wink she waggled her middle finger and then ran its nail down the center of his chest. When she circled his navel, Barry wriggled and protested, knowing where she was headed next. He was already pointing at the ceiling, and sure enough, her practiced grip sent the blood rushing up his shaft in a surge that made him suck in his breath. "Damn you, it's not fair to—"

In a flash she bound his ankles together with the end of the bandage and then quickly tied them to the foot railing. "Nothing's fair in this life, Thompson," she muttered. "Just ask any woman who has to whore for a living."

The Indian princess paused to survey her handiwork, her mood lightening. Her dark-eyed gaze roamed over his body while she crossed her arms beneath her breasts, as though deciding how to torture him next.

"All I'd have to do is holler, and there'd be a roomful of—"

"Do you want me to gag you?" she blurted. Then she chuckled and slipped onto the bed, straddling him lithely. "Some of those men would love to see you this way, marshal. A few would pay for the privilege of watching me work you over . . . a couple of them would take my place for any price I demanded. Our clientele can afford perversions you've never even heard of, and we try to accommodate them."

He'd played out many a fantasy with this woman, but he'd never heard the cold, knifelike edge in her voice before. Barry tensed. She was sliding up and down him, teasing his shaft with the dark coils of her cleft, and it occurred to him that having sex with her might be the safest thing he could do. His scab was pulling painfully across his thigh, but he undulated, probing for the opening that would make her as much his hostage as he was hers.

"No you don't," Grace said with a throaty laugh. "Since you're not paying for this, the pleasure's going to be all mine." Agile as a cat, she slipped up to his shoulders and positioned herself above his face. "Now lap at me, like the dog you are."

He'd performed this pleasure for her dozens of times, yet her blatant disregard for his comfort erased the erotic effects her earthy perfume usually had upon him. She was a woman obsessed with revenge, so cold and uncaring he wondered if Grace Putnam was going to suffocate him. If she sat across his nose and mouth, he was powerless beneath her.

Instead, she writhed against his tongue, rocking the bed with noisy bumps and grunts. "Bite me . . . harder," she commanded, and when her gyrations reached fever pitch the princess let out a blood-curdling wail.

Surely she's done. Surely Victoria will be here any minute now, Thompson thought. But when Cherry Blossom raised herself away from his face he heard piano music and laughter coming from the parlor, as though everyone in the house knew this joke was on him.

Barry opened is eyes, gasping for breath, and then his heart stopped. His tormentor wobbled on rubbery legs, wearing the smile of a sated saint—which turned demonic as she reached under the pillow and brandished a butcher knife. "We're not finished," she stated with a gleeless chuckle. "And if you want anything left to give to Lyla, you'll do exactly as I say, loverman."

Despite his distaste for sexual violence, he was throbbing painfully, desperate for release. Again the whore mounted him, this time riding one side of his manhood while she held the cold steel blade to the other side. If he didn't climax soon, Cherry Blossom could go on teasing him all day. If he did explode, he'd have some serious notches on his barrel.

"This is insane," he rasped, watching in horror as the whore pumped and writhed. "I've always treated you with respect—like a friend, because—"

"Life's hard," she replied with a flippant shrug, "and so are you, my man. My huge, passionate marshal-man. I'm gonna make you scream for it, so everybody out there'll know you're a two-bit cheat like the rest of them. Are you ready? Moan for me, Thompson. Make it sound sincere, understand?"

At that moment he realized this shameless bitch had faked her pleasure with him—how many of their times together? It was all an act. For her, he was just another paycheck. Barry suddenly knew the true meaning of degradation, understood that lusty boom towns like Cripple Creek held their prostitutes at knifepoint just as Cherry Blossom was now terrorizing him. She pressed the blade harder, her dark face alight with evil glee.

The moan that escaped him was indeed sincere, because the thought of explaining any scars on his manhood to Lyla sent anguish racing through his veins. The Indian princess resumed her ride, this time rubbing herself against him with a relish that was very real—and very dangerous, if he allowed himself to quiver with the need she was kindling inside him.

The bed shook and squeaked, both from the whore's impassioned attack and his efforts to save himself from it. Thompson gritted his teeth, squeezing his eyes shut against a sight that ordinarily drove him wild. Grace's head was thrown back and her breasts swayed rhythmically as she rode on and on, her breathing ragged.

"Moan with me. Make it a good one," she rasped.

To his disgust, the marshal discovered he had to comply. All his energies and sensations were centered on his manhood, and as his cries mingled with hers, steadily louder, he reached the point of no return.

At that crucial moment, Princess Cherry Blossom sprang away from him, her own desire pushed aside by her greater need to make him suffer. Gasping, he stared at her huge brown eyes and lips parted with longing, unable to believe she was tugging her buckskin dress on. "What the hell're you doing?"

"Leaving you. Just like you're leaving me."

"But I'm—"

"Feeling unsatisfied? Brought to the well only to be denied water?" Grace Putnam tossed the butcher knife onto the vanity and strode to the door. "Goodbye, marshal. And good riddance."

Barry strained toward her as she entered the hallway, jerking the tight handcuffs until they rattled against the brass spindles. "Wait, damn it! Where's the key?"

She turned calmly. "What key?"

"The one to these cuffs!"

Her eyes widened and then she giggled. "I honestly don't know. I didn't think to pick one up."

Chapter 16

The slamming of the door drowned out the oath he hurled at her, and the marshal fell back, exhausted. *Now* what was he supposed to do? No doubt Cherry Blossom was disappearing up the back stairs or out the rear exit, and no one would realize he was alone. After the impassioned duet the guests and other whores had heard, he couldn't lie here screaming for help. And how would he face anyone who came to his aid?

Thompson closed his eyes and tried to think of a way to escape. His bad leg was throbbing mercilessly and his arms were going numb from being curled above his head. He was tense from top to toe, the soothing effects of his massage long forgotten. Thank God Lyla didn't work here anymore so she wouldn't find him this way. But somebody would.

He tried to think of a plausible explanation for whoever stumbled in unawares, but there wasn't one. When word got out about the way Cherry Blossom handcuffed him to the bed and left, he'd never live it down, let alone convince Lyla that his reasons for coming to the Rose had started out as perfectly legitimate—strictly business.

The singing in the parlor got louder and more drunken. As time went by, Barry wondered how many hours would elapse before the New Year's revelers would realize he hadn't rejoined them . . . except they'd assume he was still being entertained by his favorite whore, a last fling before he settled down with Lyla.

The song ended in applause and laughter, and Barry was setting aside his pride to holler for help when he heard the secretive turning of the doorknob. He held his breath, watching the wooden door swing into the room just far enough for Victoria Chatterly to peek in. Her eyes widened. She looked around the suite and told someone to stay in the hall for a moment.

When the madam stopped beside the bed, she swept Thompson's body with an appreciative gaze, which lingered on his bound hands and feet. "I'd have checked on you sooner but Emily McClanahan's here, and by the sound of things, you preferred not to be disturbed. Did you ask for this, Barry?"

"Hell, no! That damn whore set me up—didn't even bring the key to these cuffs! If you think I—"

"You're in a bit of a bind, then—no pun intended," Victoria added with a twitter. She crossed her arms beneath her ample bosom, smiling as though she rather enjoyed seeing him in such a predicament. "I must say I'm impressed, marshal. Dozens of times I've envisioned you nude, spread like a feast before me, and even wounded you've surpassed my fondest fantasies."

He rolled his eyes, exasperated. "I see nothing funny about—my arms are ready to fall off, for Chrissakes, and you're just standing there!"

"What would you have me do, Mr. Thompson?"

Her crisp British accent infuriated him even more than her question. "Send somebody to my office for the damn key!"

"And have everyone know what sort of . . . *compromising* position the princess left you in? I don't think that's what you really want, dear, but you're too upset to realize that now." Miss Victoria sat down beside him on the bed, lifting her crimson skirt and allowing it to fall in a silken swirl over his abdomen. "Emily, come on in, sweetheart," she called over her shoulder. "Shut the door behind you."

Thompson felt his face turn the color of the madam's gown. His best friend's bride entered the suite, flushed and lovely from the winter wind, and then stopped to stare at his prone, helpless figure. "I swear to God this is not what it looks like," he whispered thickly. "It was a sick joke, a jealous trick."

Emily McClanahan was trying not to laugh, averting her eyes yet stealing glimpses that took in every bare inch of him. "I figured you'd be here celebrating, but I never dreamed I'd find you—"

"Enough of this, already! Where's Matt?" he snapped.

"Out asking some questions, starting the investigation because Lyla told him what really went on and that you needed his help." The slender blonde sat down on the other side of him, shaking her head. "And if you think you're embarrassed now, Barry, you just wait. Miss O'Riley told us a tale you won't want to believe."

Thompson sighed brusquely. "At this point, all I want is to be unfastened from this bed, damn it. I don't care which one of you goes—"

"Patience, dear," Victoria admonished as she pulled a hairpin from her snowy-white upsweep. Her ageless face lit up with mischief as she scooted toward his handcuffs. "I'll free your injured arm, and then we'll unfasten the other parts of you as we feel you deserve it."

"But I—" He watched the madam insert her pin into the keyhole, probe with the educated intensity of a practiced thief, and then pop the cuffs open.

"You've done this before."

"You're not the first to meet such a fate here," she replied. "Let me rub the pins and needles out of this arm while you chat with Emily. I'm sure you'll notice her good news immediately."

Barry had a hard time meeting Mrs. McClanahan's tawny gaze, let alone glancing at her waistline to see if Matt had sired a child a little earlier than he was supposed to. She brushed a loose tendril of hair from her temple, grinning, and his breath caught. "How'd you get your ring back?"

"Your beloved delivered it, along with my locket," Emily replied happily. "We had a lovely day getting to know Lyla, and we're convinced she's taking the blame for a den of sly Foxes."

He heard her cheerful prattling, only half listening to it. Somehow Lyla had secreted the McClanahan jewelry without anyone discovering it, so she *was* guilty of a minor crime, no matter how noble her motives were. But damn, she was slick! When he thought back to his brief interview in the jailhouse, he suspected she'd been covering the bulky diamond with her hand—right in front of him! And he hadn't thought to empty her pockets, or—

"You're not listening, Barry. We can't remove the other handcuff until you wipe that impudent grin from your face and give Emily your full attention."

"Oh. Of course." Thompson smiled as politely as he could under the circumstances and then focused on the blonde beside him. "You were saying?"

Emily glanced hesitantly at Miss Victoria. "Marshal, it seems that . . . well, some things went on at Lyla's cabin, and I can see why she'd feel awfully dejected since—but Matt defended you by explaining that you were probably—"

"Wait a minute," he interrupted. Her rosy color and unusually high voice suggested something was amiss. This woman had tracked her father's mur-

189

derer without batting an eye, so Lyla must've revealed some startling facts about the ambush and robbery that she hadn't felt comfortable telling him. "Spit it out, Emily. I'm hardly in a position to take a swing at you—not that I'd even think of it."

She nodded, nipping her lip. "Barry, do you recall your last night at her cabin, before she brought you back to Cripple?"

He thought for a moment. "I slept off and on. Vaguely remember her fixing the toboggan up and scaring me out of bed so I'd get into it. Why?"

"You really don't remember?" she mumbled. She toyed with her diamond, keeping her eyes on it. "It seems that when Lyla went to sleep beside you, assuming you were too tired and weak to . . . well, you weren't."

Barry raised his head to stare at her. "What're you saying?"

"It seems you made love to Miss O'Riley," Victoria cut in quietly. "And by giving her that money—"

"*What?* How can you believe I—"

"—to return to Ireland, you made her feel that your promises during a tender moment were nothing but lies."

"—could possibly . . . no, no," he said emphatically. "As much as I've wanted that girl, you think I could've had her and not remembered it? You *know* me, Victoria. I'm a passionate man, and I'm not ashamed to admit it."

The madam glanced at his nakedness with a chuckle. "Your passions have their price, it seems. And after talking with her, both Matt and Emily feel sure you claimed Lyla's virginity, amid whisperings of love inspired by high fever. Miss O'Riley can understand that, but it doesn't bring her innocence back. Think how crushed she must've felt when you offered her sailing fare rather than matrimony, Barry. Think how difficult it must've been to admit this to people she barely knew."

Miss Chatterly's grip tightened on his free arm, conveying the same concern he saw on her lovely face. As a madam, she enforced the strictest code of conduct in any parlor house in town. As a woman, she expected integrity and respect for and from her customers and ladies alike. But it was still a damn hard story to swallow.

"I—I'm sorry you found out about it this way," Emily said in a muted voice. "We told Lyla you'd be shocked and embarrassed, but that you really did love her and deserved another chance to prove it. I hope we didn't speak out of turn."

Thompson shut his eyes against the anguish that was starting to seep into his being. In vain, he tried to sift through his memories of those days alone with her . . . how could he have fondled her lush body and taken the most precious prize she could offer without recalling even a second of the sweetness they shared?

Or had he raped her?

A groan escaped him as he tried to deny he was capable of such bestial behavior. He would never force a woman. Never! Yet he'd considered Grace Putnam a loyal friend until a few hours ago, when she'd revealed a dark side he hadn't dreamed existed. Who could say what horrendous acts he'd performed, what liberties he'd taken while out of his head, except Lyla herself?

"She'll probably never see me again," he mumbled. "And I can't say I blame her. My God, I could've crushed her so she had no chance to escape—"

"To hear her tell it, it wasn't as bad as all that," Mrs. McClanahan said with a soft chuckle. She reached into the pocket of her plaid skirt and pulled out a small envelope. "She wants you to have this, Barry. You can thank us later."

His eyes bored into the envelope, trying to read through it. He didn't know whether to feel ecstatic or wary. Perhaps Emily didn't know what the note said, or was too nice to tell the whole, damning truth. Victoria was leaning over him, unlocking the other handcuff while Emily untied his ankles. Thompson watched them go with a grateful smile, until the door clicked shut and he was alone. Then he sat up, wincing as the blood rushed through his stiffened limbs again.

Barry ran a finger over the wax seal, stalling. It was incomprehensible that he'd made love to Lyla—that she hadn't mentioned it when they talked in his office.

She was waiting for YOU to say something, idiot. And you as good as sent her home to that Hadley McWhat's-his-name.

His conscience smarting and his mouth uncomfortably dry, Thompson slid his finger under the seal. "'Come to the cabin, love. I can't leave without seeing you,'" he read. "Holy socks! She wants me to—by God, she's not *going* to leave. I won't let her!"

Defying his sore muscles, he pulled on his clothes with amazing speed, stuffing the bandages into his uniform pockets. There was no time to waste. Lyla had ridden in with the McClanahans and was waiting for him. Visions of her crackling fire and cozy little home propelled him out the back exit at a swift limp. The investigation would have to wait: he couldn't put catching a few disloyal friends ahead of apologizing to—and winning—the woman he loved. Besides, Lyla O'Riley was the perfect partner, and with her help he'd be packing the thieves off to the prison in Canon City before the week was out.

He hobbled down the street, noting the crowd coming out of the Presbyterian church. People were chatting cheerily, wishing each other a happy new year, and he shared their joy. *He* was celebrating a new *life!*

The sight of Rex Adams, Theresa, and their brood

192

4 FREE BOOKS

TO GET YOUR 4 FREE BOOKS WORTH $18.00 — MAIL IN THE FREE BOOK CERTIFICATE T O D A Y

Fill in the Free Book Certificate below, and we'll send your FREE BOOKS to you as soon as we receive it.

If the certificate is missing below, write to: Zebra Home Subscription Service, Inc., P.O. Box 5214, 120 Brighton Road, Clifton, New Jersey 07015-5214.

FREE BOOK CERTIFICATE

4 FREE BOOKS

ZEBRA HOME SUBSCRIPTION SERVICE, INC.

YES! Please start my subscription to Zebra Historical Romances and send me my first 4 books absolutely FREE. I understand that each month I may preview four new Zebra Historical Romances free for 10 days. If I'm not satisfied with them, I may return the four books within 10 days and owe nothing. Otherwise, I will pay the low preferred subscriber's price of just $3.75 each; a total of $15.00, *a savings off the publisher's price of $3.00.* I may return any shipment and I may cancel this subscription at any time. There is no obligation to buy any shipment and there are no shipping, handling or other hidden charges. Regardless of what I decide, the four free books are mine to keep.

NAME _____

ADDRESS _____ APT _____

CITY _____ STATE _____ ZIP _____

TELEPHONE ( ) _____

SIGNATURE _____
(if under 18, parent or guardian must sign)

Terms, offer and prices subject to change without notice. Subscription subject to acceptance by Zebra Books. Zebra Books reserves the right to reject any order or cancel any subscription.

GET
FOUR
FREE
BOOKS
(AN $18.00 VALUE)

ZEBRA HOME SUBSCRIPTION
SERVICE, INC.
P.O. Box 5214
120 BRIGHTON ROAD
CLIFTON, NEW JERSEY 07015-5214

of carrot-haired children sobered him a bit. They were only a few yards ahead of him . . . he could ask his deputy for a word at the office, and—

No. He would not stoop to subterfuge and leave Theresa and her children at home, expecting her husband for dinner. He'd corner Rex when he returned to town with Lyla, when he had McClanahan as a backup.

As though sensing his presence, Mrs. Adams turned and spied him. "Happy New Year, marshal!" she called above the crowd's chatter. "It's good to see you looking so well!"

Bless her, she had no idea what he was about to put her through. He waved and returned Rex's reserved—perhaps nervous—nod. "It's good to be back," he replied, and then he nearly choked. Theresa's auburn hair was swept up into an intricate Psyche knot, adorned at the crown with . . . "Those turquoise combs are quite becoming," he said in the most sincere voice he could find.

His deputy leaned down to swing the youngest Adams into his arms, while Mrs. Adams beamed. "A Christmas present," she said gaily. "Rex must've been saving up for months."

Barry smiled again, but his spirits were tumbling. How many times had he removed those combs from Princess Cherry Blossom's hair? How stupid could his deputy be, assuming no one would recognize a whore's jewelry from the Christmas Eve raid?

He lumbered on toward his apartment, torn between hauling Adams in and spending time with Lyla, starting over with her. His jeans and heavy shirt went on slowly. Thompson was drained from the ordeal he'd suffered at the Rose, and the startling truth he'd learned afterward. His body told him to go to bed, to face these matters tomorrow when he was rested.

Yet he knew he'd see those turquoise combs as he

193

tossed sleeplessly, yearning to be with Lyla ... to kiss her again and pour out his heart as he should've done at McClanahan's reception.

Love won out. He took the stairs slowly, figuring he could make Phantom Canyon before dark and find the little cabin he'd never seen while fully conscious. With any luck, Doc Geary wouldn't catch him cantering off on Buck.

Something made him take the back alley to the jailhouse rather than the direct route to the livery stable. Thompson went in, satisfied that all was as it should be in his back room. He and Adams generally took turns stopping in on Sundays, so no one was in the cluttered office right now. One of the prisoners was snoring. He'd let Norbert Sykes go home, so only one other derelict was locked away, playing solitaire with a shabby deck.

Barry opened Rex's desk drawer, not sure why gut instinct told him to look inside. There were two loose keys—handcuff keys, he realized with a rueful grin. Otherwise he saw pencils and a logbook and an assortment of Wanted posters, Lyla's on top. Something rattled when he shifted the papers back into place and there it was: a Masonic ring. Sam Langston's, no doubt.

He left the evidence in place, slamming the drawer shut with sickening certainty of what he had to do— tomorrow, with Lyla and Matt.

The wind whipped at his hat as he crossed over to the livery stable. He doubted Wally Eberhardt would be there, and he was right. Thompson saddled up and rode out of the stable seen by relatively few people on this brisk New Year's Sunday. He pointed his stallion south, toward Victor and the canyon, his mind already on his reunion with Lyla O'Riley.

What would he say to her? She would assume he knew of his inexcusable deed, but he couldn't let the McClanahans' defense of his feverish act speak for

194

him. Such a misunderstanding, left unreconciled, would fester between him and Lyla for years, like a wound that refused to heal.

So he would tell her straight out that he loved her, had intended to marry her before taking her to bed. And Barry prayed she'd be lenient, and believe him. Her presence seemed so real as he rode along the snowy path . . . his hands itched with the tactile recollection of her velvet skin, the ample breasts unbound for his eyes to savor . . . her lilting brogue and laughter that danced like birdsong in the spring . . . the scent of peppermint. Lord, but he wanted to kiss those rosy lips and drink deeply of her heady nectar—

But then the breath was knocked out of him and he was falling, shoved off Buck by a man who'd jumped him from the trees. Thompson struggled briefly, at a disadvantage because he hadn't seen what hit him, then struck the ground with a force that knocked him senseless. He heard voices and felt himself being tugged up out of the snow.

"Let's hoist this sucker back onto his mount. Tie him on and be quick about it. We shoulda been out to the ranch by now."

Barry tasted blood and his face felt like a train had hit it. Buck moved beneath him, being led, and he instinctively hugged the stallion's neck to keep from falling off. *Lyla . . . oh God, honey, I'm so sorry. So sorry.*

Chapter 17

Lyla tossed, knowing her dream was the result of another night on a bad bed, yet unable to let go of it. She saw Barry at the cabin, clutching her note, looking behind every door and in the shed for signs of her. Calico was contentedly munching straw, but when the marshal realized she wasn't to be found, his face crumpled into a pained grimace: betrayed . . . again. Once more she'd left him, without giving an explanation or allowing him his. He gazed forlornly at the note. "Honey, I'm so sorry . . . so sorry," he murmured.

Her own sob woke her. As her night vision faded away, Lyla got her bearings, feeling foolish for allowing a dream to upset her so much. Now that she'd apparently ducked out on him again, Thompson wouldn't be the least bit sorry to be rid of her . . . would he? And thinking that her mare had returned to the shed at the cabin was nonsense . . . wasn't it?

Not that either of these things mattered now. She was in a rough shanty, out in the middle of nowhere. Dawn's first light revealed Kelly Jameson snoring on his bedroll, in the shadows of the far corner. Connor Foxe was seated on the floor at her feet, grinning down the barrel of his pistol.

"Nightmares, cupcake?" he asked in a suave whisper. "They're not over yet. Unless you try to run, and I put you out of your misery."

"You wouldn't kill me," she blurted. "This is all Frazier's doing and you're taking me to him. *Aren't* you?"

Connor chuckled, a gleam in his agate-black eyes. "He wouldn't mind if you had a hole in one of those luscious thighs. Wounds and scars, they sort of fascinate him, you know?"

Sickened, Lyla stood slowly and straightened her rumpled clothing. She buttoned her coat against a coldness the log walls couldn't keep out, then slipped her hands into her pockets. The bundle of twenties was still there. At least Foxe hadn't swiped it while she was asleep.

From the single window she saw endless pastureland, rolling in every direction like pastry dough powdered with sugar. The image startled her: she was so hungry, everything reminded her of food. Out here, though, there was no such luxury as fresh bread—not a tree to hide behind or a rock formation to shield her, either, should she dart away when Connor wasn't watching.

And Connor Foxe was always watching, his motives clearer and more repulsive with each hour they waited. For what, Lyla was afraid to ask.

"Where are we?" she mumbled, figuring to keep him talking. Perhaps he'd reveal information she could use to escape. And he'd have less chance to reconsider the vile suggestions he'd been threatening her with since the ambush.

"Welcome to Foxe Hollow, Miss O'Riley," he said with a sneer. "Hope you like what you see, because you'll be on this sheep ranch for a long, long time. If you're lucky."

Lyla ignored his insinuation—always hinting she'd be killed on a whim, Connor was—and clutched at a familiar straw. "Frazier raises sheep?"

"Thousands of them. After he acquired this spread, woollybacks seemed the most profitable thing to grow here." The younger Foxe looked her over as though assessing her ability to keep her mouth shut. "And it's a way to keep me busy between other little jobs he finds for me. A means for me to work off my obligation to him."

She sensed Connor's obligation wasn't something she wanted to hear about but that he was going to tell her anyway. Another reminder of his unsavory nature, in case she thought about defying him.

He settled against the shanty wall, the pistol resting on his knee. "Yeah, I was the ornery one when we were younger—but then, Frazier was such a damn mama's boy, any normal child looked like a hellion in comparison. We're stepbrothers, you know," he added matter-of-factly. "After Frazier's father couldn't defend himself during a pub brawl, our mother married the bruiser who did him in, who happened to be his brother. Guess she was desperate, and he didn't give her much choice, since she'd been seeing him on the sly—which was the cause of the brawl. I suppose that's where I got my . . . attitude about women."

Lyla nodded, hoping her horror didn't show. "When did you come to America? You could've been born here, by the sound of your accent."

"Accent!" he scoffed. "Frazier practices his—part of his mystique as a foreign businessman, he says. The types I hobnob with don't put on such airs."

Connor studied her, leary of revealing too much, yet his eyes seemed to probe for chinks in her facade. "He's nearly sixteen years older than I am. Wasn't keen on sticking around after our mother remarried, because her husband called him a pansy-ass. He has a way with money, though. Came to this land of opportunity about twenty-five years ago, and when the gold fields opened up he had enough capital to establish himself in various business endeavors. Sent for me to manage this ranch. Which was the ticket out of England I was looking for."

What horrid past was he running from? Lyla didn't want to know, but having him brag on himself was better than listening to hints of what he'd do to her when he had the chance.

"Yeah, I was always in a touch of trouble," he continued with a proud chuckle. "Frazier learned his trade in school and I picked mine up in the back streets of London and Liverpool. Never got caught at it, either, which is why I make him such a perfect partner."

Outside, the pastureland rolled on uninterrupted. Jameson's snoring missed a beat and he turned over in his bedroll. Perhaps her captor would respect her pluck if she challenged him—there was little else to break the tension while waiting for some unknown event to take place—so Lyla focused intently on him. "What line of work were you in?"

"Hired assassin." He gave her a cool grin. "When borrowers couldn't pay their loans, I'd go out to collect. If one politician threatened to take over another one's bribes or territory, I'd bump him off and disappear like a shadow. Guess how many men I've killed."

Lyla swallowed the lump that threatened to choke off her breathing. "I—I haven't the faintest idea."

Connor chuckled. "I lost count after twenty. But the women, I never forget them. They start to struggle, and their crying and carrying on makes me crazy, you know?"

The confession was intended to startle her, and it did. What sort of madman killed women, not to mention such a number of men, and spoke of these crimes as other people talked of their accurate accounts or their impeccably-kept shops? No wonder

199

Frazier never associated with his stepbrother! Connor was a man of the alleys, better left unrecognized. Lyla didn't dare ask how many people he'd murdered since he'd come to Colorado.

As though reading her racing thoughts, Foxe stood with a stealthy smile. He came up behind her and placed a hand on her shoulder, as amiable as an old school chum. "Now don't you worry your sweet little head about what I'll do to *you*, cupcake," he crooned, "because I've taken a fancy to you. Long as you stay feisty and don't turn bawlbaby on me, we'll get along just fine. Big Brother promised me a bonus for this assignment, and I figure to ask him for you instead of money. Hell, what would I do with more money? It's not like I can sashay into town and flash my cash. Draws too much attention, you know?"

Sweat trickled down her spine and Lyla managed to nod at him. All she'd done was ride after the thieves who'd stolen her necklace, and take Marshal Thompson to the doctor, and now she was trapped—part of a vendetta that was originally against Barry, and she'd been in the wrong places at the wrong times. "Why are you doing this to me?" she asked in a hoarse whisper.

Connor laughed, tightening his grip on her shoulder. "Because it's more fun than just getting rid of Thompson."

"And why are you after *him?*"

He considered her question, his roughcut features relaxing into a subtle smile. "Because Frazier finds him uncooperative. By now you surely realize his talent for hiring help where he needs it, and since several of his recent projects have been stalled by the marshal, it's time Cripple Creek found a new lawman."

Lyla scowled. "And Rex Adams will get the job?"

The outlaw hooted gleefully. "That's what he thinks. He's a man with a passel of brats to feed, and

200

no chance for promotion unless Thompson's out of the way. Right?"

"Then who—"

"You ask too many questions, cupcake," Connor said as he covered her mouth with a broad hand. "Plenty of time for those later. Jameson's asleep, and I've got an armful of soft, sweet-smelling woman, so jawing about my brother's business is the furthest thing from my mind. You know?"

His constant "you know" was wearing her thin, but it was nothing compared to the kiss he overtook her with. His mouth ransacked hers, forcing it open so his tongue could plunge between her teeth. Lyla thought of biting him, but the fates of the women who'd struggled with Connor kept her from behaving so impulsively. He turned her, unbuttoning her coat so he could press into her breasts, still plying her lips with a mounting hunger that threatened to suffocate her. When the barrel of his pistol slid between her legs she gasped and jerked away.

Foxe's arm tightened around her. "You can't tell me you've never had anything up there, you little whore. What with working at—"

"I could get shot!" she squeaked.

"Indeed you will," he replied with a chuckle. "And I'll show you things Thompson never thought of. Is he as big as the ladies claim?"

Lyla gaped, startled that he'd ask such a blunt question. But if crudeness was what he liked, perhaps feigning innocence was her best protection. "I—I don't know."

Connor yanked her back by her hair to study her face. "You're saying he was too sick to get it up at your cabin?"

She nodded rapidly, praying this was the right path to lead him down.

"Look me straight on and tell me I'll be your first. Put some feeling into it, and I'll go easy on you."

201

His coal-black eyes and dusky face lit up with a fiendish delight, and Lyla's heartbeat faltered. Even if she backed out of her lie, she was caught in this desperado's iron embrace. He obviously had a taste for untouched virtue, and her only hope now was to play along with him until she thought of a better ploy. "You'll be the first, Connor," she said in a voice that was hoarse with fear.

"Whisper that in my ear. Act like you want it, like you can't wait to give yourself to me." He backed her against the wall, his gun barrel sliding up and down between them, and then lowered his head to listen for her plea.

Lyla squirmed. The friction from the pistol agitated her even more than Foxe's insistent writhing against her breasts. When his tongue shot into her ear, she gasped. "Connor . . . Connor, please," she said with a quavery moan. "You—you'll be my first. I . . . can't wait to—"

He cut her off with a brutal kiss, forcing her down the wall until she was hopelessly entangled beneath him. Was Jameson stirring, or was that the sound of Foxe removing his pants? Frantically she fought for breathing space and a better position for her head, which was angled against the wall. "Please, let me—"

"Horses comin'!" the man across the room declared. "Get off her, Foxe. We got company."

Lyla felt the buttons of her shirt give way under his sudden grasp. Connor cocked his head to stare at his partner. "Is it Nate?"

"Who else knows we're here?" the lanky marauder grumbled. He staggered to the window, shaking the sleepiness from his head. "Yep. Nate and the dimwit from the livery stable. And Thompson, who looks poorly."

They'd caught Barry, too? Despite her fear of reprisal, Lyla's lips began to quiver with concern. He

202

was their target, after all, and with four outlaws overpowering him, the marshal's chances for survival were slim. Out here where no one would come looking for him—

"Get up, cupcake. We'll have some real fun now!" Connor crowed.

She stumbled up off the floor, relieved when he helped her out of her cramped position. But she'd no sooner found her footing than he was binding her arms to her sides, with the same lariat he'd used to catch her.

"What do you think, Kelly? Like what you see?"

The bandit's red-gold sideburns rose with his grin. "Looks like great bait to me. Thompson'll follow those knobs to kingdom come, I reckon."

When Connor stepped behind her to tie the knot, Lyla glanced down and turned hot crimson. Her coat and shirt had been shoved to the sides, and her breasts poked out between the coils of the rope, straining against her flimsy camisole. She couldn't bear for Barry to see her this way, yet when he stumbled through the low doorway, prodded by his captors, she couldn't turn her back.

His face was black and blue on one side and his shoulder wound had broken open, judging from the bloody section of shirt she could see beneath his open coat. His grimace of recognition pierced her soul. She moved toward him, but was halted when Kelly Jameson grabbed her rope. "Better tie him before he gets any ideas, Foxe. He's weak, but he's bigger than we are."

"Yeah, Lyla tells me he's *huge*," Connor taunted. "And I can see he's itching to latch onto those spigots, so we'll fasten his hands. In case he get ideas about turning her loose, you know."

Foxe had found another length of rope, and he wrapped the marshal's wrists together—in front of him, Lyla noted with an inkling of hope. Surely these outlaws realized Barry could untie her—

"Now we'll wrap it between your fingers so you can't get a grip," Connor said smugly. Then he stepped back to admire his work, chuckling when he noted Thompson's pointed gaze. "She's a sight, isn't she? Too bad you can't fondle her, but here—I'll make it so you can at least take a taste."

Pivoting on his heel, the dark-haired scoundrel grabbed Lyla's camisole. It tore when he tugged it down, leaving her exposed to four sets of leering eyes and Barry, who seemed unable to respond.

"We'll leave you two lovebirds alone for a bit. Got business to discuss," the ringleader announced. "Let's go, boys. A condemned man's got a right to his final pleasure."

With furtive glances, Jameson, Eberhardt, and the man they called Nate preceded Connor Foxe outside. The door slammed in the wind, and then the shanty was filled with a strained silence. Lyla longed to wipe the dirt from Thompson's bruised face and kiss away his agonized expression. He looked so beaten . . . when his gaze wandered to the breasts protruding from her ropes, she turned away in shame. "Say something, damn it. Don't stare like you don't know me," she implored in a ragged whisper.

Thompson struggled to breathe. The long ride, jostling against Buck's neck and the saddlehorn, had stripped him of his strength. He'd lost all hope of ever seeing his woman again, yet a nagging question dulled his joy. Lyla had apparently fallen into the same fate he had, but out here among these thieves he knew better than to take appearances for granted.

"Got your note," he said in a strangled whisper. "When Emily gave it to me, I never dreamed you were setting me up for—"

"How can you even *think* that?" Lyla whirled to face him. "I was riding back from the Flaming B, to meet *you* at—"

"Why didn't you tell me you had her jewelry?" Barry kept his face hard, determined not to give in to the waif whose blue eyes begged him to believe her, to hold her. "You had every chance to wipe the slate clean, yet you withheld stolen property. Right under my nose, if I'm not mistaken."

Her chin dropped onto her chest. The marshal thought she was in on it, a willing decoy. The men's voices came through the shanty's cracks with the wind, making her shiver with the deepest, coldest despair she'd ever experienced. If Barry believed she'd allied with Frazier Foxe, then she might as well chalk him off. She had no reasonable excuse for hiding Emily's diamond, and it was more degrading to beg for his mercy than to stand before him exposed this way.

Thompson watched her warily. More than the tear that slithered down her cheek he noted Lyla's lack of spirit, an air of dejection so unlike the Irish sprite he knew. "Lyla," he whispered.

Slowly she raised her head. When her eyes met his weary green ones, she caught the faintest glimmer of compassion.

"I guess you're not the only one who's done a few things that're pretty damn hard to explain," he said softly. "We'd better talk, before those bastards come in for us. God only knows what'll happen then."

Nodding, Lyla felt her pulse quicken. Barry smiled tentatively and held out his bound hands, forming a circle she couldn't resist. She hurried into his embrace, bumping awkwardly against him as she stepped under his arms, wishing she could return his heavenly hug.

Mere contact with her was magic. The pain stopped racing through his battered body and he emerged from the numbing fog he'd enveloped himself in during his grueling ride. Lyla, for all her wily ways, hadn't deserted him at all! She was a

205

victim of Foxe's schemes, just as he was, but at greater risk because she was a woman . . . a woman whose lush body would become a deranged man's plaything unless they could get out of this predicament.

He glanced around the sparsely-furnished shack. "Honey, let's shuffle over to that chair so I can reach you. One kiss, and then we'll fill each other in. We'll be in a bad way if we don't get out of here."

As though they were learning a strange new dance, Lyla followed Barry's lead by backing up toward the chair she didn't see until they were beside it. He sat down with a groan, and she hesitated between his parted legs.

"Climb onto my lap, sweetheart," he breathed.

"But I'll hurt—"

"Wrap your legs around me. Hold me, Lyla. God, just kiss—"

His lips sought hers with an urgency that stopped her heart, stopped her breathing. As she returned his all-consuming kiss she no longer needed those functions, and would've passed on in contentment after these few moments of his touch. She wished desperately to hold him. Her hands twitched helplessly at her hips, and only Barry's fervent embrace kept her from falling off his lap.

Thompson, too, cursed the rope that kept his fingers splayed and prevented him from completely wrapping his arms around her. Ignoring his new bruises and wounds, he squeezed her as tightly as he could while putting all the love his heart could hold into this single kiss. The dear, familiar taste of her, the rose-scented sweetness of her hair and skin—he would never get enough, but it was time to discuss their future while they still had one. "Lyla, about that time in your cabin . . . I—"

"Matt's already explained it."

"That's not good enough. Look at me, honey. Please tell me what happened," he pleaded. "You're the only one who can say, and I'm the only one who can beg your forgiveness."

Lyla sat in the circle of his arms, suddenly shy. "Well, I—I should've gone in to my own bed—"

"I don't recall but one," he said with a frown.

"Mine's in the closet."

"Where it's cold and drafty. Stop blaming yourself," Barry implored. "You were exhausted from tending me, probably afraid to sleep in the other room in case I'd wake up and need you. I guess you know I accused Emily and Victoria of flat-out lying when they told me what I did to you."

Lyla smiled. "I wish I'd been there—"

"No, you don't," he replied, recollections of his handcuffs still painfully fresh. "Tell me what happened, Lyla. Did I hurt you, sweetheart? Did I . . . force you?"

The instant flicker of shock in her eyes was some reassurance, at least. Barry glanced toward the door, wishing she'd hurry yet understanding her reticence about this sensitive subject. She shifted, and he eased her weight onto his better leg.

"It . . . it started as a dream," she began in a low voice. The memories and impressions were so vivid. What words would express her emotions and the sensations she shared while becoming his woman? "I—I thought I was imagining it when you were holding me, nuzzling my neck. We were facing the fire—"

"Both of us?"

She nodded, aware that this nearness to him was reviving the wondrous, aching torment she'd felt with him that night. "When I woke up, you *were* holding me, and despite your wounds you'd managed to open my shirt and lower my drawers. I—I was too fascinated to fight you, so—"

"Did I hurt you? God, I never meant to, honey." Thompson studied her pink cheeks and shy smile,

207

truly ashamed that he'd taken advantage of her. Then she raised her lovely blue eyes and he wished he'd at least been *conscious* while sampling the delectable banquet she'd unwittingly placed before him.

Sensing that his conscience was indeed prickling, Lyla chuckled nervously. "I'd tell you how wonderful you made me feel that night, Barry, except you'd have the idea that you could get *by* with loving me in your sleep, when I deserve your full attention."

Only when he saw a twinkle in her impish eyes did he dare to chuckle. His laughter shook them both and he pulled her as close as his rope binding would allow. "Damn right you deserve better," he whispered joyfully against her ear. "I fully intended to prove I'm capable of some restraint, intended to wait until we were married to—"

"The road to hell's paved with good intentions," she quipped softly. Then she gazed at him, unable to quit grinning. "And if this be hell, Mr. Thompson, I'll take it. And after all the endearments you murmured while loving me, you damn well *better* marry me!"

Barry blinked. "What'd I say?"

"That's for me to know and you to wonder about," she replied. "You can thank McClanahan for convincing me you were out of your head when all this happened. And after watching my brother babble incoherently after the mine explosion, when he was trying to die, Lord love him, I understand. It seems our . . . appetites have gotten us both into trouble, doesn't it?"

Chuckling ruefully, Thompson hugged her close. "I'm sorry I was such a worry to you."

"Nonsense. I had to keep you alive so we could solve this robbery," she teased. "And your murmurings were rather exciting, actually. Poor Mick chattered about chameleons and clubs, as though he were scared witless and seeing such things in his

208

hospital bed."

The marshal held her, setting his happiness aside for a moment to consider this. "There's a Chameleon Club in Cripple," he said quietly. "It's an opium den, upstairs from one of the saloons on Myers. Let's keep that in mind, but right now something else is more pressing—the matter of you becoming my wife."

Lyla's pounding heart rendered her speechless with anticipation. The green eyes above hers studied her solemnly, yet Thompson's dusty, bruised face was wavering on the brink of a huge grin.

"You seem to think a wedding is your just reward for what I've put you through, Miss O'Riley," he murmured. "Frankly, it sounds like a trap. What proof do I have that I made love to you? Or that I said anything you could construe as grounds for matrimony?"

His unexpected challenge forced her to think hard. He had a point: she alone knew what went on that night in the cabin. But Mother of God, that didn't mean this man could hold her responsible for all that had transpired between them! "Well," she replied, "you could be a cad and subject me to an examination by Dr. Geary. Or you could be a gentleman—a lover in the truest sense—and take my word for it."

"And what word is that?" he breathed, praying her wit didn't cave in, praying they weren't interrupted at this most crucial moment in all his life.

Lyla rolled her eyes, pretending to search for a response. "Yes," she whispered. "My answer is yes, Barry."

"Oh Lord, I—" He kissed her long and hard, reeling with the joy this impetuous little woman had just brought full circle. Again and again he pressed her lips, pouring out a love he hadn't dared to believe himself capable or deserving of. "Honey, I meant to ask for your hand when we were all cozy and alone, when I could put that ring on your finger and—"

"I'll hold you to that, as soon as we get it back."

"As soon as we get out of this mess," Barry promised her, "we'll have a proper engagement. A time to talk about our future, and plan the house I'm having built, and—"

"And make love?" she asked coyly. "I know you were trying to prove a point by keeping your fly fastened, but . . . well, I got your point once, and I'm not sure I can wait until the wedding before I have it again. We're an affectionate pair, Barry, and if you love me—"

"Lord yes, I do," he breathed, suddenly serious. "I love you so much it'll take a lifetime to prove it to you, Lyla." He looked at her, chuckling at the unexpected turn of events this latest ambush had produced, knowing in his heart they'd survive this ordeal and laugh about it someday. "And I promise you, young lady, that I'll be a helluva lot better lover when I'm conscious. I'll make that first time up to you."

"Again and again," Lyla assured him.

"Again and again," he repeated as he pulled her close. "I wish I could start now. Just the sight of you, and the silkiness of your hair, and—"

The door flew open, and in sauntered a grinning Connor Foxe. Familiar voices followed him inside: Frazier had pulled up in a carriage, and was exchanging pleasantries with Nate, Kelly, and a chuckling Wally Eberhardt as he handed them each an envelope. The wind made Lyla shiver in his lap, and also ushered in the cloying scent of . . . kerosene.

"Don't you two look cozy?" the outlaw jeered. "Hope you got your licks in, marshal, because this is the end of the line. Frazier wants to see you outside, cupcake."

Lyla swiveled in Thompson's arms. "Tell him he can damn well come in here if he wants—"

210

"Go on, honey," Barry said in a tight whisper. "These boys are up to no good, and I don't want you hurt."

"I'm not leaving you!" Her fears multiplied a hundredfold when she saw his face tightening with grim anticipation. "We can't let them get away with this! If the Foxes think they can—"

"Keep up your hollering," he murmured into her ear. "Go outside and cause a commotion so I can dash out of here, too. They're going to torch this shack."

Her shriek resounded like a battle cry as she slipped off his lap. Lyla charged, head down, running at Connor as fast as her binding would allow. "You bastard! If you think I'll stand by—"

"I think your nipples'll get frostbit if you—" He hit the wall with a *whumph* and then grabbed at her hair. "But those boys'd be happy to keep you warm while we watch—Jesus!"

Lyla had heard Barry coming behind her and ducked out of his way when he struck. His joined fists came down at the juncture of Connor's neck and shoulders, but the marauder was healthier and more compact, and he recovered quickly. "Get in here!" he yelled. "Tie his legs! Get him off me, damn it!"

Before she could rejoin the fray she was seized by two clutching hands and hauled backward out the door, kicking and trying to wrench free. Nate and Wally hurried inside, and as Lyla spotted the new man's rope she also saw the lethal liquid sloshing out of the red can Eberhardt was carrying. "Traitor!" she cried. "You'll roast in hell for—"

She nearly choked on the handkerchief that was stuffed into her mouth by the gloved hand of Frazier Foxe. The Englishman's face puckered with disgust when he glanced at her exposed breasts, and he stepped back to avoid her flailing feet. "Tie her ankles and for God's sake, cover her up," he ordered.

211

"What we don't need is a hysterical female foiling our plans."

Jameson's arm tightened around her, which made her struggle harder. She landed a solid backward kick on his shin, but his boot shielded him and his low laughter told her he was enjoying this sport immensely. "I wrestle rams all the time, Miss Lyla," he crooned as his hand closed over her breast, "so don't get yourself hurt by fightin' me. I can play this game all day."

Her eyes bulged and she screamed into her gag when the stockman lifted her with one viselike arm and coiled a short rope around her ankles with the other. Because one foot was tied higher, she toppled to the ground when he released her. The air rushed from her lungs when she hit, and she lay in a dazed heap at his feet.

From inside the shanty she heard the sounds of Thompson's struggle . . . stuttering footsteps, and someone thudding against the front wall. "Think about it, Eberhardt," the marshal said above the scuffle. "If I don't show up in Cripple soon, the federal marshals will get involved. You and Adams don't stand a chance, unless you cooperate and tell them Foxe is behind this."

"It'll never happen," the Englishman spoke quietly beside her. He giggled, almost girlishly. "With what I paid him, he'll be on vacation for the rest of his life. Cheerio, Thompson, old chap. I'll be hard pressed to find another quarry as challenging as you've been." His monocle glistened when he glanced down at her. "And poor Lyla. You'll be beside yourself with grief, won't you, dear-heart?"

Still gasping for breath, she shut her eyes against his insidious grin. Then there was a shout and thundering footfalls . . . and the *whoosh* of fire as it followed the trail of kerosene around the inside of the shack.

From deep inside her came a cry of abject terror. A red-orange wall of flame was dancing in front of the window and doorway, blocking any chance Barry had for escape. Lyla barely noticed the blanket being wrapped around her, or the arms that carried her toward the carriage several feet behind them. She couldn't tear her eyes from the gut-wrenching sight of the weathered wooden shack, the perfect food for a hungry fire.

Thompson was silent. She prayed he was unconscious so he wouldn't feel the infernal monster that was devouring him.

"Get her into the carriage. We'll be off now," Frazier said with quiet satisfaction.

She was too shocked to struggle when Kelly Jameson tossed her over his shoulder so he could unlatch the door. When a column of flame jumped out the window toward the roof, the delapidated shingles caught and were engulfed immediately.

Then Lyla stopped breathing, clutching the carriage door before Kelly could place her inside. A shrill whistle came from the cabin, the whine of a small, trapped animal or the wind being forced between its chinks. The other desperadoes had mounted their horses and were watching the blaze from a safe distance, but Buck remained tethered to the scraggly tree they'd used for a hitching post. The stallion reared frantically, tossing his majestic head, terrified of the flames lapping so close to him. Once more he pawed at the sky with his front legs, and with an arch of his mighty neck he snapped the leather cord that held him.

Lyla's scream pierced her heart instead of coming out. Rather than galloping away, Buck—the loyal horse who'd tolerated a harness for her and then transported them through a snow-clogged canyon after reviving his master—hesitated, and then jumped through the door of the burning shack to die

213

with Barry.

Her limbs went limp and a merciful blackness enveloped her.

"Lyla? Miss O'Riley, snap out of it now."

She was aware of being rocked . . . the steady clatter of wheels and hooves . . . a slapping on her cheek that smelled of fine leather . . . a suede finger tapping her collarbone.

"Wake up, Miss O'Riley, we're almost home. Playing dead will get you nowhere."

The man's clipped diction brought it all back: the ambush, the night in the shack . . . the unthinkable things he'd done to her Barry. Lyla blinked repeatedly and then glared at the impeccably-dressed beast seated across from her.

"I took the liberty of untying you while you slept," he said with a proprietary smile. "You could at least show your gratitude by improving your attitude." Frazier twittered at his rhyme until his monocled gaze drifted lower. "And for God's sake, cover yourself. I can't abide such immodesty. It simply won't do once we arrive."

She almost blurted obscenities about his younger brother, but then realized Foxe was baiting her. He knew damn well Connor had lashed her up half-exposed to humiliate her—and by the saints, it wouldn't work! Since Frazier apparently abhorred the sight of her breasts, she drew her tattered camisole over them with teasing slowness, making them sway while she badgered him with a come-hither look that would've had Connor reaching for his fly buttons.

Frazier pursed his lips. "You are indeed a whore, Miss O'Riley."

"And you're lower than the manure Eberhardt shovels from his stable."

With a mirthless chuckle he glanced out the

214

carriage window. "Not anymore, he doesn't. He was caving in, ready to confess, so he'll not survive the ride back to Cripple. Too bad the marshal put such an idea into his witless head. There's the estate. What do you think of it?"

Unable to stand the sight of him any longer, Lyla looked toward their destination. A steel-gray three-story house dominated the horizon, its turrets and gables giving an impression of nobility as false as she knew Frazier's to be. It was a huge, showy place with miles of white gingerbread and moldings along the eaves and veranda posts, larger than the McClanahan ranchhouse yet more like a fortress than a home. At a distance of perhaps a quarter mile stood the pens and dipping vats and outbuildings used during the sheep shearing, abandoned now because the flocks were wintering in the pastures.

"Don't even consider hiding there," her host said dryly. "Connor and his crew live in those bunkhouses year-round. And do you see that belvedere? A guard's posted in it day and night. Think of his spectacular view!"

Lyla eyed the small, cube-shaped structure perched atop the house. Frazier Foxe's elaborate security measures further proved his criminality. What rancher would need the little guardhouse they were passing through at the arched entryway, or a constant watchman in a belvedere, unless he was harboring secrets . . . or hostages? Foxe Hollow was miles from its nearest neighbor, isolated from civilization in more ways than one, she suspected.

The carriage lurched to a halt in front of the veranda steps. As though he'd been watching out the etched glass of the massive front door, a bald, reedlike man in a pinstriped suit rushed out to greet them.

Frazier gripped her shirt lapel, his gray eyes as cold as an iced-over pond. "Not a hint—not a whimper!" he warned. "Hollingsworth and my housekeeper

will inform me of your every word and deed, Lyla.
They lead a sheltered, comfortable life here, and they
won't believe what you'd tell them about Thompson,
so don't bother. I have ways of dealing with
ungrateful guests."

The carriage door swung out and the servant's
pink face lit up with sophisticated shock when he
saw her. "Welcome home, sir! I—we weren't expecting—"

"Nothing to fret about, my man. I daresay I've
surprised even myself this time." He put a gloved
hand on her shoulder, his waxed mustache lifting in
a grin. "Lyla, this is my valet—"

"Oliver Hollingsworth the Third, at your service,
miss," the man intoned with a bow.

"—and Hollingsworth, I'm pleased to introduce
Miss Lyla O'Riley . . . my fiancée."

Chapter 18

The valet's pate grew pinker as he stared first at Foxe and then, with disapproval he couldn't mask, at Lyla. "I never—gracious me, Mr. Foxe, but this *is* a surprise! I—I must go tell Miss Keating—"

Hollingsworth turned back toward the house but stopped when he saw the woman who was watching them from the door. She was tall and angular, clad in gray, and Lyla's immediate impression was that her face would crack if she attempted even the slightest smile. The woman patted her silver-streaked hair, which she wore in a severe bun, staring at them as though they'd just ruined her day.

"Well . . . perhaps you would prefer to give Miss Keating the good news, sir," the valet mumbled. "Have you any luggage, Miss O'Riley?"

"Everything atop the carriage needs to come in, and should be placed in Miss O'Riley's room," Frazier replied smoothly. He stepped to the ground and offered his hand to her as though she were the queen, his smile and bearing eloquent. "And you may have your choice of rooms, dear-heart. Should none of them suit, we'll redecorate one immediately."

Lyla's head was spinning. This man had just threatened her life if she breathed a word about Barry, and now he was offering her his world on a gilded platter—as his *fiancée!* Confused and wary, she offered Hollingsworth a weak smile and allowed Foxe to tuck her hand under his elbow.

"Try to act at least pleased that you're marrying into this," he muttered under his breath.

"A little warning would've been nice," she hissed back. She wanted to yank her hand away and run—anywhere! These people were all too old to catch her, and the servants knew as well as she did that something was terribly amiss. But Frazier was ushering her up the white enameled steps toward the housekeeper, smiling as though he were the happiest man alive.

"And this is Miss Allegra Keating, whom I'm sure you'll come to adore just as I do," he was saying. "May I present Lyla O'Riley, soon to be Mrs. Frazier Foxe."

The woman grabbed for the doorjamb to steady herself, her other hand flying to her high buttoned collar. "I—had no idea—"

"Life sometimes takes unexpected turns. Doesn't it, my dear?" he replied with a warning glance toward Lyla. "You can show Miss Lyla the available rooms, and then she'll be wanting a bath—"

"Yes, I should think so."

"—and when she's dressed we'll be ready for tea. Nothing fancy, since I realize you weren't expecting us," Foxe went on in a honeyed voice. "But even the scraps from your pantry will taste like manna from heaven, Miss Keating. As always."

The housekeeper's eyelashes fluttered at his compliment. She watched him until he passed through a door at the far end of the entryway, and then turned back to Lyla, her expression hardening again. "Well. Here you are in the vestibule."

"Yes, ma'am. It's lovely," she mumbled.

"We'll go upstairs."

Nodding, Lyla followed the taciturn woman past ornately-carved tables with sculptures and Oriental vases displayed on them. The deep green hall was bordered with gleaming woodwork, and large gilt-framed mirrors and oil paintings graced each wall. There was no time to peek into the salons they passed because Miss Keating was already halfway to the landing of the wide, carpeted stairway. Aside from the Golden Rose, it was the most magnificent house Lyla had ever set foot in.

The landing glowed with the colors of a huge stained-glass mural that depicted nymphlike ladies representing the four seasons. Frazier Foxe was obviously an art connoisseur. The sheer beauty of his home made her pause to study her surroundings—until she saw the housekeeper staring impatiently at her from the second floor landing.

"Sorry. I—I've never seen anything like it," Lyla mumbled.

Miss Keating studied her closely. "And just how did you get here, Miss O'Riley?"

She blinked. "In Mr. Foxe's carriage. I—I know I look frightful," she added quickly. Then she realized Frazier's maid wasn't referring to her mode of transportation, and by the look in her glittering little eyes she was tallying up all of Lyla's faults so she could report them to Foxe—along with every gesture and reply, just as Frazier had threatened. "It was the most . . . the luckiest day of my life when that dear man found me. Took me under his wing after my brother died in a mine explosion, you see."

With a haughty sniff, the housekeeper proceeded down the wide hallway. "Choose a room, then, so I can direct Hollingsworth where to deposit your luggage. Your bath shall be ready shortly."

Lyla almost snapped that she hadn't *chosen* to be such an inconvenience, or to sleep on a dirty floor—or to even be here at all. But voicing such frustrations could only get her into trouble. She wandered into the four spacious bedrooms, each exquisitely decorated, wondering why a bachelor would require so many. The far end of the second story was obviously

219

Frazier's suite: it spanned the front of the house and had windows on all three sides that afforded him a panoramic view of his estate. For that reason she returned to the room nearest the stairway to wait for Miss Keating.

"A wise choice," the housekeeper remarked. "Mr. Foxe does not like to be disturbed when he's in his chambers. These floorboards tend to creak, Miss O'Riley, so I'm sure you'll observe the rules of common decency during this . . . prenuptial period."

As though she'd sneak into Frazier's bedroom every chance she got! Lyla nearly choked on the irony of the woman's words and hurried to the room where a steaming tub awaited her.

A locked door and a long soak seemed like luxuries after all she'd been through. Lyla shed her coat and shabby clothes quickly, but after a few minutes she realized this bath was more of a problem than a solution: now that she was alone, images of the burning shack, and Buck jumping into the flames, and Barry's bruised, dusty face crowded all other thoughts from her mind. What did it matter how she behaved in front of these servants and their master? The man she loved was dead!

Two huge tears plopped into the bath water. It was a poor time to cry, knowing everyone else would be waiting tea, probably talking about her. Lyla splashed her face with the soothing water, telling herself over and over that this was no time to knuckle under. Now that she knew who'd assisted with the robbery and murdered Marshal Thompson, she had to get back to Cripple. Every waking moment should be spent listening and watching, searching for a way to escape. She was the only person on earth who could see that justice was done—Barry would expect, and deserved, no less.

When she returned to her room, Allegra had shaken her clothes out and hung them in the armoire. Foxe must've done some fast talking before he slipped out of Cripple. In addition to fetching her dresses and trunk from the Rose, he'd brought along three new gowns: a pale green one with pink flowers, an apricot-and-blue stripe, and a sky blue one with a violet windowpane plaid. Lyla chose the new plaid dress, wishing Barry could see how it accentuated her eyes—and just as quickly pushed thoughts of him out of her mind so she wouldn't cry in front of Foxe and his insufferable staff.

She descended to the vestibule, where Hollingsworth awaited her. The valet's eyes widened with something akin to approval, yet he merely gestured toward the parlor where Allegra and Frazier were seated around a table set for tea. Festive iced cakes were arranged on a silver plate, along with gingerbread men and cherry tarts. Scones and hot cross buns sat on the other side of the porcelain teapot, with a crystal dish of marmalade to the side.

Lyla hadn't seen such a spread since she worked at the whorehouse, and she almost said so, just to watch the housekeeper twitch at the *unseemliness* of her background. Instead, she forced a smile in Foxe's direction. "Thank you for the new gowns," she said quietly. "They were a thoughtful gift."

"I should think *that* one would suit better if you wore a corset," the housekeeper chirped as she poured tea into four bone china cups.

The silence was stifling. Hollingsworth brushed nervously at his fringe of gray hair, while Frazier was trying not to laugh. Allegra Keating set the teapot down and offered Lyla the tray of sweets, gloating as she awaited a response.

Lyla sat straighter, thrusting her bosom out, and looked the brittle housekeeper in the eye. "Ordinarily I wear one. But Frazier wasn't there to lace me up."

Two gingerbread men tumbled onto the table before Miss Keating regained her composure, and

221

Lyla snatched one up. She felt like a croquet ball surrounded by three mallets—how dare these bean-stalk Britons make fun of her figure! She bit the cookie's head off, wishing it were Frazier's.

Foxe had turned an uncomely shade of red, but said nothing. No one else spoke, either, and Lyla sensed her stay at his estate would be more trying than either of them dared to imagine unless he muzzled his help. Her cookie was dry and not nearly spicy enough, so she set it on her plate and quickly quaffed her tea. "Excuse me. I can't swallow another bite."

Striding toward the stairway, she heard Frazier making her apologies behind her. She hated to cave in to Miss Keating, but she refused to be a laughingstock . . . especially since she was suppos-edly to become the mistress of this house!

Lyla closed her bedroom door and crossed to the window. She'd unknowingly chosen a view of the sheep buildings—double torment because they re-minded her of home, and because they teased at her as a means of escape. If only Connor, Kelly, and Nate didn't live there . . . she sensed those desperadoes would be far easier to elude than Frazier, but the idea of running blind was suicidal. Better to bide her time, learning the workings of this inhospitable household, than to be hauled back in humiliation after a failed attempt at running off. She had no horse, no map . . .

No Barry Thompson to run to.

She stuffed her knuckles into her mouth and crumpled onto the bed. Such a lovely room this was, with carved cherry furnishings and olive, caramel, and cream print accessories. Items she would've chosen to decorate the house Barry said he'd be building. Just when they'd reconciled their mis-understandings and declared their love, their dreams had gone up in smoke, all because Frazier Foxe

222

resented being belittled, and Thompson refused to be bought.

Lyla's repressed grief flooded her soul and she gave in to uncontrollable crying. Barry Thompson was a good man: gentle, fair-minded, affectionate. And just when she realized how much she loved him—just when he revealed his deep feelings and wonderful plans for her—it wasn't *fair!* All the horrors she'd been forced to witness those last few moments outside the shack would haunt her forever. There was no forgiving such a callous act, no forgetting a love that would've lasted a lifetime.

Again Lyla saw his beloved face: the boyish grin, the sweet green eyes so like the hills of home, the light brown hair that framed his ruddy features, the lush, seductive mouth that would seek hers no more. She ached with the memory of his kiss, reliving each tender sentiment they'd shared this morning, shackled by captor's ropes, yet free within each other's arms.

If only she'd fought harder . . . if only she'd gone outside, as Barry had told her to, and caused a diversion so the marshal could escape from the shanty before the three thieves set it afire. If only she'd told him she loved him before he perished. So many vows unspoken; so many tender moments turned to dust.

And the worst part was that even if she got Foxe and his gang convicted of their heinous crimes, it wouldn't bring Thompson back. Once justice was done, her life would become an endless, aching void no other man could fill.

Lyla had sobbed herself out when she heard her door opening. Rather than acknowledge whoever it was, she lay facing the wall, her cheek on the wet comforter as tears dribbled unchecked down her face.

"I realize you've suffered a shock, dear-heart, but we must come to an understanding. I can't allow this behavior to continue."

A handkerchief fluttered over her shoulder, and the far side of the bed dipped with Frazier's weight. He waited for her response, and when she only hicced and sniffled, he continued in that low, cultivated voice Lyla had come to despise.

"You must put Thompson and today's events out of your mind, Miss O'Riley. Hollingsworth and Allegra will find these outbursts quite unseemly from a young woman who's to marry into such a fortune."

"Unseemly?" Lyla gasped. She rolled into a sitting position and glared at the ogre who regarded her so calmly. "How *seemly* is it for you to bring me here in the first place? I'm young enough to be—you obviously hadn't told them you even intended to—and when I appeared wearing Mick's dirty old clothes—"

"Yes, you were a shock to them, dear-heart," he said with a chuckle, "but they'll adjust. We all shall. You're the first woman I've ever brought home, so I imagine their tongues are wagging full tilt about now."

Frazier's slender legs were crossed and his gloved hands rested in his lap. As always, he was dressed to perfection in a striped suit and a crisp shirt and tie; his face appeared freshly-shaven around his waxed mustache, and his tight curls lay neatly in place. Barry's insinuations about this man's effeminate nature came back to her—since he never worked up a sweat over anything else, it made sense he wouldn't sully himself with a woman. And since he was sparing *her* no embarrassment, Lyla saw no reason to mince words about their incompatibility.

"Mr. Foxe, it's no secret that you pay the ladies at the Rose for their company, yet you never unfasten your pants," she said bluntly. "Why on earth do you want to get married—to the likes of *me*, no less?"

His expression never wavered. "Who else would

224

have you, dear-heart? You're known as a thief and a potential murderess. Unemployable. Just another vagrant from the far shores come to America and unable to support yourself."

"Your flattery overwhelms me," Lyla muttered. "And you're changing the subject. Why do you want me? According to Barry, you don't even like women."

"That's why he's dead!" Frazier snapped. "He shot his mouth off too much. Stuck his nose where it didn't belong."

Despite her grief, Lyla fought back a smile. She'd found a chink in this monster's armor and she was determined to pry at it. "And speaking of mouthiness, if I'm to be the mistress of this house, I won't tolerate Miss Keating's rude remarks. If she intends to remain here as—"

"You'll have no say concerning the running of this household or my staff," Foxe replied brusquely. "Not only because I don't want you causing any rifts, but because the wife of an extremely wealthy man doesn't concern herself with her husband's responsibilities. You've much to learn about your new station in life, Lyla. Most girls would be *giddy* with the prospect of marrying into the life of the idle rich."

"Most girls haven't watched the idle rich murder the men they loved."

"Love!" Frazier retorted with a roll of his pearl-gray eyes. "Only the young and the feeble-minded believe in such claptrap! Surely what you witnessed today taught you how useless it is to invest yourself in someone else's heart."

Lyla swallowed a sob and forced herself to focus on Frazier Foxe's monocle. Why upset herself again, when this unfeeling beast would never concede to her arguments because he'd always evade the issues she was discussing? "So," she began in the strongest voice she could find, "this will be a marriage in name only? What a relief! I thought I'd have to—"

Foxe's grin chilled her. "Actually, the only feasible

225

reason for me to bother with such a worthless institution as matrimony is to beget an heir. After amassing such vast holdings—my very purpose in life—I have to pass it on to someone when I pass on myself."

Lyla was so mortified she couldn't breathe. The thought of sharing a bed with this criminal repulsed her. After making love with Barry—even a Barry who was out of his head—how could she possibly allow his murderer to invade her body? Why, he probably wouldn't even take off his gloves, let alone—

"And so there won't be any misunderstanding," Frazier continued coolly, "I'll reassure you that I'll be no part of the necessary mating that must ensue."

Lyla lifted an eyebrow. "Surely a man with your low opinion of love can't believe in immaculate conception," she said wryly.

Foxe's laughter filled the room, and he rose to walk around in front of her. "You're clever, Miss Lyla. Too clever for your own good. And since you didn't also mention virgin birth, am I to assume you aren't one?"

She forced her face to remain expressionless, yet she felt the color creeping up her cheeks.

Foxe laughed again. "Good. Connor won't be getting everything he bargained so hard for after all."

"And what does *he* have to do with this?" she asked, although Frazier's wicked grin was confirming the boastful threats his younger stepbrother had made at the shack.

The Englishman assessed her as though she were a ewe to be considered as breeding stock. Then he shrugged. "Fornication's his favorite sport, dearheart. Since there are precious few women on this ranch—and since he so gallantly offered to forgo his bonus if he could have you instead—I saw this as the solution to my heirless state."

The ramifications of his words were too horrible to consider. "Wh—why can't you just will Foxe Hollow to Connor?" she mumbled. "He's your kin, and—"

"And die knowing my hard-earned estates and holdings would be piddled away at a poker table before I was even cold?" He adjusted his monocle, shaking his head. "Much as I despise children, I'll take my chances on indoctrinating a son before I allow Connor to control the purse strings."

Lyla was feeling paler by the minute. Not only was this madman handing her over to a professional killer, he was expecting her to go along with it! "I—what if it doesn't—what if there's no baby?"

"Oh, Connor's a proven breeder. I shudder to think how many abortions I've paid for—or train tickets, for girls too stupid to see the doctor until the baby was due." He looked her over again, stealthily. "And *you* seem healthy enough to conceive, dear-heart. Don't you see how perfect this arrangement will be? I'll have an heir, my stepbrother will have an outlet for his urges, and you'll never have to work another day in your life. As much practice as Connor's had with women, I wouldn't be surprised if you forgot all about Barry Thompson before the month was out."

Too agitated to sit still any longer, she went to the window. Once again she felt the barrel of Connor Foxe's pistol and the cruel kisses he'd forced upon her. She *had* to convince Frazier he'd regret giving her to his hired gun. Lyla clenched and unclenched her hands, thinking. Where was the catch? She had to either appeal to Foxe's baser desires or make him squirm—anything to avoid the degrading, immoral possibility of begetting a baby by one man as a commodity for another.

Lyla turned to face him, clutching at a few more straws. "If I bear a child by Connor, it won't be yours, so—"

"A son, dear-heart. You'll bear me a son I'll raise as my own because I'll have the certificates to prove he *is*."

227

"What if it's a girl?"

"Then you'll have to keep producing until I have a namesake and heir." Foxe chuckled, clasping his hands behind him as though he were extremely pleased with how things were working out. "You're not going to talk me out of this, Miss O'Riley. Better to spend your energies acclimating yourself to my household and habits. I can be delightfully kind to people who give me what I want."

Lyla lowered her gaze, thinking of her next objection. "What about Hollingsworth and Miss Keating?" she demanded. "Connor's such a braggart they're bound to find out what he's doing with me, and—"

"Miss Keating will indeed be incensed," Frazier agreed. "You'll have to either teach Connor the meaning of discretion, or live with my housekeeper's accusations. Allegra loyally reports every transgression she sees, which will assure me that an heir is on the way! She's well compensated for acting as the conscience of Foxe Hollow."

She was to endure the housekeeper's censure, to be branded as an unfaithful wife while her husband gleefully insisted upon these unholy entanglements. Frazier Foxe was even more loathesome than she'd imagined, and Lyla rued the day she'd accepted those new dresses and a job at the Rose as tokens of his concern for her. She had to escape this madhouse before—

"You, too, shall be handsomely compensated, dear-heart," her host was saying. "Tomorrow we'll draw up the papers stating the divisions of my property, as a premarital covenant between us. You take care of my needs, Miss Lyla, and I'll most certainly see to yours. Dinner's in an hour. I expect you to be at the table wearing a smile that reflects your unbounded joy and gratitude for the blessings I'm about to bestow upon you."

Chapter 19

Dinner was the bleakest meal Lyla had ever endured. She and Frazier were seated at one end of his long dining room table, suffering through course after course of Allegra Keating's abysmal efforts at cooking. The soup was lukewarm with a skin of grease congealing on it when Hollingsworth set it in front of them. The mutton was boiled beyond recognition yet still smelled gamy. The carrots, potatoes, and parsnips, cooked in their skins, had eyes and little clumps of rootlike fringe still attached. Her host apparently saw nothing unusual about any of these things and ate heartily while she took the fewest bites possible and pushed the remaining food around on her plate.

Foxe was proudly describing his sheep operation: how many thousands they sheared each spring, how many hundreds of lambs his registered ewes produced last year, how many sheepherders he employed, and how much he spent on supplies and food to make Foxe Hollow the most prestigious, prosperous ranch in Colorado—and possibly the whole West. Lyla nodded, truly impressed with the magnitude of his operation, which made her parents' herd look humble indeed.

But between Frazier's lines she heard the undercurrent from the kitchen and felt two pairs of eyes upon her. Such phrases as "obviously unsuitable" and "too young to be worthy of . . ." drifted out in Allegra's stilted whisper, answered by the valet's lower-pitched "a golddigger with the breeding and social sensibilities of an alley cat."

She wasn't particularly surprised by their opinions, but it appalled her that Foxe pretended not to hear them. When Hollingsworth appeared with dessert, he beamed up at the valet. "Give my compliments to Miss Keating for a fine dinner on such short notice."

"Indeed I shall," the servant replied as he bowed over them to set down their final course. "She was so delighted about your return that she prepared your favorite dessert—*blanc mange* with a sugar crisp. Enjoy it, sir. And you too, miss, of course," he added with a stiff nod in her direction.

The *blanc mange* was the most colorless, watery excuse for pudding Lyla had ever seen, and the cookie on her plate was burnt along the edges.

"You really should try it," Frazier encouraged as he dipped in for his first spoonful. "I don't want you getting sickly so you can't conceive. And if Allegra thinks you don't like her cooking, she'll be quite upset. She's sensitive about being criticized—and I *do* want you two ladies to get on together. Female company is scarce in these parts."

She was too wrung out from her crying spell and Frazier's earlier revelations to eat even the tastiest of meals, but she couldn't admit it. The only way she would find any peace in this house was to acquiesce to the man's whims and kowtow to his housekeeper . . . or at least appear to.

Lyla smiled weakly. "Perhaps Miss Keating was right," she said in a conciliatory tone. "Perhaps I would be more attractive if my dresses weren't so snug. You yourself said that anything more than a handful was excessive."

"I would never utter such a vile remark!" he declared. Then he adjusted his monocle and studied

230

her closely. "Actually, I find your figure rather charming. And I suspect my housekeeper was merely jealous of your endowments when she made that remark about the corset. I found your reply admirably witty, by the way. And appropriate, considering our betrothal."

He ate another spoonful of the pale pudding, chuckling to himself. Frazier Foxe was a hypocrite and a liar: he *had* made a crude remark about her breasts when Mrs. Delacroix was measuring her for her gowns. But he was complimenting her now, willing to acknowledge something positive because he thought she was submitting to his will.

And if playing up to his indecent suggestions won his confidence, Lyla would play to the hilt—and then beat him at his own game by escaping. "Aye, well . . . it wouldn't hurt to be a bit thinner. To look nice in my wedding gown, you know."

Frazier appeared dumbfounded for a moment, and then brushed cookie crumbs from his lapel. "Of *course* you'll be wanting . . . I suppose my associates would think it odd if we didn't have a ceremony that outshone the McClanahans'. Would that make you happy, dear-heart?"

"Oh yes," she whispered, "it's what every girl dreams of."

"Consider it done, then. Perhaps the planning and anticipation will help you and Miss Keating become better friends." Frazier dabbed his mouth with his napkin, chuckling into it. "Don't go turning into a stick on us, though. It's your voluptuous way of filling out a gown that Connor adores most about you."

Lyla smiled sweetly. She'd sent the younger Foxe tumbling into icy water before, and she could freeze him out again. For now it was victory enough to have Frazier mixing his twisted threats with jokes.

The evening passed slowly, but she was learning patience, taking in the details of this life that would eventually help her escape it. Frazier and Hollings-worth were engaged in a chess game that apparently continued from one night to the next, and Allegra was cleaning up the kitchen. After considering the unseemliness of helping her, Lyla instead wandered around the parlor and the other rooms on the main floor.

Off the vestibule there was a sitting room, furnished with upholstered chairs and an elegant settee, all in maroons that blended with the Persian rug beneath them. This fireplace was of pink marble—the rooms had hearths and mantels that complemented their unique decor. The salon across the entryway boasted a gleaming concert grand piano. Another room, Frazier's study, was papered and paneled and richly decorated . . . a den she'd explore when the others were too busy to notice.

Lyla passed through the large, opulent dining room on her way to the parlor, wondering if the fourteen mahogany chairs around its massive table were ever filled. Did anyone ever play that piano? All this artwork, the luxurious draperies and rugs, the tiered chandeliers that glittered like a thousand diamonds when tickled by the slightest breeze . . . who did they impress, besides Frazier himself?

When she returned to the parlor she paused beside her captor to observe the men's contest. It was Hol-lingsworth's move. Foxe glanced up at her and then remembered to smile. All part of the game, the deceit they carried out to convince his staff they were indeed engaged. When Miss Keating sat down across the room with her sewing basket, Foxe actually reached up to stroke her cheek with a gloved finger and she turned what she hoped was a telltale pink.

The housekeeper quickly looked away, pretending to be absorbed in her handwork, her pointed face a clear warning that she wanted no part of conversation. Lyla chose a book from the shelves and sat down to read, or at least to turn the pages. It was a leather-bound collection of poems by Elizabeth Barrett Browning, never before opened.

The lines about love were too painful to follow, so Lyla glanced surreptitiously at the others. It was still Hollingsworth's move, and Frazier sat back unperturbed, as though he whiled away innumerable hours anticipating his valet's strategy. Allegra's wooden hook dipped swiftly in and out of the dull brown yarn she was crocheting into an unidentifiable item . . . yarn that seemed rather curly to Lyla's untrained eye.

When the housekeeper finished a row of stitches and slipped her hook free, Lyla immediately wondered if it could become a weapon. Plenty of time to ponder that . . . the mantel clock ticked on, the two men sat motionless in their leather chairs, and the four of them seemed to be suspended in time and space and silence, a diorama in an ageless, lifeless museum.

Then Miss Keating gave a quick yank, and row by row the brown strip was reduced to a growing clump of crinkled yarn. When she'd undone the entire piece, she began winding the kinky worsted into a ball, as though she'd done it a dozen times and would do it a dozen more.

And Lyla suspected she had and would. The futility of this kind of life struck her hard: all this wealth, and for what? So four people could spend their evenings not speaking to each other, their days engaged only in the business of living a life that never changed, never lightened?

Lyla muffled a sigh and chose a different book. Her stay here already felt like an endless wake, with three corpses propped into lifelike positions rather than laid out in coffins. But she could wait and watch . . . for however many eternities it took.

The following morning, after breakfast, Frazier

steered her into his study and shut the door. "We need to conduct some business, you and I," he said briskly. "Have a seat, dear-heart, and we'll make our arrangement official—everything tidy and legal so we'll have no misunderstandings about division of property after I'm gone."

Lyla perched on a leather chair in front of his desk, thinking his mood rather jovial for a man contemplating his own death. Today his suit was a natty tan-and-green tweed which complemented his olive complexion, and his gloves were nearly the color of his skin. He sat down, swiveling to one side so he'd face a shiny black typewriter, and then pulled a sheet of letterhead from his top drawer.

"I hope you'll see these documents as protection in the event of my demise," he explained as he prepared to type. "Not only does Connor need to know where he stands, but everyone else should be informed of my wishes and stipulations. Too many unscrupulous schemers have designs on my holdings, and they'll be contesting your rights before the casket's lowered unless I spell everything out."

She nodded, slightly puzzled. "A last will and testament seems only prudent for a man like you."

"A will, among other things," Foxe replied. His fingers flew over the keyboard for a few moments, producing a rapid clatter. His lips moved slightly as he composed a paragraph on the page.

"Now then," he said as he looked at her, "I need your assurance that you have no other living relatives in this country. Is that correct?"

"Aye. My parents live in Ireland."

"Too far away to interfere. A bridegroom's fondest dream." He typed a few lines more and then smiled wryly at her. "No other kin I should know about? No estranged husbands who might appear from out of nowhere if they hear what you're marrying into?"

"I have twin brothers who'll inherit the O'Riley homeplace," she replied hesitantly. Was there, after

234

all, a chance to get out of this unholy alliance? "And there *is* Hadley McDuff. I was betrothed to him when I left."

"And why did you leave him?" Frazier Foxe's eyes narrowed as he awaited her reply.

She couldn't admit the truth—that Hadley, too, was a spinsterish old geezer who needed an heir—so she told the closest fib. "My father arranged the match without my consent so I'd have a home after my brothers took over the sheep operation. Upon meeting Mr. McDuff, I decided to take my chances here in America and I ran off with Mick."

Foxe's chortle rumbled in his throat as his hands again attacked the typewriter. "Your running days are over, my dear. But McDuff couldn't possibly offer you the life you'll lead at Foxe Hollow, so that escape was the wisest move you could've made."

After a few more lines he pulled the paper from his machine with a flourish and handed it to her. "Your signature will assure all who read this that you've entered into this marriage of your own free will and that at the time of your death, all property passes to my heir or reverts to Connor in the event there isn't a child yet. It also attests to your agreement upon all stipulations presented herewith."

Lyla read the page carefully, ignoring the fountain pen Foxe was trying to hand to her. Not only was the entire page error-free, but it was also signed by a Colorado Springs attorney, a Quentin Yarborough, near the bottom. Did Frazier keep a box of such letterhead, already affixed with a seal and a signature, for whenever he needed a quick contract?

"Will you please just sign, Miss O'Riley?" he prompted.

She glanced at the gold-trimmed pen without reaching for it. "I haven't yet seen the stipulations presented herewith," she mimicked.

"We discussed them when—"

"Put them in writing. Perhaps your attorney trusts

you enough to sign beforehand, Mr. Foxe, but I want it all spelled out."

He adjusted his eyepiece. "Are you always this obstinate, my dear?"

"Aye. If you don't like it, let me go."

Frazier's laughter chilled her. "The only way out of this arrangement is death, Miss Lyla. 'Till death do us part,' as they say."

It was a sobering thought, and Lyla sat quietly as her captor hastily added a few more lines to the page and then thrust it toward her. The new part stipulated that she was to produce a male offspring, and that any divulging of Frazier Foxe's ranching, financial, or personal affairs was license for her disinheritance. *In other words* she thought glumly, *I'll keep silent about his murders and his network of secret associates, or I'll die.*

Lyla signed the page slowly, her heart aching. This was an outright betrayal of Marshal Thompson, yet it was the only way she saw to survive. If she didn't do as Frazier demanded, there'd be no chance to escape when they went to Cripple Creek for the wedding, no chance to warn the McClanahans so they could act in her behalf as well as Barry's.

"Next is the will," Frazier continued when she handed him her document. "It's all signed and sealed, but again your signature affirms your agreement to and understanding of its contents. I think you'll be pleased, actually."

Amazed and appalled was more like it. Lyla read the precisely-typed paragraphs of legal terminology carefully to glean their full meaning, and after several minutes she glanced at Foxe, whose hands were tented in a prayerful pose just below his mustache. "The way I understand this, your various businesses in Cripple and the Springs will be entrusted to your partners until your heir's eighteenth birthday—"

"That's correct."

"—and Miss Keating and Hollingsworth are to have a home here for as long as they wish to stay—"

"Only fair, after their years of loyal service."

"—and I will inherit Foxe Hollow, its buildings, grounds, and pastureland—"

"A generous compensation for your youth, your silence . . . and your freedom."

"—but Connor inherits the sheep!" She stared at him, horrified. "He's your own kin, sir! And he *despises* the sheep!"

Frazier's head dropped back and his laughter filled the cozy study. "No one said life was fair, dear-heart. Connor despises *me*, too, yet I've met his demands and paid his debts ever since I made him manager of this ranch. I've pandered to his whims during this life and I bloody well refuse to continue in the hereafter."

"But—but what if he decides to sell all the stock?" Lyla stammered. "I'd be left without—"

"Adequate means of support?" Foxe cleared his throat, not quite covering his chuckle. "I had to leave him *something*, my dear. If I were in your place, I'd be very, very charming to Connor. It's the only way to keep him from selling—or gambling away—your livelihood. Not an easy task, considering his history of loving women and leaving them."

"This is an outrage! Bad enough that I have to couple with that criminal to produce your heir, but to be dependent upon him after your death!" Lyla stood suddenly, and in her frustration she went around to grasp Frazier's typewriter as tightly as she wanted to wring his neck. "I won't sign it! Absolutely not!"

"And what's your alternative?" he asked slyly. "Your loyalty to Barry Thompson has made you my prisoner now, Miss O'Riley, and my stepbrother's after I'm gone. We can't have you telling what you

237

know, now, can we?"

"I—I'll get him to sell his sheep to me!" she gasped.

"And what will you buy them with? My accounts are to be frozen in trust for my son," he replied smoothly. "Not only will you need to keep Connor and his sheep in Foxe Hollow, you'll have to rely upon an adequate lambing and wool harvest each year to remain self-sufficient. You'd better pray Mother Nature smiles kindly on you."

Her heart shriveling, Lyla sank back into her chair. What had she done to deserve this? Why was the estate this ogre had appeased her with now dangling before her like a noose? If she'd had an inkling of the price she'd pay for those first three dresses . . .

"There's nothing you could've done differently, dear-heart," he said gently, "except perhaps convincing your marshal to support my refinery. But things moved more quickly than I anticipated, and you were caught up in the tide of events."

Frazier came around his desk and placed the fountain pen in her hand, smiling benignly. "And don't be too hasty to assume you've sealed your doom today, my sweet. While I'm alive, I'm sure you'll coax all manner of baubles and gowns and whatever else your heart desires out of me. Actually, I'm looking forward to the role of doting husband."

His honeyed voice only infuriated her more. "Why should I believe that?" she demanded bitterly. "Each time you give me something, you take something else away!"

"Ah, come now, Miss Lyla," he crooned, brushing a wisp of her hair aside with a gloved finger. "If you don't believe, all is lost."

She reread the will in front of her to avoid his probing gaze, realizing that he was right about that: if she stopped believing she could escape and bring this villain to justice, then all was indeed lost. Her

238

only chance was to resume the docile, accommodating attitude she'd won him with last night at dinner. Saints help her to keep a civil tongue, so he'd not suspect her true motives!

Lyla signed the will beneath Frazier's own flowing signature and then folded her hands in her lap. The man beside her lifted her chin with utmost tenderness, and she thought she detected a flicker of genuine warmth as he gazed down at her.

"You're wise beyond your years, sweet child, and I truly look forward to your companionship. This house needs your sunshine, your laughter," Foxe murmured. "I realize far more fully than you do just what you'll sacrifice to become my wife. Ask me a favor, dear-heart—anything these documents we've signed will allow—and I'll grant it as a token of my esteem."

Lyla studied him warily while trying to sort out her wishes. She couldn't have Barry Thompson back, and she'd have no chance to see her friends until the wedding . . . "I—I'd like my shamrock pendant," she ventured. "My brother made it for me. It's all I have to remember him by."

"It shall grace your gown on our wedding day," he promised with a genteel bow. He lifted her hand to his lips, his kiss almost reverent. "And what would you like for now, to enjoy during our betrothal?"

If he had her pendant, Foxe also had the ring Thompson had bought! But she couldn't bear to ask for it. Too many memories . . . too many dreams that would never come true. She felt quite strange with her hand in his gloved grasp . . . best to ask for something she could truly benefit from, because his favors might run dry at any time. "I . . . I want your word that Connor will keep his distance until after the wedding. Promise me you'll enforce that."

Foxe's brow puckered. "I can understand your concern about an untimely pregnancy, dear-heart. However, the only way to insure he'll not have access to you is to remain at my side, or with Miss Keating or Hollingsworth, at all times. One step outside the house and I can't guarantee your safety, because the ranch is his domain.''

She smiled wryly, wondering if she'd ever be free of this insidious web he'd spun around her. "If that's the way it has to be . . .''

Frazier bowed slightly. Then he released her hand and went to the marble mantel, where he picked up a small velvet box. "This is the first of many gifts I intend to give you, my dear—not just for the sake of appearances, but because I admire your courage and spirit. And because, in my own way, I do love you, Lyla.''

Why couldn't it be Barry saying those precious words? Why did this man's evil nature overshadow even his compliments and kindnesses? Her hands trembled as she took the small box, because she knew it held an engagement ring—a large, showy, expensive gemstone, judging from the finery he surrounded himself with. She hesitated to lift the lid. Wearing Frazier Foxe's ring was the ultimate sign that she accepted his terms and belonged to him for the rest of his years. And beyond.

Each second that ticked by made her appear more untrusting . . . foolish . . . afraid.

Lyla opened the box and threw it onto the desk as though it were a burning coal. "You—*you!*'' she rasped, springing from the chair to bolt out of the study.

But Frazier grabbed her arm and then he freed the glistening ring from its casing. She watched, sickened, as he slid onto her left hand the diamond-encircled aquamarine—the ring Thompson had bought for her. The ring this twisted Englishman's brother had stolen at the Golden Rose, just as he'd taken her shamrock pendant!

Her captor's laugh came straight from hell, a cruel, blackhearted sound that scarred her very soul.

"The marshal had exquisite taste," Foxe remarked, turning the large, blue stone to admire it by the light of the chandelier. "And it's yours to remember him by, Lyla. Every time you look at it you'll wish for the love you lost. Each time you see it—every day, because you *will* wear it!—you'll recall his dying moments and realize that a similar fate awaits anyone who crosses Frazier Foxe!"

Chapter 20

Lyla rushed upstairs to her room, chased by her captor's wicked snickering. The man had the soul of Satan himself! She now possessed proof that he'd masterminded the Rose's robbery, but what good did it do her? Rather than bringing her joy, the glistening gems on her finger tore her apart. Not only was Foxe reprehensible enough to present the ring as his own, he was forcing her to wear it under the vilest of pretexts and to keep silent about the man who'd actually bought it for her.

Oh, Barry . . . who would ever have guessed the extent of Foxe's revenge? Who'd have guessed at his capacity for evil?

Her pent-up grief poured out, and when her sobs grew uncontrollable Lyla buried her face in the cool feather pillows of her bed. If Allegra Keating came snooping, she could give no answers to the housekeeper's questions—and who would believe the truth if she told it? Here in this lavish home, isolated from the news of Cripple Creek and Colorado Springs, Foxe's staff knew only what he told them and assumed he was the upstanding citizen everyone in town thought him to be. Her word as an outsider would mean nothing and could only get her into deeper trouble.

Footsteps creaked on the wooden stairway, paused

before her door, and then proceeded down the hall. Lyla held her breath . . . it sounded like Foxe had gone into his chambers and shut the door behind him.

Wiping her wet face with her sleeve, Lyla sat up, inspired by the view of the sheep pens and the rolling pastureland beyond. She would leave—simply change into the clothing she'd worn here and rush out before Frazier emerged or the two servants could catch her. If there was indeed a guard in the belvedere, she'd be long gone by the time he could alert the household of her escape. It meant leaving Mick's shamrock pendant behind, but this was a small sacrifice compared to what she would suffer if she remained here any longer.

As though she'd given them a telepathic cue, three men on horses galloped out of the stable toward the front gate—Kelly, Connor, and Nate! Never would there be a more opportune time to flee this gilded prison! Surely there was a spare horse, another way out besides passing the guardhouse at the arched entryway!

Lyla flung open the armoire, but the coat, pants, and shirt weren't inside. The chest of drawers held only the new underthings Foxe had provided for her. Her panic rose as she searched beneath the bed, rifled her vanity drawers—looked everywhere in her room. Everything she'd worn here was gone, along with the five hundred dollars she'd had in her coat pocket!

Without a moment's pause she strode down the hall and barged into Foxe's room. It was a spacious, airy suite done in soothing blues and greens, flooded with sunlight from the glistening glass windows. Who'd have thought a craven beast like Frazier would inhabit such an appealing lair?

He sat at an easel in the far corner, his paintbrush poised in front of a large canvas. "Why did I know you'd storm in here without knocking?" he asked in a frosty voice. "Hollingsworth was right. You need

243

some lessons in deportment—"

"Where's my coat? My clothing?" she demanded.

Frazier's face lit up with a mocking grin. "Going somewhere, Miss O'Riley? Not twenty minutes ago you were begging me to protect you from Connor, who'll most surely grab you the moment he sees—"

"He just left, damn it! Now where are my clothes?"

"They *smelled,* dear-heart," he snapped, "so I imagine they're being laundered, if Hollingsworth didn't have the sense to throw them out!"

Her heart was sinking like a brick in a well, but Lyla fought to keep a straight face. She couldn't leave now and would undoubtedly be kept under constant watch. And what could've happened to all that money? Would the two loyal servants report their find to Frazier, or split the take?

"You are the cruelest, most insidious bastard I've ever met, and by the saints you'll *pay!*" she blurted. "You'll pay for what you're doing to me—for what you did to Barry Thompson!"

Foxe sat silently, observing her with unnerving calm. "Feel better, now that you've had a little cry and vented your frustrations?" he asked lightly. He leaned forward to stroke more paint onto his canvas, and then peered at her through his monocle. "Actually, it's good you've come in. Your complexion's even lovelier in this light. If you promise not to have any more outbursts, you may step closer and see what I'm painting. It was to be a surprise, but perhaps now's the best time to show it to you."

Lyla watched warily from a few feet away. For the first time she was seeing Frazier without a suit coat. His collar was undone and his shirt sleeves were rolled to his elbows . . . *and his hands were bare!* Curiosity bit hard. She wanted to see what he was doing, but most of all she wished to know what mysteries he hid beneath the dozens of pairs of gloves he wore.

"What do you think? I daresay I've created a vision

244

of loveliness every female in Cripple will envy and any man would kill for."

Her mouth fell open but no sound came out. Frazier Foxe's hands were covered with shiny, hairless, oddly-layered skin of a ghastly red that made the bottom drop out of her stomach. They were hands that had been burned and hadn't healed properly . . . hands scorched by the fires of hell.

Frazier looked up from his palette. "Well, I'll give you credit for not screaming," he commented wryly. "What you see is the result of a little scheme that backfired, literally. Thirty years old, I was, and still didn't heed my mother's warning about playing with matches."

Lyla swallowed hard to keep the bile from rising in her throat. "So that's why you . . . pay other men to light your fires now?"

"Clever girl," he said with a wink. "One burnt offering per lifetime is quite enough. Wounds such as these raise too many questions, and since the physician of that particular town was the sheriff's brother, I doctored myself."

"Do . . . do they hurt?"

"Now that the skin's glazed over they're not nearly so painful as when the gloves stuck to the unhealed wounds. Merely stiff when I type or paint." Frazier raised an eyebrow and then applied a few more strokes. "Don't tell me you're actually feeling sorry for me."

"*No!* I—" She stepped closer so she could relieve her horror by looking at his canvas. "I know some herbal cures that might—"

"No thank you, dear-heart," he said with a knowing grin. "To prevent any chance of you poisoning me, I'd have to ask Hollingsworth to undergo your cure first. And I'm not about to show him these hands after all the years I've remained gloved in his presence. Now, what do you think? Personally, I feel it's my best likeness of you yet."

245

Lyla was too stunned to speak. The canvas glowed with fresh oils in whites and pastels, a full-length bridal portrait that featured an exquisitely-detailed gown and veil yet drew her eye to the bride's radiant face—her own! Her cheeks were like velvet roses; her periwinkle eyes shone with happiness; her honey-brown hair was pulled up into a graceful knot with enchanting tendrils peeking out from the veil's beaded edge. "But . . . how do you—"

"Oh, I used these as my models," he explained with a wave of his paintbrush. "I've sketched you countless times, my love. Your face captured my fancy from the first moment I saw you—you were at the Angel Claire when Mick was applying for his job. Which was the main reason I insisted upon taking you under my wing when he died."

His collection of sketches filled the corner behind him: all poses, all moods, some in pastel chalks, some in pencil or ink. In one she wore the red plaid dress, in another the silver-blue taffeta . . . and one showed her nude from the waist up, smiling coquettishly over her shoulder as she grasped the lavender gown beneath breasts that were lush and ripe in profile.

It was flattering to be the object of a talented artist's admiration, and yet the longer Lyla gazed at these images of herself, the more frightened she became. Frazier Foxe was a man obsessed. His impressions were amazingly accurate while being better than life: the girl in the pictures was a fantasy, rendered with romantic strokes and heightened colors. Yet Lyla recalled all the moments he'd captured—or she certainly *could* have looked this way in these dresses. A chill went up her spine when she glanced again at the nude. Mother of God, he must've been peeking into the pantry the evening of McClanahan's bachelor party, seeing her from the same perspective Barry Thompson did after she'd undone her corset!

"You haven't said a word, dear-heart," Frazier murmured. "Surely you recognize—"

"Oh yes," she replied in a strangled voice. "You have a true talent, Mr. Foxe. A marvelous eye. But I was wondering . . . well, these sketches are all from the past, yet your canvas portrays me—"

"In a dress you haven't yet seen?" The man beside her chuckled, pleased with himself as he tapped a small sketch that rested on the rack of his easel. "I designed your wedding gown, dear-heart, just as I drew sketches of your other dresses for Mrs. Delacroix to follow when she sewed them for you."

Lyla frowned. "But I'd hoped to—"

"Never fear, my sweet, I specified all the finest satins and laces. These leg-of-mutton sleeves will show you off wonderfully, and the deep vee of beaded lace on the bodice will accentuate your finest features," he said gaily. "Nothing but the best for my lovely bride . . . my sweet, lovely Lyla-bride."

Her mouth turned to cotton and took on the acrid, coppery taste of total fear. This man had taken great delight in destroying all she held dear, yet he idealized her as the picture of perfection—a picture he'd created for himself by dressing her so finely. Frazier Foxe was placing her high upon a pedestal of fantasy, and Lyla was now afraid for her life. If for one moment she defied the image he'd conjured up— if she fell below his level of expectation, or broke the premarital agreement she'd signed, he'd deem her as expendable as Barry Thompson had been.

To keep her sanity, she pursued her original point. "When you said we'd plan the wedding, I was hoping *I* could choose my gown and select my bridesmaids, and . . ."

Frazier's scowl made her falter. "You were hoping for a trip to Cripple, I take it?"

"Well, of course!" Lyla challenged him with a frown of her own. "Surely a man who has the law in his pocket isn't afraid to set foot in—"

"*I* am not the problem, dear-heart! *My* picture isn't on Wanted posters in every storefront."

"A picture *you drew!*" she blurted. "How am I supposed to have invitations printed or ask the priest—"

"It's all been arranged." Her captor's waxed mustache lifted above his grin, and he resumed his painting as though the conversation bored him. "Since Connor and his men were due for a trip to town, to buy supplies for my sheepherders, I sent specific instructions along with them. Mrs. Delacroix will receive a sketch and specifications for your gown, the chef at the New Yorker will prepare the buffet, the printer has his information, and Reverend Bailey will perform the ceremony. Any questions?"

Lyla felt her heart sinking. "I'm Catholic," she mumbled.

"You're mine," he replied coolly. "As a major contributor to the Presbyterian church, I intend to say my vows in the sanctuary I paid for."

He was becoming churlish, probably so she would leave him to his painting, but Lyla remained by his side. She hated his moods; at times like this Frazier proved just what a hypocritical bastard he was, yet these tormenting moments were when he usually revealed what she needed to know to escape him. "May I ask how the invitation will read?" she inquired bitterly.

He responded to her glare with a smirk. "We're to be wed on February fourteenth. Two o'clock."

St. Valentine's Day! Of course this madman would knot her noose on the most romantic day of the year. "And what about bridesmaids? Surely you won't ask me to stand alone at the altar."

"Grace Putnam will attend you."

The Indian princess? She'd hoped to be comforted by Emily McClanahan's steadying presence, hoped Matt could be working behind the scenes to convict Frazier before the wedding could even take place. And now she'd have one of Barry's former consorts to

248

contend with. "I suppose she's on your payroll, too?"

"No, no. Just an old friend—a kindred spirit, you might say." Frazier laid his brush aside and stretched like a pampered cat. "Grace and I met years ago in Dodge City. She had a tattoo parlor above one of the saloons—an effort to support herself without having to whore. With the clientele she attracted, however, she decided to charge for all her services rather than constantly being forced into nonprofitable situations."

"I suppose I should feel grateful that you saved me from a similar fate?" she asked archly.

"I suppose you should. But I know better, don't I?"

Was he implying she was ungrateful, or that she'd done some whoring? Lyla didn't care. He was so damned smug about pulling her strings, as though she was his pretty little puppet—as though he could anticipate her moves and twist them toward his own purposes! Her only consolation was that Frazier Foxe apparently had no desire to caress her with his horribly-deformed hands.

And as he stretched again, something even more amazing caught her eye. This paragon of the upper crust, who wore only the most fashionable, expensive clothing, sported a tattoo!

Boldly, Lyla tugged his shirt sleeve toward his elbow to get a better look. "I assume this is Grace's work?"

"Yes. Handsome little devil, isn't he?" Frazier flexed his arm to make the animal move. It resembled a dragon, in greens and blues, with a long tail and a ridged back—and a slender red tongue shooting out to encircle the bone of Foxe's wrist. "I've always admired the chameleon. Able to adapt to changing environments by altering his colors so that his prey never knows he's there until he strikes."

Even before he finished speaking, her pulse was pounding. Mick had babbled hysterically about chameleons during his dying moments, as though trying to warn her. Barry had said the Chameleon Club was an opium den on Myers Avenue. Why did she sense her captor was connected to both these circumstances in some horrendous way she didn't want to hear about, yet had to? "I . . . I suppose you belong to the Chameleon Club?" she asked in a quavery voice.

"Belong? I own it!" Her startled expression made him laugh, a humorless sound that said the joke was again on her. "I have no use for people who lie around in smoky stupors puffing on pipes. Unless I can profit from them, of course."

"That comes as no surprise," Lyla mumbled. Something told her to leave now, before this wily Foxe shattered what little remained of the life she'd cherished, but when she turned he grasped her by the wrist. The flesh of his hand was as cold and deadly as the voice he continued with.

"If you go poking under rocks, you're liable to get bit, Miss O'Riley. Or, put another way, curiosity killed the cat." Frazier pulled her against his side, his face contorted with a nasty little grin. "Your dear brother came to the club a time or two, when I was visiting the manager. Does that shock you, dearheart?"

"Liar!" she spat. "You've lied about everything else; why should I believe Mick smoked opium?"

"Dear, sweet Lyla . . . so willing to see the best in others," he crooned, tightening his grip. "It's a pity Mick didn't share your outlook. Had he taken me up on an offer, he'd be alive today."

Bile rose in her throat: he was forcing her to ask for the rest of a story she wished to remain ignorant of. "Wh—what do you mean? Why do you torment me this way?"

"Because I have no one else to confess to. Because I'm a lonely man who needs to share his blackest

250

secrets with someone who can't betray me." He kissed her hand, chuckling when she flinched. "Yes, Mick had the opportunity to be elsewhere when the Angel Claire exploded, but he balked. Nigel Grath volunteered to work for me instead."

Sweat popped out on her upper lip, yet Lyla felt a chill descend upon her. "Nigel Grath blew up the Angel Claire, and—and you *paid* him! You killed my brother! You goddamned—"

Frazier sprang from his chair and caught her in the crook of his elbow, stifling her screams with his other lizardlike hand. "Do you want Allegra and Hollingsworth to come see about this commotion, you little fool?" he demanded in a harsh whisper. "Now shut up, or by God I'll bloody well kill you, too!"

He was surprisingly strong, and in her shock Lyla lacked the strength to struggle away from him. All of Cripple Creek had speculated that Grath, the Angel Claire's maniacal blaster, was too unbalanced to carry out his devastation alone, and now she knew who had really orchestrated the explosion that had killed sixteen miners and left Emily Burnham's mine in a shambles.

"Why?" she demanded hoarsely. "Were you trying to ruin Emily so she'd be dependent upon you, too?"

"Not at all. I respected her father a great deal and didn't particularly choose his mine as my target," Foxe replied smoothly. "But Grath was willing to further my cause, and the Angel Claire was where he happened to work."

"And just what *is* your cause, Mr. Foxe?" Hot tears ran down her cheeks as she glared at the Englishman who still held her in his cruel embrace.

"Actually, I wanted to stir the miners up, to incite violence over the dangerous working conditions in all the district's mines."

"Why? So hundreds would die instead of just sixteen?"

He laid a finger upon her lips, his monocle twinkling as he clucked over her. "Lyla, Lyla . . . so gloriously beautiful when you're enraged this way," he whispered. "Connor's going to owe me—"

"Shut up about Connor! Why did you have Grath blast the Angel Claire?" she demanded.

Frazier chortled, implying that the answer was all too obvious. "It was the beginning of the end for your Marshal Thompson," he said softly. "If thousands of men wouldn't return to work, he'd have had riots and looting—more unrest than he could handle. People would've demanded a more effective lawman, someone who could restore order to prevent uprisings like we had a few years ago."

"And I suppose you had his replacement all picked out?"

"Indeed. With blessings from a friend who's a federal marshal himself."

Lyla scowled at the depth of this man's corruption. "But it didn't work. Barry had no trouble at all maintaining order, because Silas Hughes and Emily convinced their men to clear away the rubble and return to work."

Frazier shrugged. "I got my way in the end, didn't I? Thompson's gone, his deputy's come into my fold, and now that the robbery victims have recovered their valuables, Cripple Creek's ready to be ushered into a new era of industrial expansion."

"Which means your refinery will be built whether the mine owners want it or not? With their money?"

"You're one of the most astute young ladies I've ever met," he said with sincere admiration. "And contrary to Thompson's arguments, the mines will continue to produce for at least another decade, according to my geological advisors. It's not as though I'm pulling the wool over anyone's eyes."

Lyla smirked. "But you *are* fleecing them, aren't you? If it's your scheme, it has to be crooked."

Foxe's laughter climbed the scale until it was a

girlish, uncontrolled giggle. Then he steered her toward the door, his grip tightening again. "You ask too many questions, dear-heart. Surely you've learned that your inquisitive nature will only bring you pain here in my house. For your own good, I'm going to have to lock you in your room until dinner."

Chapter 21

The days dragged into weeks, and Lyla's only reason to keep track of time was the St. Valentine's Day wedding that loomed ahead. The momentous event, undoubtedly the most ostentatious occasion Cripple would ever see, would merely seal the doom she was already suffering. How could things possibly get worse? By day she was under constant watch and each night she was locked into her bedroom.

Miss Keating and Hollingsworth, often her wardens, had to know something was terribly wrong. What sane man kept his fiancée under guard and didn't allow her to set foot outside his house? Yet the two said nothing. They made the commonest of talk—"Your breakfast, miss," or "Have you anything that needs to be laundered?"—and otherwise found nothing to share with her in conversation.

Lyla felt like the proverbial bird in a gilded cage, never to be set free, nevermore to sing. Frazier appeased her with gifts, which he had delivered to the estate so he wouldn't have to leave her unattended. Fresh roses adorned her vanity and imported chocolates, scented soaps, lustrous alabaster combs, and many other offerings arrived each week, and only served to remind her of the one gift she longed for but would never receive: her freedom.

The long hours alone were sheer torment, because

when she wasn't recalling Barry's last, hellish moments she could only contemplate her bleak situation without him. Often she heard a stealthy rustling, as though someone were peeping through her keyhole, just as she often felt Allegra's pale eyes boring into her back. The aquamarine on her finger was a constant reminder of the love she'd lost. The finished portrait in Frazier's suite served as a haunting memento of the choices she wasn't permitted to make about the most important event in her life.

And Frazier's compliments, delivered with his polished, courtly eloquence, always tore her to shreds with their underlying messages. He was truly heartless. As the weeks passed and the wedding drew nearer, Lyla wondered if he hadn't planned the mine catastrophe and the robbery at the Rose to eliminate all his competition so he could feed his raging obsession for her. It was an elaborate means of making her his own, but for a man with Foxe's money and influence, such clandestine activities were merely a diversion—something to ponder as he awaited Hollingsworth's next chess move each evening.

She was allowed to ascend to the third floor once, when Allegra was cleaning there. Out of sheer boredom, Lyla took a rag and dusted the gleaming wooden balustrades and the rich, carved tables that graced the hallway. The rooms on this level were indeed a puzzle: except for Hollingsworth's quarters and Miss Keating's neat, dormered apartment, the spacious salons had never been used. A grand ballroom took up most of the space, its parquet floor unmarred by dancers' feet. A nursery and a small schoolroom waited silently for the heir she was to produce, and Lyla spent as little time as possible there.

What she really wanted to see was the belvedere and its guard. Where was the stairway that led to the small, windowed cubicle overlooking Foxe Hollow's vast pasturelands? The only people she ever saw were Frazier and his two servants, and occasionally the three men who rode in and out to tend their ranching duties.

And of course she saw herself in her vanity mirror, an Irish lass who was fading like a flower plucked and hung to dry. Since the housekeeper never failed to cook unappetizing foods, and since Lyla had no desire to eat the confections Frazier plied her with, her stylish gowns now hung so loosely they dragged on the floor when she walked. The bridal portrait was a mockery, for the rosy-cheeked young woman in the picture no longer existed.

One afternoon she parted the lace curtains in the sitting room and gazed out. Connor Foxe was riding by on his prancing sorrel stallion, framed by a brilliant blue sky. He noticed the movement in the window and wheeled his horse around to look at her. In the sunlight, the dark waves of his hair and his obsidian eyes sparkled with life as he grinned at her. He waved, and Lyla was so glad to see a friendly face—even the face of a man who sickened her—that she gave him a halting wave in return.

"Do we have a visitor?" Frazier said from behind her.

Lyla turned to see him standing in the vestibule archway, regally clad and groomed, as always. "Only Connor, passing by on his horse."

"Ah. He must be looking better to you as time goes by. Soon, my sweet . . . soon you may have as much of him as you want."

Hardened by the last few weeks of his honeyed taunts, she ignored his remark. "Why doesn't your brother ever visit the house?" she asked. "Surely, until the ewes come in for lambing, he and the men have little to do."

"He knows his place," Foxe replied coolly. "We share the same name as an accident of birth, but when I brought him to this country I set his boundaries and

256

he accepted them. By mutual consent, our only ties concern the sheep."

Lyla felt her cheeks coloring. "But you'll share your *wife* with him? You'll allow him to beget your heir?"

"Another partnership that is strictly business, dear-heart. And no business of yours to question."

"And where will this mating take place?" she demanded. "In the bunkhouse? Will I be forced to sneak out like a—"

"No. I'll escort you there myself. We'll tell the staff I'm showing you the facilities, explaining things before the flocks come in for the lambing and shearing."

Her pulse pounded weakly in her temples as she thought ahead. "To maintain appearances, we'll have to return to the house together. I suppose you intend to *watch* . . . probably take your damn sketch-pad!"

"What a capital idea!" Frazier's gray eyes glittered as he mocked her. "Who else has a visual record of the moment his son was conceived? And Kelly and Nate—why, they'd pay top dollar to have such alluring artwork on the walls beside their bunks."

"You are the most despicable—" Lyla whirled on her heel and stomped past him, nearly knocking into Hollingsworth as she headed toward the stairs.

She spent the rest of the day in her room, gazing wistfully out over pastures that were dusted with snow. The sunshine dulled with cold as evening shadows fell. Aromas of boiled beef and cabbage drifted upstairs, but Lyla refused to go down to dinner. She might as well starve . . . emaciate herself to the point that Connor wouldn't have her . . . allow herself to drift into a safe, dreamlike state where the horrors of her imprisonment would no longer trouble her, and finally pass on to her peace. It seemed the only way to escape, the only way to reunite with the man she loved.

257

When Miss Keating carried a dinner tray to her with a haughty sniff, Lyla left the linen napkin over it. Slowly she donned her nightgown, and then sat at the vanity brushing her long hair as though she were preparing for an amorous evening with Barry. He lived on in her mind, virile and strong and handsome, as he'd been during their first flirtations at the Golden Rose. It could do no harm to fantasize about him this way, since the only happiness she would ever find was the memory of his laughter and fond caress.

She climbed into bed to watch the sliver of a moon rise. She lay straight down the center of the bed with her hands clasped beneath her breast—a coffinlike pose, she realized, but it seemed so appropriate. It was January thirtieth or thirty-first—she had little need to know which. In only two weeks she'd have her last glimpse of reality at her wedding, and then return to Foxe Hollow to remain entombed here forever.

Lyla drifted off, visions of herself and Thompson sweetening her dreams. She felt the downy curls on his chest, the rough stubble on his cheeks, the satiny wetness of lips that roamed her body with the subtle sureness of a lover perfectly attuned to her wants and senses. He smelled leathery and masculine, evoking her own personal perfume with the heat of his muscled body. She ached to wrap her legs around him, to feel him thrusting inside her until they writhed in an impassioned frenzy.

She moaned, shifting beneath the sheets, which caused a rhythmic rustling that spurred her imagination, and—what was that sound on the fringes of her awareness? Footsteps? Scraping, not outside her door but on the roof, alongside her window. He was coming for her! Barry was here to rescue her from—

Lyla heard a tapping on the glass, and then the solid *thunk* of a boot heel on the casement, and suddenly her room whistled with a chilling wind that brought her out of her slumber. She shook her head, trying to focus on the lean figure that was shutting the window and then stealing through the shadows toward her bed.

But it was too short, too compact to be Thompson. Fully awake now, her eyes widened as the intruder instinctively clapped his hand over her scream.

"Ready and waiting?" Connor crooned. With his free hand he drew back the covers to gaze at her. "Satin and lace, all warm and wet from thinking about me today. God, you're beautiful. When I saw you in the window I knew you were hungry for me, too, so I—"

Lyla bit his fingers so he'd yank them away, and then she screamed as loudly as she could.

Enraged, Foxe lunged and covered her mouth with his own as he fumbled for the hem of her nightgown. "You little bitch, you know you want me—"

As he forced his tongue between her teeth, his hand stole up her thigh to the apex of her legs. Lyla struggled, hoping what she heard was a key in her door, but Connor's murmurings blocked the sounds.

Then there were rapid footsteps and Hollingsworth's loud cry. "Get off her, you foul—Frazier! Mr. Foxe, sir, come quickly!"

Connor remained sprawled over the top of her, raising only his head. "Get out of here, old man," he snarled, "this is none of your affair. I could pinch your windpipe shut before you could swing one wrinkled fist at me."

"You'll do no such thing," Frazier's crisp voice replied. There was the click of a pistol hammer, and then the room filled with lamplight and a tense silence. "Get out of her bed, slowly, with no tricks. We'll discuss this downstairs, unless you'd like me to end this embarrassment with a bullet."

Connor's face was reddened with rage, but he rose, never taking his eyes from his stepbrother. "No call to get on your high horse," he muttered. "Only

259

claiming what you promised me. I've waited long enough, by God."

As he approached the door, Frazier glanced her way. "See what comes of waving out the window? Someday you'll learn, Miss Lyla."

He left, his disgruntled brother in front of him, and Lyla hastily pulled the covers up over her exposed body. Hollingsworth was pinker than usual, averting his eyes, yet lingering in her room.

"Are . . . are you all right, Miss O'Riley?" he finally stammered.

"Yes, thank you." Lyla shuddered, not daring to wonder what would've happened had the valet not heard her cries. "You were very brave. I've seen him kill a man much larger and stronger than you. And he enjoyed doing it."

Hollingsworth's eyes widened. "I'll have locks installed on all the windows immediately, miss."

"Thank you. I—I'll be fine now."

They exchanged a hesitant glance, each realizing that too much had been said. Then the valet bowed out, leaving her alone, and more terrified than ever.

When Lyla went downstairs late the next morning, the house rang with unusual silence. The dining room table had already been cleared of breakfast—if it had even been served. She smelled no aroma from the kitchen, heard no clatter of pans or conversation between the servants. Frazier's typewriter was still, and a glance into his study told her he hadn't spent his customary time reviewing the accounts or tending to correspondence.

She turned back toward the kitchen to find Hollingsworth watching her, his hands clasped before him and his face as pink and serene as a sleeping baby's. "Good morning, miss. Shall I see to your breakfast?"

Lyla peered behind him, puzzled. "Am I so late

260

that Miss Keating's already cleared away the food?"

The valet smiled slightly. "It's the first of the month," he explained. "Mr. Foxe and his step-brother make the rounds of all the sheepherders, with their pay and supplies. They leave very early and return very late, so Miss Keating and I generally take the day off."

Already Lyla's mind was racing with the possibilities this information presented. Her pulse sped up and she fought a giddy grin as she replied to the staid servant. "Well then, I won't trouble you—"

"Oh, it's no trouble, Miss Lyla. Mr. Foxe left strict instructions that you were to be watched at all times. We drew straws, and Miss Keating will begin her shift late this afternoon."

"Oh. Of course." Disappointment choked her. How could she have been foolish enough to think Frazier would leave her unattended for even a moment? Yet there had to be a way around these elderly guardians . . .

Lyla lowered her eyes, taking on the submissive, proper attitude Oliver Hollingsworth would expect. "I—I don't know how anyone thinks I'll get very far without a coat, or a horse. And why would I want to leave? Frazier's a very generous man who took me in when I was destitute and alone."

The servant shifted, his face coloring somewhat. "I've taken the liberty of packing you some food, Miss O'Riley," he said quietly. "Your coat and pants have been laundered, and you may ride my gelding, Dickens. And might I suggest that time is of the essence?"

She stared into blue eyes that were beseeching and compassionate, yet Foxe's valet otherwise appeared to be his standoffish self. "I—I don't understand."

"If you dawdle, and Miss Keating discovers our conspiracy, all could be lost."

Her heart leaped, and she stepped forward to be sure he wasn't a phantom of her imagination.

"You're letting me get away?" she asked in a hoarse whisper. "But when Frazier finds out I escaped, he'll fire you, or—or—"

Hollingsworth shrugged. "The alternatives don't really bother me, Miss Lyla. Last night's intrusion confirmed my suspicions about the nature of your, er, *betrothal*, and I can no longer be a witness to such unconscionable acts."

Lyla grabbed his slender hands and squeezed them. "But why? Please—tell me this isn't another cruel trick."

For the first time since she arrived, Oliver Hollingsworth the Third relaxed his stiff stance and leaned into their whispered conversation. "I knew something was amiss when you arrived smelling of smoke and looking so . . . unkempt. Mr. Foxe would never tolerate such negligence in the woman he was to wed, unless he was misrepresenting his intentions. After overhearing snatches of your conversations and seeing that—*display*—of sketches in his chambers, I've come to suspect that my employer isn't the upstanding man he claims to be. And that you, Miss Lyla, will be severely compromised if you remain here."

"Thank you. *Thank you,*" she replied in a tight whisper. "I thought I'd signed my obituary when I put my name on those agreements."

Hollingsworth glanced behind him, as though he thought Allegra might be eavesdropping. "Were I in your place, miss, I'd see that those papers disappeared as well."

"But his attorney's signed—"

"That's a forgery. Mr. Foxe doesn't trust attorneys, and I daresay every document in his files is of his own making," the valet stated matter-of-factly. "His artistic talent enables him to imitate any signature he ever saw. And I've come to realize of late that he'd have no qualms about using that ability toward covert ends."

Her heart was pounding with this unexpected turn of events, but she'd get caught before she left Foxe Hollow unless she anticipated all of Frazier's snares. She released Hollingsworth's hands and paced a few steps, thinking. "What about Nate and Kelly? If they catch me borrowing your horse—"

"They've left for their monthly excursion into Colorado Springs, to squander their pay on cheap whiskey and expensive women."

Lyla chuckled at his unexpected wittiness. "And what about the guard in the belvedere? Frazier told me . . ." The valet's furrowed forehead confirmed her recent suspicions. "There isn't one, is there? That was another of his lies, another intimidation."

"I'm afraid so, Miss Lyla," he replied with a shake of his bald head. "What a beastly boring job *that* would be! Mr. Foxe goes up there on occasion to survey the pastures and remind himself how bloody rich he is. If you can be extremely quiet, we'll go up and have a look. Allegra's in her room. If she suspects what we're doing, our goose is cooked."

Silently Lyla followed him up the grand staircase, on past the second-floor landing to the third story, carefully avoiding the spots she knew to be squeaky. Hollingsworth peered toward the housekeeper's apartment. Then, with a finger upon his lips, he gestured for her to follow him to a doorway she hadn't noticed when she was up here cleaning.

The uncarpeted stairs made their footsteps echo in the short, cramped stairwell, and then they ascended into a boxlike room where the uncurtained windows were nearly as large as each of the four walls. The only furnishing was a padded windowseat that went around the entire belvedere.

Lyla gazed about, astounded at the view from this lofty perch. Foxe Hollow stretched in every direction: the sheep buildings were to her right, the arched entry gate was ahead of her, and otherwise the rolling, snow-powdered foothills were uninterrupted for as far as she could see.

Hollingsworth stood beside her, pointing between the gate and the sheep compound. "No doubt James at the guard post will return you to the house at gunpoint, if he sees you. Best to cut across—do you see that distant flock, and the canvas-covered wagon?"

She nodded, thinking they looked like toys from here.

"Frazier and his brother will have stopped there already with their supplies. That particular herder has a surly disposition, but he's your best bet for a temporary hiding place and directions out of Foxe Hollow."

"What's his name?" she murmured.

"Jack Rafferty. That's what he's told us, anyway." Hollingsworth focused his clear blue eyes on hers. "Any questions? We'd best be leaving before Allegra suspects hanky-panky."

When the old gent winked, she had to stifle a laugh. Who'd have thought Foxe's prim valet would assist her, after all these weeks when he'd seemed to have barely tolerated her presence? Lyla descended the narrow stairway as quietly as her pumps would allow, pausing at the bottom for Hollingsworth.

"And what might you two be about?" a sour voice accosted them from across the hall. Miss Keating, dressed in her perennial gray, stood watching them from her doorway as though she did indeed suspect they'd been up to no good.

Hollingsworth resumed his formal manner and tone. "Miss O'Riley became distraught when she learned Mr. Foxe had gone out for the day," he explained. "I was showing her the ranch, telling her about the monthly rounds."

"I never realized how *huge* his estate was," Lyla chimed in with a coy smile. "Why, a person could wander lost for days and die of exposure before being found."

"Keep it in mind," Allegra replied pointedly.

"These old bones tell me another storm's blowing in."

"A good day for cozying up to the fire with a pot of tea and your crocheting," the valet commented. "Miss O'Riley plans to read in her room now, I believe."

"Yes, a book from Frazier's collection." With a nod, Lyla descended the main stairway ahead of her newfound ally, careful not to betray her excitement by walking too fast. She was leaving! At long last she could escape this prison and return to reality.

"Meet me in the pantry when you've changed," the valet whispered as he walked past her. "Quietly, now. Miss Keating listens through the floor."

Lyla closed her bedroom door behind her and immediately removed her pumps. Hollingsworth had been thinking this escapade through, because Mick's clothes were neatly folded in the bottom of her armoire and her polished boots stood beside them. Within moments she was wearing the familiar clothing and hanging up her gown, so it wouldn't appear she'd left. Her heart pounded with the prospect of riding off, but she couldn't get careless or overconfident. Checking the second-floor hallway, Lyla quickly slipped downstairs, boots in hand.

The valet pressed a bundle into her arms as soon as she ducked into the larder off the kitchen. "I'd waste no time, miss. Those clouds look gray and full of snow. Take this back exit to the stables."

She gazed gratefully at the old gentleman as she pulled her boots on. "What will you tell Allegra when she finds me gone?"

"She thinks I'm a doddering old fogey. I'll take a nap while reading a newspaper, and she'll go along with it." The valet smiled, his cheeks coloring. "I . . . I proposed to Allegra shortly after we met here. Assumed she'd want some companionship in this isolated outpost as much as I did, but she only sniffed as though I were a moldy old bone. Has her cap set for

Mr. Foxe, she does, and he strings her along with his compliments, so I doubt she'll be sorry to see you go. She fancies herself as the mistress of Foxe Hollow, so your competition wasn't exactly welcome."

Lyla's eyes widened. "Do you suppose he'll ever marry her?"

"Never had the least intention of it," Hollingsworth stated. "Gives her little trinkets, buying her loyalty, but the three of us will roll about in this cavernous house like peas in a hatbox, cold and unattached until we pass on. Damned unnatural, it is. That's why you don't belong here, Miss Lyla. Now scoot, before Miss Keating comes downstairs."

"But the papers—"

"Right here. I gathered them together while you were changing."

Lyla slipped the packet inside her coat, gazing at him with a concern she never dreamed she'd feel for the stiff-lipped servant. "If—if Frazier fires you, come to Cripple. We'll find you a job. I can't possibly repay this—"

"No long good-byes, now," he said kindly. "Godspeed, and don't worry about me. I'm about to fall asleep over my paper and haven't the foggiest notion how you slipped out. Just a doddering old fogey, you know."

On an impulse she kissed his cheek and was rewarded with a flash of twinkling blue eyes she'd never forget. Then she pushed open the door and dashed toward the stables. Toward freedom!

Chapter 22

The moment she mounted Dickens, Hollingsworth's gelding, she missed Calico. Touching as the valet's generosity was, it didn't make up for the horse's skittishness or his aversion to going faster than a bone-jarring trot. Lyla urged him past the sheep buildings, and with a last glance at the mansion, she pointed him toward the open range.

First she tried patience. "Come on, Dickens, old chap," she said, mimicking his master's accent. "Pick up those hooves and show Hollingsworth what a fine gift he gave me. He's probably watching us."

The horse shook his gray head and insisted on circling back to the stables.

"No! No!" she cried. Tugging the reins across his loosely-fleshed neck, Lyla forced him back in the direction of the sheepherder's wagon. "You'd better step lively, or we'll get caught in this storm!"

The horse knew that, of course, and as the wind whipped around them Lyla understood his apprehension perfectly. The gray sky hung low with pregnant clouds that hovered just above the hills ahead of them. The poor nag was probably never ridden except on a rare trip into town, and his rolling eyes and nickers of protest made her feel truly sympathetic. But she *had* to get away from Foxe Hollow!

Reluctantly the gelding plodded on, until the first huge snowflakes struck his nose. Dickens snorted and shook, and when Lyla saw he was heading toward a grove of trees, she had to steer him away so he couldn't knock her off or scrape her leg against the rough bark. The snow thickened, and when they crested the next hilltop she grew increasingly nervous. Where was that wagon? From the belvedere, it had appeared to be on a straight diagonal path from the house, and now it was gone!

She had no choice but to keep riding. Intuition told her it was well past one, and she'd started out shortly after eleven. Even Dickens should've gotten her to Jack Rafferty's by now—if they could only find it! The snow was pelting them, blowing horizontally in a thick, white wall, and her earlier words about wandering lost until she died of exposure haunted her.

"We've *got* to locate that wagon, boy," she muttered as she turned her collar up around her neck. "I'll be damned if I'll give Frazier the satisfaction of finding me frozen!"

The horse rumbled a reply, his head lowered to keep the thick flakes out of his eyes. They'd slowed to a walk because it was pointless to proceed any faster when her visibility extended only a few feet beyond the gelding's gray nose. Her hands were going numb inside Mick's gloves. Her toes were so cold she could no longer feel them. Her cheeks and lips felt like they'd crack if she opened her mouth. Perhaps they should take shelter behind a hill until the blizzard blew out . . . but thoughts of becoming a human icicle spurred her on.

Then the horse's ears stood at attention and he broke into a trot, his nose quivering. Lyla strained to see what he'd spotted, shielding her eyes with her hand, but they were several yards farther along before she could distinguish between the white mounds

268

near the ground and the whiteness whirling around them.

"Sheep! Good boy, Dickens!" She kneed his sides, reveling in the sight of a valley filled with thousands of huddling woollybacks. Their bawling shifted with the wind, a constant, guttural sound she hadn't heard since she'd left home. In the distance, two dogs were barking as they herded the huge flock into the sheltered area behind a range of low foothills for protection.

Giddily she searched for the wagon and gasped when Dickens nearly plowed into it. The house on wheels was the size of a prairie schooner, and in the blowing snow its ribbed canvas top resembled a huge, fleecy ewe. "Easy, boy . . . let's find the side where you'll be out of the wind."

Lyla dismounted and hastily fastened Dickens' reins to a back wheel. Since the dogs were still barking, she knew Jack would also be out seeing to the sheep, so she entered his wagon without knocking.

The place wasn't fancy, but to her wind-glazed eyes it seemed a palace. The small cookstove beside the door greeted her warmly; two pairs of heavy socks were draped over its rack, which accounted for the smell of wet wool that filled the wagon. Alongside the stove was a compartment filled with firewood. Numerous sacks of flour, coffee, beans, and other supplies on the countertop told her Frazier and Connor had already been here. The opposite side of the wagon also housed food and a shelf crammed with books. An unmade bunk stretched across the far end. There was a square flap in the canvas above it, which probably served as a window in warmer weather. Beneath the bed were some drawers and a small pull-out table, which still had an egg-smeared plate and a tin cup on it.

"Well, Jack, you're no housekeeper, but you've a

cozy home anyway," she murmured. Lyla hung her damp coat over one of his two chairs and stood her wet boots beside the stove, her eyes in constant motion. Rafferty played the harmonica. Dozens of tattered dime novels and magazines were crammed into his shelf, along with works by Hawthorne, Shakespeare, Poe, and another book so worn she couldn't read its spine.

The book fell open; it was *Memoirs of Fanny Hill.* As Lyla skimmed a scene so blatantly erotic her eyes bugged, she wondered what sort of man Hollingsworth had sent her to. Gingerly she replaced the volume on the shelf and set about straightening his compact, efficiently-designed home—the least she could do as his uninvited guest. Outside, the wind blew so hard the canvas canopy above her rumbled continuously, yet the stove kept the wagon's interior quite cozy. Lyla put a few logs in the fire, started a fresh pot of coffee, and then sat across the bed to read the newspaper her host had left spread upon it.

She was immediately sorry. This issue of the *Rocky Mountain News*, dated January tenth, featured a lengthy story about the disappearance of Marshal Barry Thompson, who was presumed a victim of foul play. The story recounted his efforts to solve the Golden Rose robbery . . . mentioned her as his escort back to Cripple . . . quoted Dr. Dwight Geary about Barry's weakened physical condition following his gunshot wounds and short hospital stay.

Tears were running in a continuous stream down her windburnt face. This was almost too coincidental: the paper was out of date but still fresh enough to have been delivered just this morning. Had Frazier anticipated her escape and brought this particular issue here to torment her? Highly unlikely, yet in her exhausted, miserable state, Lyla could allow that Foxe was indeed capable of such emotional tyranny.

Laying the paper aside, Lyla pulled the quilts up

around her and sat with her back against the taut canvas wall. It was poor strategy to let Rafferty find her crying. Hollingsworth had said he was surly, had hinted that he might be using an alias, as though he had reason to hide his identity. She should remain alert and prepared. A man who entertained himself with such bawdy companions as "Fanny Hill" might forget his manners if he found a real woman in his bunk.

She reached into her coat pocket and pulled out the packet of papers Hollingsworth gave her. Here was the forged premarital agreement and Frazier's will . . . and the thick, oblong chunk at the bottom of the envelope was her stack of twenties! Saints above, old Hollingsworth hadn't stiffed her after all! Two or three other documents were folded down there, too, but sounds of movement and muttering outside the wagon made Lyla stuff the envelope and loose papers under the mattress edge behind her.

She'd hardly gotten them hidden before two dogs charged through the wagon's door, snarling and barking. Border collies, they were, the breed her family herded with at home, and the ordinarily lovable animals would tear her to shreds if she gave them the least hint she'd harm their sheep or their master.

And when Lyla saw Jack Rafferty, she was both frightened and fascinated. He approached with his Winchester aimed at her chest. Beneath his snow-covered hat glared two of the cruelest, most alluring brown eyes she'd ever seen.

"Who the hell're you? And what're you doing in my bunk?" He stopped a few feet behind the dogs, which were still growling, their hair bristling along their backs.

"I—please don't shoot!" she said in a squeaky voice. "I've nowhere else to go! No safe place to hide!"

"And who might you be hiding from?"

Lyla glanced at the snarling dogs, now at the edge of the bed, and then back to her host. She suspected that beneath his heavy, snow-covered coat he was deceptively powerful for his size. His wet black hair dragged on his shoulders and his thick mustache curved downward past his rugged chin in two menacing lines, framing a mouth that was cunning and lush despite his unwavering scowl. Could she confide in this dangerous-looking man?

"Cat got your tongue? Or shall my dogs find it for you?"

"Frazier Foxe," she rasped. "He—he's forcing me to marry him and I'd rather kill myself."

With unhurried grace he lowered his rifle. "You're smarter than you look, then. Maudie! Will! That's enough."

The dogs sat down, watching her silently as their master stepped back to shut the wagon door. After standing his rifle against the wall, he removed his coat and hat, revealing a black-and-red checked shirt and jeans that left no doubt as to his muscular, masculine build.

"Thank you, Mr. Rafferty," she murmured.

He turned, one eyebrow cocked. "And how'd you know *that?*"

"Hollingsworth told me. He—he said you'd help me leave Foxe Hollow. Without getting caught."

"What's in it for me?"

Lyla's jaw dropped. Of all the nervy—

"Get out from under those covers. No woman sleeps with me till I've had a look at her."

"*Sleep* with you? I was only—" Rankled now, Lyla tossed off the quilts and rose to her full height in front of the bunk. "If you think for one minute I came here to—"

"Do you see another bed?" Rafferty's gaze raked over her and then he looked again, slowly, assessing. "Presumptuous little piece, aren't you? I should just kick your ass out, because sure as I'm standing

272

here Foxe'll come after you."

"But there's a blizzard—"

"Should've thought of that before you left his fine mansion." Jack's coffee-colored eyes mocked her while he stroked the sides of his mustache, as though contemplating his options. "Yep, I should just march you right back to the house at gunpoint, little lady. Never figured Foxe had such fine taste in females, but you'll be worth a wad of cash if I return you. If I don't, my ass'll be grass. Foxe doesn't like it when his underlings hold out on him."

What he said was true, but she hated hearing it. As he crossed his arms, waiting for her reply, Lyla wondered if chivalry had died with Barry Thompson. This man with the brazen gaze was giving her a choice between freezing to death or returning to Frazier, even though he seemed to despise the ranch's owner as much as she did.

The two dogs watched her expectantly. Outside, the blather of the sheep was low and continuous as several moments passed. The wind whistled against the wagon's canvas top. The coffee boiled on the stove, its vapor warm and inviting. Assuming Jack Rafferty would help her was turning out to be another unfortunate mistake she'd pay dearly for. "What do you want?" she mumbled.

"What've you got?"

So many impertinent questions this man had! Lyla thought quickly, because being escorted back to Frazier's was the last thing she wanted. "I—I made you some coffee. Perhaps you'll feel more civil when you're warm."

He grunted, and using one of his wool socks as a hot pad, he poured the steaming brew into the tin cup from the table. Then he lifted the chair from in front of his dogs and turned it so he could sit facing her. "You pups go on, now. This fugitive didn't come here to visit you," he said with fond gruffness.

She quickly reached out to stroke the nearest dog's

head. "We have border collies on our sheep ranch in Ireland. Fine dogs, they are. None smarter, and extremely loyal."

"That one's Maudie," Rafferty commented, his tone gentler now. "And this tricolor's Will. Who might you be?"

She saw little point in lying, so she gave her host a hopeful smile. "Lyla O'Riley, and I—"

"What brings you to Foxe Hollow? Thought you'd latch onto Frazier's money, only to discover he's not such a catch after all?"

"*No!* I—" Lyla glared at the ebony-haired scoundrel whose mustachioed smile curved mockingly behind his coffee cup. "Foxe had me kidnapped, because I know too much. See this article about Barry Thompson in the paper?" she entreated, hoping she didn't get weepy before she finished. "Well, Foxe and his men killed the marshal a few weeks ago. And since I was a witness, he can't very well let me return to Cripple, now, can he?"

"Thompson's really dead?" Jack Rafferty eyed her warily and then reached for the stack of yellowed newspapers on the bookshelf beside him. After rapidly riffling through them he paused at one, and then stared at her. "You're *this* Lyla? Wanted for that bunged-up robbery and murder attempt on Christmas Eve?"

"The very one."

"Well, I'll be—hot *damn!*" Rafferty banged his tin cup onto the table and extended his hand, his dusky face alight with pleasure. "I've been following your story, thinking that Belle Starr's got nothing on *you* for grit. And here you are in my wagon!"

His handshake was so exuberant that Lyla gasped. Jack Rafferty had suddenly elevated her to the status of a notorious outlaw, and his excitement was contagious. Both dogs hopped onto the bunk with her, their thick tails thumping against the mattress as they pawed at her arms.

274

"That's right, pups, shake the lady's hand!" Rafferty crowed. "I've read these articles to them, and they're damn glad to meet you!"

She first shook the paw of the black and white female, Maudie, who immediately licked her cheek. Will, who was heavier and colored more like a traditional collie, gazed at her with solemn brown eyes, as though he were honored to be meeting her. Lyla laughed and looked at her host again. "None of those charges are true, you know. All I did was—"

"Hell, the papers're full of lies," he said with a wave of his hand, "but they're the best entertainment we've got out here on the range. And you say Frazier Foxe killed Thompson? Doesn't surprise me. Why, the dogs won't let him set foot in this wagon, he smells so wicked. Has to leave my supplies outside when he comes around each month, and that half-brother of his isn't much better."

It was good to be accepted as this man's friend, yet the casual way he referred to Barry's death made her lip go quivery. Lyla looked at Maudie to avoid Rafferty's gaze, stroking the dog's silky coat to soothe herself. The high-spirited heroine he'd set her up to be wouldn't sniffle forlornly, now that he wasn't going to march her back to Frazier's. But he sounded so glad Barry was gone.

Jack's dark eyes lingered on her, and in a quieter voice he said, "That fancy ring's from the robbery, isn't it? And if it hadn't been snatched, Thompson was supposed to give it to you, according to the papers. I—I don't cotton to lawmen much, but I'm truly sorry Frazier Foxe killed your sweetheart, Lyla. And I never had the slightest intention of taking you back to him. Sometimes I carry on."

He stood and took his cup to a bucket of water near the stove, and Lyla watched him wash and carefully dry it before he refilled it with hot coffee. Then he brought it to her, smiling kindly. "I reckon you need this as much as I do. Poor manners on my part, but

275

I've only got the one cup."

Gratefully she accepted the steaming, fragrant gift. Who *was* this man? One moment he seemed a threat and the next he was pandering to her. Lyla sipped the coffee and let out a sigh. "You were right about me being presumptuous, Mr. Rafferty," she said quietly. "I was so eager to escape Frazier's mansion I never gave a thought to the trouble I'd be, barging in on you. You've only limited food, and—"

"Forget this noise, Lyla. And the name's Jack," he said jovially. "I just got a month's grub, and it's a treat to have company—the likes of you, no less! Just make yourself at home."

He paused, arranging his chair so he could lean on its back while straddling it, studying her with a grin that flickered like firelight. Then he cleared his throat a little nervously. "You . . . won't be staying long, will you?"

"Why no, I—"

"Good! I mean—" He raked his hair back with his fingers, laughing under his breath. "It's just that Frazier's bound to come looking for you soon as this blizzard lifts—"

"I know that."

"—and as for me, well—" Rafferty's gaze intensified and he stroked his mustache. "Damn it, you're a fine-looking filly, Lyla, and it's been so blasted long since I had one I might not be able to keep my pants fastened. You hear what I'm saying?"

"Loud and clear," she mumbled.

"And I wish you'd button that shirt, for Chrissakes."

"Oh!" Her cheeks scalded as she glanced down at her bosom, but Jack Rafferty's loud guffaws confirmed that she was, in truth, properly covered.

His brown eyes glimmered as he wiped at them, still chuckling uncontrollably. "I couldn't resist, honey. I believe your shirt buttons must be working as hard as the ones on my fly—"

"That's quite enough of this talk!" Lyla crossed her arms, bumping the dogs' heads as she squared her shoulders. "I'm nobody's whore, Mr. Rafferty. And by the saints, if you treat me like one, I'll—I'll throw that copy of *Fanny Hill* in the stove!"

Jack's eyes widened. "You wouldn't deprive a solitary man of his finest entertainment?"

"Watch me! I've defended myself against thieves and murderers, and you'll be no trouble at all!" Where this rush of bravado came from, Lyla had no idea, and she hoped Jack didn't see through it for the facade it was. He looked humbled for now, but when night fell and dinner was over and they had nothing but each other to look at, she would be defenseless if he chose to pleasure himself in exchange for his hospitality.

Rafferty rose, his cheeks tinted with resentment. "It was only a joke, Miss O'Riley," he muttered as he placed his hat on his thick mane of hair. "Come on, pups, we'll check those woollybacks. Maybe our guest would be so kind as to rustle up our supper while we're out. Seems the least she could do to earn her keep."

Lyla watched the door close behind them, shivering in the sudden snowy draft. Mr. Rafferty had a coarse sense of humor, along with a temper that flared like wildfire. But she had nowhere else to go in this impossible weather, and no one else to help her. And only one narrow bunk in a cramped little wagon.

It was going to be a long night.

Chapter 23

The dogs kept them from becoming predator and prey. By the time the two wet, panting animals bounded into the wagon, Lyla had found milk and eggs among the fresh supplies and was stirring a bowl of flapjack batter. Bacon crackled in the cast-iron skillet, and as Rafferty removed his snow-covered coat and hat, the rich aromas seemed to soothe him.

He glanced at the food, inhaling deeply. "What's that smell from the oven?"

"Cobbler. Foxe left you a big bag of dried apples and apricots." Some of the wildness left his eyes and Lyla knew she'd done the right thing by spending the past two hours at the stove.

Jack smoothed his hair and then rubbed an old towel over Maudie and Will, baby-talking as he dried them. He stole glances at her, and watched intently as the first rounds of batter sizzled in the hot skillet. "I took your horse behind the next rise, where mine's tied. He'll be out of the wind there, and Foxe won't see him when he comes around. Storm's letting up now."

"Thank you." Bubbles appeared on the doughy tops of her pancakes and Lyla flipped them expertly, showing off a bit. "Hope you're hungry. I ended up with more batter than I intended."

278

"Woman, I can devour everything you've got," he replied with a suggestive laugh. "But I always share with the pups. And you, of course."

"Good. When I realized Hollingsworth was helping me escape, I didn't exactly sit down to a leisurely breakfast."

Rafferty apparently considered her cooking reason enough for a truce. Long after Lyla could hold no more of their simple supper, her host was sopping up maple syrup with flapjacks and stuffing whole strips of bacon into his mouth with an ecstatic grin.

Now that he wasn't badgering her, Jack was darkly handsome, a man who savored his pleasures. When he finally pushed his plate away, he sat back and closed his eyes with a contented sigh. His long, black lashes curved down to his cheeks and his lips parted slightly . . . the sheer sensuality of him made her tremble, which in turn shocked her. He could never be the kind, gentle lover Barry Thompson was, and how could she even *think* of him in that way?

He half-opened one eye, acknowledging the two dogs who sat attentively beside the table. "Will, can you ask for a flapjack?" he murmured lazily.

The dog's tan face came to life and he sat up on his haunches.

"Say grace before you eat, boy."

To Lyla's delight, the collie placed his front paws alongside his head and gave several short, rumbling barks, and he received half a pancake. "Why, you must spend hours working with him!"

"What else do we have to do out here?" Jack answered. "Maudie and Will are the only company I keep for days on end. We drive sheep together, we curl up together on these cold nights. Seems only fitting that we should be able to share our fun, too. But Maudie's the smart one—sings for her supper, don't you, girl?"

The smaller collie's ears perked up; her dark eyes glowed in a face that looked like glossy black velvet.

"Do you suppose Lyla'd rather hear 'Silent Night' or 'Swanee River'?" he asked as he reached for the harmonica on the shelf behind him. He smiled at her, his teeth white and even beneath his devilish mustache. "Or maybe, since she served up such a fine meal, we could do both. Ladies like to be serenaded, so I hear."

Her cheeks tingled and then she was chuckling. Maudie was howling soulfully, her nose pointed toward the canvas ceiling as she followed Jack's soft musical accompaniment. When the song ended, Lyla clapped loudly. "Good girl, Maudie. A touching rendition of my favorite Christmas carol!"

"You recognized it?" Jack asked.

"Why, of course!" She tore a flapjack in half and watched the dog eat it hungrily. "And I can't wait for 'Swanee River.' I suppose she dances soft-shoe to that one?"

"Why of course," he echoed, and the mischievous flicker across his face told of his approval more clearly than any words. Lyla lowered her gaze, stunned by the intensity of this man's powerful brown eyes.

"All right, girl, let's really show it off," he said as he stood up. A few bars of introduction were Maudie's cue, and then she was on her hind legs, yipping more or less to the rhythm as she and Rafferty circled each other in the center of the wagon. He was a changed man from the sinister sheepherder who'd accosted her with a rifle, a man who took proud pleasure in the accomplishments of his pets and joined in their tricks without the least concern about appearing foolish.

As she applauded with sincere delight, he took a bow and then sat down. "Good work, pups. We'll let you eat in peace now. You've had a hard day."

When the dogs' noses were buried in battered pans filled with leftovers, Rafferty cleared the table. He set a kettle of water on to heat and glanced at her as she closed the flour sack. "I truly appreciated that meal, Lyla. Where'd you learn to cook that way?"

"My brother Mick had a stomach as cavernous as the gold mine he worked," she replied quietly. "And since he was kind enough to bring me along when he stowed away to America, I raised a garden and preserved the vegetables and cooked as best I could on his worker's wage."

"A woman running from her past, eh?" he said in a teasing tone. As he started washing dishes, though, he grew more serious. "What happened to your brother?"

"He died in the Angel Claire explosion."

Rafferty's eyes mellowed as he studied her, the plate he was washing suspended above the pan of suds. "I . . . I'm sorry to hear that, honey."

Lyla's eyes were misting, but she looked up at him anyway, hoping he'd understand her desperate plight rather than complicating it. "I found out, after Foxe had me kidnapped, that he masterminded that whole ordeal. Bribed Nigel Grath with opium to blow sixteen innocent men to kingdom come. And do you know why?" she asked bitterly.

He shook his head, his expression softening.

"He wanted to stir up so much labor unrest that Thompson couldn't handle it. Get him ousted when people complained about the marshal's incompetence."

Jack scowled. "When I consider the various lawmen I've avoided, I surely wouldn't call Thompson incompetent."

"Exactly," she stated, her voice wavering now. "And when the explosion only proved what a capable, compassionate man Barry was, Foxe and his ranchhands set up the robbery during the McClanahans' wedding party. They figured to kill the marshal as he pursued the thieves, but I stitched up his wounds and got us *both* in trouble by foiling another of his plans. So Frazier struck again, and this time he . . . succeeded. I—I'm sorry."

Lyla turned away to cry, and then two arms encircled her, two damp hands pulled her back against a solid chest. Rafferty rocked her as though she were a small child, yet his tough, muscular body was only inches taller than her own.

"You cry all you want, honey," he murmured against her ear. "God knows you've earned the right, after all that bastard's done to you. And for what?" he muttered. "Meanness, that's all it is. I suspected he and Connor had more going than just sheep ranching when I signed on here, but what could I say? I didn't exactly tell them all my business, either."

Lyla sniffled and hicced, letting his low voice soothe her. His embrace was warm and comforting, but she'd give the wrong impression if she let him continue to hold her this way. Wiping her eyes with her knuckles, she turned to look at him. "A man running from his past, eh?" she repeated softly. "Yet he tends sheep and treats his dogs like his babies."

Jack eased his arms away, his smile secretive. "Men herd sheep for three reasons, honey. They've either got quirks enough that society doesn't accept them, or they've got ambitions to sink their pay into a spread of their own someday."

"Or?" She watched the inclination to lie pass over his rugged face before he focused directly on her.

"Or they don't want to be found." Rafferty's jaw twitched, yet his gaze never wavered. "I killed a woman not so long ago, Lyla. It was self-defense, and her blood'll be on my conscience till I go to my grave, but the Pinkertons and the United States marshals don't see it that way."

Lyla felt the color die in her cheeks. She no longer feared this dark desperado, but she respected the latent violent streak that must've led him to murder a woman. Rather than ask what the woman had done to him, she stepped over to the stove to dry their dishes.

"You wish you hadn't come here now?" he demanded from behind her.

"Self-defense seems an understandable motive," she replied quietly. "Better than meanness or greed or revenge, anyway."

"How do you know I'm not lying? What makes you think I won't pull a knife on you tonight?" he challenged. "That's how I killed her, you see. Right through the heart."

His mercurial moods frightened her, but she turned, maintaining what she hoped was an unflinching expression. "And what did she use on *you?*"

Rafferty stroked his thick mustache, as though he might be making the whole episode up. Yet he remained deadly serious. "A pillow."

"What?"

He chuckled low in his throat as he set the dishes on the shelf above the stove. "Seems I made a few promises to this dove—whiskey talks pretty, you know—and she didn't take it kindly when I slept it off in another girl's bed. Tried to suffocate me, and damn near succeeded."

A crime of passion in a bawdy house. She should've guessed. Lyla handed him the towel she'd dried her hands with, her voice calm. "The way I see it, I don't have a thing to worry about," she said, "because if you lift a hand against me, your dogs will attack you."

Jack's laugh filled the wagon. "Mighty cocksure of yourself, young lady. They haven't known you long enough to—"

"I have a way with animals," she stated. "They sense my kinship with them. Most dogs will defend a sympathetic female against a male—even their own master. And to prove it, I'm going to bed now."

Lyla sat on the edge of the bunk to remove her boots, smiling and crooning to Maudie and Will. She could feel Rafferty's gaze but ignored him, giving her full attention to the two border collies so like the ones she'd loved at home. She stroked each animal in turn, delighting in the silkiness of their thick coats, returning the affection she saw in their bright, curious eyes.

And sure enough, when she slipped beneath the quilts and arranged the pillow to suit herself, both dogs hopped onto the bunk. Will settled behind her bent knees and Maudie curled up against the front of her with a contented sigh.

"Well, I'll be damned," Jack mumbled. And he spent the night on the floor.

When Lyla awoke she was alone in the wagon. She felt refreshed after a night of fearless, dreamless sleep. Neither the threat of Frazier's impending visit nor ghosts of the marshal who'd gone up in flames had interfered with her rest.

She stretched from her toes up through every muscle of her body, smiling. The only sound she heard was the constant calling of the sheep and an occasional yip from the dogs. No wind . . . the snowstorm was over and today she would proceed to Cripple Creek.

The half-eaten cobbler on the back of the stove told her Jack had tided himself over and enjoyed it. Lyla smiled as she quickly washed herself with warm water he'd left in a pan. Rafferty was one of the most fascinating characters she'd ever run across. In gratitude for his hospitality, she sliced off a skillet's-worth of bacon and mixed up a batch of biscuits. He wasn't a man she could ever envision herself falling for, but she would like to leave with the memory of his seductive, secretive smile fresh in her mind.

Setting the pan of biscuits into the oven, Lyla

scowled, listening. Was that the footfall of Jack's horse? With at least two thousand sheep to move to fresh grazing ground, he had no cause to gallop.

A peek out the wagon's door made her heart lurch. As often happened, the blizzard had blown the powdery snow across the range, leaving only a sprinkling like sugar on the stubbly grass. And from the direction of the house, a lone rider was rapidly approaching.

Fighting panic, Lyla rushed to the bunk and unfastened the flap in the canvas above it. Hundreds of huddling, woolly Merino sheep covered the nearby hillsides like a moving, bleating blanket of snow. Jack was a speck in the distance and she couldn't see Maudie or Will. They were the only defense she had from Frazier: she didn't know where Dickens was tied, and searching for him on foot would make her an easy target for her approaching captor.

"Mau-audie! Will!" she hollered urgently. She gave two long, shrill whistles, as she'd often done at home, and hoped her cry for help would be heard above the blathering of the sheep. Lacing her boots on, Lyla wondered desperately if she should try to hide somewhere or just confront Frazier. The wagon's storage compartments were all full now . . . the canvas flap was too small to crawl out of. Foxe would know all these things and ferret her out, chuckling in that evil way he had when his prey was cornered.

The hoofbeats grew as deafening as her pulse and then pounded to a halt. Lyla stood, bracing herself so Foxe wouldn't get past the stove, searching desperately for a weapon because Jack had taken his Winchester. She reminded herself that Frazier was soft from his life of luxury, accustomed to battling with his money rather than his fists, and probably slow to react because of his age. The last thing he'd expect was a hellcat like herself springing at him, knocking him backwards out of the wagon—

But when the door was yanked open it was Connor's leer that turned her blood to ice. "Hey there, cupcake," he taunted. "Made it easy for me, hiding with the closest herd. And breakfast! How nice of you to—"

When he stepped up into the wagon, sheer instinct took over. With one swift movement, Lyla grasped a damp wool sock and then the handle of the sizzling skillet, and hurled it at Foxe with all the strength she possessed.

The pan thudded against his thick jacket and he swore violently when the boiling bacon grease splattered down the front of his jeans. Connor jumped back and fell out the wagon door, clutching a burned hand to his chest. "You goddamn—you'll regret this, bitch!" he howled as he rolled to his feet.

Frantically Lyla searched for something else to battle him with, because now that he was angry and injured he was even more dangerous. "You've got no right to—"

"By God, when I get ahold of you—"

Lyla seized the coffeepot, which was only luke-warm—but Foxe didn't know that. "You want your coffee now, Connor? Want a face as scarred as your brother's hands?"

Her attacker paused for just a moment to weigh the consequences of another scalding. It was long enough: from around the side of the wagon sped two snarling, savage dogs hellbent on tearing the intruder limb from limb. Will hurled himself against Foxe, knocking him to the ground, and Maudie sprang up into the doorway to defend her home and Lyla.

Connor hollered, flailing and kicking at the vicious beast who was attacking him. Praying that Jack had followed his dogs, Lyla pulled cans of food from the shelves to pelt Connor with while Maudie bristled and barked in the doorway. Just as Lyla grabbed the carving knife, she heard a dull *thunk* and a heartrending yelp. Then there was a single gunshot and silence.

Lyla clutched the knife, afraid to look outside.

"You take one more step and I'll kill you with the next one."

She let out the breath she was holding. Jack's voice was as deadly as the rifle he was pointing at Foxe's chest. He was on horseback, towering above Connor, his mustache curving around the most menacing expression Lyla had ever seen.

"Now get on your horse and get the hell out! And by God, you can tell Frazier—"

"You can't order me off my own land, Rafferty! You're fired!" Connor yelled.

"And you're *dead* if you don't get your ass in that saddle!" Jack clicked back the hammer and took aim. "After what you've done to my dog, I'd have no trouble at all putting a bullet through your brain. Or through your back, if you make a move toward Lyla."

Foxe slowly straightened to his full height, his eyes never leaving the gun Rafferty was pointing at him. His left hand was already an angry red from the hot grease, the front of his coat was in tatters, and he had a bloody gash on one side of his face. "You better be off this ranch by noon," he snarled as he limped toward his stallion, "because next time I won't come alone."

"I'll be gone before you can get to the bunkhouse to lick your wounds," Jack taunted. "And you tell your pansy-assed brother to watch his back from here on out. If I ever see him again, he'll get the same treatment you did."

Trembling all over, Lyla let the knife clatter to the stovetop when Connor Foxe wheeled his horse around and galloped away in a rage. They'd won this skirmish, but the war was far from over. And Frazier wasn't the only one who'd be looking over his shoulder for years to come. Right now, though, it was the horrible silence outside that made her throat tighten, and when she saw Jack Rafferty's face crumple as he dismounted, her worst fears were confirmed. Maudie hopped outside, but when Lyla stepped toward the doorway she was stopped by a ragged voice.

"You don't want to see what he did to Will with that skillet. I'll put him out of his misery and give him a decent burial."

Lyla covered her face with her hands, overcome by sudden, racking sobs. Will had managed to crawl underneath the wagon after his master had fired at Foxe's feet, and the single shot she heard now went straight through her heart. The dog had known her but a day and had defended her with his last burst of strength, only to be grievously injured by the very weapon she'd used to defend herself.

Jack shuffled toward the nearest clump of trees with the collie's body cradled in his arms, a spade he'd unstrapped from the wagon sticking out from under one elbow. Maudie trailed behind him, her head hung low. Lyla started outside to comfort him, to release the grip of anguish and guilt that threatened to squeeze her senseless. But Rafferty would want these last moments alone with his beloved friend.

The aroma of biscuits reminded her of all the things that needed to be done if they were to be gone before Foxe sent his hired men after them. Tears streaming down her face, Lyla shut the door and took the pan of biscuits from the oven. They would be food for the trail . . . and she sensed Jack would leave the cumbersome wagon but take everything the horses could possibly carry.

Quickly she yanked a quilt from the bunk and folded it in half on the floor. Bags of beans, coffee, flour, and other food got stacked down the center of it before she rolled it up and secured it with rope from one of the drawers. In another blanket she wrapped such supplies as matches and cooking utensils. Rafferty seemed to be wearing all the clothes he owned, so in another quilt she bundled up his books and dime novels.

She was ready to tug the sheets off the bunk when her host came inside with a heavy tread. His sorrowful expression lightened a little when he realized what she was doing. "I'll finish this," he said with quiet finality. "Got a few . . . personal effects, you know?"

She nodded, her heart overflowing with feelings she didn't know how to express. They stood studying each other, awkward in their grief, until a long, forlorn howl from the direction of Will's grave drove Lyla into Rafferty's open arms, blubbering uncontrollably. "Mother of God, I'm so s-sorry! Poor Will—wouldn't have happened had I not barged in—"

"You didn't want Foxe to bash his skull any more than I did," Jack murmured with a catch in his voice. "I should've shot the bastard. Made him die a slow, painful death like he did to my dog."

For several moments they clung together, bound by a misery that wrapped around their souls like a black velvet ribbon. Jack stroked her hair, sighing deeply when she slipped her arms beneath his coat to caress his sturdy back. "Lyla . . . Lyla," he whispered. "Here I am carrying on about a dog when it's you I should worry about. You're in more danger now than you were before you left the house."

"Don't be so sure," she stated. "Connor sneaked in through my bedroom window and came at me, or Hollingsworth would never've helped me escape. Foxe Hollow's no place for a decent person, and I hope he's not been severely punished . . . or worse, for betraying Frazier."

Rafferty chuckled wryly and pulled away to gaze at her. "You seem to inspire the bravest, most loyal support from men who hardly know you, Miss O'Riley. Now—we'd better finish packing before that bunk and your warm, enticing body make me forget about—"

When the door opened suddenly, they sprang together, sharing the fear that somehow Foxe's men had already come after them. A tall, burly form blocked the winter sunlight, and then a man in a tan hat and a sheepskin-lined coat stepped into the wagon, gazing steadily at them.

Lyla felt her face go white, as though the blood had suddenly drained from her body. It wasn't possible— not if her eyes and ears and memory could be trusted! Had the weeks of being Foxe's hostage altered her ability to distinguish between fantasy and reality, or was a phantom of the most incredibly solid sort staring at her, waiting for her to respond?

"Barry," she breathed. "Barry, is it really *you?*"

Chapter 24

His jaw twitched. "Maybe I should've knocked. Looks like I interrupted something."

Her hand flew to her mouth. And then she felt the warm gold band of a ring that was his but that he hadn't given her. Realized just how incriminating this soulful scene with Jack Rafferty must look to a man who'd returned suddenly and inexplicably, from the dead. "It-it's not what you must be thinking! I . . ."

Lyla walked out of Jack's protective embrace as though entranced, drawn by the spell of probing green eyes that pulled her by the heartstrings. He'd spoken—or was it the voice of wistful, wishful imagination reverberating in her mind? How many times had she dreamed of him, of kisses so real they stirred her wildest yearnings? How many times had his bold, virile face haunted her every thought, until death seemed her only release?

Slowly, with a hand that trembled, she reached up. She paused, afraid to trust the sound of his breathing and the pounding of her heart saying *yes, yes,* and the familiar leathery scent of his jacket. When her fingertips brushed the warm smoothness of his clean-shaven cheek, time ceased to exist.

He was real!

Thompson saw the jolt go through her and forgot

that he'd found her in another man's wagon, in another man's arms. He crushed her close, clenching his eyes shut with a prayerful joy known only to angels, and men living in the shadow of death. She felt even tinier than he remembered, and looked like a fragile shell of the spritely young woman he feared he'd never see again. "Lyla," he rasped. "Jesus, honey, I thought—"

When his lips found hers, Lyla threw her arms around his neck and felt herself being lifted, lifted . . . Barry's kiss consumed her, as though she were his first morsel of food since that fateful day they'd been shanghaied to the shack.

"I thought you were dead," she breathed, fondling the hair at his nape, hugging the sturdy breadth of his shoulders. She pulled away to drink in the sight of him, still unable to believe this unfathomable turn of events. "But—but you're not even scarred, or—"

Barry gave her another resounding kiss. Her tremulous words explained the hollows in her face and the shadows around her haunted blue eyes. And they affirmed that she, too, had suffered as only he could comprehend during the weeks he'd desperately wanted to see her. "I was lucky," he mumbled. "Eberhardt wasn't too creative with his kerosene. Only doused the edges of the shed, so even though it must've looked like a scene from hell, I had some time to plan my strategy. Got a little hair singed off coming out, but it's growing back."

Lyla listened open-mouthed. "But I saw Buck . . . it tore my heart out to think he'd break free only to go in and—"

"He's the best horse there is, Lyla," Thompson replied. He brushed the hair back from a face that was splotchy from crying and ready to pucker over again. "When he heard my whistle, he came in—flames and all, bless him—and grabbed the rope around my wrists with his teeth. I was a little stunned from the beating the blond fellow gave me, so Buck had to

292

drag me. We got out just before the roof collapsed. Good thing Foxe's desperadoes didn't stick around for the bitter end, isn't it?"

His grin sent a rush of joy through her. So many things to say, so many hopes restored because a bumbling stable manager and Foxe's three hired killers were too overconfident to be thorough! Lyla's emotions tumbled over each other: relief, gratitude, and a love that sang to the beat of her resurrected heart. Then she frowned. "If you weren't hurt, what took you so damn long to *find* me?"

If ye weren't hurt, wot took ye sae dam long t' foind me? Barry laughed in spite of an accent that pointed like a finger. She was indeed the same quick, demanding little imp he adored even as she pulled away from his embrace, awaiting a straight answer. "I holed up at the McClanahans' to let Idaho take care of my wounds—"

"You just said you escaped unharmed."

"All right, so I fibbed a little. To keep you from worrying," he said softly. "I was scorched a few places where my clothes caught fire, and my hands were a mess from that rope rubbing between my fingers, and that wiry blond worked me over pretty good with his fists. But Idaho took good care of all that, and then Matt and Emily got back from Cripple."

"That's where I was headed until Foxe's hooligans ambushed me," she said quietly. It seemed years ago instead of only weeks, but the memories were as painful as the physical harm they'd done to Thompson.

"That's what Emily said, and when rumor had it that I disappeared into thin air, and neither of us were at the cabin, Matt checked with Miss Victoria. She said Frazier'd been there to collect your clothes, so he knew you were in trouble."

Lyla listened, nodding, and then lifted an eyebrow. "All right, that accounts for a week, maybe. What about all the *rest* of that time? Especially since

293

you knew all along that Frazier had me."

Thompson cleared his throat. He'd forgotten how persistent and astute Lyla O'Riley could be, a trait he'd better get used to. "All right, so I wasn't in such good shape," he confessed. "I'd just gotten out of the hospital, remember. And then with the pounding I took, and the strain of the fire, I—well," he said with an exasperated shrug, "Matt left me at the Flaming B with Emily and Idaho to recuperate. We agreed that I was to remain unseen—supposedly dead—until we could draw Foxe out into the open. Meanwhile, McClanahan tried to get himself through the entry gate at Foxe Hollow."

Jack Rafferty grunted. "Surely his reputation as a detective preceded him."

The marshal blinked. He and Lyla had been so wrapped up in each other they'd forgotten about the dark sheepherder who'd witnessed every kiss and heard their every word. "That was a problem," he agreed, sensing a fierce protectiveness in Lyla's mustached companion. "And when McClanahan finally slipped through the boundary security and watched the house a few days, he realized that if Frazier was forced to come out and face charges, Lyla would get hurt. It's not what I wanted to hear, but we figured he'd cause her no physical harm if we didn't provoke him, and that eventually he *had* to leave his house."

"Aye," Lyla murmured, "I'm to marry him on St. Valentine's Day, at the Presbyterian church in Cripple."

That explained how his aquamarine got on her finger—that bastard Foxe! A wedding could be a perfect part of his ploy, but for now, Lyla was in more danger than he'd anticipated, and they needed to get away from Foxe Hollow.

"I'm truly sorry you had to wait so long, honey," he said. "Matt tried to send in other men with trumped-up reasons for seeing Foxe, so we could grab him when he couldn't hurt you, but even his business partners weren't allowed inside. He knew damn well someone would try to get you out of there."

The deep lines of concern crossing Barry Thompson's forehead made her sorry she'd challenged his efforts to free her. Frazier hadn't harmed her, really, and while she'd passed the endless days dressed like a princess whose only problem was loneliness, the marshal had been recovering from injuries and incidents more harrowing than he would admit to her.

"So if McClanahan's on the case, how'd *you* get here?" Rafferty challenged. The herder's brown eyes studied Thompson for details that didn't fit. He'd stopped his packing and appeared ready to fight if his questions weren't answered satisfactorily.

"Matt's on his honeymoon, and I was sick of being sick." Barry stroked his woman's warm, waist-length hair, keeping her close. The stockman had given Lyla sanctuary—and she appreciated it, judging from what he'd seen when he walked in—but he knew better than to underestimate the motives of his shifty-eyed competition.

"By the time I found the stretch of property line McClanahan told me wasn't guarded, and then slipped up to the house, the blizzard was blowing full force," he continued matter-of-factly. "Didn't want to risk finding Connor and his thugs in the barn—couldn't see it, anyway. So I tied Buck to a post on the back veranda and let myself in to what I figured was the pantry."

Lyla's eyes widened. "It wasn't locked?"

"No, and it wasn't unoccupied, either," he replied with a chuckle. "A damn skinny cook—"

"Miss Keating," she said with a grimace.

"—passed right out when I walked in on her, and when the butler heard the commotion, *he* came in."

"Hollingsworth told you Lyla was with me?" the

295

wiry herder demanded. He seemed edgy now, ready to bolt, and Thompson then realized where he'd seen this man before.

"Yeah, but I found out the hard way that you moved your flock during the storm. And I damn near got run down by Foxe's brother just now, hellbent for the house," he said in a thoughtful tone. Then he cleared his throat, returning the outlaw's defiant gaze as he tightened his hold on Lyla. "If you can forget you saw me alive, Rafferty, I can overlook the fact that you're a poster boy with rewards on your head in three states. Do we understand each other?"

Lyla jumped, astounded, but couldn't move within Barry's restrictive bearhug. How long had Thompson known—

"Sounds like a fair deal to me, marshal. Just fixing to leave for parts unknown when you walked in, as a matter of fact."

"Fine. We'll let you finish your packing." Barry steered Lyla toward the door, sensing things would get ugly if they lingered. They stepped out of the wagon and then he turned to look inside it. "I'm only doing this because you protected my woman, you know. Had you so much as unbuttoned her shirt, you'd be dead."

"Great timing and instincts. On both our parts," Rafferty replied.

Chapter 25

Lyla's thoughts raced as the buckskin stallion carried them across the endless range. It was too soon to count this a victory until the border of Foxe Hollow was crossed, yet already the morning had been the most momentous of her life. For the first time ever, she'd willingly injured a man; she'd mourned a dog with an outlaw she liked immensely and had assumed she'd take off with—until she found herself rolling with the motion of Buck's gallop. His black mane was singed short in some places and his glossy coat was marred by a few scars, yet like his master, he'd survived the horrible fire and seemed determined to triumph because of it.

She still couldn't believe Barry was holding her, saving her from eternal agony in Frazier's mansion. His arm held her close against his broad chest, his fingers slipping between the buttons of the coat Jack had tossed at her as they were leaving. His breath teased at her cheek. An occasional kiss beneath her ear sent tingles along her arms, yet still her mind refused to acknowledge that Barry Thompson was alive and rescuing her, like a fairy-tale knight on his trusty steed.

Onward they rode, over boundless stretches of frosted grass interrupted only by clumps of crystal-line trees and bushes still glazed from the blizzard.

The sky above was an intoxicating blue and the horizon beckoned, unchanged after more than an hour's ride. Lyla refused to relax. Any moment they'd come to the barbed wire border and a man who'd shoot to kill—she was sure of it. Barry, too, remained watchful, so intent on their surroundings he didn't say a word.

Thompson kept his questions to himself as he guided Buck around the foothills toward a wide, shallow stream. The clear layer of ice shattered beneath the stallion's hooves as he slowed to a trot to keep his footing in the cold, flowing water. A few miles more and he could demand the answers only Lyla could give . . . a Lyla who was oddly withdrawn as she rested against him.

Had Frazier brainwashed her into marriage? Or had she actually been in league with the Englishman all along, an attractive accomplice paid to lure him to his death?

He doubted it. If so, she wouldn't have run from his mansion during a blizzard.

Jack Rafferty was another matter, though. She and that outlaw, a lady-killer in the literal sense, had looked pretty chummy when he'd entered the wagon. The howling dog, the fresh grave, and Lyla's tear-streaked face were evidence that he'd just missed an upsetting event, which Connor Foxe had undoubtedly caused. Was she planning to accompany Rafferty to those parts unknown? Perhaps he should've asked her that flat-out—given her the choice, rather than assuming she still cared for him after all these weeks.

She thought you were dead, damn it, he reasoned. *Compared to Frazier, even a mangy outlaw with an overgrown mustache looked good. She was alone, defenseless—*

Lyla sucked in her breath when the marshal swore suddenly and urged his horse onto a traveled, vaguely familiar trail. Where was he taking her? Had he changed his mind about wanting her, after seeing her in Rafferty's arms?

Barry steered Buck off the main road toward a small abandoned cabin nestled in a grove of trees. She sensed he'd made a decision, or changed his mind about whatever he was stewing over, and she wasn't sure the turnabout in his attitude was to her benefit. "Where're we going?" she mumbled.

"To that shack."

"But—" Lyla swiveled to gaze in all directions, her heart pounding. "If Foxe's men are guarding the border—"

"That creek we crossed was the open boundary Matt told me about. We've been off his property for the past couple miles, on the Gold Camp Road."

Her eyes widened. She'd ridden Calico along this trail when she went to the Flaming B, but the scenery and landmarks looked different, coming from this direction. They were free, and she hadn't even known! Yet as they dismounted in front of a weathered little shed that groaned with the wind, Barry's ominous expression warned her this stop was no celebration party.

He gripped her shoulder as he opened the decrepit door. When Lyla's eyes adjusted to a dimness lit by stripes of light from missing boards, she saw the scattered remains of what had been a ranchhand's furniture. Some animal had made its nest in the pot-bellied stove long ago. The doors to the pie safe gaped open and the braided rug was damp and musty-smelling. Little drifts of snow lay in odd spots, and the heavy wooden table sitting in the center of the room was fuzzy with an undisturbed layer of dust.

It was here Thompson planted her, swinging her up to sit on the table's top before she could ask what he was doing. When Lyla saw the marshal's taut jaw and relentless gaze, she knew better than to challenge him.

Barry studied her for several moments, reminding himself not to let his joy at seeing her color his interrogation. With her honey hair tumbling over a jacket that looked two sizes too large, her legs dangling several inches from the floor, and her wind-pink, freckled cheeks glowing beneath huge periwinkle eyes, Lyla resembled a little girl dressed in her big brother's clothing—which she was. A precious, tempting little girl with secrets he wasn't sure he wanted to know.

But it was now or never: he could travel no farther without hearing her story. If Frazier Foxe had convinced her to keep silent, his case against the finagling financier was lost for want of a witness. And if that's how her loyalties lined up, well . . . he might as well have died in that fire.

The marshal cleared his throat, his hands resting on her shoulders. "It's time we talked," he began quietly. "I've told you how I spent this past month and a half; now it's your turn."

Lyla wasn't afraid of him, exactly, but he towered over her, restored to his full physical strength now. His coat hung open, revealing a shirt that tugged against a muscular chest, and powerful hips and thighs poised as though to catch her, should she try to escape. Barry Thompson was truly intimidating from this angle, and his stern expression left her mute with confusion.

He felt her shoulders trembling and realized he was guilty of overkill. While he'd spent his days regaining his strength, this little waif had dwindled away despite being surrounded by Frazier Foxe's lavish furnishings and finery. It didn't make sense . . . unless she'd been subjected to abuse that left only invisible scars; torture of the most excruciating sort.

Barry let his hands drift down the sleeve of her jacket until he was gripping her fingers. He raised them to his lips, kissing each knuckle, watching the aquamarine and diamond stones sparkle, feeling a

300

wistfulness beyond words. "I'm sorry," he sighed. "If it hurts too much to talk about what that miserable bastard did to you, I'll understand. But I'm confused, honey—you're wearing my ring, yet you're engaged to Frazier, and a blind man could see Rafferty had designs on you. I . . . where do *I* stand, Lyla?"

His jagged voice cut straight to her soul. She removed his hat to stroke his light brown hair and instinctively cradled his head against her shoulder. "It was my love for you—dreams of you—that kept me from going insane, even though I thought you were gone forever," she whispered against his ear. "So stand anywhere you want to, Barry. More than anything, I'd like you to be standing beside me at the altar on St. Valentine's Day."

The thought of going through with a wedding Frazier Foxe had planned repelled him, yet her intended meaning rang as clearly as her Irish accent. Barry raised up to gaze into her eyes, which were bright and unwavering now. His heart was thundering so hard he could barely hear himself as he asked, "You still want me, then?"

"More than ever, love," she murmured. "It was wanting you that made me feel alive among people who might as well be dead. Oh, Barry—"

She kissed him hungrily, as though she could never get enough. Here was the sustenance she'd yearned for while sitting at Allegra Keating's barren meals. Barry tasted as delicious as the Delmonico's dinner she'd devoured and intoxicated her like the wine, yet he was infinitely more satisfying than either. His lips responded with deep, eager pressure as his hands slipped behind her head to hold her until he, too, had gotten his fill.

"I never meant to doubt you, honey," he whispered into her hair. "I just had to hear it—wanted to fill in some gaps, and—"

"I know a gap you can fill, marshal," Lyla said coyly. She ran the tip of her tongue along his ear, giggling when he jolted against her in surprise.

It was a bolt of pure passion that nearly knocked him off balance. One moment he'd had her on the defensive and before he could breathe again she'd propositioned him! "You sound like some hussy—"

"You've bedded a few of those and liked it, as I recall."

"But—" She was slipping her coat off, gazing up at him as though she were quite serious about seducing him. "That was before I met you, Lyla. You deserve to be courted, and I—I vowed to McClanahan I was going to keep my pants on until—"

"It was too late for that a long time ago, love. And what Matt doesn't know won't hurt him." Lyla felt excitement rising up from deep inside her as she took in his shocked expression. She unbuttoned her shirt, still teasing, yet suddenly overtaken by the aching she'd felt every night she'd slept alone, wanting him. "Why, I can recall a time you were going to whisk me away from the Rose, despite the scandal it would cause . . . a certain evening I didn't think my lavender gown would get buttoned before you ravished me in the pantry."

It was true—Lord, every word brought back images of the Irish imp who smelled of schnapps and felt warm and soft as he cupped her. Those same breasts were peeking at him from beneath a sheer, lacy camisole Foxe must've bought her . . . but that hardly mattered now. Thompson felt himself straining against his pants, and then damned if she didn't reach for his fly buttons!

"Lyla—sweetheart—"

"You'd rather do it yourself? Fine!" she exclaimed with mock indignation. She drifted back onto her coat, reclining on the table so she could remove her pants. Where this wanton desperation came from, she didn't know. But she had to love him again, had to feel Barry's body caught up with the same relentless desire that was driving her to behavior she'd never dreamed herself capable of.

There she was, a lovely young woman displayed before him without the least bit of coaxing on his part. Her delicate underthings covered her with a gossamer softness he had to touch. Barry found himself tugging her boots and pants off as though he had no control over his movements, as though the sheer willfulness behind those blue eyes was manipulating him.

To think that he'd made love to this charming nymph and couldn't remember it! Her hair tumbled down over proud shoulders and pert breasts he longed to bury his face in. Lyla was thinner now, her body tapering to hips that remained lush and thighs that formed an exquisite frame around a triangle of dark curls that teased at him from beneath her dainty drawers.

Thompson gasped softly. "Jesus, you're—Lyla, honey, it's so cold in here you can see your breath, and you'll catch—"

"For a man who can do it in his sleep, you're mighty damn finicky!" She rolled sideways off the table and was stalking toward the door before he realized he should grab her. Her hair bounced over silken pantaloons that swayed provocatively with her anger. Her legs were more perfectly proportioned than many a taller woman's he'd known, and damned if she wasn't heading outside, straight toward Buck!

Lyla let out a hoot when Thompson scooped her up from behind, and then she giggled uncontrollably.

"Just where do you think you're going, dressed only in your skivvies, Miss O'Riley?" he breathed.

"Why, I was chasing after *you*, marshal," she replied, "and it looks like you caught me after all."

"You scheming little—" Barry turned her in his arms as he carried her back inside, out of the wind. She was unbuttoning his shirt, teasing his neck with kisses in all his sensitive spots as though she'd learned that trick during years of experience at the Rose.

She hadn't, of course. It was Lyla's spritely innocence that was breaking down his last defenses, and as he backed her against the wall of the cabin to kiss her, he wondered why he'd been resisting her anyway. Lyla wrapped her arms around his neck and returned his passion, play for play. Her legs encircled his waist, and he groaned. "At least let me pull my pants down before you—"

"What's taking you so long?" she demanded, her voice tight with a yearning that drove him over the edge.

"Hang on," he rasped.

"I wouldn't dream of letting you go, love."

"I—I hope I don't hurt—" Lord, he'd barely gotten unbuttoned and she was wriggling her toes into his waistband to push his pants out of the way! Barry worked himself out of his underwear flap and then yanked feverishly at her drawers, his pulse pounding. She was so tiny in his arms, he'd surely tear her apart when he—

Lyla gasped at the first touch of his hot, bare skin on hers. He was cradling her bottom in his hands while leaning her shoulders against the wall, his breathing a rapid pant that matched her own. Wrapping her ankles about him, she let herself hang loosely enough that Barry could guide her toward the joining she so urgently wanted. What were these wild feelings that set her body afire? Why couldn't she hold still and enjoy his caresses at a more leisurely—

His manhood found the moist groove between her thighs and he rocked against her, rubbing the outside of her, allowing Lyla's writhing to slicken the path he was about to lead her down. This wasn't the romantic, tender rendezvous he'd envisioned countless times these past weeks, yet—

She arched and took him in, her mouth open in a

silent cry of ecstasy. Barry crushed her hips against his, too far gone to wonder if she was ready to explode with him. She was hot and wet and wonderfully tight, so agile and light in his arms. Her whimpers drove him faster until release washed over him with a hoarse cry he wasn't sure was his own.

Lyla felt an untamed desire stalking her like a lynx, poised to pounce . . . hovering, tensing, until she leapt and felt herself flying over the edge of a climax that nearly rendered her senseless. She clung to Thompson's heaving chest, nestling against a heart that was pounding like a stampede of wild stallions.

When he could move again, Barry lifted her to his shoulder so he could turn and collapse with his back to the wall. Had he crushed her? Had the rough siding of the cabin cut into her back? Lyla was curled against him like a child, her eyes closed and one delectable breast peeping over the top of her camisole. So many things he'd meant to savor, so many endearments he'd lost in the frenzy. And all he could think to murmur was, "Next time, we're lying down."

"Ah, but wasn't it grand?"

His heart sang out at the awed sweetness of her whispered reply. She was his, this flirtatious beauty he feared had been stolen away from him body and soul, and Barry vowed more fiercely than before to get Frazier Foxe convicted of his crimes and out of their lives. He kissed the downy softness beneath her ear, marveling again that he'd pleased her. "We'd better dress, honey," he said quietly. "We're by no means out of the woods where Foxe is concerned."

Lyla nodded and let herself slide to the floor, careful not to stumble over the pants puddled around his ankles. "Where will we go? If you can't be seen—"

"To your cabin, for now," he replied. He tucked himself back into his union suit and had to chuckle when he caught Lyla watching him.

305

"To find out what you missed last time you were there?" she asked saucily.

"That, and to figure out how we'll snare ole Frazier before he retaliates for this little escape of yours." Barry hurriedly finished dressing, amazed at how drafty the shack felt now that his woman was no longer making love to him. "It'll help if you can talk about what happened while you were at the house—what you saw, what was said."

"Aye," Lyla replied with quiet determination. "It'll make your ears burn, marshal, but by the saints, I'll get him back for what he did to me! And I know just how to do it, too!"

Barry smiled, his admiration swelling within him. Lyla looked a bit haggard, yet her spirit was renewed and he had no doubt she'd succeed with whatever scheme she was cooking up. Moments later they were mounting Buck, heading back to the Gold Camp Road, which would take them to Victor and the trail leading along Phantom Canyon.

The wind whistled around them and Lyla snuggled closer. He kissed her hair, grateful for her pluck and for the fates that had brought them together again. On an impulse he turned to look back at the cabin, and then steered Buck around in a semicircle.

Lyla gaped. The ramshackle shed was shuddering in a gust of wind coming down from the mountains, and slowly, with a groan, it sagged and then collapsed.

Thompson cleared his throat. "I, uh, guess we brought the house down, Miss O'Riley."

She laughed, unable to hold her newfound joy inside her. "Well! There was never any doubt in *my* mind!"

Chapter 26

While Barry put his horse in the shed, Lyla fumbled with the lamps. The cabin was dark yet cozy in its familiarity, and as the wicks flickered and brought her belongings out of the shadows, she breathed easier.

Nothing had been disturbed. Her herbs and plants needed water, and a mouse had left his trail in the kitchen; the simple hominess of the little house wrapped its arms around her and made her feel welcome. Frazier could have his fine art and oversized mansion! Here Lyla drew her strength from the unspoiled wilderness and the green things that grew at her slightest encouragement. Here she could be herself, and she'd find a way to be free of the Foxe brothers forever.

But right now she had another man on her mind, a man whose subtle caresses and whisperings had made her feel alive with anticipation ever since they'd left the collapsed cabin. Recalling what he'd told her, Lyla had to struggle with the logs in the fireplace, her clumsiness a sign of her simmering arousal.

When the door opened and closed behind her, she continued to stack the contrary pieces of wood. Barry was silent, watching her so intently she could feel his gaze along her backside. It made her so nervous the logs fell into a shapeless heap again.

Then he was beside her, smiling as his large, competent hands arranged the pieces with the appropriate sizes and spaces in place. "I'm going to light you a perfect fire," he murmured, "a blaze that's warm and steady, that won't need tending while I make love to you, Lyla."

He struck a match while she gazed at him, speechless. The tiny light lit the laugh lines around his glowing eyes and made the blond highlights sparkle in his hair. His smile set her insides to quivering and he kissed her lightly before setting fire to the dry twigs in the center of the woodpile.

How he was going to keep himself under control until he'd pleasured every inch of her was beyond him. Crouching close by, her face lovely in the brightening firelight, Lyla looked just as nervously eager as he felt. Barry couldn't remember a woman who'd filled him with such heightened anticipation. All who'd come before her seemed to wither and blow away like petals of faded flowers, and that pleased him.

"We won't be needing these coats," he suggested quietly. He shrugged out of his own and stood to hang their jackets on pegs by the door. Glancing around the tidy little cabin, he sensed that everything in it reflected Lyla's talents and loves. Her red geraniums were blooming profusely, in the dead of winter, and the dried herbs hanging from the kitchen rafters gave the place a fresh, pleasant smell. Green philodendron stretched across the mantel, simple curtains adorned the windows. A glance at the short, single-sized bed made him chuckle.

"Can't say I remember much from my first visit," he said ruefully, "but it feels damn good to be here again, honey. Stand up. Let me take those clothes off you so I can see the woman I love."

Mute with awe, Lyla stood despite knees that threatened to knock. Why was she suddenly so shy, when his kisses and suggestions during the ride had made them both laugh lightheartedly? Barry caressed her cheek with fingertips so tender it made her want to cry out. With the lovelight shining in his eyes, intensified by the flickering fire, he was indeed a vision of love she'd only dreamed of before.

He unbuttoned her shirt slowly, wondering if she'd stop shaking when she got warmer. Lyla's eyes took up half her face; when he undid her cuffs and removed the plaid flannel, he felt like he was unveiling a priceless statue. Her filmy camisole rose and fell on the peaks of breasts that made him suck in his breath.

Barry knelt to remove her boots and pants, reveling in the warm sweetness of the firm globes that brushed his face when she held on to his shoulders for balance. The skin of her thighs and calves felt like silk as he tugged at the coarse male clothing . . . and there was that patch of curls beneath her bloomers, musky and inviting from their encounter in the cabin.

Barry inhaled deeply and ran his hands up under her camisole. "Lyla . . . Lyla honey, if you only knew what you were doing to me," he breathed.

She chuckled softly. "I've got a pretty good idea, you know. And it's obvious, the effect you're having on me."

"Not obvious enough. You don't know the half of what I plan to make you feel, now that I've got all night to show you."

Still kneeling, Barry lifted the hem of her camisole and circled her navel with his tongue. When Lyla giggled he tightened his grip and continued upward, kissing the velvety skin of her stomach, letting her lacy underwear gather lightly atop his closed eyelids until her breasts framed his forehead. Lord, but she was round and soft! With each of his palms he caressed her gently, content to breathe in her sweetness and feel her fluttering heartbeat.

The touch of Barry's tongue on her nipple made her gasp. He was kneading her with utmost tenderness, surrounding her swollen peaks with a wet heat that spread like wildfire within her. Lyla took his head in her hands, weaving her fingers through the thick waves of his hair as he worked his subtle magic on one breast and then the other.

Could there be any finer luxury than this man's touch? She doubted it, yet now his hands were lighting little fires along her sides and then slipping beneath her waistband. Barry's lips roamed lower, flickering lightly, leaving a damp trail that tickled exquisitely when his breath fell upon it.

His fingertips teased at the crevice between her hips and then he grasped them firmly. She felt her drawers loosening and looked down to see him untying the silk drawstring with his teeth.

He glanced up, grinning as her underwear slithered to her ankles. "I hope you're not in a hurry, sweetheart. Some pleasures are just too good to rush."

Lyla flushed with joy. He was leaning back on his heels, openly admiring her legs with his eyes and hands.

"You're some piece of work, Miss O'Riley," he whispered. He ran his palms up her firm thighs, savoring their softness while anticipating an experience that would be new to her. As he'd hoped, Lyla inhaled sharply when he drew his thumbs from between her legs to part the cluster of curls he longed to explore. She was inflamed, so ready . . . "Lean on my shoulders and hold tight, honey. I have a feeling you'll fly through the roof if you don't."

What on earth could he mean? Lyla watched him study her most intimate parts, wondering what could possibly fascinate him so. His sweet, boyish smile alone was driving her crazy, and when he approached her, his tongue extended, she nipped her lip.

A ripple of ecstasy like she'd never known made

her fall against him, grasping the sides of his head. Barry was kissing and gently nipping her, moaning softly as though he, too, were caught up in the whirlwind he was creating inside her. When his tongue began a firm, rhythmic caress, Lyla felt her head fall back, and her mouth opened, but no sound came out. She was afraid of falling, afraid of losing control—

"Cut loose with it, Lyla. I've got hold of you," he rasped.

His renewed attentions went straight to her head, faster than any wine. She was whimpering, writhing, opening to receive a gift made sweeter because she hadn't known enough to expect it.

With a sharp cry, Lyla gave in to him, shuddering in his grasp as she shook with one spasm after another. She was a wondrous creature while in the throes of passion, and when she collapsed he drank in her flawless beauty. Her head was lolled back, her breasts quivered beneath her gossamer camisole, and her baby-soft hair dangled around his hands as he kept a firm grip on her hips. Barry couldn't remember a more gratifying sight, and her sweet, earthy perfume made him eager for his own release.

"There's more," he said with a soft chuckle, "so I'll lay you down, let you recover for it."

Still woozy, Lyla felt herself being lowered onto the bear rug in front of the fireplace. Her whole body pulsed to a seductive beat she'd never felt before. She was vaguely aware of Barry sitting beside her, chuckling softly, but too awestruck to chide him. He'd taken her by surprise and was gloating over it! She gripped the bristly bear rug, trying to regain some clarity.

Barry removed his boots and then stood up at her feet, gazing at her. That camisole had to come off, but there was plenty of time. He reached out to touch her inner thigh with a bare toe, drawing it slowly toward himself. "You might want to open those pretty blue eyes," he drawled. "Might want to see what I'm

311

getting you into next."

Lyla exhaled slowly and then looked at him. "What *you're* getting into is more the issue, marshal," she quipped. "Pretty cocksure, aren't you?"

"That's one way to put it," he said with a soft laugh. "But it's because of you, honey. Because of the way you accept my affection and return it so freely . . . because you brought me back to life, in more ways than you know. This is how it's meant to be between a man and a woman, Lyla. I know that now, and I love you for it."

Her mouth fell open and her eyes prickled. Barry Thompson was the tallest, burliest, toughest man she'd ever met, yet now that they were alone, becoming lovers in the truest sense, his gentle sentiments filled her with grateful joy. How did he know what her soul had longed to hear all her life? Gone were his ideas about *keeping* her, like a mistress, or an orphan to be pitied. He was speaking from the heart, his tender words more binding than any of his previous plans to rescue her from the streets or Frazier Foxe.

"I believe you're a changed man, Mr. Thompson," she mumbled.

Barry smiled and shrugged out of his shirt. "I should hope so, as many times as I've stared death in the eye lately. Can you keep a secret?"

Lyla nodded, her eyes following his hand to his belt buckle.

"After Foxe and his men are in the Canon City prison, I'm turning in my badge. Life's too short to keep risking it on the likes of him."

Again her mouth fell open. "But you're the perfect man for the—what'll you do? I can't see you sitting idle, or just helping McClanahan once in a while."

Thompson let his pants drop to the floor. "My mine, the Flaxen Lassie, has a few good years in her yet. I've got plans for a house that's worthy of the wife

312

you'll make me, and then I'd like to father a few children and spoil you all rotten. Compared to the way I've lived lately, that sounds like a full, satisfying life."

Would he never cease to surprise her? Lyla gazed up at him and her breath caught in her throat. She'd seen every inch of him when he lay dying in her bed, but watching him disrobe was a different story. Barry was peeling off his union suit slowly, knowing he was taunting her and enjoying every moment, as though he had nothing more serious on his mind than flaunting his magnificence.

"You . . . you've healed quite nicely," she said in a tight voice.

He glanced down at his left shoulder, at the scar that was barely visible. "I had a fine surgeon. Something tells me she enjoyed her work, knowing she could fondle me wherever—"

"I was in a race with the Reaper himself, Thompson! I had no time for fondling!"

"Surely you at least *looked.*"

By now Barry had uncovered his arms and was lowering his union suit, grazing his sides with hands Lyla wished were her own. The swirls of hair on his chest teased at her. His muscles rippled as he pushed the cream-colored underwear to the second growth of curls and freed his erect manhood, pausing.

"Did you wonder how I would feel inside you, honey?" he whispered. "Were you curious? Afraid, because I'm so much larger than you?"

Lyla nodded, blushing.

Barry smiled kindly at her, and after he stepped out of his underwear he stood before her, glorious in his strength, glowing golden in the light from the fire. "You said you dreamed of me when you were at Foxe's. What did I do to you? What was the fantasy you enjoyed the most?"

Her eyes widened. He couldn't really expect her to admit—

"There's nothing wrong or shameful about making love to me in your mind, Lyla," he murmured as he lowered himself onto the rug. He stroked her flushed, freckled cheek and then lightly kissed her nose. "In fact, I find it extremely flattering and . . . arousing. While I was recuperating at McClanahan's, I had to take a lot of cold soaks to remain within the bounds of decency as a guest. You're potent medicine, pretty lady. I made love to you dozens of ways in my dreams, and I can't wait to try them. But right now I want to hear what *you'd* like."

Lyla remained speechless. His eyes were as serene as a sunlit evergreen forest, inviting her to share her most intimate thoughts. Hesitantly, she reached up to stroke the light stubble along his square jawline, to run a fingertip around the fullness of his lips. Did she dare express what she'd envisioned on those long, lonely nights? A man of Barry Thompson's experience would likely find her ideas childish or just downright silly.

Barry kissed the soft palm she was caressing him with, sensing her apprehension. She was no prude, but she'd never been asked her preferences—probably didn't know them yet—and he smiled, waiting her out. He kissed the pulse point of her inner wrist, so soft and pale with its delicate blue veins, and then ran his tongue lazily down her arm.

Lyla gazed, fascinated at the sensations he was creating. He was doing it again, igniting her passions with the simplest of gestures performed so tenderly she had no doubt Barry Thompson made every woman he wooed fall in love with him. But he was here, with her, speaking of a home and children. Talking of permanence and a passion that would never die.

"Barry, you make me feel like warm, drizzly honey, kissing me this way," she murmured when his lips teased the sensitive hollow of her neck.

Thompson chuckled. "So let me be the hot bread.

Spread yourself on me and do what you will, sweetheart."

He coaxed her down with him into the thick pile of the bear rug, and Lyla felt her inhibitions melting. She reached for him, wrapping her arms and legs about him, reveling in the softness of her lover's skin and hair and caress.

"What's that smile for?" he whispered.

She lowered her eyes shyly. "This is the way I saw us, love. Right here on this rug, holding each other so close before the fire."

"And this is the way I've always wanted to kiss you, Lyla." He drew her against his chest and held her head, claiming her exquisite lips softly, testing with the tip of his tongue. She was indeed like sweetest honey in his arms, flowing against him as she opened her mouth to accept his advances. He'd stolen her kisses at the Golden Rose and crushed her in his ardor at the abandoned cabin, but *this* . . . this was loving in the highest sense of the word.

Lyla responded with all her heart, her lips returning nuances she'd never dreamed of until this endearing man taught them so effortlessly. She was floating, breathless and buoyant on the waves of the desire that crested inside her. They were rubbing together, which made the hair on his chest rustle against her breasts in a hypnotic rhythm and brought the tip of him lightly against her hip, prodding suggestively. The kiss drifted on and on, subtle and sweet, until Lyla burned for more solid satisfaction.

She broke away with a gasp and wriggled lower, thrusting to take him in, but Barry stretched away from her. His low laugh told her it was another of his wiles to prolong her pleasure, but she was beyond waiting. Angling, she impaled herself with a moan she heard echoing in his own throat.

"Yes . . . yes," he murmured, overwhelmed by the miraculous rapture she gave. "I didn't know how strong my weakness for you was, honey. I want this to last and last.''

Even as she heard his plea, she felt Thompson's body straining, urging her to fly with him. She held her breath, incoherent with wanting him, and then soared forth on a burst of splendor that left her clutching his muscled body until neither of them could speak.

Several minutes passed before Barry realized just how far into another world this impassioned lass had propelled him. He drew a shuddery breath, holding her until Lyla, too, regained a sense of where they were and what wonders had passed between them.

When she looked up with her loving blue eyes, he was once again stunned by what he'd found in her—and by what he'd nearly lost to a vengeful Englishman who could still snatch her away. The thought sobered him, yet he refused to spoil this blissful moment. Lyla nestled against him and he curled himself around her, wishing this intimacy were all the protection she'd ever need from Frazier Foxe.

She turned in his embrace to stroke the long, magnificent thigh that stretched along hers. It was the most perfect of moments, yet destined to end. Lyla sensed this would be the only night she and Barry would share until they were truly free from the murderous thieves who might strike back at any time.

When Thompson took her hand, rotating his ring to make the gemstones sparkle with the firelight, she knew exactly what was on his mind, and she was now strong enough to discuss it. "It's a lovely thing, Barry. You couldn't have chosen better."

He smiled ruefully. "Matches your eyes, you know. Looks like it was made for your delicate hand, too. But I wish I'd been the man who put it there."

Lyla sighed, praying she wouldn't hurt him inadvertently as she revealed the painful details of the past weeks. "Frazier has a way of granting favors expressly so he can turn them into threats," she said quietly. "I knew he had this, and my silver shamrock, too. So when I demanded my brother's necklace, he appeased me by saying it would grace my gown—which he designed—on our wedding day. He then presented this aquamarine as a token of his admiration, he said. And in the next breath he stated I was to wear it every day, to remind me of how foolish falling in love is and of how much I lost when you died in that fire."

Thompson's gut tightened. And as he listened to her tell how Foxe had orchestrated the Angel Claire explosion to make him look incompetent, and how he'd insinuated Mick O'Riley was an opium addict, and how he'd bought men in all stations of life for the purpose of killing him, so the marshal's office would be another coin in his pocket, Barry remained too shocked to speak.

How had Lyla survived, living with such duplicity? In a trembling voice she continued her tale about how Foxe planned to beget an heir—how he'd laughed about *sketching* it, damn it! Before the robbery at the Golden Rose, Barry had considered the monocled stockbroker a pillar of Cripple society with a few pesky mannerisms. As his woman revealed one abomination after another, however, he became painfully aware of just how dishonest Frazier Foxe truly was, and, in league with Connor, how difficult he'd be to convict. No one else suspected Frazier of being an arsonist, a murderer, or an expert at forgery and chicanery. Who could say how many documents and deals he'd sealed with the name of that nonexistent attorney, Quentin Yarborough? And proving these charges would be even more of a challenge than he'd anticipated.

". . . so I figured when Rafferty steered me toward town, I'd go in as though nothing *unseemly* was taking place," Lyla was saying with a little more sparkle in her voice. "Just a bride come to check on her wedding arrangements, you see."

317

Barry blinked. "You don't really intend to go through with this wedding? Honey, you're tempting fate—"

"What else can I do?" She studied him, knowing she wasn't the only person in danger if her strategy failed. "I devised this plan before I knew you were alive, knowing the McClanahans would help me avenge your death and prove our innocence. Which is just as well, since you have to remain out of sight until we have Frazier cornered in the church."

Her talk had taken a turn while he'd been meandering down his own thought path, so he pulled away slightly to look at her. "Back up, sweetheart. You were heading to Cripple to check your arrangements?"

"Of course! Frazier made them all himself, by messenger—wouldn't risk leaving his estate, with or without me. So that'll be my explanation when he comes to Cripple to catch me," she stated pertly. "I wanted to try on my gown, and approve the invitations, and speak with the caterer and Princess Cherry Blossom. She's to be my maid of honor," Lyla added with a roll of her eyes.

Recalling his last encounter with the war-painted whore, Barry nearly choked on the irony of this. "So you're setting yourself up as bait? I don't like it. Too many things can go wrong, and—"

"What could be more wrong than having to bed Connor Foxe with Frazier looking on?" she demanded shrilly. She sat up, wondering if their lovemaking had addled his brains or if he hadn't been listening closely enough.

"I'll stop in at the Rose, have a fitting with Mrs. Delacroix—all these things to convince people that I truly am marrying Frazier, you see? But you and McClanahan will be ready to spring on him the moment I come down the aisle. It's perfect! He'll think I've been going along with his secrecy until *bang!*—the sanctuary will offer him no sanctuary after all! I have the papers you'll need to prove—to prove . . ." She'd risen to her knees, as though going for her coat, yet Lyla was now turning as pale as a pitcher of milk.

"Prove what, honey?" he asked.

She sat down with a disgusted groan, pounding the bear rug with her fist. "How could I be so *stupid?* I—" She looked at Barry's earnest face and felt utterly foolish for what she was about to say. "Foxe made me sign a prenuptial agreement concerning the division of his estate at his death, as well as a copy of his will— both papers bearing Yarborough's forged signature. That in itself would be proof of his connivery, but I left it . . . stashed behind Jack Rafferty's bunk. Along with that five hundred dollars you gave me."

Thompson clenched his jaw against the obvious question.

And when Lyla saw the jealous streak flash in the marshal's green eyes, she knew precisely what he was thinking. "I didn't want Rafferty to know the details—wasn't sure, when he first came back to the wagon, if I could trust him. And now he's off to— we'll *never* find those papers!"

Thompson pulled her onto his lap and cradled her quivering body, trying not to chuckle. This Irish imp had formulated a plan—not a half bad one—to bring Cripple Creek's most odious crook to justice, and now was forced to admit she'd forgotten the evidence. Probably because he'd shocked her by coming back from the dead as he had.

Barry stroked her silky hair and marvelous skin, indulging her in a brief cry. Lyla O'Riley would recover and proceed confidently, but meanwhile she was in even more danger than he'd anticipated. If Foxe discovered such documents missing, he'd know damn well Lyla had escaped the estate intending to expose him. And airing such secrets wouldn't exactly endear her to him.

"That settles it," he said quietly.

319

Lyla sniffled, wiping her wet cheek on his chest. "Settles what?"

"Your plan. I don't like you playing bait, but with Victoria and Mrs. Delacroix and others knowing you're getting married, you'll be too much in the public eye to be in danger for the next few days," Barry explained. "They'll be suspicious of the match—protective, if Foxe shows up acting like he's going for murder rather than matrimony.

"Meanwhile, I'll send McClanahan back to the mansion to find other evidence of fraud or forgery, and I'll hightail it after Rafferty myself. No doubt he found those papers, and since he knows better than to show himself in any towns, I'll be safer trailing him than I'd be holing up here or at Emily's ranch."

He paused, his expression softening as he took in the loveliness of Lyla's nudity on the dark bear rug, backlit by the dying fire. "And I'll send Emily in to Cripple to keep an eye on you. She's nearly as devious as you are, and I'll feel a lot better about this, knowing you two are working together."

Lyla smiled, her spirits lifting. "You think it'll work?"

"I don't see how it can miss, unless our timing gets off." He stroked her hair before standing up to stretch. More than anything he wanted to make love to her again; the anticipation of that pleasure would keep him sharp during the days to come. "You be careful, sweetheart. Stick close to the Rose, and convince Foxe with all you've got that you ran off only because you're excited about the wedding."

"Do you think he'll believe that?"

"No," he sighed, "but I know you'll outfox him somehow and get him into the church just as you planned. And Matt and I'll be waiting in the wings to grab him. Cripple's not ready for a wedding like this one," he added with a chuckle.

Lyla watched him pick his pants up from the floor, her heart thudding like a knell in her chest. It was

320

fine to plan all this derring-do when only her life was in danger, but knowing Barry couldn't get caught and live through it again made her wonder if the risk was worth it. "Do you have to go now? You'll travel faster by morning light, after a good breakfast."

Barry grasped her hands and pulled her up to stand in his embrace. "Rafferty's already several miles away, in who knows what direction by now. And traveling at night's the surest bet I won't be seen," he murmured. "Ride with me as far as Victor, Lyla. Then get some rest and take the train into Cripple. And be prepared for the stir you'll cause when you get there."

He had a point. And since she had no idea where Calico went after Foxe's men ambushed her last month, Buck was her only reasonable means of transportation.

They dressed quickly, and while Barry saddled his stallion, Lyla banked the fire and bundled up food for him and clothing for herself. She shivered in the doorway, watching until he came around the side of the cabin, looking regally tall and masculine atop Buck. By the pale moonlight she could see his stricken face, feel the loneliness that he, too, was already experiencing even as he hoisted her up in front of him.

The ride was silent, except for Buck's occasional snorting and his muffled footfalls along the canyon trail. It was a glorious, calm night. The deep azure sky formed a backdrop for black silhouettes of bare trees and evergreens decked in a silvery lace of snow and icicles. Lyla barely noticed, because she was praying that Barry Thompson's ride across the range would be short and successful, and that he'd return safely to her arms to continue the lifetime of loving they'd just begun.

When they could see the lights from the Victor taverns and hear the tinkling of a piano on the breeze, Barry halted his horse. Impulse told him to just keep

321

riding with her—disappear and start fresh, rather than risk another separation. But neither he nor Lyla would be free from Frazier's far-reaching tyranny until the Englishman was confronted and convicted.

"Well, play it safe," he said in a hoarse whisper.

"You, too." Lyla turned and met the lips that sought hers, sharing a desperate kiss within arms that squeezed her as though they couldn't let her go.

Barry broke it off reluctantly and helped her down before his need for her got the best of him. Then, with a wave, he turned toward the Gold Camp Road.

Lyla's heart lurched. Would he find Jack Rafferty? Would he return safely, to begin the life they'd both fought so hard for? Tears prickled in her eyes, until another thought occurred to her.

"By the saints, you'd better get back to Cripple in time!" she called after him. "If I've already said 'I do' to Frazier Foxe, you'll live to regret it!"

Chapter 27

Lyla hesitated with her hand on the Golden Rose's doorknob, bracing herself for whatever Victoria Chatterly and the other ladies might say upon seeing her. She'd made it from the train station unrecognized, wearing the worn brown checked dress and cape she'd rolled into her bundle, with her hair tucked up into its matching hat. She looked and felt like a frump, but these outdated clothes were more convincing attire than pants for the visits she'd make as a bride-to-be.

She stepped into the whorehouse's hushed parlor and stood for a moment. Aromas of bacon and coffee drifted in from the kitchen, but she heard no voices. It was nearly ten o'clock in the morning, which meant most of the doves would be rising soon. Best to check in with Miss Victoria before too many curious eyes and ears got her so rattled she couldn't keep her story straight. She'd taken only a few steps toward the madam's boudoir when a voice stopped her.

"My God, that *is* you! I hope those raggedy-ass clothes mean you're coming back to work instead of marrying Foxe, honey."

That cigarette-roughened bark could belong only to Cherry Blossom, and when Lyla turned she saw the Indian princess seated at one of the tables in the shadowy bar, her dark face encircled by a wreath of

323

smoke. It wouldn't do to ignore her bridesmaid, so Lyla put on a smile. "I—I'm in town to make the final arrangements for the wedding, and thought I'd stop by to—"

"And you chose me to be your maid of honor. Tell me another one." The whore's dusky gaze flickered over her outfit and then settled on her face, cynical as ever. She inhaled her cigarette, releasing the smoke with a sigh. "Look, I said some unflattering things about Thompson when I took your lunch into the jail, but Jesus! Just because he's gone doesn't mean you have to sentence yourself to life with Frazier."

Lyla managed to remain unruffled. "On the contrary, Frazier's a very interesting, generous—"

"Then why're you wearing that dress instead of a gown he bought you? He'd *shit* if he saw you looking this way."

Cherry Blossom's foul language was quite accurate, and it was clear she'd accept nothing short of the truth, which Lyla had no intention of telling. When she heard purposeful footsteps coming down the hall, she was ready to welcome anyone who'd be a diversion—anyone except Victoria Chatterly, whose porcelain features lit up with joy as she hurried into the bar.

"Lyla, dear! I knew you'd see the light," she gushed. "You may have your same bed, and a clean uniform, and start immediately. Reliable help's so hard to find, and this being Friday, we'll need to . . . whatever are you looking at me that way for?"

Knowing that Barry Thompson was alive and that she'd never again *have* to work in a whorehouse made stifling a smile very difficult. Lyla tried to control her expression while concocting a reply, but Cherry Blossom cut in.

"She's going through with it," the whore muttered as she stubbed her cigarette in an ashtray. "I'm glad Thompson's not around to see this, because he thought you were *smart*, Miss O'Riley. Must be

324

rolling in his grave, wherever he is." Cherry Blossom stood suddenly and hurried toward the grand staircase, obviously shaken.

Miss Chatterly sighed, gesturing toward a chair. "I'm afraid we're all having a hard time accepting the marshal's demise," she said with a sad shake of her head. Her aqua eyes misted over, beseeching Lyla to listen to reason. "Are you sure you know what you're getting into, dear? You're young, and I know a dozen men more suitable than . . . surely your grief is blurring your perception of this marriage."

More than anything, Lyla wished she could blurt out that Barry was alive and this charade was for his sake as much as her own! But she pressed her lips into a line, deeply touched when Victoria dabbed her eyes with a lacy handkerchief. "I know exactly what I'm doing, Miss Chatterly."

The madam patted her snowy-white hair and straightened the chain of her opal pendant as though searching for an appropriate response. "We do foolish things when we're young, things that alter the course of our lives, because we cannot—or will not—see an alternative," she said softly. After blinking away a tear, she focused directly on Lyla. "What have you to gain from this? You're throwing your life away on a—a bloody blackheart! A snake in the grass!"

Lyla's eyes widened; her story about being alone and unemployable in a town where she was accused of murder wouldn't work with this woman. "I thought you liked Frazier. He's British. Elegant and refined."

Victoria laughed harshly. "This business has taught me never to trust a man who pays for conversation. But it's our policy to provide what our clients request, and since Grace can tolerate him, I never questioned his coming here, or his bringing *you* here after your brother died. I grew suspicious, however, when he fetched your dresses and you weren't with him. Lying's not your strong suit, Lyla. Tell me what's really going on."

She was glad she'd removed the aquamarine ring before coming, because Miss Chatterly's eyes took in every detail of her shabby clothing and facial expression. "I'm sorry you feel that way," she hedged. "Frazier's been extremely gracious and kind to me, and he'd be crushed if he heard your true opinion of him. He respects you a great deal."

"He respects anyone who turns an outlandish profit, Lyla. Which makes me certain he has unsavory plans for you. What's he after, besides an heir? Frankly, I can't see him *sullying* himself to produce one."

Lyla stood, startled at the madam's hostility. It was time to leave, before she either caved in or lost this caring woman's friendship forever. "Please— trust my judgment," she implored. "There's more to this match than meets the eye, and someday everyone in Cripple will understand that."

She strode out to the street without looking back, her thoughts in a jumble. The Rose had been her first stop because her story needed polishing before she faced the dressmaker, the caterer, and other shopkeepers who were helping make this the most spectacular wedding Cripple had ever seen. Dealing with such luxury and its price tag intimidated her, because her tastes had always been as simple as her needs.

As Lyla approached Mrs. Delacroix's shop she faltered. There in the plate glass window, displayed with queenly grace upon a dress form, was her wedding gown. Frazier's creation, translated from a sketch into satin and lace and white ermine trim, made her mouth hang open. If only she were donning this magnificent dress for Barry!

She stepped closer to read the elegantly-printed card posted in the window: *You are cordially invited to celebrate the uniting in Holy Matrimony of Miss Lyla O'Riley and Mr. Frazier Foxe, Esquire . . .*

Her wedding invitation, in black ink on creamy vellum . . . Reality suddenly grabbed her by the insides: to everyone except herself and Barry, this ceremony was as sacred and binding as the McClanahans'. What if Thompson and Matt didn't return in time to stop it? What if God himself detained them somehow, and as punishment for this blasphemous deception she became lawfully wedded to a man determined to defile her?

Sweat popped out on her upper lip despite the brisk wind. She was ready to bolt, to disappear to *anywhere*, when a lightly-accented voice called out from the shop.

"*Chérie!* Miss O'Riley!" Mrs. Delacroix was waving excitedly, and then she was rushing out to grab Lyla's hand. "Do you like it? Do you think Monsieur Foxe will be pleased?" she gushed. "Such exquisite fabrics he ordered—and his design! It was an *honor* to be chosen to sew your wedding gown!"

And it was probably a year's pay, Lyla caught herself thinking. She smiled then, because people who stood to make so much money from this grandiose event wouldn't demand her justification for it. The dressmaker clutching her hand probably gossiped to all her other customers about this unlikely match, but while in her presence Mrs. Delacroix would express only praise . . . and encouragement to spend more of Foxe's money. It was an opportunity not to be missed.

"I—I really shouldn't be here. My gown was to be a surprise from Frazier," Lyla said with a little laugh. "But I couldn't stay away! The fit must be flawless, and we can't trust a man's judgment about accessories and underthings for the most important day of my life, now, can we?"

"*Mais non!*" the seamstress replied with a giggle. "Please—come in! Now's the perfect time to coordinate what you'll need. Marie!" she called to her assistant, who sat sewing at a treadle machine near

327

the back of the shop's main salon. "Miss O'Riley's here for a fitting and she needs *everything*. Have Miss Dailey and Mr. Kraus and the others come at once! We mustn't keep her waiting."

Within half an hour Mrs. Delacroix's salon was buzzing with shopkeepers drawn like bees to the golden pollen Lyla was ready to shower upon them, as befitted her celebrity status. She loved it! The finest shoes and hosiery and silk underthings were displayed by six or seven of Cripple's most exclusive merchants, and she couldn't bear to disappoint any of them. She chose the best of their lines and then disappeared into a fitting room as sedately as her childlike glee would allow.

On went lace-trimmed silk bloomers, a feather-light corset—which buttoned down the front!—and stockings of sheerest white. The leather pumps slid easily onto her feet, and when she peeked into the mirror she chuckled. Barry would be getting such a grin out of this, in more ways than one, and Foxe was in for a jolt when he saw the tab she'd run up on his accounts. And esquire that he was, he'd have to keep a civil tongue until he had her alone, which she didn't plan to let happen.

"Chérie? You are ready for the gown now?" the seamstress asked from outside the door.

"Aye! Come in!"

Mrs. Delacroix gave her an approving glance as she carefully wheeled the dress form in, holding the voluminous train over her other arm. Lyla stroked the ermine trim along the flounced front, marveling at its softness. Frazier had designed a fairy-tale gown that sparkled with crystal beadwork and shimmering white satin, with leg-of-mutton sleeves that ballooned gracefully at the shoulders. "It's so lovely," she whispered.

"Monsieur Foxe should've been a designer," the seamstress agreed as she gathered the dress into her arms.

328

Moments later Lyla was gaping at her reflection, awed by the transformation: from a pauper to a princess, by the grace of a gown. Mrs. Delacroix was humming, checking the fit at the bust and sides, her russet bun quivering with her excitement. "The others, they would like to see, if you don't mind," she suggested quietly.

"Oh—of course." Lyla smiled, and with the petite dressmaker taking charge of her train she entered the main salon.

A whispering of admiration went though the gathering like the fluttering of wings, and the shop-keepers broke into solemn applause. They walked slowly around her, exclaiming over the gown's intricate detail and exquisite materials, and Lyla felt herself flush with delight. If only Thompson were here to wink at her!

And then she stood stock-still, watching a gentleman who'd paused outside the shop window. He was gazing at her with a tenderness that was touching, a thin smile that was so familiar . . .

". . . a romantic Valentine's Day ceremony—certainly a wedding *I* won't miss," Miss Dailey was chirping, her hands clasped at her bosom.

"Nor I," another shopkeeper replied. He bowed slightly and picked up his shoeboxes. "You'll be the loveliest young woman ever to grace the aisle of a church, Miss O'Riley. Every man there will wish to be in Frazier's place, if you don't mind my saying so."

Lyla didn't mind at all—would *choose* nearly any other man. Her memory prickling, she glanced toward the front window again, but the wistful admirer was gone.

And a few minutes later so was she, once again wearing the brown checked dress and cape, once again blending into the crowd along Bennett Avenue. Her visit to the printer and the caterer would wait until she was more fashionably attired, so these men would treat her like Frazier Foxe's fiancée rather than an urchin who claimed to be the Lyla O'Riley on the vellum invitations.

She strolled along the sidewalk, smiling when people recognized her. Lyla had no trouble imagining the whispers that passed behind hands as she walked by well-heeled matrons and others who knew her from the Wanted posters—which Frazier must've ordered removed from the storefront windows. Recognition was precisely what she wanted, so Foxe would have no trouble finding her.

Crossing the street, she felt lured to the livery stable. Surely after all these weeks her mare had found another home, or met a fate Lyla didn't want to consider, but she had to satisfy her curiosity. She stopped inside the entrance, allowing her eyes to adjust to the dimness.

A stable boy looked up from shoveling manure, but otherwise there were only rows of horses as she slowly passed down the side aisle. None of their rumps resembled Calico's . . . only by some miracle would her beloved horse have returned to Cripple and been cared for in her absence.

Then a familiar whinny made her head snap up and Lyla stepped quickly along the straw-strewn walkway toward the corner. There was Calico, prancing happily in the last stall! Lyla squealed and rushed in to hug her horse, her heart pounding wildly. She'd found her mare, she'd recovered the man she loved, and only days from now the life she longed for would be hers!

"Are you all right, miss? I heard you yelp."

She turned to grin at the young stablehand. "Never finer! How much do I owe you for taking care of my Calico? I never dreamed—"

"Matt McClanahan's paid up through the end of the month," he replied with a lopsided smile. "You, uh, don't look like the girl he married."

"I'm not," she replied saucily, "but I'll certainly kiss him for doing *this!*"

The boy's scraggly attempt at a first mustache twitched. "You're—you're Lyla O'Riley! The girl in the papers! Why, it's my pleasure to feed—"

"Miss O'Riley has more important business to attend to than listening to your yammering, Tim," a reedy voice interrupted them.

Lyla looked beyond the stablehand's lean shoulders and stopped breathing. Rex Adams was surveying her, his skinny blue-uniformed arms crossed over his chest. And his catlike gaze left no doubt as to where the carroty-haired deputy intended to conduct his business.

Chapter 28

"I knew you'd show up here again, Miss O'Riley. Returning to the scene of the crime, as it were," Adams gloated as he escorted her down the sidewalk.

"If you're so smart, why do you work for Foxe?" Lyla walked proudly along, nodding to people as they recognized her. "He had Eberhardt killed, you know. He'll dispose of *you* when you're no longer useful to him."

The deputy laughed sarcastically and opened the jailhouse door. "Wally was a chucklehead and everyone knew it. When Frazier learns I've kept you from running off again, he'll see I get promoted to town marshal immediately."

"It'll never happen. Connor himself told me Frazier had no intention of putting you in that position. And what'll your wife and children do when you turn up as an accident victim, like Wally did?" She stopped beside his too-tidy desk to watch his reaction, almost grinning at how Barry Thompson's return would send this traitor into a tailspin.

Rex studied her with pale green eyes that said he, too, wondered if the gravy train might get derailed soon. But instead of backing down, he pulled a ring of keys from his desk drawer. "That's tall talk for a short woman," he scoffed. "Stupid, too. Why you'd want to duck out of a marriage to *his* money is beyond me."

Lyla shook her head, offering no resistance when the wiry deputy steered her toward the cells. "Don't say I didn't warn you. Frazier will be furious when he finds you've locked up his fiancée as though she were some whore from Poverty Gulch. You'll look like a chucklehead yourself, Rex."

"We'll see about that."

The door clanked shut on the same cell she occupied during her last visit, and Lyla gripped the cool metal bars, gazing purposefully at her warden. "I'm telling you this as a friend, Rex," she said earnestly. "I came back to Cripple so Frazier would find me and get his comeuppance. Save us both a lot of trouble and let me check into the Imperial. You won't be sorry."

"That's right. I won't be sorry for listening to my instinct instead of to you!" he said with a cocky chuckle. "As if anyone would believe what you're saying."

When he walked into the main office again, Lyla settled calmly onto the rough bunk. The cell next to hers was empty, and a grizzled stranger was snoring, his mouth ajar, in the one on the other side of it. Plenty of time to think about the startling drama that would unfold as February fourteenth drew nearer . . . today alone had been eventful, starting with Miss Victoria's lecture and being celebrated at the dressmaker's, and then finding Calico!

Her thoughts wandered back to Mrs. Delacroix's, to the warm pride she'd experienced as the shopkeepers admired her in her splendid white gown. Foxe's money couldn't buy her happiness, but it had purchased a few moments of acceptance: she was no longer a mineworker's sister or a maid at a whorehouse. She was to be a wealthy man's wife.

And she had no trouble projecting this inner radiance to the future, when her name would be Mrs. Barry Thompson. How far she'd come since New

Year's, when she'd begged the issue by saying her only honorable alternative was returning to Ireland—

Lyla's head thumped back against the wall. The face of the man in the window flashed before her: an older gentleman with a henpecked air about him, with the same slender nose and thinning hair but more wrinkles around his lusterless eyes, and a mouth not familiar with grinning.

"Mary, Mother of God," she said in a strangled whisper, "it was Hadley! Hadley McDuff, come to Cripple Creek to fetch me!"

When he heard the thunder of distant hoofbeats, Barry cocked his pistol and crouched in the shadows of the cave where he was camping. A rider would need a reason for penetrating this patch of woods, and he was on Foxe's land, so he could take no chances. He held his breath, listening to the horse pick its way through the dead leaves and close-growing trees.

Bob-bob-WHITE, came the whistle.

Grinning, Barry emerged into the bright daylight, holstering his gun. "I was beginning to think you found trouble. Did that poster of Rafferty get you through the gate?"

"Yeah—not that it did me much good." Matt McClanahan swung down from his bay and stretched, as though he'd spent the morning going at a full gallop. "The gatekeeper suspected Jack took out across the far side of the range, and his wagon was empty when I found it. Nothing there that wasn't nailed down."

"No papers stuffed behind the bunk?"

"Nope."

"Damn!" Thompson stomped the ground, because Rafferty had their most pressing evidence against Frazier Foxe—and he knew it. And God alone could guess how that murdering fugitive would put such information to use. "Any trouble getting past Hollingsworth?"

Matt grinned, showing a mouthful of even white teeth. "You should've seen the old guy's face when I told him I was investigating for Quentin Yarborough, on suspicion that his name had been forged and his services misrepresented."

"Did he cooperate?"

McClanahan shrugged. "He had no reason not to. I waited until I saw Foxe's carriage leaving—"

"Probably to find Lyla," Barry sighed.

"—so our Oliver didn't feel threatened when I asked him to find some paperwork with Yarborough's name on it."

"Didn't figure he'd be a problem, since he helped Lyla get out of there," the marshal said quietly, "but now he's in it up to his eyeballs, and we'll have to be sure Frazier doesn't retaliate. Did that bag-of-bones cook raise a stink?"

"*Cook* is not the word for what Allegra Keating does to food, ol' buddy. But at least she trusted me enough to feed me." The detective wiped his mouth with the back of his hand as though the terrible meal still plagued him. "In fact, she insisted that whatever information I found in the files would only prove Frazier's innocence. Talked like Lyla was the real criminal, for tricking Foxe into marrying her."

Barry rolled his eyes, hoping Miss O'Riley's wiles would keep Foxe off-balance, once she let him find her. "What'd you see that's useful?"

"You remember when he was spearheading the new opera house fund drive, and raising the money to bring Arizona Charley and the Mexican bullfight to the district?"

"Those projects had a pretty high price tag, as I recall."

"And all the records are signed by that phony attorney Yarborough," McClanahan replied with a nod. "Which means Foxe inflated the cost when he solicited from his wealthy friends—"

"And pocketed the difference between what we paid and the actual expense. Just like he'll do if that refinery gets built." Thompson grunted, his disgust stronger than ever. "At least we've got him on extortion. See if you can find Eberhardt's body, and I'll head north after Rafferty. He used to hang out with Butch Cassidy's gang, so I'll check out Brown's Park and Hole in the Wall."

"You damn well better be back from Wyoming before Lyla becomes Foxe's valentine," Matt warned. "It's already the fourth. If it looks like Rafferty's vanished, head on back to town and we'll lock Foxe up on the evidence we've got."

"We want to nail him so he can't wiggle out of it, though," Barry pointed out. "His will and that other agreement might stand up even if the other signature's faked, because Lyla signed them, too."

The marshal looked out over the rolling plains beyond the woods that sheltered them, hoping his woman could keep Foxe at bay long enough. "Surely his staff knows this marriage is a hoax," he said softly. "I can't imagine Frazier even touching her, or flirting like a fiancé would."

His best friend's swarthy face stiffened, and Matt hesitantly pulled a folded piece of paper from his inside coat pocket. "I . . . was going to present this little gem as a prank, at your bachelor party. Slipped it under my vest while Hollingsworth was checking the desk up in Frazier's chambers. Seems the old boy's more interested in her than we thought."

A shiver that had nothing to do with the temperature went up Thompson's spine when he unfolded a heart-stopping sketch of Lyla. Her lush breasts protruded above an unfastened lavender gown as she smiled provocatively over her shoulder at him . . . exactly as she had that first evening in the Rose's pantry.

"Jesus," he muttered. "I may have to ride night

336

and day, but by God I *will* be back in Cripple before that bastard ever sees her in a wedding gown."

Matt's jaw tightened. "Better hurry, pal—he's got a painting of her wearing that, too. So unbelievably beautiful you'll have to see her for yourself."

His insides tightened and he went into the cave to roll his few belongings into his blanket. "Take care, Matt. And thanks for showing your face where I couldn't," he said as he came outside. "Look after Lyla, will you?"

"You bet. Watch your back, Thompson," he replied solemnly. "Don't take any chances, now that she's almost yours."

Almost yours. The words stabbed at him as he hurried toward where Buck was tethered. What if Foxe wasn't the pansy he'd assumed him to be? What if those threats about turning Lyla over to Connor were only a smokescreen for what that British bastard really intended to do, once he had her imprisoned in his mansion again? Any man who drew the subjects Frazier Foxe did, with such loving, damning detail, was an enemy to be watched with utmost caution.

He swung into his saddle, vowing to smash the Englishman's monocle into his brain if he so much as laid a hand on Lyla.

"Of all the asinine—how do you think this looks, Adams? The future Mrs. Frazier Foxe locked up in jail, only minutes after she tried on her wedding gown in front of Cripple's most prestigious shop-keepers!"

Lyla came awake immediately as Foxe's voice, more clipped than usual, reached her from the office. She lay in the grayness of the dawn chuckling, picturing the hapless Rex Adams with even less color than usual in his freckled complexion.

"You could've entrusted her to Victoria Chatterly, for God's sake, or—"

337

Sitting up on the hard bunk, Lyla prepared herself for when Frazier would upbraid her, too. On and on he went at Adams, in a tirade quite unlike his usual aloof disdain. Surely his monocle was fogged, or perhaps popped completely out, angry as he sounded! She began to giggle and had to nip a knuckle to control herself when she heard footsteps and the intermittent tapping of his walking stick.

"Dear-heart, I'm so very sorry! Oh, my Lyla, my darling, I'm here for you now!" Foxe crooned as he approached the cell. His expression matched his syrupy tone as he gestured for the hangdog deputy to unlock the cell, and Lyla thought she might gag.

But of course Frazier had to play the doting, horrified fiancé, and it was best to follow his lead when they were in public. "I tried to reason with him, but he wouldn't listen," she replied archly. "I'll simply die if Mrs. Delacroix or the others hear where I landed after I left her shop!"

"Calm yourself, dear-heart. We'll see that your reputation suffers no slur because of this beetle-brain's incompetence." Frazier clamped his arm around her shoulders with another sickening smile and then glared at Rex. "And we'll see *this* nincompoop *fired!* My contacts at the United States Marshal's office will be hearing about this, Mr. Adams, and I guarantee you'll be unemployable in Colorado because of it!"

The deputy looked ready to cry, so Lyla preceded Frazier out the door without flashing the I-told-you-so smirk she'd saved for him. Her turn was coming. Foxe's stylish black carriage was parked a short distance down the street, with Kelly Jameson lounging on its driver's seat. He winked suggestively at her before she was whisked inside by her escort.

"Drop us at the Imperial and then return to the ranch, as we discussed," Foxe instructed. "And be damn sure Connor and the others are here by the thirteenth."

"Yessir, Mr. Foxe."

Frazier slid onto the seat across from her and slammed the carriage door, his true colors showing now. "You, young lady, have some explaining to do," he said in a hiss. "And when I'm finished with you, Connor has a few choice words."

"Connor deserved everything he got! I will *not* be threatened!"

"We'll discuss this in private."

"Yes, we will!" Lyla stared defiantly out the coach window, all the while feeling Frazier's disgusted gaze. Since Foxe planned to guard her here until the wedding, McClanahan had the perfect chance to gather information at Foxe Hollow. Barry would return with the incriminating documents Jack Rafferty was carrying, and she'd be keeping their target in plain sight so this ordeal would be over within a few days. She couldn't allow herself to become smug, but these aces up her sleeve would keep her confident no matter how Frazier tried to intimidate her.

He hurried her through the Imperial's lavishly-decorated lobby as though he couldn't wait to get her upstairs, wearing a fawning smile for the benefit of the few people who saw them. It was Sunday morning, February fifth, and Lyla sensed she'd be sick to death of this artificiality by the time Barry and Matt rescued her.

They entered the hotel's most exclusive suite and when Foxe shut the door the change in him was immediate. He laid his stick and derby in a nearby chair with the deliberate grace of an executioner who had all day. His cool demeanor warned her he'd act particularly nasty until she acquiesced to his wishes.

He crossed his arms over his chest, carefully, so he wouldn't rumple his starched shirt. "You were a fool to leave during that blizzard, Miss O'Riley."

"And you were a fool to assume it would stop me." She walked slowly to a table that held a vase of wine-red roses, reminding herself that she, too, had a facade to maintain. If Frazier suspected he was *her* prisoner, instead of vice versa, her cause would be lost.

"Whatever possessed you to come to Cripple, dearheart?" he asked sardonically. "Surely you knew I'd look here first. Surely you knew I'd not *stop* looking until I found you."

Lyla plucked a rose from the arrangement and inhaled its deep sweetness. She turned, widening her eyes at him. "I can't imagine you trusting the fit of that magnificent gown to luck, after spending hundreds of dollars to impress your friends with it. I'm thinner than when Mrs. Delacroix made my first dresses, you know."

He adjusted his monocle, frowning slightly. "And?"

"And what?" she asked coyly.

Frazier stalked over to stand in front of her. "How did it fit?" he demanded. "What did you think of it?"

Milking his moment of insecurity, she closed her eyes and inhaled her flower again. "I felt . . . like a princess," she breathed. "Miss Dailey and Mr. Kraus and the others *loved* it, Frazier, and so will all the guests who cram into that church to get a peek at me wearing it." She opened her eyes, speaking sincerely this time. "You're truly a talented man. Every millionaire's daughter for years to come will copy her dress from yours."

As she hoped, her profuse compliments made him forget his anger. His slender face was alight with the knowledge that his accomplishments would be lauded by the elite of Cripple Creek. What other groom could boast of not only affording such a gown, but of creating it?

"I'm glad you like it," he said quietly. "I can't wait to see you gliding down the aisle in it. And I'd appreciate it if you'd change out of that rag you're wearing immediately. Your clothes are in the adjoining room."

340

Lyla chuckled, heady with her success. She turned toward the door, forcing herself to walk rather than skip, and was stopped by Foxe's imperious voice.

"You realize, Miss O'Riley, that if you so much as attempt another escape you won't live through it."

She gave him a solemn smile, again speaking sincerely. "I wouldn't dream of leaving you, Frazier. I have far too much to look forward to."

Chapter 29

For the next few days Lyla felt like an actress in a fairy tale being performed upon the stage of Cripple Creek. She floated from one fine shop to the next, costumed in her lovely dresses, spending exorbitant amounts on anything her heart desired, at Frazier's insistence. She ordered an entire wardrobe from Mrs. Delacroix, complete with coordinating underthings from Miss Dailey's and the finest leather shoes from Mr. Kraus. Each meal was an elaborate affair at an elite restaurant. Each evening found them at a play or a concert—any place Foxe could show off his bride-to-be.

It was an impoverished immigrant's dream, and it was Lyla's nightmare. By hobnobbing with attorneys, bankers, mine owners, and Cripple's highest society—some she'd known when she was a maid at the Golden Rose—she quickly became the toast of the town. The girl on the Wanted posters only weeks ago was now the mining district's most celebrated ingenue. But she was being squired around by the wrong man!

Why hadn't Matt or Emily McClanahan contacted her by now? Where was Hadley McDuff hiding—and what would she say to him when she saw him? And why was it taking Barry so long to catch up to Jack Rafferty? Each time she set foot outside the Imperial on Frazier's arm she was on constant guard, watching for the people who could spring her from this elaborate trap. Numerous photographs of her appeared in the *Cripple Creek Times*, but beneath the bright smile she wore in public beat the heart of a frightened little girl who wanted this masquerade to end.

Frazier, meanwhile, basked in the glory she was bringing him and flashed a gleeful mustachioed grin wherever they went. Only Lyla knew he was gloating, holding her so possessively with his gloved hands because he assumed she'd flee the moment he let her out of his sight. The door between their adjoining rooms was always open; she sensed his presence in the night, checking to see that she was in her bed. She heard the scratching of his pen in the mornings, sketching her in various stages of undress, in a myriad of moods . . . in the throes of a passion he represented with aching, erotic clarity yet never showed the least inclination toward participating in himself.

Just when Lyla thought his duplicity would drive her mad, she caught sight of Emily McClanahan. A uniformed waiter was serving them tea in a secluded alcove of the Imperial's lobby, and in her excitement she nearly knocked the sterling tray from his hands.

"Emily! Emily, over here!" she cried as she sprang from her chair. Knowing Foxe couldn't stop her with other guests and the waiter looking on, Lyla hurried over to greet the petite blonde—the only friend she'd seen for days!

Emily gripped her hands, her tawny eyes wide with questions. "I was hoping I'd see you while I was in town," she said with a cautious glance toward Frazier. "You look wonderful, Lyla! And you're certainly stealing my thunder, being in all the papers and becoming the belle of Cripple Creek."

"We were just having tea—waiter! Please bring us another cup and saucer," she instructed.

The man bowed on his way to the kitchen and Lyla grinned uncontrollably for the first time since she'd come to town. Finally, someone who could tell her how Matt and Barry's search was progressing! And by the saints, she'd find a way to get Frazier out of earshot if only for a few precious moments, to hear every morsel of news Emily could tell her.

Gesturing toward the overstuffed chair beside her own, she addressed Foxe in the honeyed voice she used when she wanted to waste his money on some frivolous extravagance. "Do you believe our luck, Frazier dear? Mrs. McClanahan's in town, and she was looking for us!"

"A pleasure to see you again, Emily," Foxe replied crisply. He rose to grip her hand briefly, wary of this visit. True to his new image, however, he put on a smile and offered her the crystal plate of tarts and little iced cakes. "Sweets for the sweet? The Imperial prepares one of the most sumptuous tea trays in town."

"I really can't," Emily replied apologetically.

In her excitement, Lyla hadn't noticed her friend's pallor, and Emily wasn't the type to fret over her weight. She was wearing a jacket of burnt orange velvet trimmed in brown fur, with a matching hat that sported an ostrich plume—an outfit that would have flattered her coloring immensely if she hadn't been growing paler by the minute.

"Emily, is there anything—"

The young woman clutched her stomach, covered her mouth, and glanced frantically about before leaning toward a huge ornamental urn displayed beside her chair. It was the neatest job of retching Lyla had ever seen, but it sent Frazier up from his seat in disgust.

"Really, madam! If you were ill—"

"Frazier, for God's sake," Lyla hissed. "Get us a cold cloth instead of causing such a spectacle!"

Foxe's expression told her he suspected something,

344

but a whiff of the urn's contents sent him scurrying toward the registration desk. Lyla wrapped her arm around Emily's shoulders and guided her toward a sofa across the lobby. "An ingenious trick to get rid of Frazier," she murmured, "but you didn't have to throw up for *me*."

"It's no trick. It's morning sickness, all day long," came the barely-audible reply.

Her eyes widened and she hugged her friend fiercely. "Congratulations! Oh, Emily—"

"Shhh! Just listen, before he gets back." Emily eased herself down, her golden eyes urgent in a face as pale as the lace doily on the sofa. "Matt made it back from Foxe Hollow with evidence of forgery and extortion," she whispered, "but Barry hasn't found that Rafferty fellow or the other papers. He's gone to Wyoming looking for—"

"*Wyoming?*"

"*Shhhh!* Here he comes." Emily leaned back, fanning herself weakly with her hand as Frazier approached them. When he gingerly handed the wet cloth to Lyla, she managed a smile. "I'm truly sorry I spoiled your tea, Mr. Foxe. Dr. Geary says I'll stop erupting in a month or so, but meanwhile I'm liable to be an embarrassment."

Frazier's brow arched above his monocle. "You're . . . in the family way?"

"Yes. I just confirmed it before I came here."

"Well, I—" He seemed embarrassed, glancing toward the maid who was carrying the offensive urn from the lobby. Then he clasped his hands, composing the transparently false smile Lyla had come to know so well. "Please accept my warmest wishes, and send my heartiest congratulations to Mr. McClanahan."

Emily nodded, appearing stronger now. "Matt's at the bank, probably waiting for me," she said with a hint of mischief in her voice. "I—I hate to meet him, smelling like . . . would you be so kind as to bring me

345

a shot of schnapps, Mr. Foxe?"

His mustache twitched. "I beg your pardon?"

"Schnapps," she repeated, her eyes taking on a coyness Lyla truly admired. "It settles my stomach, you see, and the peppermint tastes—and smells—much better than what I just got rid of."

Once again Frazier's face clouded over with suspicion but he headed toward the registration desk to make her request.

"You are a *genius*," Lyla whispered gaily.

"And you're treading on thin ice," Emily warned in a low voice. "Matt says he'll check on you when he can, but of course he can't get close enough for Frazier to notice him, and he wants Barry to have the pleasure of making the arrest. Be careful," she added urgently. "If Thompson doesn't make it back before the ceremony, *bail out*. If you wait too long and end up married to Frazier—"

"It'll never happen," she replied staunchly. She pressed the cool cloth to Emily's forehead, refusing to consider the consequences if the marshal returned too late. "Come hell or high water, Barry'll be here. He promised."

Emily nodded. "I hope nothing happens. Oh, Frazier—you're a saint," she continued in her normal voice.

Foxe approached with a small tumbler of clear liquid, eyeing them, yet smiling as though nothing unseemly had transpired since she arrived. "To your health, Mrs. McClanahan," he toasted as he gave her the glass.

Holding the liqueur daintily, Emily smiled at Lyla. "To years of happiness with the man you love," she said as she lifted her drink in salute, "and to you, Mr. Foxe, a lifetime of surprise and adventure only a feisty lass like Lyla can provide."

As the next days passed in a flurry of receptions and

teas held in their honor, Lyla became increasingly anxious. Surely Hadley hadn't returned to Ireland without speaking to her, yet she never saw him in the stores or at the nightly performances they attended in Cripple's magnificent opera houses. He was a decent man at heart—certainly preferable to Frazier—but he was a bumbler, and Lyla feared he'd appear at the last moment with some trumped-up plan that would foil Thompson's rescue efforts.

And where *was* Barry? Lyla gazed out her hotel room window each morning, praying for the sight of a tall, sturdy rider on a buckskin stallion, heading toward town along one of the mountain trails. But he didn't appear.

She was losing her appetite. She was losing her nerve. Each event they attended became more diffi-cult to endure, and Lyla was sorely tempted to blurt out that Frazier Foxe was a murderer and a man who cheated his closest friends. But who would believe her? Not the millionaires whose soirées grew even more lavish as Valentine's Day approached—not after they'd watched her pander to Foxe and happily spend hundreds of his dollars every day. Exposing him without the marshal's support would be suicide . . . Frazier would see to that.

And on Sunday the twelfth, when the Foxe carriage brought Connor, Miss Keating, and Oliver Hollingsworth to the Imperial, Lyla had no choice but to keep her mouth shut and keep praying that Thompson would arrive soon. Allegra seemed more pinched than usual as she quizzed Frazier about his arrangements and her duties for the wedding. Connor, who still bore some bacon grease burns and a few toothmarks, kept his distance as though saving his revenge for when he got her alone, after the ceremony.

Only Hollingsworth carried on with his usual dignity, smiling blandly even when Frazier's nerves began to fray. There was little for him or Allegra to do, since the hotel's staff performed all the house-keeping, so he chatted or merely sat reading while waiting for Foxe to summon him.

Frazier declined invitations for the thirteenth so he could spend the morning confirming that all was ready for the ceremony and the banquet at the New Yorker restaurant. As he picked up his derby and gold-headed walking stick, he gave Lyla and Hollingsworth a pointed look. "See that my bride gets her rest," he instructed. "Tomorrow's her big day, and nothing short of radiance will do for Mrs. Frazier Foxe."

The valet bowed slightly, his face as smooth and pink as a baby's, until Foxe shut the door. Then he turned to Lyla with a conspiratorial grin. "I know you're up to something, Miss O'Riley. May I be of assistance? Is all going according to plan?"

Taken aback by his candor, Lyla studied him closely. "It's too soon to tell," she replied. "Did Frazier explode in your face when he discovered I escaped from the house?"

"I think he expected it, actually."

She nodded, gazing out the window for the hundredth time. "Does he realize I took the will and those other papers with me?"

"Not that I know of. He was too bent on catching you to check his files, and I have no intention of telling him about Marshal Thompson's appearance, or Mr. McClanahan's, either." Hollingsworth's blue eyes sparkled, showing a boyish side Lyla had never imagined. "They're helping you, aren't they? Trying to catch Foxe before he catches you?"

She nodded, sighing.

Oliver lifted her chin with a gentle finger, smiling. "It would be my pleasure to drive the coach or help you escape on the train, right now, while Frazier's out. Jolly good fun, watching him stomp about when he's been had!"

"Thank you," Lyla murmured gratefully, "but

348

only the marshal can solve my problem permanently. I can't run forever, Oliver."

He bowed slightly. "Then I'll see if I can amuse Miss Keating while you rest. Poor dear's a mess, now that she realizes the man of her fantasies is indeed marrying a little princess less than half his age."

His jaunty words were meant as encouragement, but she glanced toward the door, her brow furrowing. "What if she tells Frazier that a detective's searched his files and a marshal's been snooping about? It'll ruin everything! Barry Thompson's supposed to be dead, you know."

"She never reads the papers—didn't realize who that huge fellow was when he gave her such a fright in the pantry," the valet said with a chuckle. "And McClanahan played her like a fine violin. Complimented her luncheon, and assured her that he'd been barking up the wrong tree, where Quentin Yarborough was concerned.

"Actually, I'm glad she didn't accept my proposal all those years ago," he added with a thoughtful chortle. "Allegra's a nitpicker of the most merciless sort, devoid of humor and imagination. She'll spend the rest of her life sniveling over her lost love. Spineless, she is. And a bloody poor cook to boot."

Lyla watched him leave the suite, still amazed at the valet's loyalty. A surprising man, Oliver Hollingsworth . . . or was this another of Foxe's ploys? Perhaps he *paid* his manservant to encourage her escapes, so he'd have an excuse to chastise her in warped ways only Frazier could devise.

She gazed forlornly out the window, unable to keep a tear from dribbling down her cheek. *Barry, please—the ceremony's tomorrow! Send me a sign that you're here . . . tell me I won't be wearing that wedding dress for anyone but you, love.*

Lyla, can you forgive me, honey? Run like hell

rather than showing up at the church, because if I get to Cripple and you're married to that twisted bastard . . .

Thompson couldn't remember the last time he'd cried, but as he gazed helplessly out his window at an endless expanse of drifted snow, he was damn close to bawling. He checked his watch again. Two hours they'd been sitting here, while the plow cleared a stretch of treacherous mountain track that an avalanche had buried earlier this morning.

Taking the train had been his only hope for a timely arrival, after a thorough search of Brown's Park and Hole in the Wall turned up no sign of Jack Rafferty. Both he and Buck were exhausted. He'd hoped to catch some sleep so he could arrive rested, to rescue Lyla once and for all and retire to a life of loving her.

The conductor passed down the aisle wearing a taut smile. "Sit tight, folks," he was saying—as though they were going anywhere! "Another hour or so should have the tracks cleared, and then we'll be on our way. Your patience is greatly appreciated."

Patience, my ass! Barry fumed. All his life he'd waited for a woman like Lyla, and now, just when he was about to prove himself worthy of her love, a blizzard had stopped him cold.

He checked his watch again, and, hearing a muffled crackling in his shirt pocket, he pulled out the revealing sketch. He held his breath, gazing at Lyla's flawless beauty. Would he ever caress those glorious breasts again? Or would she belong to another man by the time he got to Cripple?

If the latter were true, he might as well be as dead as the papers speculated he was.

Chapter 30

When the swelling chords from the pipe organ drifted into the back room, Lyla's heart lurched. Her worst nightmare was coming true. Moments from now she'd be following Grace Putnam down the aisle, toward a madman bent on destroying her while he produced an heir for his empire.

Where are you, Barry?

"If you don't stop shaking so, I'll *never* get this gown buttoned," Miss Victoria fussed from behind her.

"If we had any sense, we'd be whisking her out the back door," the Indian princess retorted. Without her warpaint, resplendent in a gown of scarlet watered silk, Cherry Blossom resembled a beauty queen who was aging but not gracefully. She scowled as she brushed at the white ermine trim on Lyla's gown. "Get ahold of yourself and get out of here, for Chrissakes! Can't you see how *ludicrous* this marriage is? Foxe is a perverted—"

"It'll work out for the best. You'll see," Lyla mumbled. She blinked repeatedly to clear her eyes.

"No sense in upsetting her, Grace. She's had plenty of time to break this engagement and has chosen not to." Miss Chatterly stepped around to give her a final looking-over. "That truly is the most magnificent gown I've ever seen. You look like a fairy princess, Lyla."

"She looks like a sacrificial lamb and you know it." Grace went over to a bookcase and picked up a small, beautifully-wrapped gift. "From your beloved," she sneered. "He said you'd be expecting it."

Her hands shook as she tore away the ribbons. Had Frazier kept his word? Was it the silver shamrock pendant that had started this whole horrible affair? As the delicate chain and Mick's handiwork slithered out of its paper packing, Lyla clutched it to her chest. No matter what happened now, at least her brother's most precious gift was hers once more.

Gently Miss Victoria took the necklace and fastened the clasp behind her collar. Grace arranged the shamrock so it nestled where the lace flounce came to a vee above Lyla's breasts, her dark eyes narrowing. "This is no wedding present, Lyla. You wore this shamrock when you worked at the Rose—"

"Let her be, Grace."

"—and it was stolen on Christmas Eve, along with my turquoise combs!" Cherry Blossom's eyes hardened, reflecting the red of her dress. "Foxe was behind that robbery, and you *were* in on it, just as the papers said! Here I was giving you the benefit of the doubt because—"

"And right now you'll give her your warmest smile and your best wishes," Victoria declared as she pulled Grace back by the shoulders. "I believe our Lyla's done things she felt she had to do, and her reasons will be revealed to us very soon now."

"Thank you," she breathed. Turning from her two attendants, Lyla stood before the mirror, her heart in her throat. Never had her golden-brown hair looked more lustrous, gathered up beneath a coronet of crystal beads which held yards of diaphanous white veil that trailed gracefully over her train. The white satin of her dress glimmered when she shifted, its delicate beadwork sending little rainbows sparkling alongside the soft ermine trim. And there shone her

352

shamrock, restored to its rightful place.

I know you'll be here, Barry. Just don't be too late! she prayed silently.

The little room's side door opened to admit Matt McClanahan, who sucked in his breath at the sight of her. Glancing at the madam and Miss Putnam, he took Lyla in a careful hug.

"There's no sign of him, honey," he whispered against her ear. "Please—I'll handcuff Foxe myself and tell the crowd to go home. This is—"

"No!" she blurted, her heartbeat racing. She took a quavery breath, wording her reply carefully. "I'm fine, I tell you. It's Emily you should be concerned about. Now go on, Mr. McClanahan, before the mother of your child thinks you've abandoned her for another woman!"

With a shake of his handsome head Matt departed, taking the last of her hopes with him. What could have happened? *Why are you tormenting me this way, Thompson? For the love of God, get yourself over here!*

A few endless moments of silence passed in the airless little room. Despite the light snow outside, Lyla felt sweat drizzling down her spine and a curious weightlessness made her head float. What if Thompson didn't show?

She refused to think about it. When the door opened again and Oliver Hollingsworth poked his cherubic face inside, she let her veil flutter down in front of her and resolutely gripped her bouquet—red roses and pale orange blossoms. Perhaps their heady perfume would keep her from fainting away before this ordeal was over.

"Oh, Miss Lyla," he breathed, "when Frazier sees you—"

"He's painted me this way. Remember?"

"Yes. Of course."

With a nod, he let the madam and Grace precede them into the dim hallway that ran behind the sanctuary. The organ swelled and Lyla caught the scent of flowers and expensive perfumes and her own anxiety. Her mouth tasted like a dirty penny. She took Hollingsworth's elbow and stood in a small alcove as the ushers showed Miss Chatterly and the last guests to their pews.

"You look stunning in your tuxedo," she whispered to keep herself from going mad.

"I'd look better driving you away from here, Miss Lyla," he pleaded quietly. "The back exit's only steps away. Despite his best intentions, I fear Marshal Thompson's been detained—"

"He'll *be* here!" she insisted. Then, to calm herself as a few stragglers were seated, she asked, "How was Frazier this morning? Any second thoughts?"

"None that I noticed. Received a few last-minute well-wishers and then ate a hearty repast in his room."

"I couldn't swallow a bite," she rasped. "And how was Allegra? I didn't see her all morning."

"She was in the hotel kitchen, preparing Mr. Foxe's favorite *blanc mange*, as a token of her best wishes," he replied with a smile. "Seemed quite contrite, as though she finally accepted the fact that she wouldn't be his bride, and he finished it off with his usual flowery compliments. Ghastly stuff, her pudding. I was pleased she didn't make enough for me— saved me from flushing it down the W.C. when she wasn't looking, as I do at home."

Lyla wanted to laugh, but suddenly the organ crescendoed into an unmistakable fanfare, and with a last questioning glance at her, Grace Putnam stepped through the sanctuary door.

It was happening. Mother of God, her maid of honor was walking down the aisle—and she was next!

Hail Mary, full of grace. . . . Pray for us now and at the hour of our . . . Barry, where the hell are you?

With a resigned sigh, Oliver placed his hand over

354

the sweaty one gripping his forearm, and stepped forward. There was a flurry of movement, a gust of cold air from the church entrance as a tuxedoed man entered at a trot.

Lyla's pulse galloped to a halt. Too lean to be Thompson, damn it! The dark stranger gaped openly at her, smoothing his windblown hair before flashing her a devilish wink.

One of Frazier's friends, undoubtedly . . . one she'd gladly run off with, except he was already ducking into the end of a pew near the rear of the sanctuary.

Only then, as the organist pulled out the last stops, did Lyla realize what she was walking into. The sanctuary was packed with elegantly-attired ladies and gentlemen, craning for a glimpse of her as they stood up to watch her walk by. There was no getting out of it now. She'd cunningly set this trap for Frazier Foxe, and she herself was getting snared. It was a fairy-tale wedding every girl dreamed of, but only a *miracle* would make her happily-ever-after possible.

"Are you ready, Miss Lyla?" Hollingsworth murmured.

"Yes," she replied in the strongest voice she could manage. "He'll get here yet, Oliver. You'll see."

"I sincerely hope so. I can't bear much more of this waiting!"

She took the first step down an aisle that looked a mile long. At the end of it, in the elevated chancel, stood black-robed Reverend Bailey, his face alight with awe. A whispering fluttered through the crowd, audible above the triumphal march, as the congregation admired her.

Lyla focused on specific objects to keep from screaming: the beribboned bouquets and lacy red hearts on each pew end . . . candles flickering on tall brass stands . . . Emily McClanahan's puffy, horrified expression . . .

Connor Foxe's leer. Lord, but he looked ready to

ravish her right here in the church, his agate-eyed stare raking over her with a lust that made her stomach churn. Surely this was not to be her fate. Surely God would intervene, or the roof would collapse under the weight of this morning's snow, or—

Frazier, too, seemed to be gloating. Impeccably proper in his black frock coat, pinstriped trousers, and starched white shirt and cravat, he watched her every step with prideful wonder. He even adjusted his monocle, to fully appreciate the vision he'd so lovingly, fiendishly created, his face flushed with uncharacteristic emotion.

Lyla quailed and glanced away, only to see Hadley McDuff gazing wistfully at her from the second row. Was there no end to this hell she'd set herself up for? Why couldn't she die now and get it over with?

Barry, I love you anyway, damn it, and I always will, she prayed. The bridal march ended in a flourish, and Hollingsworth released her to assume his place in the front row beside Miss Keating. She had no choice but to take the arm Frazier was offering her.

"You are the loveliest creature on God's earth, and I adore you for it," he murmured, to the delight of everyone in the first few rows.

Lyla gave him a faltering smile, and Reverend Bailey began.

"Dearly beloved, we are gathered here . . ." The clergyman's voice carried above them, firm yet dreamlike, but Lyla was too far gone to follow the words. They weren't the Latin phrases of the Mass, so perhaps this wouldn't count. Perhaps in God's eyes this marriage wasn't real.

"—if anyone knows of a reason why this man and this woman should not be joined together in Holy Matrimony, let him speak now or forever hold his peace."

The silence screamed at her from all sides and she

felt Frazier's gaze challenging her, but her throat was glued shut. The sanctuary seemed stifling hot and the cloying scent of her bouquet made her thrust it at Grace with a vehemence she hadn't intended. As the minister motioned them toward the kneeler, Lyla glanced again at the doors on either side of the chancel, her hopes flickering like a candle in a blizzard.

He wasn't coming. God alone knew why, but Barry Thompson had stood her up.

There was a solo by an emotional soprano Lyla had heard at the Grand Opera House, not that she listened. As she mouthed the words of the vows Reverend Bailey led her in, her soul died within her. Frazier's gloved hand shook as he slipped a golden band onto her finger. "With this ring I thee wed," he said hoarsely.

What should've been the most exultant moment of her life left her feeling cold and forsaken, as though she were at her own funeral. She could feel the color draining from her face, the joints of her legs and arms going rubbery as she rose from the bench and looked up at the monster she'd just married.

"You may kiss the bride."

Frazier's head jerked and his eyes widened when he turned to face her. Apparently he'd forgotten about this part of the ceremony. He was having a hard time getting his breath, he was so nervous about bringing his lips to hers for the first time, knowing the congregation would never forgive him if he didn't. Connor coughed beside them. Grace's skirts rustled as she shifted nervously.

Slowly, with obvious trepidation, Foxe lifted the gossamer veil, his gray eyes widening like a frightened animal's. Lyla swallowed, wondering why an imposter who'd duped his friends for years would have trouble kissing his new wife in front of them, for God's sake, and then he *grimaced!* His face contorted, followed by spasmodic arm movements that

357

sent a gasp through the puzzled crowd. When he tried to retain his balance, his hands went around her neck in a death grip that left her gasping, terrified.

"He's going to kill her!" Grace Putnam screamed, and she lunged toward them, grabbing at Frazier's gloved fingers.

But Connor was already attacking from the other side. "She's mine, damn it! Let her go!" he snarled.

Lyla was losing consciousness when a startled murmuring filled the sanctuary. She was vaguely aware that Connor had freed her from Frazier's vise-like grip and that men from the front rows were rushing up to settle the situation, while Reverend Bailey stepped back, too horrified for words. She was being lifted away by arms she couldn't see, arms that cradled her against a broad, leather-scented chest and a stubbled jaw.

"Lyla, honey, I'm so damn sorry I—"

Barry! It was Barry's voice bringing her up from the depths of numbness. She groped for his shoulders so she could cling to him, sobbing with joy and relief. He'd come for her, even if he was a few minutes late!

"I don't believe what I'm seeing," he mumbled. "I've got to stop this before somebody gets killed."

Turning, Lyla heard gasps of horror and shock, some directed at her and Barry, but most of them caused by the macabre drama that was unfolding before the altar. Frazier was convulsing crazily, his eyes bugging and his arms pulled back into his stepbrother's grip. Oliver Hollingsworth had vaulted over the railing in front of his pew, brandishing the gold-headed walking stick Allegra had been entrusted with. While he clubbed a protesting Connor, Hadley McDuff sprang to his aid by tackling Frazier to the floor. Amid outcries in his heavy brogue, other voices were heard, and Rex Adams, Kelly Jameson, and Matt McClanahan were rushing forward to bring the ungodly commotion under control.

Thompson felt someone slip up behind him and

he hugged Lyla protectively.

"Marshal, I'd be pleased to help," a familiar voice drawled. "You take care of that scuffle while Gracie and I get Lyla to a safe place."

Fully conscious now, Lyla stared over Barry's shoulder at this newcomer—the rake who'd hurried into the church at the last minute! His chocolate-brown eyes sparkled in a clean-shaven face that looked vaguely familiar, yet—

"Rafferty!" Barry rasped. "Where the hell've you been?"

Jack chuckled, all the while gazing at Lyla. "Here in Cripple. Got a shave and a haircut, new duds, a room at the National. When I found those papers you forgot, I figured this'd be a wedding I shouldn't miss, and damn! Never seen the likes of it."

Thompson glanced at the ongoing fisticuffs and then back at the tuxedoed outlaw beside him. "Get her out of here so she can change clothes. We'll talk in my office after I settle this. You all right now, honey?"

Nodding, Lyla felt herself being lowered to the floor between Jack and Grace, who seemed as eager to leave as she was. Frazier was still stricken by convulsions and Connor's beastly behavior had triggered a vociferous outpouring she still couldn't believe, with Hollingsworth and Hadley McDuff the ringleaders! Voices and fists were flying, until an ominous *thunk* echoed into the high beamed ceiling and the crowd fell silent.

Deputy Adams and McClanahan took advantage of the moment to seize the two elderly attackers and pull them away from the Foxe brothers, who were both lying on the chancel steps. Connor was unconscious and Frazier . . . Frazier was arched backward, his eyes bulging as though he were in horrendous pain, yet he was absolutely stiff.

"Jesus, get her out of here," Miss Putnam muttered, and Lyla hurried out the side exit between her and Rafferty, too stunned to feel the sudden chill or the snowflakes tickling her face. Grace grabbed up her train and boosted her into Frazier's carriage while Jack hopped up into the driver's seat.

All she saw during the short ride to the hotel was Foxe, frozen in a pose that suggested he was being pulled backward into hell as punishment for his many sins. He *had* seemed unusually fidgety during the vows; short of breath, as though his collar was choking him, yet she couldn't believe the wedding he'd so gleefully staged for his peers—the ultimate of his deceptions—had sent him into such ghastly contortions.

They were in her hotel room ... Grace was choosing another dress from the armoire while Rafferty was unbuttoning the back of her satin—

Rafferty? Lyla pivoted on her heel, glaring. "And what the hell're *you* doing? And you're *letting* him!"

Grace laughed as only a sultry Indian princess flirting with a handsome man could. "He's going as far as your undies, honey, and then I'm taking over. Jack's quite good at buttons."

"And how would you know that?"

Rafferty chuckled. "Gracie and I go back to when she was running a tattoo parlor in Dodge. Small world, seeing her as your maid of honor. And what a hoot!"

"You're a fine one to talk, Rafferty," the whore teased, winking at Lyla. "He's got the nicest ass you'll ever see, honey, and a heart tattooed on one luscious cheek. With my initials inside it."

"That's a damn lie! You—"

"I always sign my work, Jack," Cherry Blossom replied slyly. "Not *my* fault you got so drunk you didn't know which end was up, and what I was writing on it."

Lyla looked from one dark-haired scoundrel to the other, laughing at the patter she suspected they'd shared to cheer her up. Rafferty deftly finished unfastening her gown while Grace stood waiting with the red plaid dress she'd worn to lunch at Delmonico's. Lifetimes ago, it seemed.

"I—I'm not sure such a bright color's appropriate."

"Red for St. Valentine's Day," the dove insisted. "And after what we just watched in that church, I don't think decorum means a helluva lot. Hurry, now, so we can get you to Thompson's office before—" The Indian princess stopped to glare at her, yet the corners of her mouth were twitching. "You could've told me he was alive, damn it! A river of tears I cried, and for nothing!"

Lyla slipped up underneath the dress Grace was holding, turning modestly when she saw Rafferty ogling her. "Why would I think you cared, after your detailed rundown of the way he broke all his promises to take you away from here?" she asked quietly.

The whore's mouth tightened, and she let Rafferty fasten the back of the plaid dress. "All right, so I exaggerated a little. I was furious with him for dropping me like a rotten potato when you waltzed into the Rose. He was one of the few friends I had, damn it, and you were snatching him away!"

The deep loneliness in her voice made Lyla pity Grace a little. She sensed this was as close as the notorious Princess Cherry Blossom would come to an apology, and she accepted it with a nod.

"Seems to me the marshal made a few promises to you as well, Lyla. But he got here too late to make good on them," Rafferty commented quietly. "What're you going to do about that?"

Staring at the glittering gold band that branded her as Mrs. Frazier Foxe, Lyla sighed. "I honestly don't know. We'd best get over to the jailhouse before every reporter in town hears what's happened. This'll be a front-page story the likes of which Cripple's never seen."

Chapter 31

The parade entering the jailhouse was one Lyla wouldn't have believed had she not seen it. First came Oliver Hollingsworth, beaming at her in his elegant tuxedo as Rex Adams led him by the handcuffs to a chair in the corner. Hadley McDuff followed, his slender, chinless face raised with defiant pride. McClanahan released him, shaking his head as the Irish aristocrat sat down beside Frazier's valet. Barry allowed Allegra Keating to precede him inside, and shut the door against the crowd that was already gathering on the sidewalk.

The marshal appeared exhausted, his clothes wrinkled from being slept in several nights, yet to Lyla he'd never looked more handsome. She could only imagine the miles of snowy terrain he'd covered and the agony he'd suffered when he'd arrived too late—all because she'd insisted on going through with the wedding instead of letting her friends help her escape!

He was tough enough to handle this situation, though, virile and tall, exuding a rugged masculinity that made her go fluttery inside. She smiled shyly as he approached the desk where she was sitting.

"That dress brings back a few memories," he

murmured. He glanced around the small office. "Are Cherry Blossom and Rafferty here?"

"They're in an empty cell, catching up on old times."

"Well—we'd better not interrupt *that*," he said with a smile. Then he sobered, sitting on the desk beside her. "Before we get to the bottom of this, I'd better fill you in. Frazier was dead before Doc Geary got to him, and Connor was gone a few moments later."

Despite the hatred she harbored for the two Foxes, Lyla's jaw dropped. "Mother of God! How?"

"That's what we're about to find out. The folks at the church were shocked, and when the New Yorker's caterer asked what he was supposed to do with all the food Frazier's paid for, I suggested everyone go there to eat, to keep them from pestering us here. I hope that's all right by you."

She nodded, sadly aware of how many decisions she faced as Foxe's widow—and how badly it hurt Thompson to acknowledge that she'd actually gone through with the wedding. "Barry, I'm sorry—"

"We'll talk about it later. After we piece together what really went on in that sanctuary." He removed his coat and hat, studying the two courtly-looking gentlemen who'd started the ruckus. "When I came through the side door I saw you attacking Connor Foxe with a walking stick, Mr. Hollingsworth, while Mr. McDuff went after Frazier."

"Yes, marshal," the valet piped up. "When I saw Connor grabbing Mr. Foxe I felt it was my duty to stop him, not because Frazier was in danger, but because Miss Lyla was. That lecherous lout had designs on her—tried to rape her once, you know—and his crude comment confirmed his malevolent intentions! No honorable man could allow such treachery to continue!"

"Aye, sir! And did ye see the way the groom

sickened at the prospect of kissin' 'er?" Hadley McDuff demanded. "'E didn't *deserve* the likes of Lyla!"

Thompson cleared his throat so he wouldn't laugh. This had to be the most bizarre interrogation he'd ever conducted, and they'd certainly taken care of the Foxe brothers for him, but serious justice had to be done. "Am I correct in assuming you're the McDuff whom Miss O'Riley was betrothed to?" he asked the little man.

Hadley smoothed the few strands of hair on his freckled head. "Aye, sir," he replied more sedately. "When she wrote home about Mick bein' killed, I felt I should come after her. She was a sheltered little lass, defenseless against you swaggerin' Americans."

The irony of these words nearly made the marshal laugh again, but seeing Lyla's embarrassed flush, he decided against pursuing such a personal topic. McClanahan had stepped up beside him to face the two suspects, and it was he who broke the uncomfortable silence that filled the jailhouse office.

"While I fully understand your protective attitude toward Lyla," Matt began quietly, "from where I stood it appeared that Connor was killed when he stumbled backward on the stairs and struck his head against the sharp corner of the altar."

"But I hit him *hard*," Oliver protested.

"I believe Dr. Geary was thinking the same way," Deputy Adams spoke up. "Such a blow to the base of his brain would be fatal. And it appeared to me that Frazier was having some sort of seizure—"

"Cold feet was wot seized 'im!" Hadley exclaimed as he hopped out of his chair. "The old gaffer was 'avin 'eart failure just *lookin'* at Lyla, lovely as she was! 'E wouldn't't've lasted five minutes in bed with 'er before 'e passed on. 'Twas a sin for the lass to be tied to such a prissy old poop, and I'm proud I did 'im in!"

Lyla stared at the gnomish little nobleman, her face aflame. Who would've guessed he held such fiery convictions about *anything*, or that he'd defend her even after she crossed the ocean to avoid marrying him? He focused his smallish eyes on her, wearing the same wistfulness she'd seen through Mrs. Delacroix's plate glass window.

"I'm truly sorry, Lyla. I behaved out of turn, I know," he continued in his low brogue. "But I could see ye lookin' for a way out even as ye came down the aisle, child. Ye're too bonnie a lass to be saddled with an old goat—me included. And I knew that the moment I saw ye tryin' on yer gown. I . . . I just wanted ye to have the happiness ye deserve, darlin'."

Lyla's eyes were hot with grateful tears, but before she could think of an appropriate response to Hadley's stirring confession, Allegra Keating cleared her throat ceremoniously and strode over to stand in front of him.

"A truly heartwarming tale, Mr. McDuff," she said with a wry smile, "but you men are all alike—conceited *twits*, just like Frazier was. I killed him myself, before either of you had the chance."

Everyone in the office was stunned beyond words. In the moments of silence that followed, Lyla noticed Rafferty and Grace coming in from their cell to listen more closely. Barry was staring at the spinster in the dove-gray suit, wondering who would be next with an outlandish confession. And these three looked so proud!

Indeed, Miss Keating was standing tall, her bun aquiver and her glittering eyes a few inches higher than Hadley's as she went on with her explanation. "I put rat poison in his *blanc mange*, Mr. McDuff. And if he hadn't made such a pig of himself at lunch he'd have collapsed sooner, saving us all the mortification of this wedding," she declared haughtily. "It's exactly what that rodent deserved for marrying this conniving little siren instead of the woman who's spent the prime of her life catering to his every whim—"

"Strychnine," Thompson murmured. "It would've blended right into that pudding."

"And it accounts for Foxe's godawful convulsions," McClanahan whispered back.

"—and what was my reward?" Allegra continued shrilly. "A home, with that little *golddigger*, for as long as I lived after he passed on. Oh yes, I read his will, Mrs. Foxe," she said, looking bitterly at Lyla. "And I'll endure imprisonment any day rather than live out my years with *you*."

Miss Keating then turned toward Barry, her skinny nose pointed up at him. "Lock me away, Marshal Thompson. And for what it's worth, you *deserve* the trouble that bosomy little bubblehead will bring you, for being a liar and a cheat yourself."

Thompson was dumbfounded. An astute, upper-crust housekeeper like Allegra Keating didn't belong in the Canon City prison with hardened criminals. Yet she'd killed a man—premeditated murder motivated by spite and jealousy—and he couldn't dismiss her with just a slap on the wrist.

"Show her to a cell, Rex," he said quietly, "until we can discuss this further. And since Connor died from his fall, in a scuffle he started himself," he added, addressing the two balding men across from him, "you fellows are free to go. Use the back alley, and take Lyla with you. The crowd out front'll never let her leave."

Lyla threw him an injured glance but then rose to go with the others. He was right to have her escorted to the hotel, and he had matters to settle with Rex Adams, who looked decidedly uncomfortable now that Foxe's murder had been solved. And the people out front were demanding an explanation only he as the resurrected marshal could give.

Seeing her disappointment, Barry reached out to

stroke her cheek. "I'll be there as soon as I can," he promised.

"Perhaps we could all ride together," Rafferty suggested, his arm around Cherry Blossom's waist. "Safety in numbers, you know."

"An excellent idea," Oliver Hollingsworth said, his voice alive with renewed purpose. "I should be pleased to drive you all to your destinations and then to accompany Miss Lyla to her suite, in case any curiosity seekers get wind of her whereabouts."

"I'd appreciate it," Barry replied with a nod. He saw Rafferty slip a packet of papers onto his desk with a wink, while the others shrugged into their coats and headed toward the back room. Then the Indian princess turned, her gaze sly as a cat's.

"Now that you've come back from the dead, marshal, perhaps you can perform another miracle and recover my turquoise combs," she said pointedly.

"I'll get right on it." He chuckled, watching her slip into Rafferty's open arm, knowing she did it as much to taunt him as to satisfy an itch that always needed to be scratched. They filed out then, all except for Hadley McDuff, who hung back, clasping his hands repeatedly as he glanced toward the cells. "Something I can do for you, sir?"

The Irishman grinned nervously. "I—would ye mind if I 'ad a word with Miss Keating? Per'aps she could use a bit of company about now."

The marshal bit back a grin. "Be my guest. Find out what we can bring her to make her stay more comfortable."

When the freckled little fellow disappeared down the hallway, he and McClanahan were left with a deputy who pointedly avoided his gaze. Adams was busily sorting through his desk drawer, his skinny wrists sticking out of a dark suit coat that made his complexion look paler than normal. Biding his time, Thompson went to sit at his own desk while Matt looked out the window at the gathering crowd.

Rex's glance darted between them, and when he realized they were forcing him to speak first he swallowed, his Adam's apple dancing a jig above his starched shirt collar. "I suppose it's only appropriate that I resign," he rasped. "It'll save me the embarrassment of admitting I was fired."

Barry was rolling a cigarette, taking his time about it. "Can't let you go until I hear your reasons."

Adams stared. "You know damn well I was in with Foxe's men, trying to help them kill you!"

"Maybe I want to hear about it from the horse's mouth, from the beginning. Maybe your story'll shed light on how Jameson and that Nate fellow ought to be dealt with." Lighting his smoke, Barry looked placidly through the haze at his assistant, waiting. There was more at stake here than Rex's pride, and he was determined to see where the chips fell before he decided the deputy's fate.

With an agitated sigh, Adams gazed at his clasped, bony knuckles. "It started as a one-time thing, a way to make a little extra cash before Christmas," he began numbly. "Frazier told me his regulars would do the dirty work, and what he wanted from me was cooperation from this office."

"He was planning the Rose robbery, then?"

The deputy nodded. "Nate, Kelly, and Connor were to be the holdup men, and once you and the posse followed them into Phantom Canyon, Nate was to divert the others while Jameson and Connor killed you."

Thompson took a long draw on his cigarette. "Where'd Eberhardt fit in?"

"He played lookout while Connor switched the stolen jewelry from the sack into the smaller leather pouch and stashed it in your saddlebag, before you got to the stable. Foxe didn't want the jewelry—he wanted you dead," Rex reminded him. "He said to leave the bag with you, so you'd die a hero and folks wouldn't be as likely to press for an investigation, since it would appear you recovered the valuables."

"It was Connor who filched the shamrock pendant and my aquamarine ring, then?"

Adams nodded. "Made some comment about his brother requesting those pieces for his own purposes—and he retrieved Frazier's walking stick while he was at it."

"So what was your part in this?" Barry asked, wishing his deputy wouldn't quake like a cornered rabbit. "Last thing I recall, you were riding alongside me up the canyon ridge and then you took out through the trees."

Rex cleared his throat for the dozenth time. "I . . . was supposed to shoot you from behind while they fired on you from their ambush positions, but I . . . I just couldn't."

McClanahan let out a sarcastic snort. "Maybe because that put *you* in their line of fire, too?"

"That occurred to me, yes," the pale redhead admitted ruefully. "But I also realized I couldn't live the rest of my life with Barry's blood on my conscience. I rode off hoping to distract the others. Or at least get him back to town before he was dead."

"But Lyla beat you to it." Thompson leaned forward, recalling how she'd found the booty in her shed and assumed the robbers would return. How she kept silent to save him from worry and did everything humanly possible to keep him breathing, all the while watching over her shoulder. "So when she returned to town and deposited me with the doc—alive—Connor and Eberhardt grabbed her and you three informed Frazier he needed a new plan. And you helped yourself to a little bonus before taking the pouch to the bank vault, didn't you?"

He nodded, cringing. "I figured Lyla would blow the whole thing open sooner or later, but it felt so good to be in *charge*—to hear Foxe promise me the city marshal's position. It seemed the only way to advance myself, to better my income. I ignored her when she told me Frazier would dispose of me as he had Wally, but when she pointed out that Theresa and the children would be left . . . well, I couldn't face that. I made up my mind to expose him at the wedding, but Allegra Keating beat me to the punch."

"Easy to say *now*, since you didn't have to incriminate yourself in public," McClanahan berated him.

Thompson heard his best friend's verdict loud and clear, but the thought of Theresa and her brood of carrot-haired chicks being left destitute weighed heavily upon him. He rubbed out his cigarette and looked Adams square in the face. "Since you weren't involved in the actual robbery, and you didn't shoot me when you had the chance—"

"He was an accomplice! He admits it!" Matt challenged.

"But he fell for Frazier's offer because he wanted a little extra for his family at Christmas," Barry pointed out quietly. "I'll be the first to say his pay's inadequate, and frankly, I'm not sure he's cut out to be a city marshal—"

Adams flushed and looked away.

"—but I'll let him keep his job under one condition."

Rex glanced up, wary yet hopeful.

"You've got to return that Masonic ring to Sam Langston and those turquoise combs to Miss Putnam. In person," he added firmly. "What you say to them is your business, but it's only right that those pieces be returned, no matter what you have to tell Theresa when you take those combs back. She was mighty proud of them."

"Yes, she was," he choked.

"So there's my offer. Accept it, or resign."

Rex loosened his collar with a shaking hand. "It's more than fair. I—you don't know how much I appreciate this, sir."

"You'll earn it. Those reporters out front'll see to that." Thompson glanced out the window at the crowd, which was getting larger and noisier. It was time to clear the slate, to give them the pertinent facts about Frazier Foxe's demise and then bow out. He'd analyzed this decision on the train and had even planned a short resignation speech, which meant little now that Foxe had been killed rather than captured.

As he stood, he saw the questions in Rex's eyes and McClanahan's scowl when the detective guessed his ulterior motive for not firing Adams outright. But as he was heading for the door to address his public, Hadley McDuff hurried from the cell area, excitement burning in his eyes.

"Marshal, may I 'ave a word?" he asked breathlessly. "This sounds irregular and a bit 'asty, per'aps, but I'm askin' ye anyway. Could I keep Miss Keating company durin' her incarceration? I—when she's free to go, I'd like to take 'er 'ome with me!"

Barry's eyebrows shot up. Not ten minutes ago the prim Miss Allegra was calling this man a conceited twit, looking down her beak at him. Glancing at McClanahan, who was chortling, he asked, "Are your intentions honorable, Mr. McDuff? This does seem hasty, since you just met her, and since she poisoned the man she always wanted to marry."

"I hope you don't need her for a cook," Matt teased.

Hadley waved them off good-naturedly. "I 'ave a cook, gentlemen, and the maids and gardeners required to keep up an ancestral estate," he explained with gleeful dignity, "but Allegra's just wot I need to spice up me old age! Kindred spirits, we are—she said so 'erself. And since she wants no part of livin' at Foxe 'Ollow, and since wenchin's gettin' a bit beyond me, I think we'll get on nicely."

Barry shrugged again, astounded by this elegantly-attired leprechaun's ideas. "I don't see why you can't visit her, but I've got no idea how long it'll be before she can leave the country. Depends upon the courts.''

"I understand that. But per'aps the fact that a nobleman such as myself's willin' to take 'er in'll convince the prosecutors to let 'er off easier.''

He'd seen stranger things happen, but a few minor points still piqued his curiosity. "Just between you and me," he began in a conspiratorial tone, "are you figuring to have children by Allegra? Lyla mentioned you needed an heir—''

"And the poor lass was no doubt afraid she'd get warts touchin' a toad like me," he said ruefully. "'Twas her father who proposed the dowerless match, and I accepted for Lyla's sake, rather than for what came of beddin' 'er. Though God knows I lusted in me 'eart."

Thompson laughed aloud, as did McClanahan, satisfied that McDuff was a respectable sort who wouldn't badger Lyla for running out on him. His gaze fell on the packet of papers Jack Rafferty had laid on his desk, and he settled down again. "As Foxe's widow, I imagine Lyla's inherited a sizable spread. That must relieve some of your concern about her.''

"Aye," McDuff replied, and then he looked pointedly at the marshal. "Which makes me wonder about *your* intentions, young man. I'll not allow her to be leeched, or to become a parlor decoration. I've known Lyla all her young life, and I shan't return 'ome till I can assure 'er father she's in good 'ands, wot with Mick bein' gone.''

"Barry's got great hands," Matt teased, his blue eyes sparkling, "but he also owns a gold mine and some property in his own right, and he told me several weeks ago that he planned to marry her. Going to build her the finest house in Cripple and fill it with children.''

"I'll *bet* 'e is.''

Hadley was studying him with stern, fatherly protectiveness, expecting him to speak for himself, and Barry felt a few butterflies in his stomach. "I have great respect for Lyla. She saved my life—"

"Then why'd she marry Foxe?"

Thompson sighed, wishing he knew the answer to that one himself. "It was part of a scheme to catch Frazier for robbery and extortion, and because of an avalanche on the train tracks, I didn't get here in time to stop the ceremony. Sounds like a weak excuse, but it's all I've got."

McDuff considered this, then nodded sagely. "And we all know Lyla could've given 'im the slip. Notorious for disappearin' when she feels trapped, she is." He smiled as though he sensed Thompson, too, had been left in the lurch a few times by the elusive Miss O'Riley. "I'll be gettin' back to Allegra, then. Just throw me out when ye need to lock up."

Thompson watched the little Irishman enter the hallway, shaking his head. Then he turned to McClanahan and Adams, who were eyeing him expectantly. "Time to meet the press," he said matter-of-factly. "What I have to report won't be as astounding as what we've heard so far this afternoon, but I've got a surprise or two up my sleeve. Care to join me?"

The pair exchanged a questioning glance before following him to the door. As Barry opened it onto a crowd that blocked the street, huddling beneath a steady sprinkling of snow, he hesitated. Behind the front couple rows of reporters stood men like Silas Hughes and Sam Langston—friends he'd shared several drinks and confidences with, friends who'd challenge the decision he was about to announce, and maybe see it as a miscarriage of the values he'd always championed. He studied their faces, pleased to be counting few enemies among them, as the newspapermen riffled their notebooks and readied their pens.

"You don't know how good it feels to be standing

here alive, talking to you again, although fancy speeches aren't my strong suit," he began in a steady voice. "You've heard by now that Frazier and Connor Foxe are dead, and I won't elaborate except to say that I've spent the weeks since the Christmas Eve robbery at the Golden Rose trailing them, on the suspicion that they were behind it. Frankly, I wish they were still alive so they could answer to me for the things they've done."

The crowd buzzed like a hive of agitated bees, scowling at each other and at him, which he'd expected. Most of these folks never dreamed the elegant Englishman who promoted so many of Cripple's civic projects was crooked, and he planned to keep their questions to a minimum for now. When he had their attention again, Barry continued.

"During my travels I was ambushed, shot, nearly barbecued after being kidnapped, and meanwhile learned that the very purpose of the Rose robbery was to do me in. What you read in the papers about Lyla O'Riley was a smokescreen, friends—another of Frazier's ploys to discredit me and the woman who saved my life."

Again his listeners murmured in astonishment, and he held his hand up, shaking his head at the reporters who were poised with questions.

"My disappearance and her wedding today were part of our plan to prove Foxe guilty of extortion, robbery, and murder, and we've accumulated irrefutable evidence of these crimes. But the investigation has cost us both, and I promised myself that if I lived through it, the Foxe case would be my last. So I hereby announce my resignation as the city marshal of Cripple Creek. Thanks for your support and concern while I was your lawman."

Barry turned before the barrage of questions began, pleased that McClanahan and Adams stepped between him and the reporters, and then followed him inside. The door wasn't shut before they were

374

hounding him.

"What the hell's *this* about? What'll you do now that—"

"So what am I supposed to *say?* All the papers will want—"

Thompson held up both hands, smiling with a sudden serenity. No more drunks to corral, no more late-night chases. He'd arrested his last recalcitrant crook, and it felt pretty damn wonderful.

"Rex," he said, his hand extended, "there'll be another marshal in here come Monday, supplied by the Springs. You'll be a top-notch deputy for him, too, and I wish you luck and that pay raise you deserve. Give Theresa and the kids my best."

The carrot-haired deputy blanched as he shook hands. "Where'll you be?"

"In and out, after I take a long-overdue vacation."

"But what'll I tell—"

"Give those reporters whatever you want, Adams. I'm sure you'll be the most quoted man in Cripple Creek for the next week or so," Thompson said with a chuckle. Then he turned to Matt, whose eyes were full of questions he wouldn't be able to sidestep quite so easily. "Let's go someplace private for a drink while we look at these papers Rafferty left me."

Matt followed him into the back room, but as they were putting on their coats, he stalled. "I know you want to get over to Lyla, and I really should fetch Emily, pal. She's feeling puny—"

"Not coming down with something, I hope?" Barry watched the emotions flicker across his best friend's face as they donned their hats.

"No, actually she's pregnant, and—"

"Son of a gun!" He grabbed the shorter man in a bearhug, lifting him from the floor in his excitement. "Congratulations, sure-shot! Didn't take you long—or will this one be a little early?"

"Will I be asking you the same question in a few months?" McClanahan teased back.

375

Sobering, Barry set him down and headed for the door. "I can't rightly say. Might depend on what these documents tell me."

Matt grabbed his arm. "You're not going to walk out on her? Not because of papers she signed when she was forced to—not after all she's been through with you?" he demanded.

Thompson's stomach tightened with anxiety. He looked McClanahan in the eye and said softly, "Do you know what it did to me, seeing my woman in that spectacular wedding gown, saying yes to another man? A lot's happened in the past few hours, and until I get some explanations, I can't answer your questions."

He stepped into the back alley, suddenly very tired from chasing across Colorado and frustrated because a jealous housekeeper had stolen the satisfaction of seeing Frazier Foxe humiliated and punished for his crimes.

"We've been friends a long time, Barry," McClanahan said from the doorway. "I thought your attraction to Lyla was another flash-in-the-pan at first, but now anybody can see you'll have a hole in your heart big enough to fall through if you leave her."

Thompson let out a long sigh, keeping his back to the jailhouse.

"Think about it before you let your pride and her inheritance come between you, pal. I hate to see Foxe ruin two more lives."

Chapter 32

Lyla sat fidgeting in her suite, watching for Barry but seeing only the lengthening shadows falling across a fresh blanket of snow. Was she a fool to assume he could still love her?

She fingered Mick's pendant, like a mother fondling every plane of a rescued child's face. No one could fault her for wishing to preserve her brother's memory, but as the dusk settled into her unlighted room she wondered if she'd sacrificed too much for a simple silver shamrock. What was the loss of a necklace compared to losing the man she loved? Had she endured threats, degradation, and abuse at the gloved hands of Frazier Foxe, only to be left as completely alone as she'd been before he'd caught her in his insidious web of deceit?

She should've refused those first three dresses and the maid's job, should've let Marshal Thompson chase the Christmas Eve bandits . . . should've run like hell when three different friends and Barry himself had warned her not to stay in church this afternoon. But she hadn't.

Oliver Hollingsworth entered to light a few lamps, graciously preserving her privacy by not speaking. A few moments later, though, he admitted the tall, burly lawman Lyla had been praying, yet afraid, to see.

377

Thompson set his hat on the highboy, glancing about the lavishly-appointed suite. He was wearing fresh clothes and smelled of shaving soap and cologne. And whiskey. The set of his jaw suggested a marshal after the facts rather than a lover come calling, and Lyla braced herself for an unpleasant encounter. "I thought you weren't coming."

Oi thot ye warnt comin'. Barry dismissed the notion that her musical brogue tickled him like an Irish ditty, concentrating on the business at hand. "I had to set things straight with Rex, and then I gave my resignation speech. It brought the house down."

Frowning, she shoved images of Barry making love to her in a dilapidated shack out of her mind. "You can't tell me anyone applauded, or let you go without asking questions."

"I left Adams to handle the press. It's his penance for a half-assed betrayal."

Lyla sensed some of the hurt in his voice was directed at her, yet he'd allowed the hapless deputy to remain employed, so there was hope: he could still rise above the shortfallings of those who hadn't followed his instructions. "What'll you do now?"

He recalled discussing this before, when they were reunited at Foxe's shack, bound by ropes yet set free by pledges of everlasting love . . . talk of marriage and children he might have to recant now. "Oh, there's always the Flaxen Lassie and the Golden Rose. I see no need to chase after Rafferty, since he was decent enough to return those papers and the five hundred bucks. And after looking over Foxe's will and that other agreement, I don't guess I need to worry about *your* welfare, either."

Her mouth went coppery and she felt the blood in her veins slowing to a trickle.

Thompson watched her periwinkle eyes mist over but he refused to fall for them, shrugging. "My attorney says the will stands regardless of the faked signature, because both you and Frazier signed it—

378

and because no heir exists to contest it. I believe that makes you the new owner of Colorado's largest sheep ranch, and with Connor dead, you've got the flocks to support it. You're a wealthy widow, Mrs. Foxe. You surely don't need a has-been marshal cluttering up that fancy house, taking up your time."

He was serious. The eyes that had once sparkled like Irish hills after a rain now reminded her of scum on a stagnant pond. Who did he think he was, sounding so injured? Lyla sat taller in her chair, determined to set a few things straight before this man sucked them both down into the quicksand of his own self-pity.

"Are you insinuating that I loved you only for your money, Marshal Thompson? That I was a poor Irish lass latching onto a swaggering American millionaire?" Lyla removed the aquamarine ring from her left hand and let it clatter onto the tabletop beside her. "Don't let me detain you, sir."

Barry heard a purposeful pride that rivaled Allegra Keating's, and when he saw no sign of Foxe's wedding band he studied her closely. "No, the thought of you chasing after my money never occurred to me," he admitted.

"What is it, then? That I'm perhaps wealthier than you are, thanks to a twist of fate?" she demanded. "I have a ranch to run, a manager to hire—"

"You'll do fine," he mumbled, stepping back when she sprang from her chair.

"But I want *you* there! Even if you *were* late getting back to Cripple," she challenged, crossing her arms beneath her breasts. "I assume some act of God held you up."

The sight of this tiny spitfire in red plaid, her breasts jutting out in her indignation as she tossed her honey hair over her shoulders, nearly felled him. But by God, she had no cause to point a finger!

"It was an avalanche, as a matter of fact," he

replied, placing his fists on his hips, "and I was tied in knots the whole time I sat helpless on that damn train, hoping Foxe hadn't already killed you for skipping out on him again. Imagine my shock when I returned to find you *married* to the bastard, after all he did to you. After I *warned* you to run before it was too late!"

And after all she'd laughed and cried about with this giant of a man, their fate came down to a shouting match: Barry was leaning over her, his nose only inches above hers as he glowered at her, and she was glaring back, her neck tilted until she was nearly toppling over backward. For several moments they remained frozen in their defiance, searching each other's souls while goading each other to break the deadlock.

Lyla gave in first . . . or at least gave the appearance of it. Barry Thompson had his pride and he had a legitimate point, given the circumstances. A lifetime of loving him was a terrible thing to relinquish, all for two such minor details. She let out a quavery sigh and turned away, hoping the truth would speak for itself and his heart would hear it.

"I wanted to run—God knows Grace and Matt and Oliver tried to whisk me away from that church, but I held out . . . for you."

From the corner of her eye she caught the twitch of his jaw. If there was ever a time to use every resource and feminine wile she possessed, it was now, when she had all at stake and everything to gain. She stepped away, and then faced him with her hands clasped, her eyes entreating him.

"I knew you'd come, knew you'd *be* there for me, Barry," she whispered. "You're the strongest, kindest, dearest man I know, and I love you. My faith in you gave me the strength to face up to Frazier, and for once in my life I didn't run when things got rough. I stuck it out to the end—waiting for *you*."

Thompson felt himself sinking, drowning in the periwinkle pools he'd never been able to resist. He'd been so incensed by a twist in timing—no more her fault than his own—that he'd overlooked the hell she had to have gone through while waiting for him to keep the promise that he'd return. His throat was so tight he couldn't speak. He slowly opened his arms, hoping.

Lyla savored her victory, but only for a moment. It was nothing compared to the warmth of Barry's embrace, the strength of arms that lifted her from the floor to kiss lips that promised a love more enduring and fulfilling than any fairy-tale ending. She clung to him with her arms and legs, reveling in the glory that this man alone could show her.

Still clutching her, as though the spritely enchantress in his arms would try to abandon him as she had the first time he saw this plaid dress, Barry lowered himself into the chair. He kissed her again, running his fingers through her silken hair, pressing into flesh that was firm and soft and excruciatingly tempting after all these weeks without her.

"I love you, too, honey," he murmured against her ear. "Guess we both had reason to panic, knowing what we stood to lose. But now that things are right between us again, a few details need to be settled."

"Like what?" Lyla sat up to gaze into his boyish, handsome face.

"Well," he sighed, "the fact that you could buy and sell me doesn't really matter, but these big old feet don't fit into Foxe's shoes and I'm not sure I'd ever be comfortable in his house, either. And I can't imagine *you* wanting to live there, after what he put you through."

She couldn't recall ever suggesting they had to reside at the ranch, but since Barry was thinking about it—and had no house of his own—it seemed a more logical alternative than letting the mansion sit empty.

"It's a lovely place, actually, and I suppose the sheep remind me of home," Lyla said softly. "'Twas Frazier and Connor that ruined my stay, and now that they're gone it seems a shame to let all those spacious rooms . . . along with the nursery and schoolroom . . . go to waste."

She picked up the aquamarine ring, watching it sparkle in the lamplight. "It's the sentiment about a thing that determines your attitude—the meaning you invest in it, rather than its actual value," she continued wistfully. "When Frazier forced me to wear this ring as a mockery of my lost love for you, the pain was only momentary. Knowing it was really *your* ring was a great comfort to me when I thought you were dead."

Thompson had a feeling she was artfully tugging his heartstrings. And since he hadn't had a chance to meet with his architect, perhaps he could live under Frazier's roof awhile, let her think she was having her way. A small concession, considering how empty his life would be without her.

Seeing the warm flickering in his green eyes, Lyla cleared her throat coyly. "Well, then, if you'd be uncomfortable in Frazier's house, could you consider living in *mine?* I know you own that acreage overlooking Cripple—"

"I do," he replied with a nod.

"—and it'd be the perfect spot for a home to entertain in when we spend time in town," she continued with her sweetest smile. "But I have an obligation to provide Hollingsworth with someplace to live, and your house isn't ready yet. And after all he's done for us, I want him to have the comfort of his own quarters, don't you?"

"I do," Barry agreed with a nod.

Lyla chuckled, loving the way he indulged her. His patient humor would make him a perfect father,

382

and she could easily imagine the laughter and love-making they'd share while begetting a houseful of beautiful brown-haired babies. But a man like Thompson was used to overseeing more than siblings' squabbles and arrangements for the next dinner party.

"Now that you've turned in your badge, you'll need something besides a Flaxen Lassie to occupy your time," she teased. "You'll have me and the children, of course, but I bet you and Buck would enjoy riding the range, seeing that the sheepherders are keeping our flocks profitable and that the grass isn't overgrazed. I envision you as an authority our employees will respect, much more than they ever did Frazier and Connor. Don't you?"

"I do."

That settled it. Thompson was raising no objections, and his vowlike replies were begging the question . . . just as his large, warm hand had found its way under her skirt and was unhooking the top of her silk stocking. Perhaps he thought he could side-track her with his advances before any intentions were exchanged, but he was wrong! She'd waited far too long and suffered innumerable tribulations for the love of this man, and she would hear him declare himself!

"Well, then," she breathed, her pulse racing as his fingers found their way beneath her lacy drawers. "If you know of any reason why this man and this woman shouldn't be united in Holy Matrimony, speak now or forever hold your peace."

Laughter started low in his chest, becoming hoarse as his desire for her rose with the color in her lovely cheeks. "I'm already holding my piece," he quipped, "and by God, she's not getting away from me ever again. I love you, Lyla. And forever won't be long enough to show you how much."

He took the ring she was holding, the magnificent

aquamarine encircled by diamonds that sparkled almost as brightly as the woman in his arms. He solemnly slid the gem onto her left hand, an act he'd dreamed of performing months ago, finally consummated.

His promise rang sweetly in her ears as Lyla melted against him, knowing Barry would always have his way with her. And giving it to him sounded like the finest of pastimes, now, and for as long as they both should live.